THE FLAMES OF TREASON
AND TREACHERY ENGULF THE
PROSPERING COLONIES

RENNO—Born among white men, raised among the Seneca, he is the great chief who must unite two worlds.

JA-GONH—Renno's pride, every inch his father's son. First he would win honor, then be forced into exile, and, finally, return triumphant to avenge his grandfather's death.

AH-WEN-GA—The lovely daughter of an aged Seneca war chief, she must live like his daughter but fight like his son.

GOO-GA-RO-NO—Renno's daughter, who follows her passion for a Frenchman and pays a bitter price.

ROGER HARKNESS—An English soldier of fortune, he comes to the New World to fight at Renno's side.

GRAY FOX—A Huron, an agent of the French, he moves through the Indian nations like a serpent wreaking havoc, fanning the flames of war.

The White Indian Series
Book V

RENNO

Donald Clayton Porter

 Created by the producers of
**Wagons West, Children of the Lion,
Saga of the Southwest,** and
The Kent Family Chronicles Series.
Executive Producer: Lyle Kenyon Engel

BANTAM BOOKS
TORONTO • NEW YORK • LONDON • SYDNEY • AUCKLAND

RENNO

*A Bantam Book / published by arrangement with
Book Creations, Inc.*

Bantam edition / November 1981

2nd printing . November 1981	4th printing .... August 1983
3rd printing ... January 1982	5th printing ... January 1985

*Produced by Book Creations, Inc.
Chairman of the Board: Lyle Kenyon Engel.*

ISBN 0-553-25154-6

Published simultaneously in the United States and Canada

PRINTED IN THE UNITED STATES OF AMERICA

H   14 13 12 11 10 9 8 7 6 5

RENNO

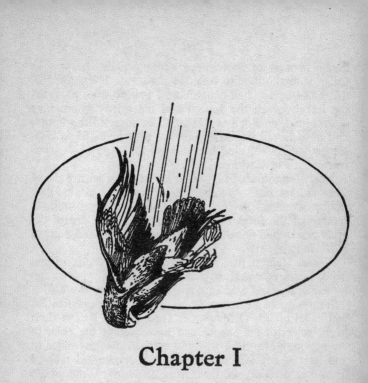

Chapter I

R enno, the white Indian, sachem of the mighty Seneca
tribe and adopted son of Ghonka and his wife, Ena,
lay asleep in his house in the main town of the Seneca.
Beside him on the corn-husk mat lay his wife, Betsy, a
Virginia heiress who had given up her life with her own
people to become the wife of Renno and the mother of
his two children. Renno stirred, sighed, then shook con-
vulsively for a moment or two.

Betsy, instantly awake, knew at once that he was
dreaming. She wanted to awaken him, which she could
have done with a single, gentle touch, but she knew
better. Renno's dreams were not those of ordinary mortals.

Somehow, in ways that not even the oldest and wisest

medicine men of the Seneca could explain, he was in touch with the infinite when he dreamed. The manitous, the half-human, half-supernatural beings who provided the link between the Seneca and the spirits whom they worshipped, confided in Renno. They foretold the future, and he believed implicitly in what they revealed to him. Never had they misled him; always they had been accurate in their revelations.

Now Renno found himself in a vast lodge with walls of stout animal skins. On the walls were great masks, grotesque wooden carvings that almost—but not quite—resembled the faces of human beings. In his dream the great masks had not only come alive but also had a grave message to impart.

"Hear, Renno, that which we prophesy," one of the masks declared in a slow, ponderous voice.

"Hear, Renno," said another, "and heed our words."

Renno could hear himself replying. "I am obedient to you in all things, O Manitous. Through you I have risen in the ranks of the Seneca and have become the chief of the nation. Never have I forgotten that I owe my place to you, just as my father, Ghonka, is ever mindful that he owes his position as the Great Sachem of the entire Iroquois League to you and to you alone. All the nations of the Iroquois bow before you. The Seneca and the Mohawk and the Oneida, the Onondaga, the Tuscarora, and the Cayuga—all acknowledge you as supreme."

His words pleased the manitous, and the great masks nodded in unison.

Then one of them said, "Listen, Renno, to our words of warning. The nations of the Iroquois form an alliance that is unlike any other in all this land. The other tribes are jealous; even the men with pale skins who have come to this land from across the sea stand in awe of the Iroquois League."

A second mask continued gravely, "The League is in great danger. Soon it may founder."

"That is true," said a third mask. "Only Renno can save the alliance on which the peace of all peoples in this land depends. If Renno succeeds, the peace will be maintained. If Renno fails, brother will war against brother, and blood will flow like a mighty stream."

Renno was horrified by their words, and he felt paralyzed by what they had revealed to him. Then, as he absorbed the information, the manitous became fainter, and the great masks faded swiftly from sight. Nothing was left but the animal-skin walls of the lodge. Then they, too, faded, and Renno found himself standing alone in the wilderness.

He was very weary. The vision had exhausted him, and he knew he required sleep.

Inexplicably, however, he awakened from his dream and realized he was in his own house with Betsy beside him. The night was warm, but he was thoroughly chilled—as cold as death.

He knew now that he had been dreaming, and he recalled the entire experience vividly, remembering every word that the manitous had spoken to him.

Their warning troubled him deeply. He debated whether to go at once to Ghonka to relate the substance of that dream but decided to wait until morning. Ghonka, as the Great Sachem of all the Iroquois nations, would have to be told. What troubled Renno most was that he, rather than Ghonka, would be required to take action of some kind in order to preserve the Iroquois nations. The manitous had not explained why he himself would be required to act.

Renno knew there was nothing to be done immediately, that there was no action he could possibly take to ward off the crisis that the manitous told him was pending. So be it.

Silently leaving his bed, he went to the door of his house and stared out past the dwellings of his people, who were sleeping. He looked past the palisade and past the fields where the corn, squash, and beans would soon be planted. He wished fervently that the manitous had given him some clue as to how their prophecy would take place, but that was not their way. He braced himself, bowed his head to their will, and swore that he would do his best for all of the Seneca when the time came for him to act.

"Death to Renno! Death to Ghonka! Death to all Seneca!"

The members of the Huron council sat hushed and in awe as the voice of the speaker rose and fell, expressing thoughts dear to all of them. How often the warriors of the Huron had wished death to Renno, the white sachem of the all-powerful Seneca, long the foe of the Huron. How often they had longed for the demise of Ghonka, Renno's father, Great Sachem of the Iroquois League, the group of six tribes that, standing together, formed the most powerful Indian body in all North America.

As always, Gray Fox knew what he was doing. He had begun his speech in a low key and was gradually increasing its tempo and his volume, little by little exhorting the stolid Huron. By the time he was finished, he would have them in the palm of his hand, willing to do anything that he wanted.

Gray Fox came by his talent naturally. In his late twenties, more than two decades younger than his arch-foe, Renno, he was the son of an Indian mother of the Huron tribe and of Colonel Alain de Gramont, long a thorn in Renno's side, long an implacable foe of the Seneca. Gray Fox—so named because he had supposedly seen a gray fox when hallucinating during his manhood trials—had been a small boy when his father had been killed, but his mother had instilled in him a fierce hatred of Renno and Ghonka. These two had stood in the way of his father's own greatness and had prevented the Huron from being victorious in campaign after campaign. The young Huron had sworn to his mother that he would continue in his father's footsteps and do the task that Gramont had found too great for him, the task for which he had died. Gray Fox was determined to make the Huron prevail over the Seneca, the most successful warriors of any tribe on the continent.

By rights, as Gray Fox well knew, all of the advantages lay with the Huron. First and foremost, they were allies of France, the most powerful of the European nations and the most generous in dealing with the Indians, showering them with such valuables as muskets, pistols, bullets, and ammunition. Also, the Huron were longtime allies of other powerful tribes, not the least of them the Ottawa and the Algonquian.

Unfortunately, France was losing her struggle for conquest of the New World, and as a consequence the Huron were taking second place to their old and bitter rivals, the Seneca.

So Gray Fox's speech was no ordinary diatribe. He had planned with infinite care for this day, and he had two distinct goals in mind. First, he intended to create dissension between the Seneca and the other nations of the Iroquois League, particularly the powerful Mohawk. At the same time, he hoped to cause bad blood between the Indian tribes and their sponsors or allies, the English settlers. His second goal was perhaps even more treacherous: to cause trouble and woe for the Seneca themselves—especially for Renno and Ghonka. How he planned to do this was not exactly clear as yet, but he already had a few ideas, and he was prepared to resort to any means, including murder.

Ultimately, as Gray Fox saw developments, the Seneca would falter; once they stumbled, the Iroquois alliance would crumble, and the English colonies would be ripe for the plucking. The Huron would be ready and willing to grasp with both hands and to win the great prize for themselves.

Gray Fox was personally ambitious, too. He hated Renno because he was a white man who had been adopted by the chief or sachem of the Seneca and had become that tribe's leader, while he himself was half-Indian yet was excluded from the inner power circles of his own tribe. He intended to batter down the barriers that separated him from the power and prestige he desired.

"For too long now have the Seneca terrorized the people of the wilderness! For too long now have they ruled the nations of our world! Their day is ending. Hear me, my brothers! Mark well the words that come from my mouth and remember them!"

The Huron sat silently, Gray Fox's words and tone enmeshing them in a web like that spun by his cunning father before him. His voice was resonant, his manner self-assured, his confidence inspiring. In spite of themselves the seasoned warriors and medicine men of the Huron listened avidly, heard what they wanted to hear, and believed.

Gray Fox knew his hold on his audience was growing, and his manner became even more assured. "There speaks to you now the son of the great Gramont—known to you as Golden Eagle—who led the Huron in their greatest battles! Golden Eagle, the last mighty warrior to win a victory over the Seneca!"

There was one member of the audience who was relatively untouched by the half-breed's rhetoric. An elderly war chief looked around the lodge, understood what Gray Fox was saying and why he said it, but remained unimpressed. He well knew that Gray Fox's father, Golden Eagle, had been a ferocious adversary of the Seneca and of Renno, in particular, but in the end he had been defeated by them. Finally the war chief could tolerate the outburst no longer. "Ghonka and Renno are protected by the most powerful manitous of all the tribes. They survive where others fall. What makes you think Gray Fox will succeed where others fail?"

Gray Fox had anticipated the question and was unperturbed. Flinging his arms wide, he struck a dramatic pose. "My brother, trust me!" he implored. "I beg you—trust me!"

Sitting quietly at the rear of the lodge, a half-smile on his face as he listened and nodded in approval, was an inconspicuous white man in buckskins. Major Henri de Bienville, the chief of French intelligence in the New World, had been given full power to represent New France in her dealings with the Indian tribes. He had been appointed by Cardinal André Fleury, the prime minister for the young King Louis XV. The young monarch, great-grandson of the Sun King, Louis XIV, shared his great-grandfather's grandiose ambitions. He, too, wanted all of North America to exist under the banner of the Bourbon monarchs of France, and Cardinal Fleury was determined to gain the territory for him. Major de Bienville, a military veteran long trusted by Fleury, was the key figure in the development of France's new scheme to dominate America. It did not matter to him that France had lost the previous rounds of the battle and that the English colonies—particularly Massachusetts Bay, New York, and Virginia—were flourishing. He, like Gray Fox, had a dream and was determined that it be fulfilled.

De Bienville had spent weeks in Quebec, the capital of New France, visiting the many tribes of the interior, traveling as far as the frontier town of Montreal in his search for the natural leaders of the Indian allies of France. There was no question in his mind that Gray Fox was such a leader. De Bienville had no idea what specifics the man had in mind, but his challenge to the Seneca was a bold, daring maneuver that struck just the right chord, and Bienville waited impatiently for the meeting to end. Unaccustomed to the interminable Indian rhetoric, he was forced to endure more than an hour of repetitious speech-making before Gray Fox, slightly hoarse but still filled with enthusiasm, finally concluded.

Bienville waited until the leaders of the tribe left the lodge, and then he fell in beside Gray Fox. "You are a very impressive orator," he said. Gray Fox had been conscious of the French official's presence but pretended indifference and nodded, then inclined his head.

"You truly intend to defeat the Seneca?"

Gray Fox shrugged. "They are warriors, hence they are men. They are not immortal. When they are struck with a tomahawk or an arrow, they bleed, and they die."

Bienville raised an eyebrow. "You truly think you can get rid of the great Ghonka and of Renno?"

Gray Fox smiled. "They, too, are mortal men," he replied.

"I have seen the sachem of the Ottawa quail at the very mention of the mighty leaders," the major declared.

7

"I have seen the great war chief of the Algonquian tremble like a leaf high on a tree in a strong autumn wind when the names of Ghonka and Renno are spoken. Are you so sure that you have magic that will prevail against them?"

Gray Fox looked sideways at the French officer. "Magic? What magic?" His voice was derisive. "My late mother saw to it that I was educated in the ways of the French, my friend. I do not hold with the ignorant superstitions of the Indian tribes. I use them to my advantage when it suits my purposes, to be sure, but I trust I am more advanced than that."

Bienville was increasingly certain that this was the leader he had been seeking. "Gray Fox," he said, "I may be of assistance to you. You can call on me for help, and I will give it to you."

Gray Fox halted abruptly before a hut that stood at the end of the street. "What is the price I must pay for your help?" he demanded.

Bienville smiled. "My friend," he said, "we seek the same goal. My fee is victory for France."

Gray Fox took the other man's measure, liked what he saw, and was quick to recognize the potential worth of a relationship with him. "Any man who seeks the death of the leaders of the Seneca and the end of Seneca domination is truly my friend," he said, and extending his hand, he gripped the Frenchman's wrist, Indian style.

Henri de Bienville knew better than to ask what the half-breed's scheme was. He doubted that Gray Fox would confide in him, but he felt certain that the man had evolved some plan that would be effective. Eventually Gray Fox would come to him for money, for arms, and for ammunition. Then he would be in a position to demand to know the half-breed's secret and would be able to pass judgment on it. Until then, he had only his instinct to guide him—and his instinct told him that Gray Fox, of all the Indian allies of the French whom he had encountered, had the best chance of accomplishing the near-miracle of putting the Seneca and their Iroquois allies in their place and asserting the dominance of the

Huron. Certainly France would not succeed in the New World without the Huron, and the Huron, in turn, seemed to depend on the wily son of Alain de Gramont, who was still regarded as one of the best operatives France had ever had in the New World.

George I, King of England, Scotland, and Wales, Lord of the Channel Isles and monarch of England's overseas possessions, was an affable Hanoverian, interested in his family, his food, his other creature comforts, and the gossip of the small court that had been the center of his life for so long. He had accepted the rule of Great Britain, but that didn't mean he was interested in the people or their problems. He vastly preferred to leave such matters in the able hands of his ministers.

He was fortunate indeed that these able servants of the Crown included such men as Charles, Viscount Townshend, the King's secretary of state, who allegedly knew all there was to know about the affairs in any part of the world that might affect King George or his subjects.

It was said that Lord Townshend had no personal ambitions other than to govern wisely and well, and even his enemies in Parliament had to admit that his stewardship of the affairs of state was almost flawless. He arrived early in the morning, seven mornings a week at his office, where he breakfasted while dictating correspondence to a battery of clerks. More often than not he wasn't seen again outside the confines of his Whitehall domain until late at night. Apparently he required very little sleep and needed no time for recreation.

Townshend surrounded himself with men of like temperament, and one who was remarkably similar was Sir William Gooch, the governor of the Royal Colony of Virginia in North America. Although Sir William loved a joke as much as he loved a good meal and a journey through the wilderness, his mind was always on business, and his loyalty to Lord Townshend—and therefore to the Crown itself—was unquestioned.

When Governor Gooch came to London from Virginia

in the spring of 1727 to confer with government leaders, humorists declared that they would hate to be present when he and Lord Townshend were throwing statistics at each other. "God help anyone who can't stand up to the barrage of facts and figures that either of that pair is capable of hurling," they said.

The humorists, as always, were badly mistaken. They would have been very surprised to find that Sir William spent the better part of an hour discussing the tobacco crop of Virginia and his own theories on how to increase it. This inspired Townshend, an amateur agriculturist, to hold forth on a new breed of turnip that he was developing. In fact, he waxed so enthusiastic on the subject that it was late afternoon before he and his visitor got down to the subject that had brought the Virginia governor so far.

Sir William, impeccably dressed as always, flicked a speck of lint from his satin waistcoat and leaned back in his chair. "If the truth be known, milord, I don't like the situation in the colonies. I don't like it in the least."

Townshend, shaggy and disreputable as always, raised a bushy eyebrow. "How so?" he demanded in his low, rumbling voice.

The governor of Virginia smiled slightly. "Things are going far too well for us."

Townshend hooked a thumb in a waistcoat pocket. "I think I see what you mean," he muttered.

"I look at it this way," Sir William declared. "The economy of Virginia is sound. Tobacco, in which I obviously take great interest, is flourishing and is bringing us an income greater than any we have ever before enjoyed. New York is booming, both as a shipping and as a manufacturing center. Massachusetts Bay is growing faster than we can keep track of her expansion. Boston is already the largest city in the New World and is larger than many in England itself. We are—to the best of my knowledge—at peace with everyone."

Lord Townshend smiled thinly. "Well," he said, "I'll admit that we're not at war with France at the moment, but that is no fault of Cardinal Fleury or of his young master. From all the information I glean, the young King is as ambitious as his great-grandfather and covets all of the New World for himself."

Sir William nodded. "That's exactly why I'm uneasy. Our colonies are establishing themselves so firmly," he said, "that sooner or later the French will once again attempt to take control. And only a war would dislodge the British and enable the French to take possession. We have never been so strong, particularly since our relations with the Indian tribes are as stable as they are these days. As you well know, our alliance with the Iroquois has always been the keystone of our position. As long as we have been associated with the six nations that make up the Iroquois League, the colonies have been solid and secure. As long as we and Ghonka, the Great Sachem, have stood together firmly, we have been invincible. The French tried to do their damndest, and we defeated them. The Spaniards fulminated and frothed at the mouth, but they could do nothing, either. The other Indian tribes have conspired against us, but they were no match for the power of the Iroquois."

"Is our relationship with Ghonka still so solid then?" the secretary of state asked.

"Most definitely yes," Sir William replied. "His son, Renno, is a white man who was adopted at birth by Ghonka. He has grown to manhood and has distinguished himself as a Seneca. He is married to a woman who comes from a family of prominent Virginians, and his own children follow in the same traditions that have led him and Ghonka for so many years. I say that as long as that family remains at the helm of the Iroquois, England and her colonies will have staunch allies in the New World. They and we, standing together, have a strength that no other force in America can question or challenge. But I fear the French have never learned their lesson and will challenge us once again, even if it means the greatest war ever fought in the New World."

Townshend ran a heavy hand through his rumpled hair and stared up at the high ceiling of his plainly furnished office. "I understand your concern," he said, "and I'm uneasy, too. I grew up seeing France ruled by Louis XIV, who was a conniver and a troublemaker. Now, unfortunately, thanks to Cardinal Fleury and the young King, the spirit of Louis XIV still lives. Their intelligence, as well as the lengths to which they'll go in order to gain possession of the entire New World, should never be underestimated."

William Gooch was not smiling now, and his dark eyes were brooding. "I never underestimate a potential foe, milord," he said, "but in this instance I don't quite know how to cope."

Lord Townshend demonstrated why he had become the King's secretary of state. "I do!" he said energetically. "You'll be in London for several days, I assume?"

"I'm at your service, milord," Sir William replied.

"Very well, then. In the next forty-eight hours I shall send a young man to you who will be an inestimable help in the cause of peace in the colonies." Townshend was vague—deliberately so—but he sounded very sure of himself.

Sir William forgot all about the secretary of state's offer until, two days later, he was scheduled to meet Lord Townshend for dinner at the Red Hart, one of the town's most popular taverns. He was late for the appointment, having miscalculated the heaviness of traffic on the Strand en route to the place. As he entered the tavern he stopped briefly, allowing his eyes to adjust to the semidarkness. A bar in the front of the establishment was crowded, and Sir William was forced to edge past a number of men who were standing as they drank and chatted.

Suddenly he received a violent shove that almost knocked him from his feet. He blinked at a burly, well-dressed man who had charged him with the ferocity of a raging bull. Paying no further attention to the middle-aged victim, the man started to hurry to the exit.

Something in his manner alerted the governor, who felt for the purse he kept suspended from a belt at his waist. To his dismay he found it was missing. "Stop, thief!" he shouted.

Others at the bar were too stunned to respond, and it appeared that the burly thief would escape unscathed. But one guest reacted instantly to the challenge. Tall and slender, with dark, wavy hair and lively, intelligent eyes, this man appeared, at first glance, to be something of a dandy. Dressed in the uniform of a captain of the Grenadiers, he wore boots that were so highly polished one could see one's reflection in them. His satin breeches fitted him snugly, as did his ornate waistcoat and coat. His hat was tilted rakishly.

But there was nothing foppish about his reaction. Reaching for a long sword he carried, he drew it as he ran, and he was almost abreast of the thief by the time they reached the door. Using the sword to trip rather than to harm the man, Sir William's savior sent the fellow stumbling. As the thief fell, the tall young man reached out, snatched the purse that had been neatly cut from the governor's waist, and said, "I'll relieve you of this if you don't mind."

By now other guests had come to life and surrounded the thief, but the young man quickly came to the thief's rescue. "We'll leave the fellow alone," he announced cheerfully. "The money he inadvertently appropriated has been recovered, and he appears to be in too delicate health to withstand a siege at Newgate Prison." The other gentlemen obviously were disappointed, but there was nothing they could do in the face of the young man's odd behavior. The thief needed no encouragement and hurried off to safety, racing out to the street and disappearing in the crowd.

The young man hurried to Sir William's side, removed his hat, and bowed low. "Your humble servant, Governor," he said.

"You know me?" Gooch was surprised.

"I've been keeping watch over you for two days," the young man said, grinning broadly. "Captain Roger Harkness at your service, sir." Suddenly Lord Townshend hailed them from a nearby table. "Ah, Sir William!" he called. "I see that you and Harkness have already met."

The young man was completely at his ease as they

approached the table. "I was able to do a small service for His Excellency, the governor," he said modestly.

"A small service indeed," Sir William replied. "I was carrying over two hundred pounds in my purse, and you've saved the entire sum for me."

The young man shrugged. "Glad to be of help," he said.

A smiling Lord Townshend explained his identity. "Captain Roger Harkness is on leave from the Royal Infantry and holds a special position in the military hierarchy. He has seen active duty as an espionage agent in France and is thoroughly familiar with the doings at the court of Louis XV. I am sending him to the American colonies on a special, roving assignment: he will go wherever he chooses, nosing out trouble, and will report to you, Sir William. Presumably, if trouble should be brewing he will learn of it in time to forestall or circumvent the difficulty."

Harkness raised his tankard of ale in a toast. "May our relationship prosper, Governor," he said. "May we have no problems, and may the troubles that arise be easily solvable." He looked as though he didn't believe his own words.

Sir William Gooch suspected that Roger Harkness was the kind of man who brought his own troubles with him.

Ja-gonh was hunting a deer, and his entire being was devoted to the sport. He crept silently through the limitless forest in the land of the Seneca, making no sound, every muscle in his lithe, lean body tense as he moved closer to his quarry. This was a great day for Ja-gonh, son of Renno and Betsy. Anyone unfamiliar with his background would have been surprised to see a tall, sunburned man in his late twenties, his hair and eyebrows a pale blond, wearing a loincloth, headband, moccasins, and war paint. Like Renno before him, Ja-gonh was first and foremost a Seneca, although he had English blood on both sides.

He was born for such a day, Ja-gonh reflected. The

thrill of the hunt, the surge of joy he felt at outsmarting his foe, the smell of the damp earth, the feel of the warm sun filtering through the trees on his bare skin, all combined to make him glad that he was alive, glad that he was a Seneca.

Ja-gonh was fortunate and knew it. He had recently been promoted to the rank of senior warrior, a rank of considerable honor and responsibility. Now he was eligible to sit in the council chambers of Renno, his father, and of Ghonka, his grandfather, although he knew that they probably would not be seeking his advice for some time to come. Nevertheless, he rejoiced because he and his uncle, El-i-chi, Renno's younger brother, had gone hunting for the sheer sport, and Ja-gonh as usual had shown unerring instinct and almost immediately had unearthed a quarry. Now he was closing in, and soon he would be returning to the main town of the Seneca with a plump deer. His grandparents would welcome the meat, and his sister, Goo-ga-ro-no, would be able to make a new dress of deerskin.

Demonstrating the sensitivity and acuteness that were the hallmarks of the Seneca warrior, Ja-gonh sensed rather than saw or heard El-i-chi nearby. He halted, raising one arm in a signal to his uncle, warning him that the deer was nearby and that he intended to strike soon.

Reaching over his shoulder for an arrow from his quiver, he fitted it into his bow, braced himself, and let fly. The arrow sang through the air, and the deer was no more. Ja-gonh was not surprised by his own skill; in fact, he would have been amazed had he failed to kill the beast with a single shot.

El-i-chi materialized beside the younger man, and together they prepared the carcass for carrying. It was customary, after a hunt, for the successful hunter to return to the town carrying his own spoils, and Ja-gonh slung the carcass of the deer across his back, staggered under the weight of his burden, and then regained his balance. As he straightened he happened to glance up at the sky, and suddenly his heart beat faster.

There in the distance, so far away that only someone with extraordinary eyesight could even see it, was a hawk. Ja-gonh knew of nothing more important than the appearance of a hawk. The bird had been his father's guardian and now was his, too.

In their wisdom the manitous had chosen the hawk as a symbol of their presence, of their guidance, and of their protection of Renno and, ever since his son had become a junior warrior, of Ja-gonh, as well.

So the young Seneca rejoiced doubly. It was a good sign that a hawk had appeared at this particular moment. Apparently the gods were pleased with him, and he would be able to tell his family that all was well. Unmindful of his burden, he stared up at the hawk for some moments, watching it as it circled slowly and lazily in the sky overhead.

Suddenly, to Ja-gonh's horror, the great bird faltered and fell.

It was an amazing spectacle. One moment the hawk was soaring, proud and free, the next moment it acted as though a giant hand had reached out and snatched it from the sky. It reacted as though it had been attacked fatally by another bird of prey or had been decapitated by a giant tomahawk. Whatever the reason, it plummeted to earth.

Ja-gonh was terrified, and he dropped the carcass of the deer to the ground. He had faced enemies in battle without flinching and had fought with distinction against both the French and their Indian allies. He had taken part in more raids on enemy strongholds than he cared to count and had always done his duty, always sure of himself, always stout-hearted.

But the hawk was no ordinary bird, and its tragedy was no ordinary occurrence. His flesh crawled as he realized there were supernatural elements at play. The spring day was warm, but suddenly he was bathed in a cold sweat, and a chill ran slowly up his spine. All at once Ja-gonh became aware of El-i-chi standing nearby. "Did my uncle see?" the young man demanded hoarsely.

El-i-chi was renowned as a fearless warrior, but he, too, was badly shaken. He folded his arms, stared off into space, and said, "I saw." Obviously he did not care to discuss the incident or its possible significance.

Ja-gonh understood all this without being told. He knew he would be required now to warn his parents and his grandparents of the strange death of the hawk; perhaps they would be able to solve the mystery for him. He glanced up at the sky and was about to start off for the main town of the Seneca at a trot, but El-i-chi smiled faintly and tapped him on the shoulder. "You forget your prize," the older warrior reminded him.

Ja-gonh was embarrassed. He was so shaken by the incident that he had almost forgotten his deer. He picked up the carcass, shouldering it easily, and started off toward the town at a trot, a pace he could maintain for hours at a time without faltering, even when carrying such a heavy burden.

Ordinarily this would have been a joyous occasion. Ja-gonh had gone hunting, his trip had been successful, and his family would reap the benefits of his day's labor. But he was deeply troubled. It was impossible for him to imagine the significance of the proud hawk's sudden disappearance from the sky. Nothing that he had ever undergone had prepared him for such a catastrophe.

There was still a spring in Ja-gonh's step as he came to the fields where some of the women were busily at work, cultivating the earth for the planting of corn, squash, and beans—the three vegetable staples of the Indian diet. Many of the younger women looked in admiration at the lithe warrior. Ordinarily Ja-gonh might have been tempted to flirt with some of the prettier girls, but his mind was too full, and he paid no attention to them.

Wasting no time, Ja-gonh went directly to the house of Ghonka. The Great Sachem was as grave and distinguished in appearance in his old age as he had been in his younger days. His forehead was broad, lined with furrows, and crow's-feet showed at the corners of his dark eyes. It was said that he was extraordinarily wise, and

Ja-gonh did not doubt it. In his mind his father and grandfather had capabilities far beyond those of other men.

Ghonka had been dozing, but he awakened slowly when his grandson came into the house, and a slow smile filled his face. It was no secret in the family that Ja-gonh could do no wrong in his grandfather's eyes.

The young warrior laid the slain deer on the ground, and his grandmother, Ena, hurrying into the house, took one look at it and nodded happily.

"Ah," she said, "we shall feast tonight."

Ja-gonh nodded but was not interested in a discussion of his luck in the hunt. All he wanted to do now was to find Renno, who, he knew, would advise him well. There was a bond between father and son that went even beyond that of Ja-gonh and Ghonka, so the young man took leave of his grandparents and hurried to tell his father the news.

Renno was aging gracefully. His torso, shoulders, and arms still had the power of the natural athlete, and his legs were muscular and sturdy, still capable of marching untold miles through the wilderness. But his blond hair was growing sparse now, and it was no longer necessary for him to shave as carefully around his scalp lock. There were also signs of gray in his eyebrows. When Ja-gonh found him, he was seated in conversation with some of the senior war chiefs of the Seneca, discussing a future hunt.

Seeing his son approach, Renno looked up at him and felt great joy. Ja-gonh was not only a source of pride to his father but was also the hope and future of the Seneca nation itself. Sensing that his son had something very important on his mind, Renno excused himself from the group of warriors and went with Ja-gonh to a place where they could talk privately.

Suddenly the words tumbled out of the young man as he related the strange occurrence.

Renno listened soberly to what his son told him. He still remembered vividly the dream of a few nights ago, which he had discussed with Ghonka at great length. The

18

two men had realized that there was nothing to be done until a clear path presented itself, but now, with Ja-gonh's experience, there could be no doubt that trouble was imminent.

When Ja-gonh had finished his account, Renno looked into his son's eyes and said solemnly, "Ja-gonh, repeat this tale to your grandparents tonight when we meet for dinner. The manitous have given us a warning, and we must heed it, or we shall pay a terrible price."

Ja-gonh nodded.

"Perhaps," Renno continued, "your grandmother will give us some guidance." It was well known that Ena, the matriarch of the ruling family, was more familiar than anyone else with the manitous and their ways.

For the rest of the day, Ja-gonh busied himself at the lodge of the Bear Clan, where he now resided, and he did not appear at the house of his grandparents until about an hour after darkness had fallen. As he approached the house the smell of roasting venison told him that Ena was putting his deer to good use.

As was the Seneca custom, none of the family members spoke during the meal, but Ja-gonh could tell from his mother's concerned expression that she had heard the news of what had happened to him.

Betsy was still a beauty. Certainly she did not look like the mother of two grown children; she looked as if she could be Goo-ga-ro-no's sister rather than her mother. Although she smiled at Ja-gonh, Betsy was troubled.

It was difficult for her to acclimate to the superstitions of the Seneca. She had grown to womanhood as the daughter of the late Brigadier General Austin Ridley, who had also been a prominent shipowner, and he and his wife, Mary—who had died a few months after her husband—had seen to it that their daughter's education and background were those of an upper-class Englishwoman. Over the years, however, Betsy had found repeatedly that many of the Seneca's beliefs about the manitous were accurate. She could not explain them, for they defied logic, but they nevertheless were very real. So she often was torn, and that was how she felt now, not wanting to give too much credence to her son's experience and yet not dealing lightly with it, either.

After they had finished their dinner, the family continued to sit in a circle around the fire. Renno came to the point at once. "Let the son of Renno speak," he said. "Let him say what befell him this day in the deep woods."

Ja-gonh plunged into his story, relating the incident directly and succinctly.

El-i-chi, who sat across the fire from him, listened carefully and nodded. "The words that the nephew of El-i-chi speaks are true words," he said. "That which happened to the hawk happened as he has said it."

As Renno had anticipated, all the family members turned to Ena to hear what she had to say. "I do not pretend to know the meaning of the omen," she said slowly. "I do know that it means no good for us."

Ja-gonh cleared his throat. "You think there is evil in store for us?"

Ena shook her head slowly. "The manitous do not know evil from good," she replied severely. "The manitous do not judge as humans judge. The manitous have their own standards, their own thoughts, their own ways. It is not for us to understand them. It is our place but to obey them. And I say to you that the omen you saw today is very, very serious."

Ghonka folded his arms across his broad chest. Like Renno, he was pondering the two messages the manitous had sent, first to Renno, then to Ja-gonh. Betsy, meanwhile, was torn between implicit belief and a total denial of the supernatural power of the bird of prey. But she was as shocked as everyone else when her daughter broke the silence.

"I think the words of my brother and the words of my grandmother are nonsense!" Goo-ga-ro-no cried. "Anything could have happened to the hawk. He could have fallen ill. He could have simply died. Why must we ascribe all sorts of terrible powers to a mere bird?"

No one spoke or moved. Renno's face darkened, and his pale eyes glowed at his daughter's temerity. He loved

Goo-ga-ro-no dearly, but she was going too far and deserved to be treated accordingly.

Before he could speak, however, Ghonka raised his voice, as befitted the head of the clan. "Goo-ga-ro-no is foolish, as only maidens can be foolish. She speaks words that will make the manitous angry, that will require them to obtain vengeance. Let her apologize to them at once! Let her go at once to the shrine beyond the cornfield and there pray that the manitous will forgive her."

Everyone present understood that Ghonka was issuing a direct order that under no circumstances could be disobeyed.

Goo-ga-ro-no jumped to her feet, her eyes—as pale a blue as those of her parents—flashing. She hurriedly left the house and raced off into the night, never once looking back as she left the palisade of the town behind her and headed across the open fields.

She had no idea whether or not the incident involving the hawk had any significance; she had deliberately goaded Ghonka because she had hoped she would be sent to the shrine. She had a special reason for coming into the forest.

Hurrying past a thick stand of silver birch, Goo-ga-ro-no smoothed her dress of doeskin and ran her fingers through her long blond hair, which seemed so incongruous in an Indian maiden. She came at last to a hollow surrounded by several large elm trees, and there she halted, drew in her breath, and whistled, giving a fairly credible imitation of a lark.

She did not have long to wait. Soon another lark called in answer to her cry, and a moment later a handsome, swarthy white man in his late thirties emerged into the clearing.

Pierre Fanchon smiled at the young woman. "I had just about given up hope of seeing you tonight," he said.

She shook her head. "I told you I'd be here, didn't I?"

"Well," he said, "I took you at your word, so I was patient. Now my patience has been rewarded."

They looked at each other for a moment, and then Goo-ga-ro-no moved uncertainly into the man's arms for his kiss.

She knew her parents would be shocked beyond measure if they had any idea that she was meeting Pierre in private. Certainly this was the first time in her life she had ever lied in this way, but she had her reasons. Chief among them was the fact that Pierre Fanchon was of French descent. To Renno, Pierre's ancestry would be like waving a red flag in front of a bull. Renno had fought the French in innumerable campaigns for as long as he had been a warrior, and he regarded them as his permanent, implacable foes. In Renno's opinion no Frenchman could be a friend.

Realizing this, Goo-ga-ro-no was afraid to tell him of her growing involvement with Pierre Fanchon. Certainly she could not tell her mother, either, because she knew Betsy kept nothing from her husband and would be sure to reveal her daughter's secret to Renno.

But as far as Goo-ga-ro-no was concerned, she was doing nothing wrong in caring for Pierre. She was determined to lead a life of her own, free of the hatreds that had caused so many wars for the men of Renno's generation.

Chapter II

General Jeffrey Wilson and his wife, Adrienne, had succeeded his late parents, Andrew and Mildred, in far more ways than one. Not only were they the principal landowners on the Springfield frontier, where their estate was sufficiently large to raise a variety of crops and cattle, but Jeffrey also had replaced his late father as the head of the Massachusetts Bay militia.

"One of the first things to learn about the New World is that nothing is quite what it seems," he said, smiling at his dinner guest, Roger Harkness. "Renno, the sachem of the Seneca, probably the most ferocious and certainly the most capable field general in all the Indian forces on the continent, you would assume to be a typical Indian. Renno, however, is as white as you and I, and although he is a Seneca by background, he is certainly a Caucasian by nature."

Captain Harkness shook his head. He had been in the colonies only a short time when he had been sent by Governor Gooch to visit Fort Springfield and to confer with Jeffrey Wilson about conditions on the frontier. So far there had been no indications that France or her Indian allies were planning any kind of offensive campaign, but all the same Roger Harkness was learning a great deal.

"There are many contradictions in the New World," he now said, "but I'm learning little by little that these are what give the colonies their great vitality."

Two young ladies, who sat at the dinner table on either side of the young officer, had been notably silent. Patience, the Wilson's elder daughter, had inherited her mother's glorious red hair and cream-colored complexion, as well as her father's chiseled profile. But her solemn nature was her own, and she had refused many requests of marriage because she was so demanding. Margot, her younger sister, was elfinlike, and never for an instant was she silent. In particular, she loved to tease the refined and beautiful Patience, who had so many ardent suitors, and the raillery between the sisters was a common occurrence in the Wilson household. Now Margot felt she had been excluded from the conversation long enough, and she couldn't help butting in. "You know," she said, "Renno isn't the only Seneca white Indian. Ja-gonh's grandparents were Virginians, and if ever there is a conflict between the colonists and the Seneca, I'm not sure which side Ja-gonh would be loyal to." She stopped speaking long enough to glance slyly at her older sister.

Patience shook her head. "That is nonsense," she said. "Nothing will ever disrupt the alliance between the English colonists and the Seneca. And," she added, "Ja-gonh is totally loyal to the Seneca at all times and in all things."

Margot refused to be denied. "What about Goo-ga-ro-no?" she demanded.

Patience sighed gently and made no reply. Adrienne

24

Wilson raised an eyebrow and glanced at her daughters in turn. The Wilsons had been good friends with Renno and his family for many years, and they knew of Goo-ga-ro-no's obstinacy and her dissatisfaction with many of the Seneca ways. But it was improper and impolite to discuss the private business of good friends in the presence of a stranger, and both Margot and Patience recognized in their mother's expression a warning that they should not go any further with the conversation. Patience felt rebuked and stared down at her plate. The irrepressible Margot, however, grinned and looked across the table at her father.

"Are you going to take Captain Harkness out to visit the land of the Seneca, Pa?" she asked.

Jeffrey couldn't help smiling at his spirited younger daughter. "I really haven't made up my mind yet. Why?"

"Well," the young woman replied playfully, glancing at her sister, "if you were planning such a trip, I think I know someone who would love to come with you."

Patience glared at her. "I don't think you're in the least amusing," she said, "and you know very well I never ask to be taken when Papa goes on a business or military trip."

Jeffrey understood now and smiled broadly. "Ah, so that's it," he said. "Patience seems to have an unquenchable thirst for the land of the Seneca. It exerts a tremendous magnetism that keeps drawing her there."

Margot winked at her sister and grinned mischievously. "The magnet," she said, "is Ja-gonh." Patience rewarded her with a smirk, and Margot had the audacity to wink again.

A short time later they adjourned to the parlor, where Jeffrey Wilson discovered that he'd used the last of a bottle of brandywine and needed to replace it. He asked his younger daughter if she would be good enough to fetch another from his liquor supply.

Margot was on her feet instantly. "Of course," she said promptly. "Captain Harkness, could I prevail on you to accompany me?"

The captain was slightly surprised by her request but

was sufficiently civilized to agree smoothly. Patience again rewarded her sister, this time by glowering at her.

The pert Margot did not speak until they reached the pantry and were out of earshot of the parlor. "I just wanted an excuse to speak with you privately. I hope you don't mind, Captain Harkness."

Roger Harkness was not surprised by anything the mercurial young woman did or said, and he shook his head.

She lowered her voice. "You can tell me to mind my own business, and I wouldn't blame you in the least," she said, "but I've been watching you since you arrived here, and I've noticed your interest in my sister."

Harkness seemed to adjust a heavy weight on his shoulders. "I don't think that's so unusual," he said lightly.

Margot shook her head so vehemently that her dark curls danced. "Oh, not at all," she said. "Patience is one of those women who always attract all the men. I'd have been surprised indeed if you hadn't developed an interest in her, sir. Everyone who sees her automatically falls in love with her."

Roger Harkness nodded but made no comment. Certainly he had no intention of revealing the state of his feelings to Patience's nosy younger sister.

"I just wanted you to know," Margot went on brightly, "that you're wasting your time."

If Harkness was surprised he didn't show it, and he elevated one eyebrow. "Oh?" he asked, his expression noncommittal.

Margot removed a full bottle of brandywine from her father's wine rack, then leaned close to the visitor. "Strictly between you and me," she said conspiratorially, her voice slightly above a whisper, "Patience is in love with Ja-gonh!"

Harkness couldn't help showing his annoyance. "Why do you tell me all this?" he demanded.

"Well," she said, chattering at high speed, "I like you very much, you see, and I hate to see you wasting your time. There are other people who have been disappointed because Patience won't look at them twice. She has eyes only for Ja-gonh." Margot raced on as fast as she could speak, her voice a trifle breathless. "Mama and Papa would love it if a romance developed between Patience and Ja-gonh," she said. "That's because Renno is their oldest friend, and they're very close to Betsy, too. But it will never happen that way. I know that much."

In spite of himself, Harkness was amused. "You seem to know a great deal," he said.

She looked fleetingly like Patience as she nodded solemnly. "It's very simple, you know," she said. "When Ja-gonh wants to act like a settler and wears European clothes, he's rather wonderful. In fact, I could fall in love with him myself. But he doesn't often satisfy himself that way. He *is* a Seneca, you see—he truly is! I know it's difficult to understand how a white man can be so thoroughly Indian in all he feels and thinks, but there's no doubt about it: Ja-gonh is an Indian through and through, and that will be too much for my sister in the long run. She cares more about civilization and creature comforts than she realizes." She stared out the pantry window at the rolling fields of the Wilson estate, then suddenly remembered that her father was awaiting her return with the bottle of brandywine. "Anyway," she said brightly, "now you know all there is to know, so the rest is up to you. If you have the forbearance to wait until Patience realizes that Ja-gonh isn't for her, maybe she'll look at you twice." She blithely started back toward the parlor.

Chuckling quietly, Roger Harkness followed her. She had given him a great deal to digest, far more than she knew, and he was in no hurry to assimilate the information. He found Patience Wilson extraordinarily attractive, but his mission came first, and everything else had to take second place to it. In addition to which, he expected he would be in the New World for a long time to come. Long enough surely for Patience to work out the romantic complications in her life.

*   *   *

Sun-ai-yee, the greatest of living Seneca war chiefs, the grizzled fighting man about whom so many songs and legends had been passed into the lore of his people, had made an accommodation that enabled him to live as ordinary mortals lived. That is to say, he did exactly as he was bidden by his wife, Talking Quail, and obeyed her injunctions in all things pertaining to family life. In return, she did not interfere when he went off to recount his glorious exploits with the tribe's elders.

Talking Quail was a representative of the small, southern Biloxi tribe; hence her ways were still somewhat alien to the Seneca, in spite of her many years of marriage to Sun-ai-yee. This certainly was true of her cooking. She had a knack for baking fish, for example, that tasted unlike any fish prepared by anyone else. The herbs in which it was packed gave it a piquant, spicy flavor that Sun-ai-yee enjoyed.

Now, as he ate his meal, Sun-ai-yee looked across the table at the grave and lovely Ah-wen-ga, his elder daughter, who had inherited his fearlessness and her mother's beauty. The war chief was privately amused to note that Ah-wen-ga did precisely what her father was doing: she pretended to be listening as Talking Quail—who ignored the Seneca custom of remaining silent at meals—described an incident that had taken place in the fields late that afternoon. If necessary, the young woman, like her father, could have repeated her mother's words verbatim, but in actuality her mind was far away.

Listening to every word her mother was saying, however, was White Deer, Talking Quail's younger daughter. Just twelve years old, the girl was tall and scrawny, but she had inherited her mother's gift for speech. It was said in the longhouse of the adolescent girls that White Deer could speak as rapidly as the manitous who were charged with keeping the language of mortals.

Sun-ai-yee took his cue from his elder daughter. When Ah-wen-ga smiled at something in Talking Quail's recital, the elderly war chief nodded and chuckled benignly. When Ah-wen-ga looked concerned, he frowned. The young woman knew, of course, what her father was doing, and she entered wholeheartedly into his conspiracy, as she did in all things that concerned him. Neither cared whether or not Talking Quail knew that they were paying no attention to her story; it was sufficient, they presumed, that Talking Quail had an audience, and the price, they reasoned, was little enough in return for a far better tasting dinner than was being served anywhere else in the Seneca town.

At last Sun-ai-yee could hold back no longer, and he interrupted the long diatribe, asking Ah-wen-ga softly, "You heard about Ja-gonh and the hawk?"

Her already enormous dark eyes seemed to grow still larger as she nodded. "I have heard," she replied solemnly. "I could scarcely believe that which I heard, but the story was told to me by Goo-ga-ro-no, so I know it was true."

"It is true," Sun-ai-yee declared flatly.

"What does it mean, my father?" she inquired.

He shrugged his massive shoulders. "The manitous have not chosen to confide in me," he said ponderously. "If they have their secrets, they have reasons for them. All will be revealed in due time to those who believe in them."

Talking Quail's voice did not falter, but she displayed the rather remarkable knack of being able to listen to the conversation between Sun-ai-yee and Ah-wen-ga, even though she was still speaking at a rapid rate. Certainly she had her own views of the manitous. Although she wouldn't dare tell her husband, she believed that the Seneca were rather fanatical in their religion, and that they placed far too much emphasis on what the manitous approved and disapproved.

"Perhaps nothing untoward will come of the strange incident," Talking Quail said, breaking off her own narrative.

Sun-ai-yee did not deign to enter into active speculation

with her on the subject. His massive shoulders rose and fell in a mighty shrug. The manitous would decide, and he would tend to his own business in the meantime.

Suddenly someone stepped out of the shadows of the cooking fire. Ja-gonh stood before the family, his arms folded as he bowed respectfully to Sun-ai-yee. It would have been unseemly for him to recognize the presence of anyone else, but as White Deer was quick to observe, his eyes darted repeatedly to Ah-wen-ga. Certainly he was very much aware of her proximity.

"Greetings, Ja-gonh, son of Renno," Sun-ai-yee said cordially.

Ja-gonh stood immobile. "I have been asked by the sachem of the Seneca to serve as his messenger," he said. "Members of the other tribes of the Iroquois have begun arriving in the land of the Seneca, and I am to tell you that the Council will meet this night at the Lodge when the embers of the cooking fires burn low."

After Sun-ai-yee nodded and murmured his thanks for the message, Talking Quail said quickly, "Would you like to join us for some fish, Ja-gonh?" she asked.

He looked at her with genuine regret. He knew, as did everyone else, that no one in the land of the Seneca was Talking Quail's equal as a cook. "I thank you most kindly," he said, bowing to Talking Quail, "but I have already eaten. Besides, I am required to deliver the message of my father to other members of the Council." He somehow summoned the courage to turn and look directly at Ah-wen-ga.

Ordinarily she might have flinched and certainly would have looked away, but he had challenged her, and she felt compelled to meet that challenge. She met his eyes boldly, and for a long moment they stared at each other, neither of them blinking, neither of them showing any expression.

Then, just as suddenly as he had arrived, Ja-gonh vanished. There was an electric silence finally broken by White Deer's high-pitched laugh.

"Mother," Ah-wen-ga said, "if you don't silence that

horrid child, I shall be forced to take a tomahawk to her!"

"Behave yourself, White Deer," Talking Quail said absently, then looked at her husband.

Sun-ai-yee pretended to be unaware of the significance of her look, but he was fooling no one. Deep within him burned the hope that someday his elder daughter would find it in her heart to mate with the son of Renno, his oldest friend and closest companion in war as well as in peace.

But these matters were not discussed, for Ah-wen-ga could not tolerate the bringing of such thoughts into the open. So the family ate the rest of their meal in silence, not even Talking Quail enlivening the proceedings with a rambling account of her day's activities.

The odors of venison roasting, of corn bread baking, and of squash, beans, and corn bubbling over a fire in their own liquid drifted through the wilderness. In the background could be heard the faint throbbing of a drum. The sound was quiet yet intense, even though the drummer did not increase his volume.

The drum was a sensitive instrument to the Seneca. It signified war or peace, it told of treaties made and treaties broken, and it told of alliances, victories, and disasters. A single drum, played lightly for several hours, carried a far different message, however, and those who heard it, particularly the young, were highly pleased.

This was the night when the Seneca would hold one of their spring festivals, and members of the tribe were invited to attend. This was a time for celebration and, above all, for dancing.

The activity in the lodges of the maidens was frantic. They were scurrying about madly, adding makeup to their dark-rimmed eyes' and juice-stained lips, changing into their best dresses of doeskin and elkskin. Similarly in the lodges of the young warriors, no time was being wasted. Men shaved carefully on both sides of their scalp locks, applied quantities of yellow and green paint, and made sure that they looked their most ferocious.

Renno was grateful that a meeting of the Council afforded him the opportunity to avoid attending the festivities, and Betsy felt the same way. They had eaten and danced through enough ritual functions.

Deputized to stand in for them were Renno's sister, Ba-lin-ta, and her husband, Walter Alwin, a native of Fort Springfield, who had gained both his hearing and his powers of speech in the land of the Seneca and consequently was living proof to the devout of the powers that resided in the manitous. They had been unable to have a child, though they had longed for one, but they reconciled themselves to their lot and continually gave thanks for their constant devotion to one another.

Attendance at the festival was by no means compulsory, although no self-respecting unmarried member of the tribe would have been absent. The attendance was limited by age, and children of White Deer's generation, for example, were strictly forbidden to attend. This made it necessary for these preadolescents to conceal themselves among the bushes and observe as best they could.

The entertainment was very simple. When enough maidens and warriors had gathered, the drummer would be joined by three or four colleagues, and all would play together. Young, unmarried warriors would come one at a time into the open fields and there would strut and dance in any way that pleased them. They were privileged to invite maidens of their choice to dance with them, and almost without exception they availed themselves of the opportunity. The older women disliked the festivals because it was so difficult to maintain a semblance of decorum and order. Warriors and the maidens of their choice had a habit of disappearing and creating problems for the women of high morals, who kept guard over the purity of the nation.

Ja-gonh was very reluctant to attend. He told himself that he was still too concerned over the incident of the plunging hawk, but he knew this was only an excuse. His real reason was that he felt, because of reasons he could not analyze, he had arrived at too serious a point in his life to attend a frivolous social event and make light of a young woman by asking her to dance with him. He was fast-approaching a crisis of some sort, and he well knew it, although he did not understand what it was. All he knew was that he would have preferred to avoid the festival completely, though such avoidance was out of the question. He was young, he was unattached; no one, including his parents, would have understood or approved his refusal to attend the function.

Ah-wen-ga swiftly dressed and applied makeup for the event, knowing that, as always, she would prove to be one of the most popular maidens present. If the usual took place, four or five warriors would vie for the honor of dancing with her and would surround her when she caught her breath.

But Ah-wen-ga was more troubled tonight than she was willing to admit. She could shrug off very easily the attentions of warriors who did not interest her. What distressed her was that long look that Ja-gonh had given her at the home of her parents, a look in which he had said so much without speaking a single word. She knew that she was entering deep waters with strong currents, and she would need all of her judgment to stay afloat. Was she ready for a serious, mature relationship with Ja-gonh? Well, she knew only that she wanted him, and she hoped that he wanted her as badly. Beyond that she could not look.

One who suffered no doubts about what she was doing was Goo-ga-ro-no. Her expression radiant, she crossed the fields to the open space where the dancing would take place, and Ba-lin-ta, her aunt, looked at her in whole-hearted approval. To her, Goo-ga-ro-no represented all that was pure in a maiden of the Seneca.

She had no idea that her niece slipped away into the wilderness as soon as she reached the shadows at the far side of the field. Racing madly on silent feet, the young woman soon reached her hidden rendezvous with Pierre Fanchon, deep in the forest.

Materializing out of the shadows, Fanchon tenderly

embraced her, although he felt extremely apprehensive. If the Seneca discovered his presence this close to their main town, if they even guessed his relationship with the daughter of the sachem, it would be the end for him. They would ruthlessly snuff out his life, and he would not be allowed to appeal for clemency or mercy.

Fanchon knew that he was dealing with a volatile, highly dangerous matter, so he wasted no time. "Dear one," he murmured, "I cannot wait for you forever. You have promised to come with me, and I must hold you now to your word. Each day that I linger here the chance that I will be found becomes greater, and the risks I take are enormous."

Goo-ga-ro-no knew he was not exaggerating, but it was a wrench to give up all that she knew for the sake of this tall, mysterious stranger who had won her heart. "Must we leave the land of the Seneca for all time?" she asked.

He shook his head. "Not for all time, only until we are married and establish ourselves properly. Until then, however, we will be too vulnerable, and we need to protect ourselves. So, I say, in two weeks from now we will leave and go to New France together."

"Two weeks!" Suddenly time was racing so rapidly that Goo-ga-ro-no felt she was losing control of the situation. She certainly could not blame Pierre for his eagerness, and she respected his desire to deal honorably with her. He had promised from the outset to marry her and, much to her surprise, had made no attempt to bed her. Therefore, the least she could do was to agree to his schedule. "Where will we go?" she whispered.

Pierre had no intention of revealing that their destination would be Quebec; he did not want Goo-ga-ro-no to leave a farewell note, telling of their whereabouts. "We've got to move one step at a time," he said evasively. "It's enough that we're going to New France and will build our lives there together."

"It's more than enough," the young woman said. She pressed close to him again for a long moment and then, breaking away, retraced her steps through the wilderness to the scene of the festivities. There she would dance with any number of single warriors and would succeed thoroughly in fooling anyone who looked at her.

As Goo-ga-ro-no stole back on the scene, additional drummers joined in playing the intense, primitive airs, and the throbbing sounds permeated the consciousness of everyone present. A number of young braves, who recently had been elected to the rank of senior warrior, could not help showing off their new positions with their headdresses of three feathers, and to the amusement of their elders, they strutted out onto the field. Most lost no time selecting partners. A brave and a young woman faced each other and, never touching, moved back and forth at will, improvising and inventing steps as they saw fit, each challenging his or her partner to keep the pace and the rhythm.

Ah-wen-ga took her time coming to the open field; she didn't want to admit it, but she had no desire to dance with anyone other than Ja-gonh tonight and, if necessary, was prepared to refuse everyone else. This was an uncommon insult and would not be lightly regarded by any warrior who was spurned. But she was in an increasingly reckless mood, willing to leave her destiny in the hands of fate.

Ja-gonh, meanwhile, told himself stubbornly that he had no intention of joining in the dancing. He had nothing to prove; he had no reason to celebrate. So while other warriors stepped out onto the field, he stood with his arms folded and his face impassive, watching them.

His uncle, Walter Alwin, materialized beside him. "Did you injure your foot, perhaps while you were hunting?" Walter inquired solicitously.

Ja-gonh got the hint at once and shook his head. "I am sound of limb," he said.

Walter clapped him on the bare shoulder. "I'm glad to hear it, boy," he replied, then went off for some of his favorite food, a bowl of steaming corn soup.

Goaded, Ja-gonh took a deep breath, and as he moved out onto the field, he heard a murmur arise from the ranks of the maidens. This in itself was sufficiently disconcerting to cause him to want to flee, but he reminded himself that he was the son of Renno, the grandson of Ghonka, and that he would be a laughingstock if he ran from the group of women. Instead, he gritted his teeth, raised his head high, and moved onto the field.

Ah-wen-ga's belief in the omnipotence of the manitous was promptly confirmed. Through no attempt of her own, through no conscious effort by Ja-gonh, suddenly he stood facing directly toward her. He could not help gazing at her, just as she could not help gazing at him in return. It was as though the manitous had preordained this confrontation between them.

Their eyes locked and held, and Ja-gonh, feeling as though he had been immersed in ice water, gasped aloud.

Ah-wen-ga discovered to her astonishment that she was trembling slightly, and she devoted all of her strength, all of her being, to curbing that feeling. She succeeded sufficiently well to raise her head and, as she returned Ja-gonh's gaze, to smile at him.

He was never conscious of her smile; all he knew was that he felt an overwhelming urge to dance with her instantly, and he was suddenly afraid that some other warrior might beat him to her side. So with a show of unseemly haste, he crossed the intervening space quickly and grunted an invitation.

Ah-wen-ga felt as though she had been robbed of the power of speech and could only nod as she accompanied him onto the field.

Little by little the young couple lost their sense of self-consciousness. The music had its effect on them, their proximity cast a potent spell, and soon they were immersed in the dance.

Talking Quail, who always attended such functions, was quick to notice her elder daughter and Renno's son. They were so absorbed in each other that they had lost all consciousness of everyone else, and something stirred within Talking Quail. For once she had the good sense to keep silent, and as she watched them, her own pulse beat more rapidly.

Neither the young man nor the young woman was even remotely interested in improving on the dance. Their feet moved in rhythm, their bodies swayed without effort, and neither was conscious that they were perfectly attuned to each other. All they did realize was they were in the grip of a turbulence that was so threatening, so powerful that it swept all else from their minds.

There was no need for conversation. They responded to each other instinctively, without words. It did not cross Ja-gonh's mind until much later that he did not speak, and it didn't occur to Ah-wen-ga, either, that she, like the young warrior, spoke not a word.

At last the drums fell silent, their throbbing sound still pulsating on the quiet night air. Ja-gonh looked at his partner and was overwhelmed.

Ah-wen-ga seemed to sense his reaction and was similarly stricken. They stood for a long moment, still devouring each other with their glances, and then Ja-gonh broke the spell by reaching out with his thumb and middle finger, with which he encircled Ah-wen-ga's wrist. He led her back to her companions, lightly grasping her in this way, and she willingly allowed herself to be led.

Abruptly they parted. Neither exchanging farewells nor looking at each other again, they went their separate ways. But both of them knew that a bond had been established between them that night, a strong bond that, although they could not define it, would prove to them in time what they were just beginning to suspect about themselves and each other.

It was very quiet in the Seneca town. With most of the inhabitants attending the festival, only the lodges of the preadolescents were full. A fire burned brightly in the Council Lodge, and the Iroquois chiefs attending the meeting—which was routinely held at least once each season—reviewed the treaties with their English allies. Everyone present was well pleased with the state of affairs. Indeed, the alliance between the Iroquois and the English had never been stronger, and the tone of tonight's meeting was festive.

Now Ghonka, Great Sachem of all the Iroquois, asked

if there were any concluding remarks that the chiefs wished to make. All eyes turned toward Renno, who, as sachem of the Seneca, had achieved great renown not only as a warrior but also as an orator. Renno, realizing he was expected to address the others, rose and spoke softly.

"My brothers," he began, "it is with a happy heart that I speak to you tonight. There has been a long peace with our neighbors and a long peace in our homes. With our friends the English, the Iroquois are the greatest power in the land. Let future generations refer to this present state of peace as the happy time. Long may the happy time continue!"

There were shouts of approval, and the medicine men shook their rattles. Then Renno led the other chiefs in a prayer of thanks to the manitous. As he bowed his head he tried hard not to think of the unsettling dream he had had recently, and he prayed fervently for the continued unity and peace of the Iroquois League.

Finally the meeting was terminated. Renno hurried off to his own house, where Betsy would be waiting for him, and most of the other Seneca Council members rejoined their families. Meanwhile, the members of the visiting tribes returned to their camps outside the palisade, where they would spend the night before departing for their homelands.

Ghonka and Sun-ai-yee, however, lingered, taking their time as they left the solidly built Lodge. The evening was cool, so Ghonka wrapped himself in his feathered buffalo robe, the symbol of his high office. The Great Sachem had more than four-score years, but his body was still powerful, and he carried himself as proudly as ever as he strolled out into the open with his old companion at arms, Sun-ai-yee. Both were in a reflective mood.

They made their way to Ghonka's quarters, and there they sat on the ground outside the building, propping their backs against it as Ghonka slowly and methodically lighted his long pipe.

"As I grow to the end of my days on this earth," he

said, "my thoughts turn more and more forcibly to the future of my people."

Sun-ai-yee nodded.

"My heart is light," Ghonka declared, "to know that the son of the Great Sachem, Renno, has led the Seneca well. This, I know, he will do always. For many years I was worried about Renno's son, because Betsy insisted that her children be educated in the ways of the settlers from England, as well as the ancient ways of the Seneca. But Ja-gonh has also done well. It is true that he understands the mind and heart and spirit of the settlers, but he is not one of them. He is like his father and his grandfather." He paused and added with great pride, "He is a Seneca."

Sun-ai-yee nodded comfortably. He, too, felt that Ja-gonh had excelled during his transitional training and was fit to represent the Seneca anywhere. He was less certain about Goo-ga-ro-no, particularly in view of the rumors that he heard from his wife about the young woman's strange absence from many Seneca gatherings, but he didn't feel it was his place to mention her problems to Ghonka.

"So I am satisfied now," Ghonka continued, "that Ja-gonh will also serve his people well, as will his son after him. There is no longer any question in my mind."

"I quite agree," Sun-ai-yee said. "Ja-gonh is a proud bearer of the torch that you and Renno have carried for so many years."

Ghonka puffed on his pipe in silence and stared up at the sky, which was filled with shimmering stars. "What I have been wondering is who will be a fit mate for Ja-gonh."

Sun-ai-yee was startled. This was not the sort of subject that old warriors ordinarily discussed with each other.

"I know," Ghonka declared, "that Jeffrey Wilson of Fort Springfield would be pleased if Ja-gonh married his daughter. Surely she would be a fit mate for any warrior, were he not the son of Renno and the grandson of Ghonka."

Sun-ai-yee felt he had to speak frankly. "That is so," he admitted. "The Wilson woman comes from an excellent family, and her father is one of the staunchest allies of our nation, but what does this young woman know of our ways? It is true, Renno's wife is white, but Betsy is unique and is truly a Seneca."

Ghonka did not raise his voice, but there was a ring of familiar authority in it when he said, "Ja-gonh must find a mate who knows the ways of our people. Ja-gonh will marry a Seneca! There is no other way! He has no choice!"

Sun-ai-yee accepted the pipe from the Great Sachem and puffed on it reflectively. Talking Quail, he thought, would be delighted when he repeated this conversation to her.

"Is it possible that the daughter of Sun-ai-yee has inherited from her father the cunning of the fox and the courage of the lion?" Ghonka sounded innocent.

Sun-ai-yee adopted a modest approach. "Ah-wen-ga is a maiden," he said, "so she has had few chances to show her cunning or her courage, but it is my belief that she is truly the daughter of Sun-ai-yee."

That was precisely what Ghonka had wanted to hear, and he nodded complacently. "In the days to come," he said, "I will not be too busy. The Council of the Iroquois will not meet for another three moons, so I will have a little time to myself. Perhaps Sun-ai-yee will tell his daughter that it is my wish to become acquainted with her."

Sun-ai-yee nodded solemnly. "She will be told," he said.

The issue was settled, and conversation languished. After a time Sun-ai-yee yawned, and Ghonka knocked out the ashes of his pipe onto the ground. The grizzled war chief hauled himself to his feet. "May Ghonka enjoy the sleep of the just," he said as he raised his left arm in stiff farewell.

Ghonka returned the gesture smartly, in spite of the arthritis that made it difficult for him to straighten his arm. Then, sighing, he stared at the dying fire. He would enjoy its warmth for a few minutes more, he decided, before he would join Ena and obtain his night's rest.

As Sun-ai-yee made his way home, he thought about the conversation. He knew that Ah-wen-ga was being called on to give a command performance and that if she passed the test, her marriage to Ja-gonh was a certainty. He rejoiced silently, and he knew Talking Quail would share his delight. They could ask for nothing more for Ah-wen-ga than membership in the most distinguished family in all the land of the Seneca.

As Sun-ai-yee made his way across the deserted town, he saw a tall, sinewy figure heading in the opposite direction and frowned because he failed to recognize the man. Then he saw that the young warrior's face and torso were smeared with the vermilion paint of the Mohawk, and he relaxed. The Council meeting had been attended by representatives of the other Iroquois tribes, including the Mohawk, and Sun-ai-yee assumed that this young man had been present at the meeting. He couldn't be certain, but that did not trouble him; as he grew older he found that young warriors, whatever their nationality, resembled one another more and more. Without thinking any more about the stranger, Sun-ai-yee went into his house and closed the door behind him.

Gray Fox breathed more easily after he passed the aging war chief, and he continued to cross the town without incident. He had been afraid that the barrel-chested warrior might challenge him, but his task was proving to be easy—far simpler, far less complicated, and certainly far less dangerous than he had imagined back in the land of the Huron, when he had finally decided how to cause the downfall of both the Seneca and the Iroquois League. Disguising himself as a Mohawk, Gray Fox had taken advantage of the Seneca festival and Council meeting and had arrived in the town unquestioned.

A feeling of great joy took possession of the Huron when he saw Ghonka sitting alone on the ground in front of the fire before his house. His fortune was almost too good to be true. For more than a half-century the Huron had been intimidated by Ghonka. Now, at this very moment, Gray Fox would obtain vengeance for all that Ghonka had done to subjugate his tribe.

Ghonka looked up, saw the war paint of the Mohawk, and nodded pleasantly, waiting to be greeted. To his astonishment the stranger reached beneath his short cloak, and his hand reappeared, grasping a razor-sharp tomahawk.

A faint cry of exaltation burst from Gray Fox's throat as he released the tomahawk. It flew a short distance in the air and was true to its mark; an era ended when it found its target.

Ghonka knew instantly that the tomahawk was going to hit him, and he met his fate with the same quiet resolution that he had displayed so often in battle. He did not try to evade the inevitable; and he refused to flinch. The tomahawk caught him in the forehead, felling him instantly, and his blood dampened the soil he had fought so often and so hard to protect. A low, penetrating moan escaped his lips.

Inside the house Ena heard his cry of pain and hurried into the open to find her husband near death. Her loud scream of terror and anguish alerted the whole community to the tragedy.

Gray Fox knew the instant he released the tomahawk that his mission had succeeded far better than even he had dared to hope. Ghonka, the implacable enemy of the Huron, was no more. Now only one thought filled Gray Fox's mind: he had to make his escape swiftly. Turning away from Ghonka's house, he retraced his footsteps as he made his way toward the palisade that protected the town from the wilderness. He knew better than to hurry, but he did not linger, either, and walked at a brisk, even pace.

His resolve was tried to the utmost when he heard Ena's scream. He knew that within moments the entire town would be aroused, but he forced himself to continue the same pace until he came to the field where the dancing had taken place. Only then did he allow himself to break into a trot.

As it happened, Ja-gonh had stood in a daze after he and Ah-wen-ga had concluded their dance, and only now did he stir. Shaking himself, he started toward home and was mildly curious when he saw an unfamiliar warrior wearing the paint of the Mohawk, trotting across the field and passing almost within arm's length of him.

Ja-gonh had no idea what called his attention so forcibly to the stranger. All he knew was that it was very strange, indeed, to see a Mohawk running through the fields beyond the palisade, and he turned to stare over his shoulder. There was something about the man's run that engraved itself on his mind. It was a loose-limbed, deer-like run, and as Ja-gonh watched, he knew he would recognize the runner if he ever saw him again.

War chiefs, senior warriors, and junior warriors, all in full battle array, lined the streets of the Seneca town. In every house, in every lodge, in every longhouse, lights were burning, and the muted sound of weeping could be heard. The inconceivable had happened: the invincible Ghonka was nearing his end.

The Great Sachem's family gathered outside his house and stood in silence, awaiting the opportunity to bid a final farewell to the man whom history would call the greatest chief of all the Iroquois.

Ba-lin-ta and Walter walked solemnly into the hut and paused beside the simple bed of corn-husk mats, covered with a blanket. Ba-lin-ta's heart felt as though it had been ripped to pieces; only now did she realize how much she loved her father, how much she would miss him. Her lifelong training did not help her conceal her emotion, and she wept miserably as she looked down at him.

"Do not grieve for me, my daughter. Do not grieve for me, my son," Ghonka said. "I have lived far longer than most, and I have received great joy from both of you. This fills my heart with satisfaction." He raised his left hand, palm outward, in a salute, and they accepted the gesture of farewell. Controlling her tears, Ba-lin-ta bowed her head, and she and Walter crept quietly out into the night.

The next to enter was El-i-chi. He walked briskly to conceal the emotions that threatened to overcome him, and he scowled fiercely as he looked down at the badly wounded body of his father.

"To you, my son, I wish what I wished for myself. You have fulfilled all my wishes and all my hopes. If the manitous are pleased with me, it is because you have fulfilled your obligations as a Seneca, as a warrior, and as a man."

Tears streamed down El-i-chi's face now, and he wept without shame. He bent his head, and Ghonka reached up, feebly touching his forehead. El-i-chi fought for self-control and refrained from giving vent to the great sob that welled up within him.

Goo-ga-ro-no now entered, dreading the lecture she thought certain she would receive from her grandfather, but even now Ghonka's great wisdom did not desert him. There was a hint of gentle humor in his voice as he said to her, "Well, young woman, perhaps you will admit now that the signs given by the manitous are true signs and should be heeded."

Unable to reply, the young woman was racked with sobs and was so overcome with grief that her father and brother had to help hold her up. She began to see that she would be deserting all that Ghonka had held dear when she ran off with Pierre Fanchon, though as she saw it, she had no choice and had to obey the call of her own destiny. She wished now that Ghonka were going to live a little longer. The realization dawned on her that he, of all the family, would understand her absolute need for independence. But it was too late now. Her grandfather's life was ebbing rapidly.

Ghonka's closing words to Betsy were succinct: "You came to the land of the Seneca a stranger, and now you are my daughter. I can ask for no greater boon than that. I am proud of you, and I share Renno's joy in you."

Ena, Ghonka's mate for more than half a century, was

dry-eyed when she entered his presence, as befitted the wife of a Seneca warrior. She did not flinch as she gazed at his tomahawk-battered face.

Ghonka addressed her softly. "We will meet soon again, in the land of the hereafter," he said. "I will wait for you in the happy hunting ground of our ancestors."

Ena nodded, and there was only a trace of huskiness in her voice as she replied. "Ghonka will not have long to wait," she said evenly. "He knows that Ena will come to him, as she has always come to him."

Their hands touched fleetingly, and she was gone while she still retained her composure.

It was only fitting that Ghonka should reserve his greatest candor for Renno, his elder son. "My heart is troubled as I leave this world, my son," he said. "He who killed me with a tomahawk wore the paint of the Mohawk. I do not know this man; I do not know his grievance. But I know that the Seneca will cry for vengeance against their brothers, the Mohawk, and the alliance of the Iroquois will be spattered with much blood."

"It is true that the warriors of the Seneca will feel great hatred in their hearts for their brothers, the Mohawk," Renno said. "I will speak with them; I will tell them it is my wish and the wish of Ghonka that they live in peace with all other Iroquois, but I cannot guarantee that they will listen. They have loved the Great Sachem with a deep and pure and abiding love, and in their grief they will strike out, as the bear, who has seen her cub killed before her eyes, strikes out."

Ghonka sighed faintly. "I know you will do your best, my son, as you always do your best. That is enough for me to ask of you."

Father and son exchanged a long, lingering look, and when Renno emerged from his father's chamber, he smeared ashes on his forehead, the bridge of his nose, and the backs of his hands. He would wear these signs of mourning until they wore off.

Only Ja-gonh, of all those near and dear to Ghonka,

had not yet bid him farewell. It was the young man's turn now, and his whole being surged with emotion as he stood beside his grandfather's bed.

"Do as you have done," Ghonka directed him, "live as you have lived, and in that way you will find favor with the gods and with men."

Ja-gonh could curb his emotions no longer. "In the names of all the manitous," he cried in a loud voice that carried easily to those outside of the sickroom, "I swear I will avenge the murder of Ghonka, my grandfather. I will not rest until he who slew Ghonka is dead—as he deserves to die!"

Even Renno was somewhat appalled by his son's temerity. Such an oath, taken on Ghonka's deathbed, had to be fulfilled. There was no way of avoiding or evading the inevitable: Ja-gonh had promised to find and inflict justice on Ghonka's killer. Ja-gonh had assumed an obligation, sacred and inviolable, and could not rest until he satisfied it.

Those who heard his anguished cry agreed that it was only right and fitting that Ja-gonh—who represented the future of the Seneca—should seek the murderer and wash clean the stain on his people's honor.

Never had such a large crowd assembled in the town of the Seneca. Warriors, their wives, and their children came from every community in the land of the Seneca to pay their homage to their greatest leader. Other Iroquois were present in vast numbers, too. In fact, so many of them came that it was necessary to erect tents in the fields beyond the palisade to accommodate the crowds.

But the Indians were not alone. General Jeffrey Wilson appeared on behalf of Massachusetts Bay, wearing his full-dress blue and gold uniform and accompanied by an honor guard of forty militiamen.

Drums began to beat as soon as the first gray streaks of dawn appeared in the sky, and they seemed to throb everywhere in the wilderness, as though dozens of men were playing the slow, mournful dirge. A funeral pyre nearly twenty feet high had been constructed beyond the cornfields and was piled high with kindling and cornstalks. On it Ghonka was laid out in his most handsome feathered war bonnet and his feathered buffalo robe. It was only right that he should wear these into eternity. The immediate family gathered at the base of the pyre along with representatives of each of the Iroquois nations. A fire was started by these brothers of the Seneca, and a flaming torch was handed to Ena. She walked forward a few feet, her steps never faltering, and after muttering a short prayer in which she consigned her husband's life to the care of the gods, she thrust the burning torch into the midst of the kindling above her. It caught, and there was no sound but the crackling noise of the fire as it spread.

Suddenly the flames flared high, and the remains of Ghonka were consumed.

Renno made certain that his mother was not faint or otherwise unwell, and when Ba-lin-ta and El-i-chi assured him of her well-being, he moved to the head of the procession, folding his arms and staring off into space, his forehead, nose, and hands still bearing traces of the ashes he had spread on them. He stood for what seemed like an eternity as the leaping flames destroyed and consumed the last earthly remains of his great father. He knew that his dream had been in anticipation of this day, and he realized, too, that an enormous burden would now descend on him and his son.

The drums continued to throb at the same even pace, and of the immediate family only Goo-ga-ro-no wept aloud. The sky and the elements, it appeared, were in sympathy with her because a faint drizzle fell, and many Seneca women commented that the manitous were mingling their tears with those of humans.

In only one respect was the funeral of Ghonka similar to that of the great statesmen of the more civilized nations. When the last of the funeral pyre had disappeared and the simple ceremonies were at an end, everyone adjourned to rough-hewn tables, where cold meats and breads, baked for the occasion, were available. The Iroquois leaders sat together, and ordinary Seneca by the hundreds crowded forward to express their condolences to Ena.

It was a miracle, as Renno admitted in a low voice to Jeffrey Wilson, that no blood had been spilled at the funeral. The anti-Mohawk feeling was running so high that it seemed impossible to contain it. The fifty Mohawk warriors who had attended as escorts for Mi-shal, the sachem of the Mohawk, received so much abuse that Renno was certain open hostilities would flare at any moment. Mi-shal, however, proved to be exceptionally competent and was able to keep his men under control. Only by exerting great effort could Renno prevent his own warriors from taking a knife or tomahawk to Mohawk visitors.

Now, with the funeral itself ended, only one function remained. The sachems of each of the Iroquois tribes, attended and accompanied by their principal medicine men and senior war chiefs, went into a secret conclave to elect a Great Sachem of all the Iroquois.

Hundreds gathered outside the Council Lodge to watch the leaders as they entered, and Renno, marching at the head of the Seneca delegation, had no doubt that the sentiment against the Mohawk was continuing to run dangerously high. At his request El-i-chi and Walter were actively patrolling the lines, keeping impetuous young warriors from hurling themselves at the Mohawk, who, ostensibly at least, were their sworn brothers.

The tensions were plain to behold in the Council Lodge. The Seneca delegation was greeted with warm sympathy by the majority of other Iroquois, and Renno noted that only the Oneida held back. That was quite natural. There had always been a rivalry between the Seneca and the Oneida, and it was normal enough in a time of tension for the Oneida to side with the Mohawk. But, Renno realized, herein lay a great danger, as well. The strength of the Iroquois League lay in the absolute equality of all of its members. The playing of politics, the balancing of one tribe against another, was unheard of, but it appeared that that was the danger in the present situation.

The elderly sachem of the Onondaga, the most senior official present, acted as chairman and felt compelled to deliver an interminable eulogy in which he extolled Ghonka's many virtues. Everyone had to hear him out, of course, and listened in polite silence. Finally came the real business of the occasion, the election of a new Great Sachem.

Sun-ai-yee was on his feet instantly. "I place in nomination a Seneca who was so close to Ghonka that his name is inseparable from that of Ghonka. I give you Renno."

The nods of the Cayuga and Tuscarora indicated that they were in hearty approval, but Renno was astonished. It had not occurred to him that he might be called upon to succeed his father when there were so many sachems his senior. Now that he faced the possibility, however, he had to admit it had its advantages. Certainly if he were in a position of greater authority, he would be in a better position to control the surging tides of emotions.

Then an elderly Mohawk medicine man lumbered to his feet and, without further ado, placed the name of Mi-shal in nomination. The choice of the Mohawk leader was a good one, Renno had to admit. Mi-shal was approximately his own age, in his early fifties, and had a long, distinguished career of service both to his own people and to all of the Iroquois.

Unfortunately, however, his nomination at the present time seemed to pit the Seneca even more sharply against the Mohawk, and the confrontation that Renno had wanted to avoid now appeared inevitable. Tempers were bubbling and boiling near the surface. The Oneida were openly siding with the Mohawk, who felt the hostility of their other colleagues and were responding in kind. It seemed likely that the leaders of the mighty Iroquois might shed blood before the meeting ended.

Renno and Mi-shal were asked to withdraw so their

nominations could be discussed freely. They consented and made their way together past the large area where ceremonial fires were lighted on state occasions.

Renno saw no reason to be less than candid. "I don't like this situation," he said.

Mi-shal was equally open. "Neither do I," he admitted.

"It seems to me," Renno said, "that we lose far more than we stand to gain if the Iroquois League is harmed in any way."

"Granted," the Mohawk declared.

"Perhaps," Renno said, "both of us could refuse the nomination. That would open the door to some candidate whose nation is less likely to arouse unseemly emotions."

Mi-shal smiled and shook his head, and his words promptly demonstrated that he was a true statesman. "If any man deserves to become Great Sachem, the honor—such as it is—should go to you. Your experience and background have trained you for it. Frankly, I don't relish the prospect of holding such a position, so the easiest and simplest way out of the dilemma is for me to refuse the nomination. This will leave clear the path for you."

Before Renno could stop him, Mi-shal turned, hurried back to the conference, and interrupted the startled representatives by delivering a short, pungent speech in which he rejected the nomination for himself and urged that the election of Renno be made unanimous.

Then he astonished the entire Council when he said, "It is not easy to be a Mohawk in an assemblage of Iroquois these days. I do not pretend to know the identity of the Mohawk warrior who, it is alleged, is responsible for the death of our beloved Ghonka. It is not enough for me to say that the whole Mohawk nation decries this act and looks with hatred upon the perpetrator. We realize that it is essential that the unity of the Iroquois be preserved. That unity is fragile at this very moment, when brother would plunge his knife into the heart of a brother. So I beg you to accept my offer and to allow me to work with you, for the common good of us all."

His speech was greeted with silence, and then with one accord there was a roar of enthusiastic approval. His statesmanship was beyond question, and his farsightedness was making a valuable contribution to the cause of allied Indian unity.

Renno was immeasurably grateful to Mi-shal and lost no time in making his feelings known. "If we avert bloodshed, my brother," he said, "it is you who have prevented it."

Mi-shal smiled faintly. "I take no credit where credit is not due," he said. "The Mohawk stand alone, you know. The Oneida lean toward us, but if there were an emergency, they would side against us with all the others. Rather than see the Mohawk cut off and isolated, I prefer that they rejoin their brothers of the Iroquois League."

He was very wise, Renno decided, because leading the Mohawk in an isolated fight for recognition surely would be a battle in a losing cause, and the Mohawk ultimately would suffer great damage. But the rift could not be entirely healed in a single day, and Renno said, "I think it would be wise of you, Mi-shal, if you and the Mohawk depart quietly, during the funeral banquet tonight, while all others are occupied. In that way there will be no exchanges of words, no exchanges of blows, and we will avoid the shedding of blood."

Fortunately the Mohawk leader could see the wisdom of the suggestion, and he agreed—with some reluctance, to be sure—to follow Renno's scheme.

Thus it happened that Renno began a term of office as successor to his father, under conditions that appeared to improve hour by hour. He led the sachems and other leaders of the Iroquois nations from the Council Chamber, and there was a murmur from the crowd as people saw his war bonnet with many feathers and recognized his feathered, long cloak of buffalo skin. There was a shout of approval from the crowds, and without discussion it was agreed that justice of a sort had been done. Ghonka had been cruelly and unjustly murdered, but his place as leader of the Iroquois League had now been taken by his son.

RENNO

In a move that was regarded as almost anticlimactic, Sun-ai-yee was elected to replace Renno as sachem of the Seneca. This was the first time within the memory of living man that either Ghonka or Renno had not been directly at the nation's helm, but Sun-ai-yee had been so closely associated with Ghonka and his son that everyone agreed the future of the Seneca was secure.

Renno, as always, was concerned only with practical matters. "Have Mi-shal and his warriors left as yet?" he wanted to know.

Sun-ai-yee nodded. "They required a little prodding," he said. "But they are gone, and I am grateful to the manitous for their departure. I was sure blood was going to be spilled before this night was ended."

"So was I," Renno said, then sighed in relief. He knew, as did Sun-ai-yee, that though their positions held great honor, they also bore enormous responsibilities in exceedingly troubled times.

Chapter III

One visitor who could not arrive in time for the funeral itself but who nevertheless came to the land of the Seneca to pay his respects to Ghonka's family was Betsy's brother and Renno's good friend, Colonel Ned Ridley. Now commander of the First Regiment of Virginia, Ned had ridden long and hard through the wilderness to be present in a dual capacity: both as official representative of the governor of Virginia and on his own behalf, as one who had so long admired Ghonka.

Ned, along with Jeffrey Wilson, sensed the great tension caused by the death of Ghonka, and Renno spoke freely with his friends, his oldest colonial associates. "I find it difficult to believe—impossible, really—that the Mohawk actually engaged in a conspiracy of some kind to

53

do away with Ghonka," he said. "They revered him almost as much as the Seneca. I cannot believe that any Mohawk warrior would conspire against him."

"Are you suggesting," Jeffrey Wilson asked, "that the murder was the work of a madman—or someone whose reasoning was in some way defective?"

Renno shrugged. "That is always possible," he said, "but the way the killer made his escape was very clever. It obviously was well planned. There is more to all this than meets the eye, more by far than we know."

Ned thought to himself that Renno truly was a Seneca in all of his ways. He was showing no impatience whatsoever in solving Ghonka's murder but seemed to take the attitude that if the killing had been committed by someone other than a Mohawk, that fact ultimately would make itself known. He had acquired the incredible patience of the Indians, and it was serving him in good stead.

One development that resulted unexpectedly from the visit of the colonists to the land of the Seneca was the growing bond between Ja-gonh and Roger Harkness, who had accompanied Jeffrey Wilson to the Seneca village in order to learn more about the colonists' esteemed allies. He had sent dispatches on two occasions to the Virginia governor to say that although the leader of the Iroquois had been assassinated, there was no evidence of anything untoward on the part of France or her Indian allies. But little did Roger or any of his associates suspect that one of the greatest—and most devious—offensive campaigns against the New World was already being put into motion.

Ja-gonh was assigned by Renno to look after Roger and to act as his host, and in the course of several days of hunting and fishing together in the wilderness, the pair discovered that they were kindred spirits. To Ja-gonh's surprise Roger had the ability to remain very silent when he was hunting and to show the patience of a true warrior. The pair developed a quick, mutual respect for each other, as well as a deep understanding.

But their rapport was almost destroyed inadvertently

by Roger one afternoon when they were returning to the Seneca town after a jaunt that had taken them far into the wilderness. Ja-gonh secretly had been testing the young Englishman's stamina and was surprised to discover that Roger could march without tiring for far longer periods than the average white man. They bagged several rabbits, as well as a pair of plump geese, and consequently were well satisfied with their day's efforts. As they approached the town they slowed their pace when they came to the vegetable fields, where a number of the women were at work, as usual. Roger halted abruptly and muttered something under his breath. Ja-gonh was surprised and noted that the Englishman was staring hard at someone across the field. Roger half turned to him and spoke softly. "Good Lord," he said, "I don't think I've ever seen a more beautiful girl anywhere."

Ja-gonh was shocked to realize that his friend was staring at Ah-wen-ga. Long experience with the unmarried young settlers in Massachusetts Bay and in Virginia had taught him their attitude toward Indian women, whom they regarded as suitable objects for conquest and whose desires and feelings they were inclined to ignore. He had no idea whether Harkness shared these views but decided to speak very cautiously on the subject of Ah-wen-ga.

"The maiden is very comely," he said flatly.

Harkness was struck by something in his tone that was a shade remote and alien, and he became slightly confused.

"She is the daughter of the new sachem of the Seneca," Ja-gonh went on. "She is a woman who stands apart from other women here."

Roger immediately assumed that it was her father's new rank that gave her additional stature, but Ja-gonh quickly disillusioned him. "She has always been very different from the other maidens of the Seneca," Ja-gonh said emphatically. "He who befriends her is my friend. He who would take advantage of her is my enemy. I would cut out the heart of any man who harmed Ah-wen-ga."

Roger Harkness swallowed hard as he realized that he had blundered into a situation far more complex than he had known. "I will remember the words of my friend," he said hastily. "And I will make certain that I always treat the maiden with great respect."

Ja-gonh was satisfied and was convinced that at the very least he had saved Ah-wen-ga from possible embarrassment. He knew that she was aware that she was under discussion and was pretending to ignore him and his colonial companion, continuing her work in the fields. But Ja-gonh had no desire to tell her about the conversation he had just concluded because he had no right to act as her protector. So he looked away from her and continued toward the town.

Unfortunately, she was sure to resent being talked about behind her back, and the new-found amity that he had established with her would be destroyed, but that couldn't be helped. Perhaps he would find some way to hint that he had been trying to help her rather than harm her.

When he arrived at the house of his parents, Ja-gonh handed the geese and rabbits to Betsy. Then he and Roger proceeded to clean their weapons. Meanwhile, Renno was deep in conversation with Ned, his brother-in-law.

Renno's manner in dealing with the many subordinates who had come to him from time to time throughout the day was confident and self-assured, but Ned was not fooled. He and Renno had undergone many trials and had shared numerous adventures over the years, and the Virginian consequently knew him better than anyone else. He kept his opinions to himself, but ultimately he said quietly, "You're much more concerned over the murder of Ghonka than you are letting anyone know, Renno."

Renno's pale eyes seemed to bore into Ned as he nodded.

"You really face a serious situation, then?" Ned asked.

Again Renno nodded. "In the years that I was growing to manhood," he said, "there was one factor that was constant above all others. It was a fundamental of life, as certain as the fact that the sun rises in the morning and sets at night, and that was the solidity of the Iroquois League. The nations of the Iroquois were tied together with bonds of steel that could not be broken. This I knew. This every warrior in every Iroquois tribe knew." He sighed gently. "Now, however, the League has been shaken to its very foundations. Regardless of the identity of the man who killed my father, there is bad blood between the Seneca and the Mohawk—blood that calls for the spilling of more blood. The Iroquois unity that has existed for so many years has been shattered. The Seneca demand vengeance for the death of Ghonka. The Mohawk feel guilty over his death. In their anger they, too, wish to strike out blindly. I am afraid that the peace that has existed in the lands of the Iroquois for so many decades may be disturbed at any moment."

Ned was deeply concerned. "Are you telling me that you expect that the Seneca and the Mohawk will go to war with each other?" He realized that the very idea of such fraternal warfare would have been unthinkable previously.

Renno folded his arms across his chest, and his eyes became thoughtful. "There will be no formal war," he said, "because Sun-ai-yee will control the Seneca and Mi-shal will curb the excesses of the Mohawk, but when the tempers of brave warriors are ragged, many men may die without war having been declared. Frankly, Ned, I don't know what to expect, but I am reluctant to take steps in advance to prevent a disturbance. Merely by taking those steps I will be encouraging the creation of such a disturbance."

"I see what you mean," Ned replied. "I wish there were something I could do to help. The very possibility that the Iroquois League is shaky is enough to send tremors through every colony in North America."

"Yes," Renno replied, "that is my greatest concern. Once our old enemies, the French, learn of such a disturbance, they will be sure to use it to their advantage."

Ned's lips tightened, and he nodded. "I have talked with Governor Gooch at length about the possibility of a war with France in the New World. It is his opinion, and the opinion of the secretary of state in England, that France is as ambitious as ever and will wage war sooner or later—and my guess is it will be sooner, if the rift among the Iroquois is not healed."

Both were relieved when Betsy rejoined them in the house, making it possible for them to change the conversation to a topic less forbidding and gloomy. As usual, she had more immediate concerns on her mind. "I suppose that both of you noticed," she said, "how Jeffrey Wilson's conversation at supper last night kept reverting to Patience."

Renno smiled absently. "That's only natural," he said. "She is his eldest child, and he has always been very fond of her." Ned nodded, indicating his agreement, but Betsy stared at her brother, then at her husband and shook her head. "Men," she said, showing mock indignation, "are so thickheaded that I can't believe it. Jeffrey had one subject, and only one, very much on his mind. He would like nothing better than to arrange a marriage between Patience and Ja-gonh."

Ned grinned but kept his opinion to himself, having learned that his sister had a sixth sense when it came to affairs of the heart. Renno, however, laughed aloud and shook his head. "I think you exaggerate a bit, Betsy," he said. "I believe that Jeffrey and Adrienne would be happy enough if Ja-gonh asked for the hand of Patience, but I do not think they actively seek such a union."

His wife answered tightly, "You are totally mistaken. They seek such a tie for many reasons, not the least of which is that it would bind the Iroquois and the colonists of Massachusetts Bay more or less irrevocably. For another thing they undoubtedly are having trouble finding an appropriately eligible suitor for Patience. Her position in Massachusetts Bay is extraordinary. I know what I'm talking about because I was in more or less the same position in Virginia, before I married you. It isn't easy to find a suitor for an heiress, you know. I happened to be lucky in that I met and fell in love with a renowned Seneca warrior."

Renno exchanged a warm glance with his wife, then looked away and stuffed his pipe. Adopting a stern tone, he said, "Ja-gonh will make up his own mind regarding the woman he wants to marry. I refuse to allow political considerations to influence him."

Betsy lowered her voice so that Ja-gonh and Roger Harkness, who were still cleaning their weapons outside the house, would not hear her. "I don't know whether Ja-gonh knows it or not," she said, "but I think he has already made up his mind regarding his future wife."

Renno looked at her sharply. "You hadn't told me," he said.

"I've just become aware of it myself," she said. "I think he's strongly attracted to Ah-wen-ga, but I don't know if he's conscious of it."

Renno was pleased. "Perhaps I should have a word with Sun-ai-yee in private," he said.

Betsy glowered at him. "You shall do no such thing," she said.

Ned grinned. Renno might be the Great Sachem of all the Iroquois now, but Betsy was still Betsy and would tolerate no nonsense from him.

"Ja-gonh is capable of looking after himself," she said, "just as you were capable of it at his age. Remember, you and I were married when you were Ja-gonh's present age."

Renno had thought he had been much older but was not prepared to argue the point with her. Long experience in marriage had taught him that Betsy inevitably was right and invariably won such arguments.

"If he really prefers Ah-wen-ga," Renno said, "I shall find it necessary to have appropriate words with Jeffrey sooner or later. He is too old and too good a friend to be hurt, and I don't want him to get the idea that Ja-gonh doesn't think Patience is good enough for him."

Betsy took her husband's hand, and again they looked at each other with a love that had not dimmed in all the years they had been married. There were probably few people in the entire New World who understood each other as well as Betsy and Renno, and there was nothing they couldn't discuss. Now they were in complete agreement about the manner in which to deal with their son's romantic leanings, and the lovely Virginia woman—now nearly as much a Seneca as her husband—couldn't help admiring Renno anew. He was able to show his concern over affairs of the heart, even while he was preyed upon by his worry for the future peace of the Iroquois League.

Major de Bienville took a bag of gold from his belt, weighed it in his hand, and then slid it across his desk in the Citadel, the great fort that guarded Quebec, the capital of New France. "You deserve all this and more," he said.

Gray Fox quickly scooped up the leather bag and, not taking time to count the gold it contained, hid it beneath his buckskin cloak. He nodded and bowed his head, but he remained silent.

Bienville thought Gray Fox was being modest, but his face was averted, and the Frenchman could not see his eyes, or he would have realized that the half-breed was being far from humble. In fact, he was quite brazenly relishing his situation.

"I don't know how you accomplished so much so easily," Bienville said, "but I think it's miraculous. Not only is Ghonka out of the way, thus disposing for all time a leader who struck fear into the hearts of French allies everywhere in the New World, but you also have the Seneca and the Mohawk at each other's throats, too. This is almost too good to be true."

Gray Fox sat back in the handsome leather chair that he actually found both comfortable and attractive and allowed himself the luxury of a faint smile. "I believe," he said, "that troubles are just beginning between the Seneca and the Mohawk. Soon, I think, all of the Iroquois will be squabbling, perhaps even fighting."

Bienville shook his head. "Whatever you've done and however you've done it, you've accomplished more in a short time than anyone has been able to do in a period of years. What's next on your schedule?"

Gray Fox stared out the long French window at the Saint Lawrence River, which gleamed in the spring sunlight; occasional ice floes could still be seen here and there bobbing up and down on the waters, but soon the river would be clear again, and furs—the lifeblood of New France—would be pouring into Quebec from the interior.

"I think," the half-breed said softly, "that I would like muskets for all of the warriors of the Huron. They will need many months of practice before they become proficient with these modern weapons of the white man, but eventually such arms will give them a decided advantage in the battles that they are going to be fighting with the Seneca."

Bienville raised an eyebrow. "You seem rather certain of the future," he commented dryly.

Gray Fox's eyes glittered. "I know only that a climactic war between the Seneca and the Huron must come," he said. "The two nations have been enemies for as long as living man can remember, as long as France and England have been enemies. All that I do, all that I plan has but one goal in mind. I am weakening the Seneca to ensure the victory of the Huron when the warriors of these nations finally meet."

Bienville was silent and suddenly made up his mind. "Very well," he said. "You shall have your muskets. It won't be easy for me to justify their purchase with the paymaster general of the army in Paris, but that will be my concern."

Gray Fox nodded and made no comment, taking care to keep his pleasure well hidden.

"What is the next step that you are planning?" Bienville demanded.

Gray Fox bore an almost startling resemblance to his father, Alain de Gramont, as his lips creased in a small, tight smile. "I do not care to reveal my plans," he said. "It is enough for you to know that the Seneca, who are already reeling from the death of Ghonka, are about to suffer another blow to their prestige." In truth, he was not yet too sure of the details himself, and even if he were, he certainly had no intention of letting even a trusted French officer in on such a secret.

Bienville shrugged. Certainly the half-breed was a rascal, and anything that he planned would do the Seneca little good. Perhaps it was as well to remain in the dark. Bienville was curious but contained himself, sure that in Gray Fox he was backing the one Indian leader capable of destroying the predominance of the Seneca.

The interview having come to an end, Gray Fox departed swiftly. He had done well: the promise of arms for the Huron was heartening, and the gold he had received was his alone, to be shared with no one. Unlike his father, who had died a poor man, he intended to accumulate great wealth for himself, and if he could do it at the expense of the Seneca, he would be striking double blows.

Leaving the headquarters of the high command, Gray Fox mounted a handsome horse and made his way quickly through the streets of Quebec, then out through the town gates. There he spurred his mount to a gallop, and soon he arrived back at his own headquarters, a modest hut in the nearby town of the Huron. As he dismounted, a young warrior gestured to him. "A Frenchman awaits you," he said.

Gray Fox lost no time. "Who is he?"

The Huron brave shrugged.

"Where is he?"

"He waits in the house of Gray Fox."

Gray Fox had no idea who might be awaiting him and was surprised when he entered his hut to find Pierre Fanchon sitting cross-legged on the floor. They stared at each other in silence.

"You have been absent from New France for a considerable length of time," Gray Fox said, a hint of accusation in his tone.

Fanchon nodded comfortably. "Quite so," he said. "I hope you have a good dinner you can give me. I've been traveling through the wilderness at considerable speed and am going to retrace my steps as soon as I've finished reporting to you."

Gray Fox didn't believe in giving rewards prematurely,

but he was dealing with a Frenchman, not with an Indian, so he had to make an exception. He reluctantly walked to the door, called the young brave to him, and ordered a meal brought to the house for Fanchon without delay.

A short time later Fanchon was making himself thoroughly at home as he tore chunks of dripping, steaming venison apart and stuffed them into his mouth.

Gray Fox watched him with interest. "You have been hungry?" he asked.

Fanchon nodded and grinned. "Oh, I've had enough food to survive," he said. "But I've been living on cold meats and fish for longer than I care to remember. I thought it unsafe to cook meals when I've been living so close to the main town of the Seneca."

Gray Fox raised an eyebrow. "It's true, then, as you reported to me, that you actually resided very close to the Seneca?"

"I never lie," Fanchon replied stiffly. "I made an arrangement with you, and I am prepared to keep it."

His tone was imperious, and Gray Fox took exception to it. Like all Frenchmen, Fanchon considered himself superior to a mere half-breed, and a deep resentment welled up within Gray Fox. He was himself smarter and more courageous than any Frenchman he knew, but he was condemned, apparently, to second-rate citizenship in New France because of his mother's Indian birth.

"I've promised you one hundred gold francs if you would strike a severe blow at the Seneca," he said. "So far you have chosen to surround your mission with mystery, and I know literally nothing about your plans. If you expect more than a meal from me, you'll have to be more open and direct."

Fanchon continued to eat in silence, relishing his meal, and then he licked his fingers. "I think you'll be very well satisfied," he said. "In fact, I'm providing you with an even bigger victory than you thought possible. I'm willing to make you a deal right now. I'll tell you what I have done and what I have in mind, if you'll pay me fifty gold francs immediately."

Gray Fox stared hard at him. "I'm listening," he said.

Pierre Fanchon smiled again. "I return tonight to the land of the Seneca," he said. "I shall come back to Quebec permanently in less than two weeks. When I come back, I will be accompanied by none other than the daughter of Renno."

Ordinarily Gray Fox would have remained inscrutable, but the news was so startling that he could scarcely believe it. "Surely you joke," he said.

Fanchon shook his head. "I give you my word," he replied. "Goo-ga-ro-no, the daughter of Renno, who is now the Great Sachem of all the Iroquois, is coming to Quebec with me."

Gray Fox digested the information. "What will you do with her once you bring her to Quebec?"

Fanchon laughed. "That," he said, "really does not concern me. In fact, I'm considering dropping her completely and allowing her to flounder, in order to make her degradation all the more complete." ·

Gray Fox decided not to ask too many questions. If the man was telling him the truth—and there was no reason to believe that he was lying—he was about to achieve a very considerable victory. Indians, the Huron and the Seneca in particular, prized their daughters and put a great value on their virtues. The mere fact that the daughter of Renno would be leaving her home with a Frenchman and would accompany him to the capital of New France would be a cause for irreparable loss of face. This blow, of course, would strike Renno personally, but because of his new and exalted position, anything that reflected on him would have a meaning far greater than it would for the ordinary Seneca. For him to suffer such shame, so soon after the murder of his father, would further besmirch the reputation of the Seneca and would be of inestimable value in raising the Huron in the eyes of all the tribes of North America.

Gray Fox concealed his elation. Certainly he didn't want Fanchon to know how important a blow he was about to strike. Reaching into the purse he had just been given by Major de Bienville, Gray Fox feigned great carelessness as he counted out fifty gold francs and threw them onto the ground in front of the spot where the buckskin-clad Fanchon was sitting cross-legged. "Here you are," he said. "Keep your word, and you shall be paid accordingly. If you fail—no matter what the reason—I will expect immediate repayment of these funds."

Pierre Fanchon chuckled as he picked the coins up out of the dirt and dropped them, one by one, into his purse. "Never fear," he said. "You shall owe me another fifty before two weeks end, and I suspect that if my scheme succeeds as well as I hope it will, you'll be pleased to give me a handsome bonus, as well."

Gray Fox was irritated at this Frenchman, who was trying to take advantage of him, but he was damned if he was going to give in to any such nonsense. He didn't care in the least what Fanchon did with Renno's daughter once he took her away from her people, and he was equally indifferent to Pierre Fanchon's fate. His own goals were clear, and he was determined to let nothing come between him and them. Certainly he wasn't going to be deceived into paying more for services rendered than they were worth. He might be only half-white, but he was not a fool.

Fear of reprisals from the Iroquois had acted as a restraining influence on the tribes that lived along the frontier of the English colonies. Now with that fear suddenly removed because of the rift between the Seneca and the Mohawk, the whole wilderness seemed likely to go up in flames, as Indians threatened to act up and make up for lost time, evening the scores for grievances real and imaginary.

News of the rift between the Seneca and the Mohawk traveled swiftly. It moved north to the Maine district of Massachusetts Bay, just south of the border with New France, and the Abnaki and Algonquian rejoiced at the lack of faith suffered by their old enemies, the much-feared Seneca. They were emboldened by the news, and they made plans to return to the warpath.

The word also spread south with equal speed, and when it reached the land of the Pimlico, it caused an immediate reaction there. The warriors of the tribe gathered, and their position was made plain by one elderly war chief, who rose to his feet and said, "For many years, for many moons, we have been at peace with the men of England because we have feared the wrath of the Seneca if we took to the warpath. We have not followed our own inclinations in this, but we have been motivated only by our fear of the dreaded Seneca and of their allies. Now their alliance has crumbled like dust. At last we are free of the chains that have bound us. I say to you, my brothers, let us strike the bonds that have tied us to the English. The English are as weak as women and will not punish us themselves! The Seneca are no longer able to punish us! So we will tear our treaty with the English to shreds, and we will spit in their faces."

Two days later, colonists in the city of Norfolk, Virginia, were startled when a delegation of Pimlico warriors, carrying a white flag, gained admission past the sentries who were on duty, and shocked the captain of the guard by spitting on the ground at his feet, then hurling at him a copy of their treaty with Virginia and departing without saying a word.

Without delay, they reported the unhappy news to the governor. It was all too clear that the peace of the Virginia frontier was about to be broken, that the Pimlico no longer felt themselves bound by their treaty. This, coupled with the recent dispatch from Roger Harkness describing the death of Ghonka, caused Sir William to fear the worst, even though nothing had yet been learned of French war preparations. But if conditions continued to deteriorate as they were doing, a French attack was a certainty.

Although Colonel Ned Ridley was in the land of the Seneca, the governor called Ned's regiment of militia to duty immediately. Ned's wife, Consuelo, was badly upset by these developments, and her sister-in-law, Anne Cooke, the younger sister of Ned and Betsy, immediately invited Consuelo to dinner that same evening with her and her husband, André. Consuelo and Ned's son, Linnick, now in his twenties, had married and moved with his bride to the South Carolina Colony, where he was trying his hand at growing cotton. Thus, with her husband and son absent, Consuelo arrived alone at the Cooke home.

Anne and André's two teenage sons were boarding at their school in nearby Williamsburg, so the adults were able to discuss the recent events freely. "I hate to admit it," Anne said as they were seated around the dining room table, "but the mere prospect of new troubles with the Pimlico fills me with terror." There was no need for her to remind either her husband or Consuelo that she had been kidnapped by the tribe when she had been very young, and only Renno's intervention had saved her.

Consuelo nodded. "I know what you mean, my dear," she said. "Ned told me all about that nightmare period when the Pimlico were at war with the Virginia settlers."

André, a long, lean man, smiled faintly as he ladled turkey, sweet potatoes, boiled onions, and turnips onto plates. "The trouble with you ladies," he said, "is that you're spoiled. I realize my own background was a trifle unusual because I lived alone deep in the wilderness for so many years, but you Virginians have been at peace with the tribes for so long that you've forgotten the normal dangers of day-to-day living."

Anne looked across the table at him. "What will happen now?" she asked, trying to disguise the growing alarm she felt.

André shrugged. "If you ladies will pardon the expression," he said, "I'll be damned if I'm going to get scared half to death just because the Pimlico frown. If they want to break their treaty with us, let them go ahead and break it. Personally, I hope that they do overreach themselves a bit. They deserve a good thrashing. It will teach them a lesson and enable us to have peace here for as many years as we've enjoyed it, under the protection of the Seneca."

Consuelo started to cut her meat. "Will Ned's regiment see action soon?"

"I don't know," André said cautiously, then turned apologetically to his wife. "I don't quite know how to break this to you, Annie," he said, reaching out for her hand, "but I have decided to take advantage of Ned's long-standing offer of a commission in his regiment. When I received word this afternoon that the call had been issued, I immediately offered my services, and I'll be leaving home in the next day or two."

Anne's face fell, and for a moment she thought she would begin crying, but she made a valiant effort to look and sound cheerful. She knew that after many years of a sedentary life, working on their land and being a considerate, loving husband, André was eager to come to the assistance of the colonies. "I'm sure you'll be a very valuable addition to the militia, André. You know so much more about the forest than even the most experienced hunters and trappers, and the troops will have a very definite need for you."

"Yes," Consuelo said, nodding, "I know that Ned will be delighted to have your services, André. I'm sure he'll start for home immediately from the land of the Seneca as soon as he learns of this development."

André grinned. "My guess is that a decisive action won't develop for quite some time."

Anne raised an eyebrow. "Really?" she asked.

He nodded. "You've got to understand the savages. The Pimlico have now embarrassed us. That in itself is sufficient to satisfy them for a time. They aren't really thinking in terms of fighting a war. I'm sure their orators have fired them up with belligerent speeches, but they have become accustomed to peace for a long period of time, just as we have. So the way I see it, it will take a little time for a real martial spirit to build up on both sides of the frontier. A war is inevitable now, of course; they've knocked the chip off our shoulders, and we've got to meet the challenge or live under a perpetual threat of a Pimlico attack. But I think that Ned will have ample opportunity to organize the regiment for a campaign in the field after he returns from the land of the Seneca. I'd be very much surprised if the Pimlico are really prepared to do battle with us immediately."

André had succeeded in dampening both Anne's and Consuelo's worst fears. Actually, he had no idea whether the Pimlico would go to war immediately or would take their time. The possibilities were equally strong either way, and the one thing he did know was that a campaign, when it was fought, would be extremely vicious. The Pimlico had been building grudges for years and had been prevented by their fear of the Seneca from striking retaliatory blows. Now that that fear was removed, they were certain to start attacking individual homesteads on the frontier, and certainly no family living alone would be safe. From now on, every man and every woman would be forced to carry a rifle at all times.

In the town of the Seneca, Renno watched with dismay as the era of peace, so carefully engineered by his father, fell apart. Jeffrey Wilson had returned to Fort Springfield to mobilize his regiment for border duty, and Ned Ridley had received the urgent summons from the governor of Virginia. Renno conferred at length with representatives of the other Iroquois nations. He also spoke repeatedly with Sun-ai-yee, but Renno came to no firm conclusion.

The balance that Ghonka had achieved had been based on universal respect of all Indian tribes for the prowess of the Seneca. With that missing, the whole delicate, subtle structure was falling apart.

Gradually ideas began to form in Renno's mind. He knew the situation was extraordinary and that extraordinary means were required in order to solve the urgent problem. Certainly he recognized the fact that the English colonies would not deal leniently with any tribes who broke the peace. Colonists would die unnecessarily, and then warriors would meet a similar, senseless fate. These tragedies had to be avoided if at all possible.

While Renno wrestled with his new responsibilities, he was further distracted one day when Betsy came to him in tears. She had learned the stoicism of the Seneca and rarely gave in to her emotions, but now nothing seemed to stem the tide, and she wept copiously as she handed him a brief document.

As he read it, he grew pale. Goo-ga-ro-no had written

to say that she had fallen in love with Pierre Fanchon, a citizen of New France, and that he also loved her. She had joined him, she said, and they were going to journey together to New France, where they intended to make new lives for themselves. She closed on a rather pathetic note, saying, "I know it is too much to expect your forgiveness now, but I hope that in time your hearts will turn and you will accept me and the man I have chosen for my husband."

Renno was infuriated, but for Betsy's sake he concealed his feelings, and gathering her into his arms, he comforted her quietly.

"Is there nothing we can do?" she demanded. "Is there no way we can get our daughter back?"

"The sun now stands almost directly overhead," Renno said. "No doubt she and this man left the town of the Seneca early this morning, so they have spent about five hours in travel now. It is true that I could assign warriors to overtake them, and I have no doubt that they would be successful in this mission. Surely they can travel far more rapidly than can a woman and a white foreigner. But I wonder if we want to intercept them."

Betsy gazed up at him in astonishment and was too stunned to speak.

"We know nothing about this man," Renno went on. "It is enough for our purposes that Goo-ga-ro-no loves him—or at least thinks she is in love with him, which is the same thing. If we separate her from him forcibly, she will hate us for it and will yearn all the more fiercely for the man. I am afraid that we will cause more complications than we solve."

Betsy dried her eyes and struggled to regain her composure. "You're right, as you so often are," she said. "I'm afraid that we must give Goo-ga-ro-no great freedom if we are to regain her confidence."

"When one wishes to catch a large, strong fish," Renno said, a half-smile on his lips, "one gives the fish ample line—as much line as it seeks. Then as the fish tires one draws in the line little by little. That is how we must deal with Goo-ga-ro-no. We have no friends or other connections in New France, so we must wait now until she contacts us."

Betsy was obviously deeply troubled as she looked up at him. "You mean we make no attempt to find her or communicate with her?"

"Exactly," Renno declared. "She has taken the initiative in running away, and she must take it again when she wishes to see or speak with us. It is wrong for us to seek her now, so we have a difficult time of waiting ahead of us."

Betsy shuddered, then pulled herself together with an effort. "I'll try to be as strong as you, my dear one," she said, "but I can't promise that I'll succeed. This is the last thing on earth that I expected, and I'm still reeling from the blow."

Renno knew how she felt, and sympathized with her. He, too, was badly hurt and disappointed by what Googa-ro-no had done, but a problem of far greater import loomed ahead and required his attention. As the new Great Sachem of all the Iroquois, he had taken upon his shoulders the grave responsibilities that Ghonka had borne for so many years. Now, somehow, he had to find a way to prevent needless killing, needless suffering.

One idea occurred to him; it was bizarre and outlandish, but he suspected it might be effective. He talked with Sun-ai-yee, who agreed there was everything to gain and little to lose.

So Renno sent swift messengers to all of the other Iroquois tribes, summoning their sachems to a special conclave. They responded at once, coming to the town of the Seneca with only small escorts and standing on no ceremony.

At Renno's insistence, protocol was held to a minimum, and on the night that the sachems gathered, he made a welcoming address at a dinner that he and Betsy gave for them. But he dispensed with the usual displays of medicine men, the dances of the young people, and other festivities that ordinarily marked a gathering of the leaders of the Iroquois.

Early the next morning he addressed his peers in the

Council Lodge and avoided using the rhetoric that was customary on such occasions. "I propose," he said, "that each of the nations of the Iroquois provides a force of one hundred and fifty warriors. These should be our best, our most efficient men. Let us choose with care those who have the greatest stamina and can march for the longest hours without tiring. Let us select those who are the best shots, those who willingly face an enemy without fear, those who are willing to take risks. In all, this force will consist of nine hundred men. I will augment it with an additional one hundred Seneca, bringing the total number to one thousand. I intend to lead this force myself. We will go everywhere on the frontier where danger threatens. If it is true that the Abnaki or the Algonquian are about to attack one of the settlements in Maine, we will intervene and will stop them, even if it means that we attack them ourselves. We will interrupt the Erie, who undoubtedly are preparing a considerable campaign against our English colonial brothers. We will dissuade the Pimlico and will go far to the south to the land of the Choctaw and make it plain that they will have inherited a hornet's nest of Iroquois if they attack any of the towns or farms in South Carolina or Georgia."

"In other words," Sun-ai-yee added, "it is the thought of the new Great Sachem that this force will explain itself. It will be made up of fine, young warriors from all of the Iroquois nations, who will work together. Together they will give the lie to those who say that the Seneca and the Mohawk quarrel so badly they cannot work side by side anymore."

Renno nodded gravely. "It is my wish," he said, "that all of the tribes who live on the frontier will see for themselves that the Iroquois still stand united and are prepared to fight against common enemies, shoulder to shoulder like the true brothers they are. If we act quickly and decisively, I think the ferment that affects the nations of the frontier will die away. They will reconsider, they will take new thoughts into their heads, and they will decide that it is the better part of wisdom to keep the peace with the English colonists, as they kept it when

Ghonka wore the feathered bonnet of the Great Sachem."

The idea was received by the other Iroquois leaders in total silence. This was no time for rhetoric, no time for posturing, no time for heroics.

At last Mi-shal of the Mohawk rose to his feet and looked around the Council Lodge, studying the chiefs in the light of the fire that flared in the stone pit in the center of the chamber. "The plan of Renno is a good plan," he said. "I approve of it. I need not confer with the warriors of the Mohawk. I say here and now that the Mohawk will join hands with the Seneca in this enterprise."

His agreement had an almost magical effect on the others. One by one the tribal leaders of the remaining nations rose and pledged their total support for the unusual enterprise.

And so it was that a strike force, capable of achieving great mobility and speed, was formed. To the surprise and secret delight of Renno, his idea became reality within a scant ten days. He himself chose the warriors who would take part in the extraordinary campaign, and one of the first he selected was Ja-gonh. He also unhesitatingly chose El-i-chi as one of his two subordinate war chiefs. He knew that Sun-ai-yee was disappointed at being left behind, but Renno refrained from telling the senior war chief that he had grown too old for the rapid movements that he expected his task force to make. It was far preferable that Sun-ai-yee's feelings be injured than that he suffer real disgrace by joining the band and discovering he was incapable of performing with the speed and vigor of younger men.

Renno sent brief communications to the militia heads of the various colonies and then, without further ado, led his special task force from the main town of the Seneca. He felt bad having to leave Betsy behind to grieve alone for their daughter, and he actually felt twinges of guilt when he realized that his own activities were keeping him from dwelling on Goo-ga-ro-no's fate, but he tried to console himself with the realization that if he succeeded, his mission would be well worth the effort. Renno's first destination was Fort Springfield, on the western border of Massachusetts Bay, and he lost no time in striking out for it. He kept his column in motion day and night, traveling at a trot, and the young warriors responded as he had known they would: not one of them faltered on the wilderness trail. What he did not know was that they marveled at his own strength and stamina. It was remarkable that a man of more than fifty summers could remain in motion, day and night, without tiring, but Renno appeared to be as fresh and as inexhaustible as the youngest member of his command.

When he and his men crossed the Connecticut River in barges that the militia supplied for them, Jeffrey was on hand with his entire staff to greet the new arrivals.

"If I know you," Renno said, smiling, "you're planning all sorts of banquets and other fetes for my special unit. I must ask you to change your plans."

Nothing Renno ever said or did surprised Jeffrey. "How so?" he replied.

"We intend to spend as little time here as possible," Renno replied. "If you can, give one quiet banquet. See to it that the sachems of the Algonquian and the Abnaki are present; the Ottawa, too, if they can be weaned away from the side of the French. Let it be understood that the banquet will be held in three nights' time from the present. I'll grant you that it's short notice, but I can promise you they will appear because they are curious to see whether the Seneca and the Mohawk really intend to break bread together."

Jeffrey Wilson grinned and shook his head; as always, Renno was absolutely right in his reasoning. Militia couriers were dispatched at once to the towns of the Algonquian, Abnaki, and Ottawa.

Three nights later the banquet was duly held on the Wilson property, with Adrienne and their daughters discreetly absenting themselves and staying in the house. Aside from Jeffrey and the members of his immediate staff, the only white colonist who attended the banquet was Roger Harkness.

The whole meal was held in a subdued atmosphere,

and there were no speeches and none of the usual chest-pounding rhetoric that was customary at Indian gatherings. It was enough for Renno's purposes that the Seneca and the Mohawk warriors who were present fraternized freely with each other and obviously were on good terms. That gave the lie to the many rumors about the relations of the two tribes, which was all that Renno needed. The representatives of the Algonquian and the Abnaki saw for themselves that their dreaded foes were still united, and they drew their own conclusions. Thus, the Massachusetts Bay frontier continued to simmer, but at least there were no open hostilities.

Renno made up his mind to employ the same technique elsewhere. Explaining to his warriors that they would fight only if absolutely necessary, he was able to convince them that they were temporarily enrolled as diplomats rather than warriors.

Accompanied by Roger Harkness, who asked permission to march with the task force, Renno led the men from Fort Springfield to Fort Albany, in the heart of the country dominated by the Mohawk. From there they continued south into the new colony of Pennsylvania, where they put on a similar show of friendship in the land dominated by the Erie, long the implacable enemies of the Seneca.

So far, the scheme appeared to be fairly effective. The leaders of local tribes who were invited to dine with the task force saw for themselves relations between the Seneca and the Mohawk were not strained, and they promptly abandoned their new belligerent stance toward the English colonists. It appeared that, without anyone actually striking a blow, Renno's scheme would succeed.

Then one night when the task force had worked its way as far south as the young colony of Maryland and was meeting with the Chickahominy and other minor tribes, misfortune struck swiftly and unexpectedly.

The coming of trouble, although Renno failed to realize it, was anything but accidental. Gray Fox had made it his business to trail the warriors and judged that the time was opportune for him to intervene. He guessed that these young, virile fighting men would be slightly bored with the pacific roles that they were being obliged to take and that it would be relatively easy for him to stir up unrest. He was aided in this by a stroke of good fortune: he was able to purchase some strong fermented berry juice from the Potomac tribe for a very small sum. That night he disguised himself as a Seneca simply by daubing on Seneca war paint. As a Huron, he knew that his speech and accent were already virtually identical to those of the Seneca. He took care to make the fermented berry juice available to anyone who wanted a drink but carefully did not identify himself as the donor. As he expected, a number of the young Seneca dipped their gourds freely into the tubs of the alcoholic beverage, and the young Mohawk followed their example.

The rest was all too easy. Going to a group squatting beside a fire while waiting for their evening meal to cook, Gray Fox muttered something about the insults that he had just endured at the hands of the Mohawk.

The young Seneca, assuming he was one of their number, were duly incensed.

He continued to play on their sympathies until they became thoroughly aroused, and then he cautiously beat a retreat into the deeper recesses of the forest, where he removed his Seneca war paint and trusted in the momentum of the thrust he had inaugurated to have its own effect.

That it did. Before anyone quite realized what was happening, Seneca and Mohawk were hurling insults at each other, and a violent fistfight broke out. Among the participants was an incensed Ja-gonh, who threw himself wholeheartedly into the fray.

Serious damage was averted only by the swift intervention of El-i-chi, who acted before warriors of either party could draw weapons and shed blood. He moved boldly into the seething mass of combatants and, speaking in a loud, crisp voice of authority, ordered the Seneca to desist at once.

The discipline instilled in the warriors was stronger by far than the fermented berry juice the young men had

consumed, and they obeyed El-i-chi's order. Calm was
swiftly restored, and El-i-chi had the unenviable task of
reporting the incident to Renno.

The new Great Sachem listened carefully, his eyes
narrowed to slits. After El-i-chi had finished, he rose
swiftly. Motioning for El-i-chi to follow him, he walked to
the campfire of Mi-shal. "It grieves me," he said, "to say
that bad blood exists between your warriors and mine."
At Mi-shal's nod, El-i-chi told the sachem of the Mohawk
what had happened.

Mi-shal, also, was deeply disturbed. The journey of the
task force had been so successful to date that it was a
shame even to think that something might be interfering
with the continuing success of the venture.

Renno folded his arms across his chest. "Who was
responsible for the squabble?" he demanded. "Was it the
Seneca or the Mohawk?"

El-i-chi answered truthfully. "It was the Seneca who
first called names and insults. It was our warriors who
said that the warriors of the Mohawk were like wom-
en."

Renno's expression didn't change. "Can you identify
the leaders?"

El-i-chi nodded, realizing too late that he had not made
clear to Renno that for reasons beyond his comprehension, Ja-gonh had been rather deeply involved.

"Fetch them!" Renno demanded, and his voice carried
a great distance through the wilderness.

El-i-chi hesitated for a moment, then turned on his heel
and made his way back to the campfires of his younger
colleagues.

Roger Harkness had become aware of the trouble and
made his way silently to a place near Renno and Mi-shal.
This was the first time he had seen the legendary Renno
in action, and he was curious as to how he intended to
handle those who had dared to disturb the peace and to
place the entire task force in jeopardy.

El-i-chi returned, four young warriors walking rather
sheepishly behind him. He raised his left arm smartly in a
salute. "I have done as the Great Sachem has bidden," he

said. "Here are the leaders of those who heaped insults on the warriors of the Mohawk."

Renno looked from one to another, and there was no sign of recognition in his eyes as he peered at his own son. "Do you deny that you incited trouble with our brothers of the Mohawk?" he demanded.

Each of the four young men in turn shook his head. All regretted their part in the stupid venture, and certainly none was sorrier now than Ja-gonh, who was making no excuses for his conduct. That was not the Seneca way.

Renno drew in a deep breath. "Are you aware what the consequences of your rash behavior might have been?" he demanded.

Again the four young warriors nodded.

The Great Sachem turned to Mi-shal. "They have admitted their guilt," he said. "I leave to you the decision of how they shall be punished for their transgression."

Mi-shal well knew that Ja-gonh was Renno's son, and the Mohawk chief had no desire to come between them. It was significant enough that Renno was showing no favor to Ja-gonh, and Mi-shal was sufficiently impressed to be willing to call off any reprisals that he might have in mind. He shook his head. "The Mohawk," he said, "do not seek vengeance against the Seneca."

His point was so well taken that Renno had to nod in agreement. "Well said, my brother," he declared. "The manitous will applaud your generosity, but I cannot permit those who have strayed from the path of righteousness to go unpunished. We are engaged together in an enterprise that will determine whether the English colonial frontier will be at war or at peace. These thoughtless young men have placed our enterprise in jeopardy; therefore, they must be made to pay a price for their failure."

Mi-shal was startled. Apparently Renno actually intended to inflict punishment of some sort on his own son. El-i-chi, also, was amazed and felt a strong urge to intervene. Renno had expressed himself well and had made it clear that a principle was at stake, but he surely did not intend to inflict humiliation on Ja-gonh for a thoughtless deed.

But Renno's face looked as though it was carved of stone. Now, of all moments, he was conscious of the heritage that was his, of the burden that had descended to him from Ghonka. He was the Great Sachem, and his position was so exalted that he could not and must not show favoritism, even to his own flesh and blood. He knew Betsy would be hurt and upset by what he was about to do, but that could not be helped. He was a man, dealing with men, and principle was of paramount importance, now and always.

He looked at each of the four young culprits in turn, his gaze resting longest on Ja-gonh. "Hear my words and heed them," he said. "Until the new moon, you are forbidden to take up arms with the warriors of the Seneca. Until the new moon, you stand alone, in isolation, and may not participate in the battles fought by the bravest of the brave." He looked at each of the quartet again, and his expression was unchanged as he stared at Ja-gonh. Then Renno turned on his heel and stalked away, heading toward his own campfire without hesitation.

Nothing he could have said or done would have impressed Mi-shal as much as the punishment Renno unwaveringly inflicted on his own son. The best man by far, Mi-shal thought, had been selected as the Great Sachem. Renno was a worthy successor to Ghonka.

El-i-chi felt a surge of sympathy for his nephew but wasted no emotions on him. He, too, was a son of Ghonka, and he knew in his heart that what Renno had done was right and just.

Ja-gonh felt as he had when he had been a little boy and had twisted his ankle on the trail. He wanted to burst into tears, but he was a grown man now, a senior warrior, and he did not weep, he could not weep. He had to do what was required of him, he had to accept his punishment like a man and make no protest. He folded his arms across his chest, lowered his head, and, his step unwavering, trudged back to his own campfire, making no word of complaint, giving no sign of the dismay that he felt.

Roger Harkness was thunderstruck. He had heard many things about the Seneca from Jeffrey Wilson, who had regaled him with countless tales. But what he had just seen had engraved itself on his mind, and he knew that he would never forget it. He sympathized with Jagonh, whose innocent prank had caused no real harm, and he was in awe of Renno. Never before had he encountered anyone so devoted to principle, so determined to put his standards ahead of his personal feelings. It was not accidental, surely, Roger thought, that the Seneca had achieved greatness and stood head and shoulders above all other tribes.

Pierre Fanchon thought of purchasing horses to make the journey from the land of the Seneca to Quebec easier, but good mounts were exorbitantly expensive. And when he learned that Goo-ga-ro-no, like the other members of her tribe, did not ride horseback, he had the perfect excuse to abstain and to plan to make the journey instead on foot.

For two days they wasted little time on the trail, and Fanchon set a brisk pace as he headed through an impenetrable sea of trees. Goo-ga-ro-no needed no explanation of his haste, understanding that he was putting as much space as he could between himself and the Seneca, for fear that a party would be sent out to capture her and return her to her parents.

Fanchon had no illusions regarding his own fate if he fell into Renno's hands. He was gambling for big stakes and well knew it. He had spent his whole life on the periphery of big events and had just missed fire. Now, at last, he was participating to the hilt.

The son of mixed parents, one of them English and the other French, Fanchon had been an outcast for the better part of his life until he had lived down his heritage. He had an older brother whom he had not seen in over twenty years, and from time to time he couldn't help envying his sibling. The older brother had accepted his status without a murmur and had built his own life accordingly. Pierre was uncertain as to his present whereabouts, but knowing his brother's preference for using English rather than French as his spoken language, he assumed that his brother had cast his lot with the English settlers.

Not that his present whereabouts mattered in the least. Their paths were unlikely to cross ever again, and Pierre was busy making his own way in the world. He had been fortunate in finding a possible mentor in Gray Fox, and he sensed that Major de Bienville might prove exceptionally useful to him in time to come, too. The young woman who trudged so willingly beside him through the wilderness was merely a means to an end, not an end in itself. In spite of his many protestations, she meant nothing to him, and he didn't care what became of her. She was too sweet, too simple, too straightforward for him and didn't in the least appeal to him. If the truth be known, he preferred the company of the ladies of easy virtue who made their homes in Quebec and earned substantial sums from the soldiers of the Citadel and from the fur traders.

Sooner or later, Pierre knew, he would have to decide how to break the news to Goo-ga-ro-no that their future was not what he had led her to believe. But a sixth sense warned him not to act prematurely, to wait until they either reached Quebec or were very near to the city.

They maintained a blistering pace, and somewhat to the young Frenchman's surprise, Goo-ga-ro-no was easily able to keep up with him, never tiring and never faltering. She was, after all, a Seneca, and her training made such travel through the wilderness mere child's play.

They subsisted entirely on jerked venison and parched corn, which Fanchon had purchased in Quebec before setting out to pick up the young woman. Goo-ga-ro-no wondered why he did not pause on the journey to catch fresh fish or bring down some of the game that was so plentiful, but she was so much in love with him that she assumed he had his reasons and did not question him. She would have been surprised to learn that he was neither an expert hunter nor a skilled fisherman and was just as satisfied to limit their food and save time and effort on the trail.

She knew, however, that her own expertise in traveling through the vast reaches of the continent was far greater than his. At night, after a hard day's march, she was still wide awake and spent hours thinking of his lovemaking once they were married. But Pierre was so exhausted that he dropped off to sleep beside the small campfire that he made, ostensibly to keep hostile animals, like wolves, at a distance. Goo-ga-ro-no did not have the heart to tell him that such fires would attract wolves and bears rather than repel them.

By the fourth day of their journey, there was no question that they were in New France. When they came to an occasional farmhouse, the young woman was thrilled to hear Pierre exchange greetings with a farmer and his family in French. She had learned the language during her visits to the Wilson home in Fort Springfield, where Adrienne frequently conversed with her daughters in the tongue of her parents. Goo-ga-ro-no realized that she was now far from home and in an alien land in every sense, but her faith in Pierre was so great that she felt sure they would overcome all obstacles together.

A bitter disillusionment awaited her when they reached Quebec. Fanchon, for want of anything better to do, took her to his own rented quarters. They made their way through the winding, twisting streets, climbing ever higher on the steep hill that formed the better part of the city of Quebec, which was crowned by the Citadel.

Goo-ga-ro-no was ill at ease as she looked at the pedestrians whom they passed, at the officers on horseback, and the women in silks and satins who seemed to be great ladies but were actually courtesans from France who lived with high-ranking officials. She realized that she was creating more than a fair share of attention, her blond hair and blue eyes contrasting sharply with her Indian doeskins. But she remained close beside Fanchon and felt relieved when he climbed a flight of rickety stairs and unlocked the door of what appeared to be a private dwelling.

Inside was a single room equipped with a small four-poster bed, a plain table with several unvarnished chairs, and a pile of fur skins in one corner. Fanchon busied himself at a hearth on which he threw several logs and kindling. "Make yourself at home," he said brusquely. "It will soon be warm."

Goo-ga-ro-no looked around the cramped room. "Is this where you live?" she asked.

He nodded, and Goo-ga-ro-no had to hide her surprise. The Virginia house of Uncle Ned and Aunt Consuelo had many rooms, and they were large and handsomely furnished, but this one room was very cramped and obviously was used for sleeping, eating, as well as living.

Although she kept her views to herself, her face was expressive, and Fanchon flushed. "Quebec," he said stridently, "is an expensive town. I haven't been able to afford better than this!"

Goo-ga-ro-no was abashed. "I meant nothing amiss," she said.

It might be useful, Fanchon decided, to provoke an argument with her, since actually his task was only half completed. He had succeeded in persuading Goo-ga-ro-no to accompany him to Quebec, but that was just the beginning. Now he had to get rid of her. So he glared at her but made no comment. The infatuated young woman remained highly apologetic, however. "I think this is a very cozy little place," she said, walking up to him and smiling warmly. "And it seems to suit you. Are we going to live here after we're married?"

Fanchon hooked his thumbs in his belt and looked her up and down slowly. "Whether we marry or not depends on how well we get along with each other."

Goo-ga-ro-no was stunned by his tone. Nothing had prepared her for his sudden change in attitude, and she didn't know what to make of his hostility. She blinked at him in astonishment, trying to absorb his harsh statement.

The scheme was working out even better than Pierre

had hoped. It was clear he was estranging the young woman from him, and he had an idea how he could alienate her even more. He smiled and advanced slowly across the room toward her.

She read his intention in his eyes and shrank from him. Certainly she enjoyed his kisses and invariably yearned for more of them, but something in his eyes warned her that he had no intention of stopping with kisses. Goo-ga-ro-no liked to think of herself as being rather worldly, but the truth of the matter was that she was very much an innocent. Certainly she had been reared in the most strict traditions of the English colonists and of the Seneca. The thought of having an affair with a man before she was married to him was too much for her.

Fanchon continued to move toward her, and she hastily retreated to the far side of the heavy table and grasped a chair, which she placed in front of her. "What has come over you?" she murmured, unable to reconcile this new attitude with the man she had come to know.

Fanchon smiled broadly. "I'm a man," he said, "and a very human one at that. We have spent many days and nights together traveling through the wilderness, and now I seek my reward."

Goo-ga-ro-no was appalled. "Reward?" she gasped. "Is that how you refer to our coming marriage?"

Fanchon halted abruptly, and his voice became harsh. "You don't seem to understand," he said. "I haven't decided whether I'm going to marry you or not. That will depend on how thoroughly you cooperate with me right now."

His meaning was clear—all too painfully clear—and the young woman gave in to the sense of deep panic that welled up within her. She thought she loved this man, and, therefore, it should be simple enough to give in to him; if the truth be known, she wanted him as badly as he wanted her. But he was so crude in his demand, so unyielding that something within her caused her to rebel. His attitude indicated that he thought it was his right to take her. He seemed to be denying their mutual love for each other. She needed time to sort out her thoughts, and it was obvious that Pierre had no intention of granting her that time. He started forward again, his lips clamped together, and she knew that she was incapable of yielding to him.

Thrusting the chair in his path, she maneuvered toward the door.

"I suppose," Pierre said, sneering, "that I'm suddenly not good enough for you."

She had to control herself to keep from bursting into tears. "Not at all!" she cried. "What on earth has come over you?"

He planted his feet apart and jabbed a forefinger at her to emphasize his words. "Let me make my position very clear," he said. "Either you will make love with me right now—as it is my right to demand—or you may go to the devil."

She drew herself up slowly. "What does that mean, sir?" She was no ordinary creature, after all, but was the daughter of Renno, a person of considerable consequence.

Fanchon, however, seemed to have his own ideas regarding her stature. "I don't care to argue the matter with you," he said. "Either we go to bed or you can get out of here, for all I care, and what becomes of you is your concern, not mine!"

There was a long, stunned silence. Goo-ga-ro-no absorbed his ultimatum and made up her mind. She had no choice, really, and her whole background dictated her response. Not looking at Pierre again, she picked up the buckskin sack that contained her few belongings and slung it over her shoulder. Then moving swiftly so her resolve would not weaken, she went to the door, opened it, and slammed it hard behind her.

Perhaps they were suffering a misunderstanding and were having a typical lovers' quarrel, Goo-ga-ro-no tried to tell herself, but she knew better. A dreadful, hollow, sinking feeling in the pit of her stomach told her that she had made a major error. She had totally misjudged the character of Pierre Fanchon.

Now, as a result of her mistake, she was hundreds of miles from home, far from her fellow Seneca, equally far from the English colonists to whom she was related. She was in an alien city populated by men and women who regarded both the English and the Iroquois, particularly the Seneca, as their enemies. She had no idea how she would survive in this hostile, strange place, but she was determined to live and somehow compensate for her terrible blunder in judgment. Wandering down the stairs to the strange street, she walked aimlessly to the commercial center of Quebec and knew only that as bleak as her outlook appeared, she could not and would not give in either to her own panic or to Pierre Fanchon's unreasonable demands. She was a Seneca, the daughter of Renno, the granddaughter of Ghonka, and somehow she would manage to overcome the seemingly insurmountable odds that threatened her well-being and security.

Chapter IV

Immediately after his return to Virginia, Ned Ridley learned that a dangerous situation existed far to the south. The Choctaw, by far the largest and most belligerent of all tribes in the area, were showing signs of great restlessness, and Ned felt, as did the officials of South Carolina, that it was necessary for the Seneca to make some demonstration of strength to prevent a sudden uprising of the tribe. He immediately sent a message to his brother-in-law, and when Renno received it, he promptly changed his own plans. Instead of going on to Williamsburg for a meeting with the governor and dealing with the Pimlico while there, he decided to proceed by forced march, without delay, to the land of the Choctaw.

While Renno's task force made ready for the long

march, Captain Roger Harkness came to him and seemed somewhat troubled.

"If it's all the same to you," Roger said, "I think I should report to Governor Gooch right now, so I prefer to go directly to him rather than accompany you on your march farther south."

"By all means," Renno said agreeably.

Roger hesitated. "I must ask a favor of you in order to accomplish this goal. I'm none too familiar with the wilderness—in fact, one stretch of it seems identical to the next. With your approval, I would be grateful if you would assign Ja-gonh as my guide on this journey."

He was being very discreet, which pleased Renno. The suggestion, the Great Sachem knew, was made to order to solve his own dilemma: by assigning Ja-gonh to accompany the young officer, the warrior would be gainfully occupied and there would be no need to embarrass him further by letting him accompany the special unit, knowing all the while that if a battle developed he was forbidden to take part in it. So Renno immediately approved, writing to Ned to tell him of the relative success of the special task force.

The pair set out at once, carrying the deerskin pouches of jerked meat and parched corn on which they would subsist in the forest. Ja-gonh was armed with his bow and arrow, two tomahawks, and a pair of metal-handled knives, but he carried no firearms, explaining to Roger that he vastly preferred the traditional weapons of the Seneca to what he called the "war tools of the English and the French."

Ja-gonh made his way quickly through the luxurious foliage of the Virginia wilderness, which was much fuller and greener than it was in lands that lay farther to the north. He traveled at a trot, his pace never varying, no matter what obstacles he had to overcome in the forest.

Roger was far less fortunate. He found the New World forests far different from the so-called "wilds" of Europe with which he was familiar. Here there were countless hidden traps: fallen logs concealed by dense underbrush, holes in the ground made by small animals, and even rocks that could not be seen easily.

Ja-gonh seemed indifferent to food and drink. He was capable of going for long periods of time without tasting anything, and when his companion suggested that they eat, he was agreeable enough but didn't seem to need sustenance. If Roger had not already known it, he would have become convinced that the Seneca truly were a remarkable breed. Just how extraordinary they were, however, was something that he learned while on the march.

One afternoon when Ja-gonh, as usual, was setting the pace and Roger was following as best he could, the young warrior suddenly halted, then raised a hand for silence. Not bothering to explain, he seemed to melt into the foliage. Even though Roger was only no more than an arm's length from him, he found it difficult to make out Ja-gonh's exact location.

Ja-gonh revealed himself long enough to indicate in pantomime that he wanted his companion to do likewise. Roger had had no experience in forest camouflage, but with Ja-gonh's subtle help he discovered that he, too, was able to conceal himself exceptionally well.

Ja-gonh, he noted, had drawn a tomahawk and held it firmly in his right hand. Roger drew a pistol, cocked it, and looked at his companion for approval. Ja-gonh grinned and nodded; the pistol indeed might come in handy.

Moments later, Roger was electrified when a half-dozen warriors appeared suddenly and silently, seemingly out of nowhere. Their faces and torsos were smeared with blue paint, which, as the young Englishman later learned, was the distinctive color of the Pimlico. The warriors were all heavily armed, and they all carried long spears with slender shafts and exceptionally sharp metal points. They seemed to be on the trail of something or someone. They halted, studying the ground and then conferring in undertones.

The realization dawned on Roger that he and Ja-gonh

were the quarries for these braves. They had been followed, and now that they had disappeared, the warriors were somewhat confused.

Ja-gonh stared at his companion, their eyes met, and Roger read the young Seneca's meaning plainly. Ja-gonh intended to launch a surprise assault and wanted Roger to follow his example.

Roger took a fresh grip on his pistol, his heart hammering against his rib cage as he waited.

Suddenly Ja-gonh was in action: his tomahawk flew through the air, striking one of the braves in the forehead and sending him sprawling. Before his companions could react, two others were severely injured as Ja-gonh hurled his knives at them with deadly accuracy.

The signals were more than sufficient for Roger, and he raised his double-barreled pistol, firing point-blank at one of the braves, who dropped to the ground at once, and then taking a considerably longer shot at a second brave. To Roger's chagrin, the warrior sustained only a minor shoulder wound and was still on his feet and seemed to be more or less intact.

But Ja-gonh's and Roger's initial assault was as devastating as it was unexpected. They quickly gained the initiative and did not lose it. Ja-gonh pulled his second tomahawk from his belt, and Roger drew his sword. The injured brave and a companion fought ably but were no match for the grim, dedicated pair, and the two braves escaped into the forest. Three other Pimlico warriors were dead, and another, who seemed to be their leader, was dying.

Roger was startled when Ja-gonh, acting with swift ruthlessness, scalped each of the dead warriors in turn and placed their scalps, still dripping with blood, in his belt. He was far more of a savage than Roger had realized.

The Pimlico leader, suffering from severe wounds inflicted on him by Ja-gonh, tried to stand but stumbled and fell, then tried in vain to rise to his feet again. Resigned to inevitable death, he propped himself up against a tree.

Ja-gonh neither slew him with a final blow nor did he elect to scalp the Pimlico prematurely, which was something any good Seneca would have done. Far more civilized, according to European standards, than he appeared, Ja-gonh waited patiently for the Pimlico leader to expire.

The warrior was surprised by his consideration and was grateful for it. Bowing his head, he murmured, "I thank you for the boon."

Ja-gonh was embarrassed and replied with a shrug of indifference.

"Had we known there were Seneca in the vicinity, we would not have been so careless," he said. "We heard a rumor that a large party of Iroquois was on the march through our territory, but no one specifically mentioned the Seneca. It is not true, then, that the Seneca are finished and that their days as fighting men are ended?"

Ja-gonh shook his head solemnly. "It is not true," he said. "You have seen what a Seneca warrior can do."

The dying Pimlico warrior sighed deeply. "Much more blood of my people will be shed because the Seneca continue to roam at will through the forests of our homeland," he said. "If I could I would warn our sachem and our war chiefs, but it is too late."

Ja-gonh's interest was immediately piqued. "Why should it be too late, O Mighty Man of the Pimlico?" he asked softly.

"We of the Pimlico know better than to trust the voices of old women, who cackle like hens," he said. "We should have ignored the stories that said the Seneca were finished. The Seneca are still powerful. Now our finest warriors will die because we have been careless."

Sure that he was on the track of something significant, Ja-gonh managed to speak very calmly. "What is all this talk of death?" he demanded.

Again the Pimlico warrior sighed. "We have plotted long and well," he said, "and we have laid an ambush for the man who leads the settlers of Virginia and who bears the name of Gooch. Perhaps he will die, but the Seneca surely will obtain vengeance for his death, and many

Pimlico will go quickly to the land of their ancestors."

Ja-gonh concealed his excitement. "When is this ambush of the governor to take place?"

"This very night," the Pimlico replied. "That is why it is too late; nothing now can stop this terrible catastrophe from taking place." His head fell forward suddenly, his eyes closed, and he slumped to the ground.

Ja-gonh made certain that he was dead and then lost no time in swiftly and expertly removing his scalp.

The lack of emotion that the young Seneca showed was what really astonished Roger, who found it hard to believe that Ja-gonh could be engaged in earnest conversation with the Pimlico one moment and could, without showing any feelings whatsoever, take his scalp the next.

Now Ja-gonh quickly translated his conversation with the Pimlico into English, and Roger stared at him. "Do you mean to tell me that they're setting an ambush—tonight—for the governor?"

"So it appears," Ja-gonh said, shrugging.

The young officer's face hardened. "I have no idea how far we may be from Williamsburg, but we've got to get there before he's attacked. We can't allow him to be brutally murdered."

Ja-gonh seemed lost in thought for a moment. "Then we must hurry," he said. "We still have a long way to travel."

Without further ado he took to the trail again, paying no further heed to the sprawled bodies of the Pimlico. His pace was far more rapid than it had been previously, and Roger was hard put to keep up with him. Forced at times to run at full speed, the Englishman crashed through underbrush, unmindful of the noise that he was making. His one objective now was to reach the governor in time, and he didn't care how much commotion he caused.

The ground seemed to vanish rapidly beneath their feet, and they overcame countless obstacles, making their way through huge bramble patches, scrambling up and down hills, and even fording two swift-running rivers. By early evening Roger was exhausted, but Ja-gonh seemed as fresh as he had when they had first started their journey; the young Englishman thought seriously of requesting him to go on alone.

Suddenly, however, he caught sight of a large, substantial-looking shadow directly ahead, and he grinned feebly when he realized that they had come to the palisade that protected Williamsburg.

"Who goes yonder?" a sentry demanded in an authoritative voice.

"Captain Harkness and a Seneca guide," Roger shouted hoarsely. "We bring an urgent message to the governor."

The officer of the guard was summoned, and a few moments later the two travelers, the dirt of the wilderness still clinging to them, were taken to the governor's mansion. There, in the library, they found Governor Gooch and Colonel Ned Riley sipping glasses of brandywine as they exchanged news. Ned stared in open-mouthed wonder at Ja-gonh.

"Your Excellency," Ned finally said. "Permit me to present Ja-gonh of the Seneca, who happens to be my nephew."

Sir William exchanged greetings with both Ja-gonh and Roger. Then taking note of their travel-soiled condition, he demanded, "What brings you two to Williamsburg at this time of evening?"

"I thank God we're in time, sir," Roger replied. "There's a plot on your life."

Wasting no words, Ja-gonh succinctly filled in the details that he had learned from the dying Pimlico.

The governor and his militia chief exchanged a long, significant look. "Our situation," Gooch said, "appears to be graver than we had any idea it might be."

Ned nodded solemnly. "Indeed, sir," he said. "With fear of the Seneca removed, I'm afraid the Pimlico are growing slightly mad, and they've selected you as their obvious target."

Sir William chuckled. "I enjoy life far too much to abandon it without a struggle," he said. "I hate to disappoint the Pimlico, but I'm afraid I have other plans."

Ned grinned as he studied the two young men. "Are you two too tired for any further duty tonight?"

Roger replied for both of them. "After coming all this distance with a warning, we have no intention of missing out on the action."

Ned took immediate charge of the operation. "How the Pimlico intend to pass our sentry lines tonight is beyond me, but we needn't be concerned with such details," he said. "It's enough that they do intend to surprise you here. I assume they'll be launching an attack on you in this house, and I think we might prepare a little surprise for them."

The governor entered into his scheme with gusto, and soon the arrangements were complete. Roger, armed with a brace of pistols and a pair of knives, was hidden behind thick drapes at one end of the windows, while Ja-gonh, refusing any weapons other than his own, went into a clothes closet. When last seen, he was fashioning a garrote out of a length of rawhide.

Ned Ridley summoned the officer of the guard and several of his assistants, and they, too, took up hiding places in the library. When all was in readiness, there was nothing left to do but to pretend that this was an ordinary occasion—and wait for the surprise attack.

The warning had not been received too soon. Less than a half hour after Roger and Ja-gonh appeared, Ned heard scraping sounds outside the window of the governor's residence. Continuing to speak conversationally, he nodded in the direction of the outdoors and at the same time silently loosened his sword in his scabbard.

Sir William's behavior was extraordinary. His life was at stake, but he displayed no nervousness, no apprehension, no fear. If anything, he seemed to be enjoying the occasion, and he grinned as he reached for a dueling pistol with a very delicate hair trigger that rested within arm's length on his library desk; he intended to give far better than he received.

As Ned Ridley subsequently remarked, he had never seen an Indian operation better planned, mounted, or executed. The Pimlico displayed great cleverness in managing to sneak a score of warriors past the sentry lines of the Virginia militia. The braves moved swiftly toward the governor's house and headed directly for the library, where lamps were burning and a fire blazed in the hearth. Then as they poured into the room, all hell broke loose. Of all the governor's defenders, none was the equal in valor, speed, or dexterity of Ja-gonh. Here was an opportunity for a Seneca warrior to show his mettle, and Ja-gonh responded superbly. Before the Pimlico quite realized what had happened, two of their number had been garroted and lay still on the floor. A third succumbed to Ja-gonh's tomahawk attack, and a fourth fell back under his blistering assault with a long knife. Then the other defenders stepped into the fray, and a brief, vicious free-for-all ensued. The upshot, as Ned Ridley remarked, was "very satisfactory." The attacking force was totally wiped out, the defenders suffered only three or four minor casualties, and most important, the governor and Colonel Ridley were untouched.

Sir William was lavish in his praise of Ja-gonh, who accepted the compliments with a stolid indifference that was not feigned. He had done only what any Seneca warrior would have done, and could see no reason why he should be singled out for special adulation.

An inadvertent remark made by Roger Harkness led Ned Ridley to inquire more closely into the circumstances that had resulted in his nephew's traveling with the young Englishman, and he chuckled aloud. "You're much like your father, Ja-gonh," he said. "His good fortune in battle was always extraordinary, and you seem to be similarly blessed. I can assure you that you'll no longer be under a cloud in the ranks of the Seneca. The letters that the governor and I will write will give you a new standing that will make even Renno proud of you."

Ja-gonh did not care about the letters, but he did not refuse them. It was enough for him that his uncle was satisfied with what he had done and that he had compensated for the blunder that had forced his father to punish him.

The assassination attempt had been foiled, but Governor Gooch and Colonel Ridley were far from satisfied. "It seems to me, sir," Ned said thoughtfully, after reading the letter sent to him by Renno and hearing Roger Harkness's report to the governor, "that the supremacy of the Seneca has got to be reestablished the same way for the Pimlico as it was for the northern tribes. This would-be attack on you tonight is merely one symptom of the disease that Renno and his task force are attempting to subdue before it spreads along the entire frontier. I shall ask Renno to visit us after he has seen the Choctaw."

At Ned's insistence Ja-gonh and Roger accompanied him to his own home, and there Ja-gonh was inundated with affection by his aunts, Consuelo Ridley and Anne Cooke. Both were secretly amused to hear of the punishment that Renno had inflicted on him, and both were delighted for his sake that his heroic conduct in saving Governor Gooch more than compensated for his misbehavior.

Observing Ja-gonh with his white, civilized relatives, Roger Harkness began to understand the complexities of the young warrior's character somewhat better. But he knew that men like Ja-gonh and Renno were unique and stood alone in the New World. They were blessed with the best of both the Indian and the colonial cultures, and they were consequently members of a superior breed.

Roger was forced to review his opinions of white men in the New World after meeting André Cooke, now a major in the Virginia militia. Tall, silent, and brooding, André was the only white man Roger had ever seen who seemed to fit as naturally into the strange and exotic patterns of the wilderness as an Indian. From Ja-gonh, Roger learned that André had lived alone for years in the wilds as a trapper and hunter and that he was held in the greatest of respect by Renno and Sun-ai-yee, for whom he had fought so valiantly in a campaign years earlier against the Spaniards and their Indian allies.

All of this information had an effect on Roger, who discovered, to his surprise, that his own standards were changing. He was acquiring new respect for the men, both Indian and white, who struggled for the leadership of

New World forces, and it dawned on him that the stakes for the colonists representing the major powers of the Old World and their Indian allies were very high. It also seemed clear that if the deterioration of frontier conditions did not come to a firm halt, the French would be sure to take advantage of the situation and attack. The shape of the world to come would be determined by that battle.

He tried to express his thoughts at dinner at the Ridley home. "It seems to me," he said, "that he who controls the New World establishes control of all of the Old World as well. He who rules America also will rule Europe."

Ja-gonh, sitting at the dinner table and using a knife and fork with the expertise of lifelong experience, merely shrugged. "I'm not all that familiar with the Old World," he said, "but what I've seen of her representatives has not impressed me. They are petty men engaged in petty conceits and quarrels."

"That isn't quite true, lad," Ned Ridley told him. "Roger has come closer to the mark than have you. The potential of this country is so enormous it is staggering. Whether it remains free under British rule or whether men are forced to live in fear under French rule will determine the history of what is to come."

"The Seneca," Ja-gonh said proudly, "support the English colonists for only one reason, because they, like the Seneca, believe in freedom for the individual. That is why we shall always prosper and be strong."

Ned didn't want to disillusion his nephew, so he remained silent. What Ja-gonh failed to realize was that the very base of Seneca power was threatened and that unless Renno was able to produce near-miracles, the influence of the Seneca would soon be destroyed. Then the French, who had needed very little provocation in the past to attempt to wrest control of the New World from the colonists, would be sure to attack. The future for the colonists and their children, as well as for generations of Indians yet unborn, would be determined in the struggle.

Ned had great faith in Renno and good cause for that faith, but he realized at the same time that his brother-in-law, no matter how gifted he might be, faced circumstances that might be too powerful for him to overcome. It was possible that the years Ghonka had spent as Great Sachem of the Iroquois would go down in history as an era of good feeling, unique in the history of the New World. It appeared that old alliances were breaking up and inevitably new alliances would be formed. There was no way of knowing how the story would end. The New World was indeed entering a critical era.

Despite the show of good faith that the Seneca and the Mohawk managed to display for the other nations of the north and the south, misunderstandings continued to plague the relationship between the two tribes. Bad feelings, lack of faith, and loss of tempers all contributed to a steady deterioration. This was certainly true in Renno's special corps, where two more outbreaks between warriors occurred, necessitating harsh, immediate action from him and from Mi-shal, the sachem of the Mohawk. But even more disturbing was the decline in the relations of the two tribes at home. Warriors of the Seneca took care not to stray into the land of the Mohawk, and the Mohawk returned the dubious compliment. For the first time, representatives of one or the other tribe were cursed in the towns of their colleagues, and in one incident that could have had serious repercussions, a Seneca visiting a Mohawk town was reviled and almost hanged.

So the tensions that Renno's task force had attempted to subdue started to break out again, and Indian nations from the north to the south once again flaunted their authority and openly challenged Seneca supremacy. Only Gray Fox rejoiced, and the French were convinced that a miracle was somehow taking place that permitted the tribes loyal to them at last to achieve the upper hand in the constant jockeying for position in the wilderness.

Governor William Gooch of Virginia was gravely concerned about the steady decline in the fortunes of the English colonies' staunchest allies. He conferred at great length with Ned Ridley but was forced to agree that he was almost powerless to stem the growing tide of bad feeling. It was impossible, he discovered, to combat opponents who were almost nonexistent, wraiths who appeared briefly, only to vanish again. Had any tribe put up firm opposition, he could have countered them. But instead, the Indian nations of the continent were resorting to new tactics. They did not oppose a colony directly but instead sent their warriors to hunt on the farmlands established by colonists and to steal grains, meats, and vegetables from the provisions accumulated by the farmers.

The only way to stop them would have been to declare open warfare, and that would have put the colonies at war with virtually all of the tribes of the continent. This was something to be avoided. The only hope, Gooch decided, was to sit back calmly, refuse to become overly alarmed, and to give Renno the opportunity to reestablish the controls that so long had been exercised by the Iroquois. He had a difficult time convincing the militia leaders that this was the wisest course of action, and he had his hands full persuading them to remain cool and not to start hostilities.

Believing that his was the best way, Sir William wrote at length to the governors of South Carolina, New York, and Massachusetts Bay, and at Ned's suggestion he also enlisted the aid of high-ranking militia leaders. He wrote a long explanation of his policy and the reasons behind it to General Jeffrey Wilson, and again at Ned's suggestion, the letter to Jeffrey was given to Ja-gonh and Roger Harkness to deliver. As Ned explained subtly to his nephew, by the time that the communication was delivered and Renno and his column had returned to their own land via Massachusetts Bay, the ban that Renno had established on his son's activities would be ended.

So Ja-gonh and Roger again acted as couriers and took the governor's communication to Fort Springfield. They traveled in summer, and their journey was an easy one. Food was plentiful, and not only were game and fish ample, but Ja-gonh showed his companion how to gather berries, nuts, and a variety of edible roots.

"No Indian becomes thin in the summer," Ja-gonh said. "That is an old saying of the Seneca, and you can see why it is true."

Jeffrey and Adrienne Wilson made the two young men welcome, and Patience was secretly very pleased. The visitors were assigned to share quarters in one of the many spacious guest rooms in the Wilson house, and Adrienne took the precaution of warning Margot, her younger daughter, not to speak out of turn.

Roger was delighted to see Patience again and made no secret of his feelings. Ja-gonh, however, reacted rather strangely. Still smarting because of the punishment he had received at the hands of his father, he elected to become more Indian than ever. He was long accustomed to the civilization of the colonists, but no one seeing his reaction would have known it. Rather than bathe in the hot water provided in tubs by the Wilson maidservants, he insisted on swimming in a lake on the Wilson property. Rather than wear colonial dress, he wore Seneca buckskins and used a Seneca knife for cutting and eating his food.

His attitude bewildered Patience. Her father tried to explain to her, although he was unfamiliar with the circumstances.

"It is very difficult for Ja-gonh to know himself," Jeffrey Wilson said. "He must go through an inner war constantly, with one force tugging him toward our civilization and another toward the ways of the Seneca. I know his father had that problem until he became as old or older than Ja-gonh is now and finally decided to cast his lot totally with the Seneca. How Ja-gonh will react and in what way he'll tend, I don't know, but he must be allowed to find his own way." Patience agreed, feeling great sympathy for the young Seneca, but she couldn't help contrasting his ways with those of Roger, and as a consequence, she found herself more and more interested in the young Englishman.

Her preference was obvious and resulted in driving Ja-gonh still farther into his Seneca shell. He spoke English under the Wilson roof because it was convenient for him to do so, but in all other ways he was a Seneca.

Patience would not have been surprised had she seen him sitting cross-legged on the floor when she encountered him in the parlor.

"I can't quite explain it," Patience said to her mother, "but it's as though Ja-gonh is going out of his way to stress his Seneca nature. He seems to be insisting on calling attention to it."

Adrienne looked slightly troubled. "I well remember periods when Renno did the same thing," she replied. "They must take a stand regarding their identities, I suppose. Goodness knows it can't be easy for them."

Patience sighed and shook her head, and her mother looked at her searchingly. "Do I gather that the strong emphasis on his Seneca background makes Ja-gonh somewhat less attractive to you?"

Her daughter hesitated, then replied carefully. "I wouldn't say that," she replied. "On the other hand, I must confess that I find myself more drawn to Roger Harkness than ever before. So make of it what you will."

Affairs came to a sudden, unexpected head one morning when Patience announced that she had to go into town on an errand. Ja-gonh courteously offered to escort her. The various horses, ordinarily found in the Wilson's stable, were in use, so the young couple decided to walk. The summer day was lovely, the breeze was invigorating, and it would not be a hardship to make their way on foot from the farm into Fort Springfield.

Patience soon wondered if she had been wrong to accept Ja-gonh's invitation. He was moody and withdrawn, and it was difficult for her to make conversation with him.

They walked along the path that skirted the edge of the Wilson property and led them beside the east bank of the Connecticut River. Ordinarily both of them would have enjoyed the stroll, but they were beset by hidden pressures, and Ja-gonh's silence certainly did not help ease the tensions. As they turned a bend on the trail, they paused when they saw a huge, bulky man approaching. According to his war paint, he was a warrior of the small

Mahican tribe, and he stared with considerable interest at the couple.

Ordinarily Ja-gonh would have been quick to take offense at any stranger who paid too much attention to Patience, but he tried to curb his feelings. The warrior halted in the middle of the path, making it impossible for them to squeeze past him. "Well, what's this?" he asked in a booming voice. "Since when does the daughter of the great General Wilson lower herself to be seen with a Seneca?"

The insult was as deliberate as it was unnecessary, and Ja-gonh felt as though he had been slapped in the face. Still trying to avoid trouble, he clamped his jaw together and made no reply.

The Mahican appeared determined to make an issue of the matter. "All the people of the wilderness know," he said, "that the day of the Seneca is done. Once they were a brave and powerful people, but that time is ended. Now they are weak, and it is said that even their finest warriors behave like squaws."

Ja-gonh knew that he could tolerate no more, particularly in the presence of Patience. He walked slowly up to the giant, who towered above him, and looked hard at him, scrutinizing him carefully from head to foot. Unwilling to dignify the man's comments with an answer, he suddenly spat, full in the warrior's face.

The challenge to personal combat was unmistakable, and personal honor demanded that the Mahican do something at once. His angry roar reverberated through the woods, and he reached for his tomahawk. Before he could draw it, however, Ja-gonh had his own tomahawk in hand, ready to wield it instantly.

The Mahican realized he had been outmaneuvered, and glowered at the man. "The honor of my nation demands your blood," he said.

Ja-gonh's eyes glittered, and his expression remained unchanged. "It is too bad," he said, "that the warrior of the Mahican must die, but so be it. We will meet here at this very place when the sun stands directly overhead."

Not waiting for a reply, he turned on his heel and

rejoined Patience. As they resumed their walk into Fort Springfield, both were conscious of the huge warrior standing where Ja-gonh left him, a half smile on his face as he carefully measured the man who had become his foe.

Patience was badly upset. "You're going to have a fight to the death?" she asked.

Ja-gonh grunted in assent.

"I hate to be the cause of bloodshed," she said. "I wish you wouldn't fight."

Ja-gonh spoke succinctly and savagely. "There is no choice," he said. "What must be, will be. The Seneca have been insulted, and I find this intolerable." As far as he was concerned, that was the end of the matter.

Word of the impending fight spread quickly, and close to noon, Jeffrey Wilson and several of his aides approached the site, accompanied by Roger Harkness. Patience, obviously wishing she were elsewhere, nevertheless felt compelled to return to the scene with Ja-gonh, who seemed thoroughly at ease.

Hoping he could stop the fight before it started, Jeffrey questioned his daughter at some length regarding the incident that had sparked the dispute. Patience replied truthfully and in detail, and when she had finished speaking, she saw that her father was deeply troubled.

He shook his head as he turned to Roger Harkness. "Not only must I allow the fight to take place," he said, "but I find it essential that Ja-gonh win."

The young Englishman was startled.

"If I could," Jeffrey continued, "I would even resort to chicanery of some kind to make certain that he is the victor."

Before Roger could register his astonishment, the general continued.

"There was a time, not so long ago," Jeffrey explained, "when the Seneca were held in more than universal regard by the other Indian tribes. They inspired awe. Now, thanks to their altercations with the Mohawk and the eagerness of other Indians to see the mighty fall, they are held in disrepute. The big Mahican warrior acted deliberately, insulting Ja-gonh freely until he forced a fight challenge out of him."

"I understand all that," Roger said, "but why is it so necessary that Ja-gonh be the winner?"

"The peace of the Fort Springfield area depends on it, unfortunately," Jeffrey Wilson said. "If Ja-gonh wins decisively, the myth of the prowess of the Seneca is restored, and the tribes of the area will continue to watch their steps. If Ja-gonh should be defeated, however, that is virtually a guarantee that the Mahican will create trouble—lots of trouble. They'll begin raiding outlying farms on the frontier almost immediately, and there will be general hell to pay by the time they're through." He sighed, shook his head, and looked gloomy.

Roger Harkness smiled grimly. "I know Ja-gonh," he said. "You have nothing to fear. I've never seen him in personal combat, but I daresay he can hold his own."

"In an ordinary fight, I'm sure he can," Jeffrey replied. "But he's facing an opponent who weighs almost twice his weight, who stands a head taller, and has a reach far longer. I don't see how he could have the skill and stamina to beat the Mahican. The man is no ordinary warrior. His name is Sa-ra-ro, and he is reputedly the most ferocious of all warriors in the Mahican tribe. I'm afraid that Ja-gonh is going to have his hands full."

Looking at the giant, Roger was able to understand some of the complexities of the situation. Sa-ra-ro was surrounded by a half-dozen of his fellow Mahican warriors, who stripped him to his loincloth and anointed his entire body with bear grease. Their attitude was admiring, their spirits were jocular. It was obvious they expected him to win a decisive victory over the Seneca who had had the temerity to challenge him.

Ja-gonh removed his clothes quietly, and when Roger went to him to offer his assistance, the young Seneca smiled slightly and shook his head. He not only was making his preparations alone, but it was obvious that he wanted it that way. He was deliberately calling attention to the difference between the champion of the Mahican nation and himself.

The crowd continued to grow as word of the impending combat spread. A number of uniformed militia men drifted to the area, as did the various townsmen and a number of young women who had nothing better to occupy their time.

The Mahican were preparing for the fight in a holiday atmosphere. Sa-ra-ro joked with his colleagues, and they roared with laughter at virtually everything he said. Ja-gonh, on the other hand, who was now wearing only his loincloth, seemed sober and preoccupied as he astonished the onlookers by engaging in a form of what appeared to be calisthenics. Roger secretly approved of what he was doing and thought he was wise to be as ready as possible.

Jeffrey, increasingly worried, made a serious attempt to persuade Patience to return home. "This is no place for you," he said. "You've never seen one of these Indian grudge matches, and I can assure you, they can be very vicious. I don't think you'll particularly enjoy the sight of blood."

"Ja-gonh was escorting me when he encountered the Mahican," she said. "And I'm sure it was because of me that the big bully deliberately created a scene. I would be unfaithful to my obligations to Ja-gonh if I ran away now."

"I'm not suggesting that you run away," her father told her. "I just think you'll be better off if you avoid a spectacle that may become sickening."

She set her lips firmly and shook her head. It was quite apparent that nothing would stand in the way of her continuing presence at the fight.

To Roger's astonishment both of the combatants kept their tomahawks and their long-handled knives, which they placed in belts above their loincloths. He could scarcely believe his eyes as he asked General Wilson, "Surely they're not going to fight with arms?"

Jeffrey Wilson laughed without humor. "You must understand," he said, "that Indians have their own, different approach to life than we Anglo-Saxons. They are primitive people, and their ways are barbaric. A fight like this is a grudge match. Put two colonists against each other and they'll fight in a nasty free-for-all, using their feet and their teeth, but when one of them has won a clear-cut victory, that suffices. The honor of Indians, however, demands a fight to the death: either Ja-gonh or Sa-ra-ro must die. There is no alternative."

The combatants, it appeared, were in no way limited as to space. The onlookers cleared an area at the top of a grassy slope, and they took care not to enter an area that led down to the bank of the Connecticut River from the crest. Apparently the fight would take place wherever Ja-gonh and Sa-ra-ro wished.

As the tensions mounted, Roger instinctively moved closer to Patience and took his place beside her. Her father went to her other side, touched her arm, and looked at her in silent appeal.

The young woman set her mouth firmly and shook her head. Nothing would dissuade her from witnessing the combat that might result in Ja-gonh's death. The spectators became increasingly excited, and the buzz of conversation grew louder and more insistent.

Sa-ra-ro seemed well aware of the stir that he was creating and obviously relished it. He waved to colonists whom he knew, and winked at several attractive young women. Ja-gonh, on the other hand, seemed to be concentrating on his coming task with single-minded intensity. Roger was startled when he heard Ja-gonh speaking very softly and realized he was uttering a prayer to the manitous who protected the Seneca, quietly asking them for their help.

The combat had no formal beginning, as such. Suddenly Sa-ra-ro decided the time had come to begin, and he literally hurled himself at his more slender opponent.

If he hoped to catch Ja-gonh off guard, however, he was doomed to disappointment. His face showing no expression whatsoever, Ja-gonh easily sidestepped several inches, and his huge opponent brushed past him but left him intact. The fight was under way. The Mahican cheered their champion vociferously and roared their approval, emitting several ear-splitting war cries when Sa-ra-ro slowly drew his tomahawk. Apparently he intended to end the combat almost before it had begun.

Ja-gonh seemed totally unconcerned and stood quietly, his arms folded, seemingly in a trance. Roger noted, however, that he was balanced on the balls of his feet in the manner of a duelist and that he was prepared to move rapidly in any direction and at any time.

Sa-ra-ro did not conceal his intentions. Drawing back a powerful arm with exaggerated slowness, he took careful aim with his tomahawk and let fly. To the astonishment of everyone watching the spectacle, he missed his target very badly, for Ja-gonh, exerting very little effort, threw himself to the ground and then bounded instantly to his feet again. He accomplished the entire maneuver so swiftly and so gracefully that anyone who did not happen to be watching him closely would have missed his action.

The significance of what had just happened was lost on no one. Sa-ra-ro was no longer armed with a tomahawk, but Ja-gonh still carried his and consequently had a great advantage. The Mahican champion promptly tried to compensate for his lack by rushing his opponent, both of his massive arms flailing as he advanced.

Ja-gonh stood motionless, awaiting him quietly, and Patience gasped aloud, thinking he intended to meet his opponent's onslaught face to face.

At the last possible moment before Sa-ra-ro made contact, however, Ja-gonh again moved, and his agility was as great as his speed. He ducked under the hammer-like blows so that they didn't touch him, and he astonished the giant by ramming him in the chest with his head and shoulders, then withdrawing again instantly.

Sa-ra-ro lost his balance as well as his breath and sat down hard on the ground. Several of the colonists laughed, which infuriated the Mahican and outraged his colleagues.

It was evident, however, that Ja-gonh was toying with his opponent deliberately, making him look foolish in the hope that he would lose his temper. Again the young Seneca darted forward, and this time butted Sa-ra-ro in the stomach with his head before moving beyond the larger warrior's possible grasp. Sa-ra-ro was furious. Bellowing with rage, he unleashed another war cry and then drew a stone-handled knife from his belt. Patience shuddered as she watched him advancing ponderously, slowly placing one foot before the other as he sought his slender foe.

Ja-gonh, however, was totally unimpressed, and the contempt on his face was plain as he awaited the fresh onslaught. He stood silently, his arms at his sides, and waited for the larger man to attack. In fact, he became overly confident, and that very nearly caused the young Seneca's downfall.

Patience shuddered when Sa-ra-ro, unexpectedly adroit and quick, lunged with the knife that he held in his grasp. The brave approached so suddenly that he caught Ja-gonh unaware, and only Ja-gonh's quick reflexes prevented his death: he threw himself to the ground just as the warrior pounced on him, and the knife cut his cheek but did not seriously wound him. Now, before he could rise, Sa-ra-ro pounced again, and Roger was reminded of a huge bear seeking its prey.

The Seneca's agility, however, was little short of miraculous. He grabbed Sa-ra-ro's wrist just as the blade was about to descend and, with a sharp twist, forced the burly warrior to release the knife, which was kicked aside in the scuffle. Now for the first time the young Seneca took the initiative. Fighting in the style of the English colonists, he unleashed a furious flurry of hard punches, delivering bruising lefts and hard, smashing rights in quick succession. His fists pounded Sa-ra-ro's head, face, and torso, inflicting considerable punishment in a remarkably short time: Sa-ra-ro's left eye was swollen, and blood was streaming from a cut on his jaw as his opponent again retreated beyond his reach.

The tactics employed by the young Seneca were so bewildering that the Mahican warriors who were witnessing the combat and had been anticipating their champion's easy triumph were stunned. The colonists were equally surprised, but they recovered in time to cheer for the young man who was succeeding against such heavy odds.

Ja-gonh was concentrating exclusively on Sa-ra-ro and paid no attention whatsoever to any of the onlookers. Again he moved forward, and Sa-ra-ro, somewhat groggy, prepared to stave off another attack of fists. But Ja-gonh varied his strategy, and this time he unleashed a swift, powerful kick that caught the giant in the pit of the stomach and felled him, sending him sprawling on his back.

This was the opportunity that Ja-gonh had been awaiting. His foe was temporarily immobilized, and his onlookers grew very quiet as he drew his own razor-sharp tomahawk from his belt.

Patience shuddered, braced herself, and for a moment closed her eyes.

Crouching down, Ja-gonh straddled his opponent and raised his tomahawk for the kill. The only question in the minds of his onlookers was whether he intended to first dispose of Sa-ra-ro or whether he intended to remove the man's scalp while he was still conscious.

Brandishing the tomahawk, Ja-gonh held the blade lightly against his opponent's throat. If Sa-ra-ro made the slightest move now, he would destroy himself.

To the astonishment of everyone present, Ja-gonh spoke in a loud, clear voice. "Hear me, champion of the Mahican," he said. "Let your brothers open their ears and hear, also. You defiled the good name of the Seneca. For this you deserve to die, but you knew no better. You heard tales about the Seneca that were false, and you believed them. You were stupid. The Seneca do not kill their foes for stupidity but for arrogance. Therefore, you will be spared." He amazed the onlookers by unexpectedly thrusting the tomahawk into his belt.

Jeffrey Wilson could scarcely believe his eyes, and Patience was in a daze. What they were witnessing would be a subject of discussion in Fort Springfield for years to come, and a legend was in the making, a legend that would be repeated whenever men spoke of Indians.

"Heed my words well and remember what I say, O warrior of the Mahican!" Ja-gonh declared. "Hereafter walk humbly when you are in the presence of the mighty Seneca. Do not tempt them, do not arouse their anger. You live because the Seneca are just and merciful. They do not kill just for the sake of killing. They believe first and always in the cause of justice. Live justly, O warrior of the Mahican, and your days will be long." He rose nimbly to his feet and placed his tomahawk in his belt. The onlookers stirred, but none spoke, and in the silence that followed, people watched numbly as Sa-ra-ro hauled himself slowly to his feet.

The giant had never known defeat in combat, and this fact, coupled with the unexpected sparing of his life, left him dazed. He cleared his throat, folded his arms across his chest, and spoke with the great dignity of which only an Indian brave was capable. "Hear me, O Seneca," he cried. "Hear me, my brothers of the Mahican, hear me you who are strangers and have chanced upon this scene. I swear by all the gods of my people that I will be the blood brother of the Seneca who spared my life. For the rest of my days, I will honor him. I will follow him into battle; I will do his bidding." He bowed low before Ja-gonh, then drew his one remaining knife from his belt and extended it to the Seneca hilt first, in a gesture of surrender.

Ja-gonh shook his head slowly. Taking the knife, he reversed it, thrust it at the Mahican, and quickly drew one of his own knives, which he also offered to the huge warrior.

Patience watched with shining eyes. Never had she seen anything more heartening, and she was proud of Ja-gonh, proud of her association with him. She saw the cut on his face, of which the young warrior seemed to take no heed, and she realized that Ja-gonh would have a scar on his face for the rest of his life. But the scar would be a mark of honor, and anyone who saw it would be reminded of the greatness of the Seneca.

Roger Harkness was equally impressed. The Seneca were less barbaric than he had assumed when he had witnessed Ja-gonh's scalping of the Pimlico. What he wondered and had no answer to guide him was whether all the Seneca were as noble as Ja-gonh and his great father or whether Ja-gonh and Renno displayed such nobility because of their English colonial background and associations. Whatever the reasons, they were extraordinary, and Roger felt he was privileged to be associated with them. More than ever, the young Englishman could understand why Renno and his family were so universally admired everywhere on the American frontier.

Goo-ga-ro-no despised Pierre Fanchon as she had never in her life hated anyone. Too late to do anything practical about it, she realized that he had deliberately tricked her for reasons she couldn't quite fathom. All she knew was that he had delighted in humiliating her, and she realized her current predicament was grave indeed. She was without funds, she was many hundreds of miles away from home, she had no training that would enable her to earn an honest living, and she knew no one in Quebec who would befriend or help her.

As she wandered the streets aimlessly, the young woman thought hard, considering her dilemma, weighing her chances, and wondering what to do next. The possibility of returning to the land of the Seneca was virtually nonexistent. She would be taking far too many risks if she ventured alone into the wilderness and tried to cross territories controlled by the Huron and the Ottawa.

Ultimately, perhaps, she could find some way to arrange for an escort of some sort and make her way home—if indeed she had a home any longer. Until that time, however, she had to have food and a place to sleep.

Near the base of the hill on which the Citadel stood was a large eating establishment that, Goo-ga-ro-no noted, seemed very popular. It was crowded with men in rough-hewn buckskins, obviously trappers, and was also patronized by the bateaux men whom she came to recognize as the expert professionals who paddled the long canoes of the French Canadians up and down the Saint Lawrence River. Soldiers ate in the establishment, too, and it was crowded with a motley variety of civilians. The very popularity of the place attracted the young woman, and she studied it more closely.

She had left the town of the Seneca with precisely twenty-five cents in cash—a quarter of a dollar, coined in Virginia, that her Aunt Consuelo had given her as a good luck token. She was reluctant to spend her only capital but knew it was necessary. Going into the eating establishment, which bore the name The Maple, she held her head high. Seeking and finding an empty table, she sat there, but to her surprise no one appeared to wait on her. Looking around cautiously, she realized that the waitresses were preoccupied with serving the male clientele, who no doubt gave the servingwomen generous tips, but she also saw that many patrons here simply helped themselves to their food. They went to a counter at the far end of the establishment and selected various dishes for which they then paid a busy woman who sat at a small, high desk. Rising slowly to her feet, Goo-ga-ro-no made her way to the counter, and there she stared in bewilderment at a variety of meats, fishes, and other prepared dishes, all of them delicious if appearances were to be judged. Anxious to see to it that her quarter of a dollar went as far as possible, she debated at length and finally took a bowl of a hearty soup with a meat base and a slab of bread. She carried them to the woman at the desk and smiled at her timidly.

Phyllis Bouchard, the wife of the proprietor, Etienne Bouchard, was necessarily a keen judge of character, and she looked with interest at the stunning young woman who incongruously wore Indian attire but who, with her blond hair and fair coloring, in no way resembled an Indian. "You have chosen well, my dear," she said. "The soup is the best buy of the day." She took the quarter dollar and handed the girl a fistful of change, most of it in pennies.

Goo-ga-ro-no stammered her thanks. Phyllis Bouchard

studied her more closely. "You are a stranger in Quebec?"

Goo-ga-ro-no nodded.

"You have relatives here or good friends, perhaps?"

The young woman shook her head. "I know no one," she muttered.

Phyllis Bouchard looked around the establishment until she found her husband, a deceptively meek-looking, short man who was bringing more food from the kitchen. She caught his eye, and he came to her at once. Without speaking, she indicated Goo-ga-ro-no.

"You'll forgive me for interfering in something that is none of my business, but I hope you have made appropriate living arrangements," the Frenchwoman said. "Quebec is a strange and cruel city to strangers, and you're far too pretty to be wandering alone here. Let me just tell you that the harbor is full of merchant ships from France. There are many bateaux men and fur traders in town, and a new half regiment of troops has just arrived, too."

Goo-ga-ro-no looked stricken, and Phyllis was convinced that her initial judgment of the maiden was correct. By no stretch of the imagination was this young woman a prostitute. She smiled encouragingly as she awaited an answer.

Goo-ga-ro-no drew a deep breath. "I'm afraid I have no funds to rent quarters," she said. "How I landed in this dreadful predicament is a long story, but I'm afraid it is irrelevant. The only money I had, I spent for this soup and bread."

Phyllis again looked at her husband, her deep eyes lidded. She had the ability to communicate silently with Etienne, and he grasped her meaning at once. Rubbing his hands together, he asked gently, "Are you interested in honorable, gainful employment?"

Goo-ga-ro-no felt that her prayers had been answered. "There's nothing in the world I seek as much as I do a position that will help me support myself," she said fervently.

Phyllis Bouchard smiled. "You are prepared to work hard?"

"Very hard, madame!"

Etienne did some rapid mental calculations and saw an opportunity to hire an exceptionally attractive young woman for a very low fee. Like his wife, he noted that she was dressed in Indian attire, which indicated that she was the poorest of the poor. He took a deep breath and said jovially, "Suppose we give you all of your meals and a place beside the hearth in our kitchen to sleep, would payment of ten sous per week strike you as sufficient?"

Goo-ga-ro-no was overcome by the offer. "You're very generous, sir," she said.

Etienne knew she was totally lacking in worldliness, as well as impoverished. By no means could his offer be called generous, but he had no desire to quibble, and held out his hand. "Consider it done, then," he said. "We have struck a bargain. You will begin by helping my sons, Georges and Philippe, who are busy cooking in the kitchen."

She quickly finished her meal. Then he escorted her past the food counters to a room where vast quantities of food were cooking over two large brick hearths. She was surprised to see that the Bouchards' sons, Georges and Philippe, were only a few years her senior. Neither asked questions about her identity, and both started to give orders at once.

"I need vegetables cut and placed in this pot to simmer," Georges said. "Quickly, quickly!" He shoved a small kitchen knife at Goo-ga-ro-no and practically hurled a bunch of carrots, several onions, and a head of cauliflower at her.

"I require that the stew being prepared in the big black pot be tested at once," Philippe said. "Here, take this," he said, thrusting a fork at her, "and taste the meat. If it is ready, move the entire container to a smaller fire."

Goo-ga-ro-no didn't know what to do first, but one thing was certain: she was being accepted totally, and the question of her immediate future was solved. Logically, it was inconceivable that the daughter of Renno, the leader of the Seneca, and of Betsy, who was related to one of the most powerful families in Virginia, should be working in an inexpensive eating establishment in Quebec as a scullery maid, but that was Goo-ga-ro-no's lot in life, and she was very grateful for it. She actually smiled as she plunged into her work, and Etienne Bouchard later discussed the situation with his wife.

"We are in luck," he said. "The young woman must be very poor to be wearing Indian clothes, but I think we will refrain from asking her too many questions. She is a willing worker, and we have hired her for a small fraction of what we would have had to pay someone else."

Phyllis Bouchard nodded. She was curious about Goo-ga-ro-no's background and situation, but her story could wait. In the meantime, Goo-ga-ro-no would give full measure at The Maple, and that was all her employers could ask of her.

Chapter V

Renno's special task force returned home at last from its long journey. Although the new Great Sachem of the Iroquois was less than satisfied with the results, he had to admit that he had accomplished his basic purpose. Everywhere he had gone the local tribes had thought better of their possible insurrection and had not gone on the warpath, although the tension in the land was still great.

Someone else who observed the progress of the task force with particular interest was Gray Fox, who, emboldened by his earlier successes, was about to strike another major blow. Even his immediate subordinates were startled when they learned of the plan, but they unhesitatingly followed orders, and as soon as the Iroquois warriors returned to their various tribes, Gray Fox set his bold plan into motion.

Fifty warriors sneaked down across the Canadian border from the land of the Huron. Traveling through New York Colony, they crossed the site that was to become in the years ahead Fort Ticonderoga—where key battles of the French and Indian War and the American Revolution would be fought. Here they donned the distinctive war paint of the Mohawk, then continued to march south rapidly, until they saw at last the high wooden palisade of Fort Albany, on the upper reaches of the Hudson River. Gray Fox timed their approach so they arrived opposite the fort about two hours after nightfall. The warriors paddled out in the canoes they had carried with them for the purpose, and soon were crossing the river and approaching the palisade.

Fort Albany had been at peace for a very long time. The treaty with the Iroquois had been scrupulously observed by both the English colonists, who made their headquarters at Fort Albany, and by the Mohawk, whose lands adjoined those of the settlers. Aside from minor infractions, neither side had broken the peace for at least a generation.

Consequently, the sentries on duty in the watchtowers of the fort were neither alarmed nor upset when they saw the warriors crossing the narrow silver band of the Hudson River. By the light of the half moon, they made out the Mohawk war paint and assumed that a party of visitors was approaching the fort. To their astonishment, when the canoes were almost within arm's reach of the fort, the warriors suddenly unleashed a hail of arrows. Four militiamen were wounded in the unexpected attack, two of them seriously. Then, before the officers in charge could rally their men, the braves sent burning arrows into the open windows and gun ports of the wooden fort. The attack was as dramatic as it was unexpected, and three fires broke out almost at once, one of them spreading rapidly toward the large complex of offices and dormitories of the fort that stood behind the front bastion. The militia were so taken by surprise that they were forced to concentrate all of their efforts on trying to put out the fires; retaliation against the Indians for the unprovoked, unexpected attack would have to wait. After scrambling and scurrying for a considerable time, the militia extinguished the fires and were able to concentrate on their unexpected foes. To their surprise, however, the Indians had retreated beyond the range of the militiamen's rifles. When last seen from the windows of the battered fort, the canoes were rapidly making their way to safety upstream.

It was too late to try to follow and punish the braves who had taken part in the assault, and the enraged militiamen watched helplessly as the warriors landed far upstream and vanished into the wilderness.

A subsequent study showed that damages to Fort Albany had been severe. The fires had burned out several rooms, destroying furniture and other property that would be difficult to replace. The authorities still had no idea why the attack had taken place.

The civilian mayor of Fort Albany was furious, and his indignation was shared by the major of militia who commanded the garrison. Naturally they assumed that the Mohawk were to blame, and they reasoned that for some cause, which they did not know, the powerful, populous tribe had elected to break the treaty that had been in force for so long.

Gray Fox was well satisfied with his night's work. His men immediately swam in the Hudson and removed all traces of Mohawk war paint. Then, carefully avoiding all other Indians, they set out as rapidly as possible for the border of New France. Crossing without incident into Canada, they finally resumed their identity as Huron and made their way home. There was no doubt in the mind of any warrior who participated in the venture that serious problems had been caused for the Mohawk and that relations with the English colonists had been badly disturbed.

The Fort Albany leaders communicated first with their superiors in New York Colony and then with the authorities of other colonies. The shock waves spread quickly. Everywhere, officials were stunned by the senseless attack and, even more important, by the recognition that the assault constituted a serious breach of the treaty with the Iroquois nations, thereby threatening the entire structure of peace that had held together for so long on the frontiers of the English colonies.

The other tribes of the Iroquois League were bewildered about the incident, as were the Mohawk, who were completely innocent of wrongdoing. None had any idea that the leaders of the colonies conferred seriously and at great length before deciding on a plan of action. It was determined that Colonel Jeffrey Wilson would act as spokesman for all of the colonies, and because of his long and close association with Renno, he would go directly to the new Great Sachem to complain about the conduct of the Mohawk. In order to emphasize his peaceful intentions, Jeffrey was accompanied only by a small squad of troops. Roger Harkness also went with him and was designated as his special aide.

They made their way directly to the main town of the Seneca, and there Renno greeted his old friend warmly. Ja-gonh, who had completed his term of punishment and who had been highly praised by Renno for his exploits against the Pimlico and Mahican, was pleased to see Roger again, too, but both he and his father were bewildered by the obvious coolness that Jeffrey and Roger displayed to them from the outset. The Seneca knew, of course, about the raid on the fort, and Renno realized that Jeffrey would want to confer with him, but the attitude of his colleague and friend indicated that Jeffrey had something more on his mind.

Not until after they had finished eating an informal dinner together that night around the fire in front of Renno and Betsy's house did the truth come out. Jeffrey spoke forcefully and bluntly about the unexpected, unprovoked raid on Fort Albany and made clear that the consequences were grave.

"Naturally I don't hold you to blame in any way, Renno," he said. "But I hope you understand that this attack necessarily changes our whole relationship."

Renno was still surprised at Jeffrey's coldness, but first

he had to absorb all the details of what he had just heard. "If you please, Jeffrey," he said, "tell me again what you know about the assault. Include every detail, if you will."

Jeffrey nodded to Roger, who read at length from the official report of the major commanding the Fort Albany militia.

There was a long silence when Roger finished speaking. Betsy looked shocked, and Renno's lips were compressed, although he retained his composure. Now he realized that his friend's aloofness was a result of the belief that the Iroquois were engaged in some kind of a conspiracy. So Renno spoke firmly and decisively.

"I find it difficult to believe that any Iroquois nation would foolishly place the League's treaty with the English colonies in jeopardy," he said. "It is true that tribes like the Choctaw and Algonquian sometimes conduct raids without reason, but I have always assumed that the nations of the Iroquois were too intelligent to behave in such a barbaric and irresponsible manner. It is obvious that I was mistaken." He raised his voice slightly. "Jeffrey, I shall convey to you and to all of the militia leaders of the English colonies my sincere official regrets for this stupid incident, and I give you my assurances that the attack will not be repeated. Unofficially, I intend to get to the bottom of this matter at once and make sure that not only the perpetrators are properly punished but that there is no repetition of something that places our relationship with the colonies in the greatest jeopardy."

He excused himself, then went off to the lodge of the council for a consultation with the elders of the Seneca. The result of that meeting was a stiff note addressed to Mi-shal of the Mohawk, demanding an explanation of the outrageous assault.

A messenger departed at a trot for the land of the Mohawk at dawn the following day and was instructed to await a reply before returning home.

Jeffrey Wilson trusted Renno implicitly and accepted his word without question, writing to the governor of Massachusetts Bay and to the leaders of several other colonies to the effect that he was convinced that there was no Iroquois conspiracy against the colonies and that he was certain that the Seneca were in no way involved.

While they awaited the reply of the Mohawk, Ja-gonh and Roger Harkness hunted and fished together in perfect amity. Roger also accompanied the young Seneca on a visit to the house of Ah-wen-ga for the purpose of being presented to the Indian maiden, and he was much impressed by her. He had to admit that he approved thoroughly of Ja-gonh's taste in the opposite sex, be she an Indian like Ah-wen-ga or a colonist like Patience Wilson.

Roger's own relationship with Patience, however, was far from certain. He was still residing in the Wilson home and reporting back at intervals to Governor Gooch. Naturally he saw Patience often, and he was as attracted to her as ever, but now, after Ja-gonh's victory over the Mahican warrior, it seemed all Patience could do was talk about the young Seneca.

The Seneca messenger returned with very bad news. Mi-shal and his council were taken completely by surprise and resented deeply Renno's communication. The Mohawk were innocent of all wrongdoing and saw no reason to be forced to justify themselves before their peers. The tone Mi-shal employed had been both austere and harsh, and he scarcely bothered to refute the charges. What infuriated him the most was the lack of faith shown to the Mohawk by the Seneca, and he made no secret of his deep resentment.

Renno was taken completely off guard by the nature of the Mohawk reply, and he reacted sternly, strongly, and immediately to it. He regarded the communication from Mi-shal as an admission of Mohawk guilt and was angry because it was not accompanied by any explanation of Mohawk conduct. Wasting no time, he immediately called an emergency meeting of the leaders of all of the Iroquois tribes.

They traveled quickly to the town of the Seneca, and when they were all gathered, they went into secret session in the Council Lodge. There Renno explained what had happened, telling them of his shock when he had learned from Jeffrey Wilson the details of the incident at Fort Albany. He read his letter to the Mohawk, and then, as the leaders of the tribes sat in a hushed silence, he read Mi-shal's hasty, bad-tempered reply. There was a silence, and no sound was heard but the hissing of the logs burning in the Council fire.

Then Sun-ai-yee rose to his feet and addressed his colleagues in a ponderous tone. "I grieve to see the day," he said, "when the all-powerful Iroquois League founders. It brings tears to my eyes when the ship of state that is the symbol of the Iroquois smashes and is reduced to useless birch bark on the sharp rocks of Mohawk perfidy and two-faced cunning."

Mi-shal jumped to his feet instantly, intending to rebut Sun-ai-yee's remarks, but the portly Seneca leader gave him no chance to interrupt. "In my lifetime," Sun-ai-yee declared, "I have led troops; I have led warriors of all our nations into battle more often than I can count the times. Always I have held my head high; always I have been proud to be a leader of Iroquois. That day is ended. I would cringe with shame now if I were asked to lead the Mohawk into battle. Why? Because the word of the Mohawk cannot be trusted. They break their sacred pledge, and by so doing they cause trouble for all the rest of us." He glowered at Mi-shal, then sat down abruptly.

Mi-shal's reply was inconsiderate and ill-advised. Smarting under the unjust criticism of a revered colleague, Mi-shal struck out blindly in a fury and said a great deal that he would later have cause to regret. He insulted the Seneca, then went on to say uncomplimentary things about all of the other Iroquois. He made it clear that in his opinion, as well as in the opinion of his subordinates, it was the Mohawk who were responsible for not only holding together the Iroquois League but also for whatever prestige that alliance had gained.

The meeting quickly degenerated beyond control. The sachem of the Tuscarora was a hot-tempered warrior who resented Mi-shal's comments, which he took personally, and he responded to them viciously. Soon all of the leaders were exchanging insults and making vicious comments. Renno tried repeatedly to restore order, but on this occasion it was impossible. Not even Ghonka could have achieved such a goal.

The upshot was dramatic and sudden: Mi-shal stormed out of the meeting, and summoning the members of his party, he promptly led them out of town. This was the first time that anyone had walked out of the Council of the Iroquois. The other sachems were nonplussed, but at Renno's suggestion they did not make an issue out of Mi-shal's withdrawal for fear that the entire Iroquois League would certainly crumble and would fall apart. At best, that union was very fragile, and its preservation was dubious.

So Jeffrey Wilson and Roger Harkness returned to Fort Springfield, leaving the land of the Seneca in as solemn a mood as when they had arrived. That night Renno could not sleep, and he paced his house through the small hours of the morning. "I did not agree to succeed my father as Great Sachem of the Iroquois only to see the whole League crumble," he said to Betsy, who quietly stayed by his side throughout the night. "I've got to do something."

Betsy knew better than to ask him what he had in mind. She understood him well enough to realize that he was in torment as he struggled in vain to preserve the fabric of a structure that had meant so much to the peace of North America. She could not advise him, nor, she knew, could anyone else. He faced a dilemma that was as impossible as it was cruel, and she had no idea how he could go about solving it.

Her faith in him, however, was unbounded, and she felt confident that somehow, in some way, Renno would triumph and would perform a miracle, as he had done so often in the past. If only the leaders of all the Iroquois tribes felt as she did, Betsy thought, the problem would be solved!

Gray Fox met with Pierre Fanchon and paid the Frenchman the money promised him, even going so far as to give the man a bonus. Certainly Fanchon's taking of

Goo-ga-ro-no away from her homeland and letting her flounder in Quebec was no mean feat, undoubtedly causing Renno and all the Seneca to grieve. No, the money was well spent, and Gray Fox was sure he had got the better end of the bargain.

Gray Fox also received a detailed report on the state of affairs in the town of the Seneca from a spy he had planted there, and he listened carefully as the man told him of Mi-shal's hasty, angry departure and the outrage of the Iroquois leaders who had remained behind. He showed no elation but privately rejoiced. At last his careful plans were coming to fruition. The League was in grave difficulty—and would be in even more trouble after he carried out his latest scheme.

Gray Fox made it his business to visit Major de Bienville at his office in the Citadel, and there he spoke bluntly. "The Iroquois League is virtually shattered," he said. "The Seneca and the Mohawk are becoming enemies. The Mohawk have actually withdrawn from a meeting of their allies."

The news was almost too good to be true. "What next?" de Bienville demanded.

"Certain events will occur," Gray Fox said, "that will drive the Seneca to take up arms against the Mohawk."

Major de Bienville regarded him closely. "This is not a subject for joking," he said, shaking his head dubiously.

Gray Fox returned his gaze steadily. "I do not jest, I assure you," he said. "I think I can guarantee that within a short time warriors of the Seneca will launch a large-scale attack on the towns of the Mohawk."

The major leaned back in his chair and stared up at the plastered ceiling. "If that should happen," he said, "it will give France the biggest boost we have ever had in attaining mastery of the New World. If the Seneca and the Mohawk actually go to war with one another, the Huron and the Ottawa will emerge as the most powerful tribes in America, and the Iroquois alliance will no longer be worthy of its name."

Gray Fox's lips parted in a bloodless smile. "I gather that such a development would not be unwelcome to you

125

or to Cardinal Fleury or to His Majesty at Versailles?"

Bienville almost lost his temper. "You know damned well," he snapped, "what every last one of us would think of such developments!"

"In my youth," Gray Fox said, "I remember hearing about a visit my father made to France. There he visited the great-grandfather of the present King, at his palace in Paris called the Louvre, and the King invited my father also to visit him a second time at his country home, the Palace of Versailles. What magnificence! What dazzling splendor! What great wealth! When I heard about all this, I realized that the King of the French must be one of the richest men in the world; and the young King is wealthier by far than his great-grandfather from whom he inherited so much."

The major knew what was coming and braced himself.

"I am not greedy," Gray Fox said, "and I certainly do not yearn for the vast riches of a king, but it would be very pleasant indeed to be made a gift of gold and silver and gems that a rich monarch wouldn't even miss but that would mean so much to someone in my position. Do you think, Major, it might be arranged for young King Louis to show his appreciation?"

There was a long, pregnant silence, and Major de Bienville said, "I think that if the Seneca and the Mohawk actually come to blows and thus not only terminate the Iroquois alliance but assure our own allies of mastery—I'm quite sure His Majesty would be appreciative. I cannot speak for the extent of his generosity because one does not bargain with a king, but I am told he is much like his great-grandfather. Therefore, I am convinced he will be exceedingly generous to those who serve him well."

Gray Fox's eyes gleamed avariciously. "I believe I can guarantee that King Louis will be delighted when he hears the news from the far side of the borders of New France. I think I can guarantee that the Seneca and the Mohawk will come to blows in the immediate future!"

Bienville was almost overcome with curiosity but held

himself in check. So far Gray Fox had managed to keep his word, and although what he was now proposing would have seemed preposterous a few months earlier, it certainly seemed within the realm of the feasible now. Bienville did not trust the half-breed but grudgingly was forced to admire him. The man had imagination, courage, and daring to carry out his outrageous schemes.

The town of the Seneca was in a wild ferment: a band of Mohawk warriors had been seen approaching the town shortly before sundown. Whether they actually had entered the community or stayed in the nearby wilderness was uncertain. All anyone knew for sure was that Sun-ai-yee's elder daughter, Ah-wen-ga, had vanished into thin air.

Her disappearance was not discovered for some hours. Her parents did not see her at supper and assumed that she was eating at the lodge of the unmarried maidens. Similarly, there was no sign of her at the lodge, but the occupants took it for granted that she had gone to the house of her mother and father.

The news of her loss emerged almost by accident. Talking Quail wanted to give her daughter a message and went to the lodge of the maidens, only to discover that Ah-wen-ga had not been there for a number of hours. Inquiries then revealed that she had almost literally disappeared from the face of the earth at about the time that the Mohawk warriors had been seen.

Talking Quail lacked the self-discipline of the Seneca and burst into tears, so it required some little effort for Sun-ai-yee to get the news from her. He was horrified and, losing no time, went straight to Renno, who was sitting in a discussion with Ja-gonh.

Sun-ai-yee spoke at length indignantly, his voice booming in anger and frustration. Renno listened carefully and then remarked, "It appears to me that the Mohawk who were seen loitering near the town must have kidnapped her."

His son, heartsick and angry, nodded slowly. "It makes

no sense, but I'm forced to agree with you, my father. Ah-wen-ga has been abducted by the Mohawk."

"They took her," Sun-ai-yee said, "as a way of making all Seneca lose face. They chose her because I have been made the sachem of our nation by our people, and by losing my daughter, by being forced to beg the Mohawk to return her unharmed, I will lose stature in the eyes of all the Iroquois. The Mohawk do this deliberately in order to make the whole Seneca nation lose stature."

Renno nodded. "It is so," he said, and his voice had a metallic ring, "but I will not tolerate this insult."

Ja-gonh gripped the handle of his tomahawk. "The Mohawk have gone too far," he said. "I was punished for quarreling with them on the march, but I am willing to risk even greater punishment now. I will go to them, and I will demand the immediate return of Ah-wen-ga. If they do not give her to me at once, I will burn their town to the ground."

Renno and Sun-ai-yee exchanged alarmed glances. "No, my son," Renno said, "that is precisely what you will not do. We are making great efforts to preserve the alliance of the Iroquois. Some Mohawk are acting unwisely and irrationally, but their stupidity is no reason for us to reply in kind."

Sun-ai-yee nodded gravely. "I think," he said, "it will be best if I send a communication to Mi-shal. I shall be polite, but I shall also be firm. He will understand that he must control his own people. If Ah-wen-ga is not returned, I will hold their sachem responsible." His tone and his expression indicated that the Mohawk would be in for a rough time indeed if his daughter was in any way harmed and was not returned promptly.

Renno indicated his approval of the plan, and Sun-ai-yee wrote a letter at once. At Ja-gonh's request he was permitted to act as messenger, and no sooner was the communication on paper than he immediately set out for the neighboring land of the Mohawk.

He traveled at a rapid trot and reached the principal town of the Iroquois allies in the remarkable time of less than forty-eight hours. He was ushered into Mi-shal's presence and silently presented him with Sun-ai-yee's communication.

The leader of the Mohawk promptly lost his temper. Loudly proclaiming that he was tired of seeing his people accused of deeds they had not perpetrated, he swore that his men were innocent.

Ja-gonh listened to him carefully and could not help being impressed with his sincerity. Either Mi-shal was an actor of extraordinary talents, or he was an honest, indignant man. Certainly no Mohawk had ever been known for his hypocrisy, so Ja-gonh was inclined to believe that what he was saying was the truth.

Preoccupied with Mi-shal's flat statements, Ja-gonh returned to the land of the Seneca, but before reporting to Renno and to Sun-ai-yee, he decided to do something that should have been done when it had first been discovered that Ah-wen-ga was missing. He searched the underbrush in the wilderness until he found the tracks that told him the whole story of the abduction. Six braves had participated in the venture, and he could read their marks with the utmost clarity. He followed the path Ah-wen-ga had taken, and knew precisely where she had been caught unaware and captured after a brief struggle. Then he followed the tracks for a time, and he was even more thoughtful when he finally made his way to the town and reported to Renno.

Asking that Sun-ai-yee also be present, Ja-gonh explained that he had been impressed by Mi-shal's protestations of Mohawk innocence and had delayed his return home to search for signs that would tell him more about the incident.

"The men who captured Ah-wen-ga," he said, "did not take her to the land of the Mohawk; they did not travel to the southeast. Instead, they moved very quickly toward the northeast."

Renno was astonished by this revelation. "Are you quite certain of your facts?" he demanded.

His son nodded, then explained that he had followed the tracks of the abductors for several miles.

Sun-ai-yee was totally bewildered. "I do not understand," he said. "Why should warriors of the Mohawk take my daughter elsewhere than to their own homeland?"

"I cannot answer that question," Ja-gonh said. "But it makes sense to me only if the kidnappers were not truly Mohawk and tried to create fresh troubles between the Mohawk and the Seneca by pretending they were Mohawk."

Renno nodded, and his mouth set in a grim line. "I know of only one people—the Huron—who would try to create troubles of that sort," he said, "but I do not want to jump to hasty conclusions. You are following a lead that could prove fruitful, so I urge you to continue your investigation."

Sun-ai-yee frowned uneasily. "It may be," he said, "that you and I have personal enemies, Renno, who are trying to cause trouble between the Seneca and the Mohawk. I do not object if Ja-gonh tries to find the enemies, but I do know that if Ah-wen-ga is not returned to me in the immediate future, unharmed, I will ask your permission to send an army of Seneca braves out to look for her."

Renno nodded. As sachem of the Seneca, Sun-ai-yee had the right to make such a request.

Meanwhile, Ja-gonh followed up on his original lead and began tracing the trail of the kidnappers. To his astonishment it led in the direction of Fort Springfield. He reported this to Renno, who urged him to follow through as best he was able and to report his findings to no one else.

Gray Fox exercised greater caution than he had ever before shown. He well knew that if the kidnapping of Sun-ai-yee's daughter could definitely be attributed to the Huron, the Seneca would attack their neighbor to the north instantly and without mercy. Therefore, he took great pains to conceal the presence of Ah-wen-ga in the midst of his warriors.

They traveled by choice in the direction of Massachusetts Bay and avoided all trails that led to the land of the Mohawk, Gray Fox reasoning that the paths would be crowded with Seneca seeking revenge.

Similarly, he took pains to conceal his identity and that of his braves from the maiden. She was kept blindfolded at all times as a precaution, but although Gray Fox did not realize it, this did not handicap her. Ah-wen-ga had been reared as a Seneca, and she knew in spite of the covering over her eyes precisely where she was being taken each day. She could have drawn a map of the route that her abductors took.

Gray Fox allowed his subordinates to speak freely in front of her, and as nearly as she could tell, the language they spoke was that of the Seneca. It occurred to her that her kidnappers might be Huron, since their language was so similar to that of her own people.

At no time did she see the faces of any of her kidnappers, and at Gray Fox's strictest orders she was treated with great delicacy. At night, in particular, no fewer than three warriors stood sentry duty over her at any given time. Gray Fox well realized that the complications could be endless if one of his warriors gave in to temptation and actually bedded the young woman. If Ah-wen-ga lost her virginity, the Seneca would have just cause for a major war.

Gray Fox faced a peculiar dilemma. He had succeeded in kidnapping Ah-wen-ga and had fulfilled his goal of further worsening the bad blood between the Seneca and the Mohawk. What bothered him now was what to do with the Seneca maiden. He could not release her for fear she would make her way home; he did not dare to have her escorted to the land of the Huron, where her whereabouts could not be kept secret for very long. He wished there were some way he could deposit her in the land of the Mohawk. But whatever he did, he realized that he would be wise to get rid of her. Therefore, he let it be known to the local tribes through whose area he was passing that he had a choice Seneca maiden for sale and would part with her for a reasonable sum of wampum, plus some modern firearms. His goal was to protect himself, as well as to make a small profit in return for his trouble.

So it happened that word was received by the Mahican that unidentified warriors wearing no war paint whatsoever were prepared to sell a maiden of the Seneca. This news was greeted with a measure of astonishment, since the Seneca had been victorious in so many battles that no members of the tribe had been placed for sale as slaves within the memory of anyone now alive.

Ja-gonh, painstakingly following the trail left by the abductors, found himself in the land of the Mahican, not far from Fort Springfield, and he was somewhat confused but continued his search for the kidnappers. He customarily began his search each morning at daybreak and continued until sundown that evening, covering ground far more rapidly than anyone other than a trained Seneca would have deemed possible. Although he didn't know it, he was within thirty miles of Ah-wen-ga and her abductors.

He sat one evening before a small campfire he had made, ready to eat a brace of wild ducks he had shot, cleaned, and baked in clay. While his meal cooked, he drank from a nearby stream, then dug up the roots of several edible plants.

His sharp hearing detected the approach of a lone warrior, so he reached for his tomahawk, placing it on the ground, conveniently close at hand. He registered no surprise when Sa-ra-ro, his opponent in the vicious free-for-all fight, came into the clearing and saluted him.

Ja-gonh knew that the Mahican brave had probably learned from sentries of the Seneca's presence and had sought him out deliberately. He acted casual and calmly returned the salute.

"Welcome to the land of the Mahican," Sa-ra-ro declared. "It has come to my attention that my brother, the Seneca, searches the forest diligently each day as though looking for something or someone."

"That may be," Ja-gonh admitted laconically.

The Mahican giant sat down beside the fire unbidden and crossed his legs, making himself at home. Ja-gonh made the best of the situation by inviting his former opponent to join him at supper. Fortunately he had an extra duck on the fire.

Sa-ra-ro was pleased by his hospitality and promptly responded to it. "It may be," he said, "that I know something of those whom my brother the Seneca may seek."

Ja-gonh inclined his head but made no reply.

Sa-ra-ro stared out across the treetops and made no move as his host removed the two hard-baked clay balls from the fire and, after they had cooled, cracked them open with a sharp rock. The odor of duck that had cooked in its own juices was delicious, and Sa-ra-ro's eyes gleamed.

"It is said," he declared, "that a party of strange warriors is in the vicinity. They wear no war paint, and their nation is unknown."

Ja-gonh managed to match the other man's seemingly serene behavior. "What language do these strangers speak, I wonder?" he said softly.

Sa-ra-ro shrugged. "It is said they speak the tongue of the Seneca. I do not know for a fact if this is true because I have not met them myself, and I find it strange that Seneca would go through the wilderness without wearing the war paint of their great nation."

"I, too, find it strange," Ja-gonh said. "What business do these strangers seek to do that makes them interesting?"

Sa-ra-ro lowered his voice. "When I took an oath to be your brother for all time, I meant every word," he declared. "I swear now before my gods that my oath was sincere. Now I shall prove it. The strange warriors offer a Seneca maiden for sale."

Ja-gonh was stunned. Apparently he had followed the kidnappers of Ah-wen-ga a considerable distance only to learn that they wanted to be rid of her. "What price do they demand for her?" he asked gruffly.

Sa-ra-ro smiled deprecatingly. "Two kegs of parched corn and one of jerked venison, as well as some modern firearms," he said, sounding a trifle apologetic. "I know the price is not high; in fact, it is low, absurdly low, for a maiden of the Seneca, but I repeat to my brother what I have been told, and I do not try to insult or shame him."

Ja-gonh contained his excitement. "I would like to see these strange warriors," he said. "I would also like to see the maiden they offer for sale, in order to determine whether she is truly a Seneca. Could a meeting be arranged between them and the Mahican?"

Sa-ra-ro was becoming more involved than he wanted to be, but he saw no graceful way to avoid giving in to the request. "I think," he said, "that arrangements can be made."

Ja-gonh concluded the plan quickly as they ate. They arranged to meet the following day in a hollow some half-mile or so from Ja-gonh's present campsite. There Sa-ra-ro would pretend to be interested in purchasing the Seneca maiden, and Ja-gonh, who would conceal himself in the wilderness nearby, would be able to see the maiden and her companions without himself being discovered.

So the Mahican warrior went off saying he would communicate with Ja-gonh if he could not make the necessary arrangements. Meanwhile, the young Seneca spent a tension-filled night and morning.

As the time for the rendezvous approached, Ja-gonh occupied himself by honing the blade of his tomahawk, sharpening his knives, and testing his arrows. He had no idea what might be in store, but the prospect of coming face to face with Ah-wen-ga's kidnappers caused him a grim sense of anticipatory pleasure; he hoped that he might be able to rescue Ah-wen-ga and at the same time give her kidnappers the thrashing they deserved.

Sa-ra-ro awaited him at the rendezvous, and Ja-gonh immediately concealed himself in the nearby brush. There, in tense silence, he awaited the arrival of the strangers.

In due time Gray Fox appeared and studied Sa-ra-ro carefully. "You are the warrior who has expressed an interest in purchasing the maiden?" he asked.

The heavyset Mahican nodded.

Gray Fox insisted on examining the merchandise that

Sa-ra-ro was offering in barter, and while he looked at the grain and the jerked venison that Sa-ra-ro had taken care to provide, Ja-gonh peered from his hiding place at the man. He did not recall having seen Gray Fox before but would never forget his features again. What was puzzling was that the man wore no identifying war paint of any kind, which was unusual, and that he spoke the tongue of the Seneca without an accent.

At last Gray Fox was satisfied. "You also are willing to exchange firesticks of the Western Europeans for the maiden?"

Sa-ra-ro was more clever than Ja-gonh had given him credit for being. "I make no promises," he said. "You have seen two casks of fine corn and another of the best quality of jerked venison, but I have not yet seen the maiden. How do I know she will be a suitable slave in the lodge of my wife and children?"

The time had come when Gray Fox was obliged to produce the captive, and he sighed gently, then gestured to the wilderness behind him.

Two subordinates came forward out of the underbrush, each of them holding a leather thong, the opposite end of which was attached to one of Ah-wen-ga's wrists. The young woman was blindfolded and had no idea what was happening but walked, as always, with her head held high.

Ja-gonh recognized Ah-wen-ga instantly, and his pulses raced. It was almost too good to be true that he had stumbled upon her abductors, and he intended to set her free at the first possible instant.

"She is here," Gray Fox said. "You may examine her all you please. Now I would like to see the firesticks that will complete our bargain."

Ja-gonh could restrain himself no longer and came into the open, his bow bent, an arrow already notched in it. "Firesticks are unnecessary," he said.

Ah-wen-ga recognized his voice instantly, raised her head, and smiled broadly. Realizing he had been tricked, Gray Fox didn't waste a second. Shouting an order to his two subordinates, he dove into the underbrush, and they followed quickly, dragging the helpless Ah-wen-ga with them.

Too late Ja-gonh became aware of his opponent's strategy: by disappearing with Ah-wen-ga, Gray Fox was making it impossible for the Seneca to shoot his arrow, for fear of striking the young woman.

A crashing sound in the underbrush told him that the quarry was escaping. Ja-gonh lost no time and plunged after them, intent on delivering Ah-wen-ga from the hands of her tormentors.

Sa-ra-ro hesitated. It was true that he had sworn perpetual brotherhood, but this affair was becoming far too complicated for his taste. In fact, he knew that a vicious fight would take place between Ja-gonh and the strangers, and he wanted no part of the battle. So he refrained from following, and the other two Mahican braves, who had agreed to participate in the scheme with him, also lagged far behind.

Ja-gonh knew he was outnumbered but recklessly did not care. He knew, also, that he had to exercise great caution, for fear that the strangers would kill or seriously injure Ah-wen-ga in order to facilitate their own escape. So he deliberately allowed the fleeing Huron to pull away from him, and when Ja-gonh emerged into the open at the crest of a hill, he could see them clearly in the distance.

There were seven warriors in the party, all of them armed and none wearing identifying war paint. They were leading the still-blindfolded Ah-wen-ga by the thongs attached to her wrists, and it was miraculous that she was able to keep on her feet in the underbrush. Only someone of vast experience in the wilderness could accomplish that feat.

As Ja-gonh concentrated on the leader of the group, who was covering the rear as he ran away, his blood suddenly ran cold. He recognized the loose-limbed runner and was stunned as he recalled that this was the man he had seen wearing Mohawk war paint the night Ghonka had been murdered. This man, whoever he might be, was not only the abductor of Ah-wen-ga but was also the

killer of Ja-gonh's beloved grandfather. A cold, hard
resolve formed in the pit of Ja-gonh's stomach. Crouching
low, he sped forward, making no sound whatsoever.

The fleeing kidnappers' pace was slowed by the presence of Ah-wen-ga, but thanks to the extraordinary cunning shown by Ja-gonh, they had no idea that he was
following their trail. One by one they became convinced
they had left him behind. Even the cautious Gray Fox
was forced to believe they were correct. They sped to the
bank of the Connecticut River, and for an instant Ja-
gonh's heart stopped beating. Then he breathed more
freely when he realized they had no canoes awaiting them
and were intending to go upriver on foot. He doggedly
continued after them, determined to obtain vengeance for
the killing of Ghonka, as well as the abduction of Ah-
wen-ga.

For several hours the chase continued. Ja-gonh performed his self-assigned task easily. He found it no chore
to keep the fleeing party within earshot and to make his
own approach soundless. Sooner or later, he knew they
would be forced, because of Ah-wen-ga, to call a halt for
the night. He had to smile when he caught an occasional
glimpse of the young woman. She knew what her abductors did not, that he was following them. Her own training in the forest stood her in good stead, and she could
hear what they could not.

Furthermore, she was assisting Ja-gonh in a clever,
subtle way by pretending to a clumsiness that was alien to
her. Using her blindfold as an excuse, she tripped over
hidden roots and fallen branches and thus made it necessary for the warriors accompanying her to travel at an
even slower pace.

At last Gray Fox called a halt for the night, and rations
of parched corn and jerked venison were distributed.

From his vantage point Ja-gonh noted that Ah-wen-ga
was given a fair share of meat and grain to eat, although
her wrists remained bound and the blindfold was not
removed from her eyes. All that remained now was a
demonstration of patience, and Ja-gonh had learned patience from the time he had been a small boy. He ate a

little parched corn and jerked venison of his own, then loosened his tomahawk and his knives in his belt. Realizing that the odds were seven to one against him, he also took a strip of rawhide from its place as an extra thong for his bow and quickly fashioned it into a garrote. He would need to dispose of his foes silently when the time came.

The Huron gradually settled down for the night. Two of their number had been assigned as sentries, Gray Fox electing to keep Ah-wen-ga close beside him so he could deal with any emergency that might arise.

Ja-gonh coolly and rationally figured out his plan of battle. As Ghonka and Renno had taught him, he did not allow emotion to influence his judgment in any way. "War," his grandfather had often said, "is a science, and the warrior who knows it best and acts accordingly will be sure always to triumph." At last all was in readiness, and Ja-gonh crept forward very slowly, pausing to make certain he had not been overheard, then advancing again. Seeing the taller of the two sentries looming directly ahead of him, Ja-gonh deliberately waited until the man turned his back. Then with lightning speed he dropped the leather thong over the warrior's head and tugged on both ends with all his might. The garrote was so effective that the Huron choked to death without making a sound. As he died, his body slumped, and Ja-gonh caught him and silently eased his body to the ground.

Ja-gonh decided on another means for dispatching the remaining sentry, and he pulled out a sharp, double-edged knife. He crept closer to his quarry, then moved closer still, and suddenly he struck with methodical precision. The blade buried itself in the brave's chest, and the man died instantly, sucking in his breath briefly and then expiring silently.

Withdrawing his knife grimly, Ja-gonh wiped it clean on the body of the brave he had just killed. Now the odds were reduced to five to one, but with every moment that passed, the dangers became greater. Thus, he quickly located Ah-wen-ga in the clearing and then made his way toward her. Both of the thongs attached to her wrists were tied now to the sleeping leader's wrist. Ja-gonh took in the situation at a glance, then stepped forward silently and slashed the thongs, setting Ah-wen-ga free.

As he had hoped, she was wide awake and had anticipated just such a maneuver on his part. He slashed again, removing her blindfold with a single cut of his knife, and she met his gaze evenly, boldly. She was prepared for any action that he might dictate.

Ja-gonh assessed the situation swiftly. The murderer of Ghonka was within reach, but it would be the height of foolishness to attack him now while he slept. Four other warriors remained in the group, and Ja-gonh knew his good fortune would not hold forever in hand-to-hand combat with them. He would have to allow his grandfather's killer a respite so that he could more certainly rescue Ah-wen-ga.

He motioned to the young woman, and she stepped over Gray Fox's prostrate body, then over the body of another sleeping brave as she joined him.

It was unnecessary for Ja-gonh to gesture for silence. He retreated hastily, and Ah-wen-ga proved herself equal to the challenge. She moved with quick grace and made no sound as she followed the young Seneca.

And so they put a considerable distance between themselves and the members of the Huron party. Then they paused long enough for Ja-gonh to cut the last of the leather thongs from Ah-wen-ga's wrists. He did not smile as he handed her one of his knives, and as she gripped it firmly in her small hand, the expression in her eyes indicated that she would not hesitate to use it if need be. Suddenly there were two Seneca ready to do battle against the abductors, not one.

"We will head immediately toward the west, where the forest is thicker," Ja-gonh murmured. "Every moment is precious. Let me know when you tire, and we will stop so that you may rest."

Ah-wen-ga shook her head fiercely. "I need no rest," she replied.

Ja-gonh found it difficult to control his temper. "When you grow tired," he said, "you become careless and your feet make whispering sounds in the underbrush, sounds that the enemy can hear. Do exactly as I tell you, and do not argue with me."

The young woman knew she deserved the rebuke and nodded contritely.

Without further ado, Ja-gonh set out toward the west. They were far from the land of the Seneca, but he wanted to put as much distance as possible between them and the men who had abducted Ah-wen-ga. When they discovered she was missing, they would set out in pursuit, and the advantage, as Ja-gonh well knew, would switch to the abductors because they could make far better time without being hindered by the young woman's presence.

He traveled as fast as he dared, paying particular attention to Ah-wen-ga's techniques. He had to admit that he approved heartily of her ability to handle herself in the forest. She did not travel without making any sound; this would have been too much to ask of her, but he guessed that she did as well as any junior warrior of the Seneca could manage. It was astonishing that any mere female could be so adroit, so adept, so at home in the wilderness, and Ja-gonh felt great pride in Ah-wen-ga for being a Seneca.

His attitude communicated itself to her, and for the first time since he had rescued her, she smiled at him, her limpid eyes huge. There was no need for words; he returned the grin, and they established a close rapport.

Ja-gonh set the pace according to the best speed that Ah-wen-ga could muster, and he marveled privately at her ability to move so quickly and at such length, without pause. Granted that her life was at stake, she was still a remarkable person, and his appreciation of her grew. She asked no questions, did as she was bidden, and uttered no complaint. There was no more that he, as a senior warrior, could have asked of any junior assigned to him. They went on for hours, and only when Ah-wen-ga suddenly stumbled, did it occur to Ja-gonh that she had used her reserve of strength and was continuing on sheer nerve. She had deliberately refrained from telling him that she was tiring, but he had learned the truth in spite of her, so he took full responsibility. He waited until they reached a natural minifortress made by several large boulders, and there he called a halt.

"Drink from the brook," he directed. "Drink very slowly, and do not take too much water, or it will make you ill. Then sit and stretch your legs."

Ah-wen-ga obeyed without a word.

He regarded her curiously. "What can you tell me about the men who abducted you?" he demanded.

"Very little," she confessed. "I stupidly was careless and allowed myself to be taken prisoner, but my only excuse was that I had no idea I would be in trouble so close to the main town of the Seneca."

He silenced her with an impatient wave. "I am not blaming you," he said. "I merely want to know all that you can tell me about these men. What nation are they?"

"I'm not sure," she replied. "I often wondered myself. I eavesdropped on them because I've had so little else to occupy me, and I suspect that they may be Huron, but I wouldn't swear to it."

Huron. Ja-gonh mouthed the word silently, and on his lips it was a curse. The enormity of the plot against the Seneca, the plot that had resulted in the untimely death of Ghonka and the bad feeling between the Seneca and the Mohawk, began to become apparent. He couldn't see the scheme in its entirety, but his instincts told him what was being done. "Who is this man who is their leader?" he demanded.

Ah-wen-ga shrugged. "They were very careful not to mention names in front of me," she said, "but two or three times some of the warriors slipped. I think his name is Gray Fox."

"Gray Fox," Ja-gonh said. "He is the man who killed my grandfather in cold blood. I will not rest until I have sent him to damnation for all time."

She stared at him in wonder. "You could have killed him when you rescued me, but instead you elected to save me," she said in wonder.

"Of course," Ja-gonh replied. "My first duty is to the living."

Ah-wen-ga knew better. She had been present when he had sworn to avenge the death of Ghonka, and she recognized the sacrifice he had made for her sake. Lamely, rather haltingly, she tried to thank him.

Ja-gonh silenced her with a brusque wave. "Save your breath," he said. "You'll need it. We have a long journey ahead of us to the land of the Seneca, and you can be sure that these warriors, regardless of whether they are Huron or whatever they may be, will be on our trail. They will be very unhappy to discover two of their number already dead, and I don't think we can expect too much mercy from them when we meet again."

So he had disposed of two of the band. He spoke so calmly that Ah-wen-ga shook her head. He was a remarkable young man, and it occurred to her that perhaps the manitous had arranged for him to rescue her. Her father would call such a notion pure rubbish. Although Sun-ai-yee knew a great deal about warfare, he could not understand the way a young female felt.

Suddenly Ja-gonh's tone became brisk again. "We will start out again anytime you're ready," he said. "And we'll march all night if need be. Can you manage the bear trot?"

The bear trot, as it was called, was the famous mode of travel used by warriors of the Seneca. They moved at a steady trot for hour after hour, their pace never varying, and somehow they did not tire as they went on and on. This was their greatest weapon in dealing with their foes, and it was flattering to Ah-wen-ga that Ja-gonh thought her capable of managing to move in such a manner. She considered the question and replied honestly. "When I was younger," she said, "my father taught me the bear trot. I think it was because he so badly wanted a son and instead had me, a daughter. In any event, I can keep it up for quite a time. I'm not as expert as you, but I don't think I shall give you cause to be ashamed of me."

Ja-gonh opened the pouches that contained parched corn and dried venison and offered them to her. "Help yourself," he said. "It will be easier for you to eat now than it will once we're on the trail again."

She helped herself to the food, and he noted with great approval that she took very limited quantities of both the grain and meat. Obviously Sun-ai-yee had been an exceptionally competent teacher.

He ate a light meal, too, following it with a swallow or two of water, and then they were in motion again, making their way through the wilderness. Ja-gonh's ability to see at night was little short of miraculous. Ah-wen-ga had heard stories about Renno and Ja-gonh being able to see in the dark, and she had always taken such tales lightly. Now, however, she accepted them as truth.

Ja-gonh noted everything. At one point he slowed his pace slightly, raised a hand in warning, and soon they passed a small herd of buffalo drowsing on an open plateau. How he had seen these huge, shaggy beasts in the almost total darkness was beyond Ah-wen-ga's comprehension.

Toward morning he suddenly hurled his tomahawk without slackening his pace, and the young woman was astonished to see that he had killed a large rabbit. They halted soon thereafter at daybreak, and after first testing the wind, he and Ah-wen-ga made a fire, then placed the rabbit on an improvised spit. "We're in luck," he said. "The wind blows to the west, so even if we're being followed, this fire won't give us away."

Ah-wen-ga could not remember when a meal had tasted so good. She was weary beyond measure, however, and Ja-gonh, recognizing the fact, allowed her to sleep for a few hours. He himself remained wide-eyed as he stood guard over her. Before they resumed their journey, after Ah-wen-ga awakened, Ja-gonh silently crouched close to the ground and placed his ear near the fertile soil. Cupping his hand and listening intently, he made no move for a long time. Then he frowned. "They come," he said. "We are being followed. Now we shall find it necessary to use the cunning of the Seneca in order to throw our foes off the trail."

He suited action to words. They came shortly to a shallow but swift-moving creek, and at his direction Ah-wen-ga removed her moccasins. He did the same, and setting the example, he waded into the middle of the stream and followed it for several hundred yards until the icy water began to make his feet numb.

Ah-wen-ga needed no explanation of his conduct. She knew that the Huron—or whoever her pursuers might be—were searching the trail that she and Ja-gonh had left and that by traveling in the midst of the brook, they were leaving no sign of any kind.

When they emerged onto dry land again, Ja-gonh had the young woman take the lead, and he followed, carefully rearranging branches and twigs, making certain that he uprooted blades of grass that she inadvertently trampled. This was slow, painstaking labor, but once again he was destroying evidence that they had passed this way, and his meticulous attention to detail was awe-inspiring.

It was true, of course, that these efforts did not completely obliterate signs that he and Ah-wen-ga had traveled in this direction, and no one realized it better than did Ja-gonh. He knew that any brave who was accomplished in wilderness travel would be able to follow the signs that the couple left, even though they would not be easy to read.

His hunch proved correct. Late in the second day, Ja-gonh spotted a wisp of smoke on the horizon. He studied it at length, then put his ear close to the ground and listened carefully. When he rose to his feet again, he was solemn. "My fears are proving all too true," he said. "The enemies who abducted you are on our trail."

Ah-wen-ga was dismayed, but she concealed her feelings. "What shall we do?" she asked, content to leave the ultimate decision up to him.

Ja-gonh did not hesitate. "We cannot outrun them," he said, "so we must fool them."

Ah-wen-ga looked puzzled.

He shrugged. "When the time comes," he said, "we will act. Until then, we shall continue on our journey." He resumed the lead, and his pace, as always, was blistering.

Late that night it became apparent that Ah-wen-ga was tiring once again. Ja-gonh, who seemed well aware of her condition, appeared to be spending most of his time staring up at the sky, which led Ah-wen-ga to believe that he was looking for signs of some sort from the manitous.

Finally he halted near the base of a mammoth elm tree and grinned broadly. "At last," he said, "I have found what I have been seeking."

Ah-wen-ga had no idea to what he referred and looked blank. He gestured toward the tree. "Can you climb this?" he asked.

She sniffed contemptuously and, instead of replying, went to the tree and shinnied up it, swinging from one stout limb to another with the agility and ease of one who had grown accustomed to such sport in childhood.

Ja-gonh watched her in admiration and then, after covering any tracks they might have made, followed her up the tree. "Higher," he said. "Much higher."

She responded by making her way to branches that stood at least seventy-five to eighty feet above the ground. This was as high as she dared to go, since the branches were becoming smaller and she was afraid they would not bear her weight.

At last Ja-gonh halted her. "This," he said, "will be just right." He indicated an L-shaped limb against which she could support her back, and she made herself as comfortable as she could. He grinned at her and pointed down at the ground.

At last she understood his strategy. He had placed them high above the trail, but they could still see the ground clearly from their vantage point and could observe their pursuers.

Feeling relatively safe at last, and exhausted from her arduous journey, Ah-wen-ga dozed lightly. She had no idea how long she slept, but she awakened suddenly when Ja-gonh hissed softly to attract her attention.

She opened her eyes, and she saw him gesture for silence. Then she realized that he had notched an arrow into his bow and was aiming it at the trail that led beside the base of the elm.

Ah-wen-ga watched in silence as the five Huron marched single-file past the base of the tree, with Gray Fox in the lead.

The Huron leader made a perfect target for Ja-gonh, who undoubtedly could have dispatched him with the single arrow in his bow, but the young Seneca made no move and continued to follow the Huron's progress carefully, ready to act if need be, yet restraining himself. Ah-wen-ga thought his reaction was very odd, and when the truth finally dawned upon her, she was shocked.

It was for her sake that Ja-gonh was refraining from firing a lethal shot. He was conscious of the fact that the Huron was accompanied by four allies who would immediately become aware of the presence of their foes above them in the tree and would attempt to bring them down with their arrows. So strictly for the sake of her safety, Ja-gonh was forbearing from committing the act of vengeance he had sworn an oath to take. Nothing that he could have said or done would have impressed Ah-wen-ga as much as that simple act. Her heart went out to him, and her appreciation of his thoughtfulness overwhelmed her. Whether she lived for years to come or died within the next few moments, this unselfishness on the part of Ja-gonh was something she would not forget.

Ja-gonh made no move, and his face remained blank as the Huron passed in single file on the ground beneath him. When all had gone, he nodded slightly and relaxed his hold on his bow but did not return the arrow to the quiver that he carried over his shoulder. Instead, he waited for what seemed like a very long time and then silently motioned to Ah-wen-ga that the time had come for them to descend. Ja-gonh climbed down carefully, until he reached a point about ten feet from the ground, and then he dropped silently to the mossy bank below. Ah-wen-ga, whose agility certainly matched his, followed him, and when she made the final leap, Ja-gonh put out a steadying hand to help her.

They touched, and although neither of them knew precisely what was happening, they promptly melted into one another's arms. Eagerly, Ja-gonh's lips sought Ah-wen-ga's, and she returned his kiss with the same eagerness. Their exhaustion was forgotten, the extreme dangers of recent days were blotted out of their minds, and nothing existed for either of them but the other.

At last they drew apart, both shaken by the experience. They looked at each other in wonder, and then Ja-gonh suddenly remembered their circumstances. Grasping his bow and fitting an arrow into it, he sped to the top of a nearby hill and searched the area for their foes. He located the Huron, about one hundred yards away, traveling more slowly and with far less certainty now that Gray Fox had lost track of any signs of the fleeing couple.

Putting himself in the enemies' position, Ja-gonh reasoned that the Huron would soon be retracing their steps, so he moved quickly into a thicket of underbrush and gestured sharply for Ah-wen-ga to follow him.

This she did, ignoring several long, nasty scratches on her bare arms and legs made by the thorns on the brambles.

She stood close to Ja-gonh as the Huron retraced their steps, and the young Seneca warrior felt her tremble when Gray Fox passed within view. Never had Ja-gonh exerted such self-control as he was forced to exercise now. He wanted to place his arrow between the eyes of his grandfather's killer, but he knew that he would be inaugurating a full-scale battle that he had little chance of winning. There would be other opportunities to even the score with the Huron in the future; for the present, the safety of Ah-wen-ga was paramount.

Again the five Huron disappeared from sight, and gradually the sounds of their footsteps faded.

At last Ja-gonh spoke. "I would not swear it," he said, with no more than a faint hint of satisfaction in his voice, "but I believe we have eluded them."

"They will not come this way again?" Ah-wen-ga asked softly.

"They are confused. They will cross their own tracks many times, and in crossing them they will obliterate the tracks that we ourselves created. This is one of the oldest tricks known to the warrior who is hunted, and it seems to be succeeding. Come."

He returned to the trail, and although it was dark now, he led the way confidently through the gloom of the wilderness. Sun-ai-yee had told Ah-wen-ga, long ago, that Ghonka possessed a sixth sense on the trail and that both Renno and Ja-gonh also had this marvelous faculty. Ah-wen-ga had believed privately that this was one of the conceits harbored by her father, who admired Ghonka, his son, and grandson inordinately, and she had paid scant attention to the boast. Now, however, she discovered that what Sun-ai-yee had said was all too true. Ja-gonh truly reacted instinctively to hidden forces and to unseen stimuli, and the young woman, recognizing his strange and awe-inspiring talents, placed herself completely in his hands, knowing she would be safe.

After they had spent four or five hours on the trail, they came to a region of rocks and high hills where they had to slow their pace. Suddenly, for no apparent reason, Ja-gonh halted, turned sharply to his right, and unerringly led Ah-wen-ga to the entrance of a cave. He squeezed inside, barely managing to get into the narrow opening, and beckoned for her to follow.

It was easier for Ah-wen-ga to work through the opening. As her eyes became accustomed to the gloom, she realized that they were in a fairly large cavern, perhaps the size of a Seneca lodge or even bigger. Water was running freely in a stream at one side, and when Ja-gonh invited her to drink, she realized that she was far thirstier than she had imagined. They knelt side by side and consumed quantities of the cold, pure water. Then Ja-gonh said abruptly, "Wait here," and a moment later he was gone. Ah-wen-ga had no choice, and shivering slightly, she kept the knife he had given her within arm's reach.

After a time Ja-gonh returned, and to the young woman's astonishment he carried the carcass of a freshly slain young deer. While she butchered the meat, he gathered

148

wood and started a fire near the base of an opening in the roof of the cave, and soon their meat was cooking.

Now Ja-gonh was able to relax completely. "I am certain that we're safe," he said. "Your abductors—whoever they may be—will not be able to find us."

Ah-wen-ga nodded. "Never have I seen anyone as resourceful as you, Ja-gonh, and never have I encountered anyone as considerate. You could have kept your pledge and killed the murderer of Ghonka. Instead, for my sake, you let him live—for now."

A faint trace of a smile appeared at the corners of Ja-gonh's mouth. "Now that I have seen this man and know him, he will not escape from me," he said. "I think he may be a Huron, but regardless of his nationality, I will find him again and will demand justice in the name of my grandfather. My first task is that of returning you to Sun-ai-yee and Talking Quail, who are badly upset by your disappearance. They will rejoice when they find that you are safe."

"They will rejoice," she said softly, "because Ja-gonh has proved he is truly the son of Renno and the grandson of Ghonka. If I know my sister, she will write a song about your exploits, and all of the children will sing your praises."

He flushed slightly as he turned the meat on the spit.

At last their food was ready. They were both ravenous, so they ate heartily. As they ate, they both became increasingly aware of the other's presence.

Both were thinking similar thoughts, and Ah-wen-ga broke the silence. "We are Seneca," she declared, "so both of us well know the rules that govern conduct of our people."

"That is so," Ja-gonh agreed solemnly. "A warrior and a maiden may want each other, but they learn to resist temptation because only those who will marry and spend the rest of their lives together are permitted to sleep together."

Ah-wen-ga did not dare look at him as she said, "The manitous arrange the destinies of men as they see fit.

Perhaps it was my fate and your fate for you to find and save me. If that is the case, we are not to blame for the strange and powerful yearnings that we feel in our loins."

Certainly Ah-wen-ga's argument seemed valid. Through no fault or connivance of their own, they were nearly a hundred miles from the land of the Seneca, isolated in a secure but remote cave, and were relaxing for the first time, having escaped from enemies who were bent on their destruction. The manitous who guided the destiny of the Seneca undoubtedly knew and recognized the yearnings that this young man and young woman felt. So, Ja-gonh reasoned, perhaps it would not be wrong to give in to his desires and Ah-wen-ga's. He was not certain of the ground on which he stood, and wanted to make his position clear. "It may be," he said, "that the day will come when you and I will wish to be married to each other. I make no promises, nor do I expect promises from you."

"I am able to give you none," Ah-wen-ga replied quickly. "It may be that you are destined to become my husband and I am destined to become the wife of Ja-gonh and the mother of his children, but this we do not know. This lies in the future and is a question that neither of us is able to answer now."

He looked at her, reached out a hand tentatively, and took hold of her shoulder.

She returned his gaze steadily and moved a fraction of an inch closer to him. This, then, was her answer. She was willing to go as far as he wished, and she would place no limits on their relationship. The future they would leave to the manitous who guided the destinies of both of them.

The hour that followed was, forever after, rather vague in the minds of Ah-wen-ga and Ja-gonh, and when they recalled the occasion, it had a dreamlike quality. Motivated by forces beyond their control, driven by forces more powerful than any they had ever before known, they kissed, then stretched out together on the floor of the cave. Tenderly they undid each other's clothing, and they felt no embarrassment as they studied and caressed each other's bodies. Gradually their lovemaking became more frenzied. The feel of Ah-wen-ga's warm, firm body excited Ja-gonh almost beyond control, and she was equally aroused as he slid on top of her. She held him to her tightly, feeling them become one. She let out a gasp and then began to cry out repeatedly as Ja-gonh's powerful legs and arms encircled her and his thrusts became more insistent. Then Ja-gonh also began to cry out, and their shouts rang in their ears and echoed and reechoed in the cave.

They were aware of nothing but each other. This act of union was a fitting ending to all that had preceded it, and they felt no guilt, no shame, no sense of wrongdoing. On the contrary, it confirmed their deep affection for each other, and they were brought together far more closely than they would have been in a formal betrothal. Finally their passionate lovemaking reached its crescendo, and they both let out a final cry of ecstasy. Then there was no sound in the cave but that of their exhausted breathing, and they remained coupled for some time, then drew apart.

They slept for a while, and they made love again. Then they ate another meal, drank water, and resumed their journey. As Ja-gonh had predicted, there was no sign now of the Huron, and the couple covered ground rapidly as they marched all that day and part of the next. Then suddenly Ja-gonh smiled, halted, and putting his hands around the girl's slender waist, lifted her off the ground. "We are safe now," he said. "May the manitous be praised, we are safe."

Ah-wen-ga looked at him in surprise.

"We have crossed the borders of the Seneca, and we are safe now in the land of our own people," he declared. "No enemy warriors, no matter how courageous they may be, would dare to follow us here." He grinned at her. "Listen!"

Soon Ah-wen-ga heard the steady throbbing of a drum and made out the import of a message being sent by a Seneca sentry. The daughter of Sun-ai-yee and the son of Renno, the sentry declared, were traveling together and were heading toward the main town of the Seneca. Both appeared to be in good health.

Ah-wen-ga knew that her parents would rejoice, and she realized that the fact that it was Ja-gonh who had saved her would cause many complications. That they had actually slept together was their own business, but it would further complicate their future.

They traveled swiftly for the rest of the day, the drums of sentries keeping pace with them and announcing their proximity.

Dusk was falling when they finally approached the vegetable fields outside the main town of the Seneca. A crowd had gathered, and Sun-ai-yee was the first to recognize his daughter. He said something to Talking Quail, who stood a pace behind him, and they moved forward rapidly to meet their daughter.

Ah-wen-ga cast aside her dignity and suddenly began to run, sprinting toward her parents at top speed, hurling herself first at Talking Quail and then at Sun-ai-yee.

The grizzled sachem of the Seneca grinned broadly as he clasped Ja-gonh's forearm. "I should have known," he said, "that you would be responsible for her safety. I should have known."

His tone was so firm that Ja-gonh was startled. Why Sun-ai-yee should have assumed that he would rescue Ah-wen-ga was beyond his comprehension.

Renno, who awaited him and next clasped his forearm, did little to alleviate his sense of the mysterious. "It was your destiny," Renno declared. "Some things are decided by men and others by the gods. You are fortunate because the gods are determining the paths you will follow."

A large crowd gathered, and the returning couple were forced to tell their stories, Ah-wen-ga relating how she had been kidnapped by a band of strangers and Ja-gonh relating how he had managed to follow her trail and rescue her from her abductors. They alternated in telling what had happened to them after they had engineered her escape, omitting, of course, any reference to the intimacy they had enjoyed.

Soon thereafter, Ah-wen-ga returned to her home with her parents and her little sister. White Deer was enthralled by all that had happened to her and exclaimed, "You have all the luck! Nothing so exciting has ever happened to me."

Sun-ai-yee did not know whether to laugh or frown at his younger daughter. "I'm sure Ah-wen-ga wasn't looking for this kind of excitement," he declared.

"Indeed I wasn't," Ah-wen-ga said. "I was frightened half to death the entire time and had to struggle in order not to show it."

Talking Quail nodded wisely as she studied her elder daughter. "I couldn't have arranged a better ending to your adventure than that which happened," she said. "To think that Ja-gonh rescued you is almost too good to be true."

Sun-ai-yee was afraid that his wife was pushing matters slightly and looked at her over Ah-wen-ga's head, silently telling her to watch her step.

Ah-wen-ga shook her head solemnly. "It was the will of the manitous," she said, "that Ja-gonh came to my help, but his appearance and his great assistance to me will mean nothing for my future."

Her mother raised an eyebrow. "Nothing?" she inquired.

Ah-wen-ga shook her head firmly. "I would not want Ja-gonh to feel, now or ever," she declared emphatically, "that he was in any way obligated to me. It is enough, more than enough, that he came to my rescue when I so badly needed help. I would be filled with shame if I took advantage of his generosity and courage to obtain a proposal of marriage from him."

Talking Quail could only stare at her elder daughter, and even Sun-ai-yee was taken aback. He was unable to understand Ah-wen-ga's seeming indifference to the young man, but he knew of no way to refute her argument.

Meanwhile, much the same situation faced Ja-gonh. He joined Betsy, Renno, and his uncle, El-i-chi, for dinner, and his mother was still talking about his experience.

"Perhaps all things that happen work out for the best," Betsy said. "I have been heartbroken since Goo-ga-ro-no ran off with a Frenchman, but now perhaps my son will provide me with a healing balm. Do I assume that we can now arrange for your marriage to Ah-wen-ga?"

Ja-gonh noted that she looked happily expectant and that his father seemed to be pleased, too. He had no wish to hurt either of them, but he felt compelled to say, "In view of what has happened, you should not approach Sun-ai-yee and ask for permission for me to marry Ah-wen-ga. They feel obligated to me because of the help that I gave her, and therefore they would agree. It is wrong, I believe, for any warrior and maiden to be married under those forced circumstances."

Renno looked hard at his wife and son, then turned blankly to his wife. He well understood the logic that motivated his young son, and he was sure Betsy did, too, but he couldn't help feeling disappointed that a marriage between Ja-gonh and Ah-wen-ga could not now be arranged.

Ja-gonh hastily amended his statement. "I do not say," he declared, "that Ah-wen-ga will not become the wife of Ja-gonh. It well may be that we may marry one day. All I wish to make clear to you is that I want to feel under no obligation to marry her, and even more importantly, I want her to feel under no obligation to marry me. We will lead our normal lives now, and we will soon see whether she will become my wife. In the meantime," he added, his voice hardening, "there is a matter of far greater import to discuss."

Renno and El-i-chi listened in shocked silence as Ja-gonh explained that the leader of the band of Ah-wen-ga's kidnappers undoubtedly had been the murderer of Ghonka. "I do not know if this man is a Huron," he said, "but I must find out. I intend to follow him to the ends of the earth and make good my pledge to avenge the soul of my grandfather. Whoever this man is and wherever he may be, I will find him, and I will mete out the justice to him that he deserves."

Renno glanced across the table at the white-faced

Betsy and nodded solemnly. The manitous worked in strange ways, but he knew that vengeance was near and that the days of Ghonka's slayer were numbered. Perhaps now there could be peace in the land.

Chapter VI

Renno conferred at length with Sun-ai-yee and then wrote brief, urgent communications to the leaders of the English colonies, including Governor Gooch and Ned Ridley of Virginia and Jeffrey Wilson of Massachusetts Bay. He had learned of a great conspiracy that had far-reaching implications, he declared, and he asked for an immediate conference with them. He sent off the letters by messenger and, not waiting for a reply, set out with Sun-ai-yee for Fort Springfield. He deliberately held down the size of his escort and gave the command of the unit to Ja-gonh as a way of placating his son and keeping him occupied. Otherwise, Ja-gonh would have gone off of his own volition immediately to the land of the Huron. Swiftly the party traveled eastward through familiar territory, and when they crossed the border into the land of the Mohawk, Renno was in no way surprised to be apprehended by a large, heavily armed band of the braves of that nation.

Calmly instructing his own Seneca not to engage in a battle and not to provoke the Mohawk in any way, he allowed himself to be taken under heavy guard to the main town. There Mi-shal awaited him.

Renno wasted no time on formalities but plunged at once to the heart of the issue. "It may be," he said, "that I have discovered the mystery that has plagued our relationship. I think we are victims of a conspiracy initiated by the Huron for the purpose of disrupting the Iroquois alliance."

"Why would the Huron seek to do this?" Mi-shal demanded.

"It's very simple," Renno said. "If my theory is correct, they are working on behalf of the French, who again are showing their insatiable greed."

Their recent enmity quickly forgotten, Mi-shal immediately proposed a joint military venture against the Huron.

Renno smiled and shook his head. "Not so fast, my friend," he said. "Perhaps we will come to that. The honor of the Seneca and the Mohawk certainly needs to be upheld, and I would be the last to object to such a campaign, but first I wish to confer with the English colonial leaders and to obtain their views of the situation. I hope to learn from them how best to deal with what we all face. I don't think that a simple military campaign is necessarily the answer."

Mi-shal was forced to agree. The following morning an escort of Mohawk was added to Renno's Seneca, and both groups accompanied him to Fort Springfield, where the Great Sachem was delighted to find that the English had reacted instantly to his news. Ned Ridley, acting as the personal representative of the Virginia governor, as well as the commander of the First Regiment of the Virginia militia, had already arrived at Fort Springfield, Jeffrey Wilson was on hand in his capacity as chief of the Massachusetts Bay militia, and the commanding officer of Connecticut, Rhode Island, and New York were also present.

The Wilson mansion was the only place in town large enough to accommodate the various dignitaries, and Adrienne Wilson, long accustomed to entertaining her husband's colleagues, acted as hostess with her daughters' able assistance. The entire group met informally at breakfast, and the discussions began over Adrienne's very special French pancakes. Then the participants adjourned to the library, where Jeffrey, acting as chairman, convened them in formal sessions. "We are here, gentlemen," he said, "because our ally and good friend, Renno, has informed us of some very serious difficulties that may await us. If he is right in his estimate of a Huron conspiracy, it can only mean that New France is becoming active again and that a new attack or series of attacks is going to be launched on our colonies from French soil. I suggest that we hear first what Renno has to say and then that we evaluate the situation accordingly."

Renno repeated what he knew. Then, realizing he could give his son no greater honor than to ask him to speak to the assembly, he nodded in Ja-gonh's direction and asked him to relate his own experience.

Ja-gonh was attending a meeting of colonial leaders for the first time, and he was startled to find himself the center of attention, but he told in full detail about the warrior he had seen the night Ghonka had been slain and about his certainty that the same man had been responsible for the abduction of Ah-wen-ga.

"I cannot say with certainty, gentlemen," he declared, "that this man and his associates are Huron, but it is logical to assume that they are, and it is logical to assume that they will be active against us and the Mohawk. In order to make certain, it will be necessary for me to go to the land of the Huron, and this I propose to do as soon as Renno, the Great Sachem, releases me from other duties. As he well knows, I will not rest until the killing of my grandfather is avenged."

The militia chiefs studied the situation at length and

came to the conclusion that the only way to determine whether the Huron indeed were actively taking part in a campaign against the Seneca and the Mohawk was to send a representative to the Huron nation, where he could scout out the situation for himself.

There was no question that Ja-gonh would be given the assignment. He had the full and enthusiastic support of Renno and was also backed by Sun-ai-yee. One by one the militia chiefs became convinced that he was the best of all possible candidates for the risky assignment, and they agreed to dispatch him.

Jeffrey Wilson came up with an addition to the plan. "It seems to me," he said, "that we also have a great deal to gain by sending an officer to Quebec to determine what the French are up to. That way, we'll learn not only about the possibility of a Huron conspiracy but also the extent to which the French are involved."

Roger Harkness, who had been listening in silence to the discussion, suddenly raised his voice. "I volunteer for the post," he said. "I think that I am as right and natural for the Quebec assignment as Ja-gonh is for scouting out the Huron."

His superiors all looked at him.

"I propose," he said, "that I make no secret of my identity when I go to Quebec. I will travel as myself. Perhaps I might even go in uniform and pay courtesy calls on the commanders at the Citadel. After all, England and France are officially at peace now, so I know of no reason that I should conceal either my identity or my profession."

André Cooke, who had accompanied Ned Ridley from Virginia for the meeting, grinned and shook his head. "I've got to admire Captain Harkness's courage," he said, "and I'm impressed by his ingenuity. If I know the French, and I am better acquainted with them than most, the more open his mission, the less he will come under suspicion."

Roger nodded. "I think that's pretty much the case, Major," he said. Then looking at Jeffrey again, he added, "When Ja-gonh has completed his survey of the Huron and has learned all that he can about them, he can come to Quebec and compare his information with mine."

Jeffrey looked at each of the militia commanders in turn and took his time responding. "I see only one thing wrong," he declared. "The scheme is ingenious, exceptionally clever, but once Ja-gonh goes to Roger, he reveals not only his own mission but also the fact that Roger is acting as a go-between. This could place both of them in considerable jeopardy."

Roger winked at Ja-gonh and then said, "I believe I have the solution to that problem, also. The moment Ja-gonh comes to me with information he has gleaned regarding the Huron, both of us leave Quebec at once and shake the dust of New France from our boots. We have no reason to tarry there, and the sooner we get back here, the better we'll be able to evaluate and disseminate the information that Ja-gonh has collected."

The overall scheme was subjected to very close scrutiny again, and the participants could find no major weaknesses in it. So it was decided that Ja-gonh would become, in effect, an espionage agent and would report his findings to Roger Harkness.

Roger set out at once for Quebec, accompanied by a small detachment of General Wilson's troops, who would escort the Englishman to Boston. From there, Roger would sail in a ship to Quebec, and he would establish himself in the capital city before Ja-gonh actually set out on his own mission.

And so the conference ended on an inconclusive note. The colonial leaders were agreed that it was idle to speculate and that they would be in a far better position to judge the situation once they were armed with facts. They communicated this to the governor in Virginia, and so for the time being, all the colonists could do was wait.

Renno and Sun-ai-yee departed at once for the land of the Seneca, accompanied by their Iroquois escort, and Ja-gonh remained in Fort Springfield, where he would linger for two or three days to give Roger a head start in reaching Quebec, and then would set out on his own journey.

Patience Wilson was in a vile humor. She had been very pleased that Roger Harkness had been staying with her family while visiting the colonies, and she felt their relationship was growing and deepening. Then, totally unexpectedly, he had departed in great haste and offered no reason for his abrupt leave-taking. Certainly her mood was improved in no way when her father refused to explain where Roger had gone or why, and she felt very much left out.

There was an unexpected compensation, however. The conference broke up in mid-morning, and most of the participants were on their way home before noon, with only a few remaining at the Wilson house for dinner. Patience was surprised that Ja-gonh had stayed, and she learned from him that he would be a guest for a few more days.

Overcompensating without realizing it for her disappointment over Roger's leave-taking, Patience reacted more strongly than she otherwise might have done and flirted more openly with Ja-gonh than ever before.

She had no way of knowing, of course, that he was very much in a mood to respond. He had been upset because his own sense of honor had compelled him—as it had forced Ah-wen-ga—to see less of the Seneca maiden, but he had been deprived of an alternative. It was essential that he and Ah-wen-ga have complete freedom to do as they pleased; only in this way could they eventually come together of their own free will.

Now he was regretting his genuine impulse, knowing he had volunteered for a very hazardous mission and aware that it was possible that he had seen Ah-wen-ga for the last time.

So it happened that he responded with greater enthusiasm than he otherwise would have done to the innocent overtures that Patience made. She was delighted, particularly because his conduct contrasted so sharply with the way he had behaved when she had last seen him.

Nature took its course. Both Patience and Ja-gonh were young, lively, full of spirit, and certainly endowed with considerable charm and magnetism. It was only natural that they should enjoy each other's company. It was only natural that they went a trifle farther than either intended in their flirtation.

Margot Wilson was the only person who saw clearly what was happening, but she chose on this occasion to keep her mouth shut. She was more than slightly enamored of Ja-gonh herself and was living vicariously through her sister, so she made no comment and watched the couple with avid, all-seeing eyes as the Wilsons gathered in the library before supper.

Jeffrey offered Ja-gonh a drink as a matter of course, and the young Seneca absently but firmly refused it. Patience looked at him curiously. "I've noticed," she said, "that you never touch spirits, not even a glass of wine or a cup of porter or ale with your meals. Why is that?"

Ja-gonh had assumed that everyone knew his reasons, and he explained flatly, "It has been found that liquor and the Indian temperament do not mix well."

Patience absorbed his comment in silence, then couldn't help saying, "But you're an Indian by choice, so to speak. Your parents are both white, as white as mine, so I can't see that a drink would do you any harm."

"Perhaps not," Ja-gonh replied. "It's a question of habit I suppose." The young man had no intention of revealing what had happened some months earlier when he had taken a drink and had gotten into a brawl with a Mohawk brave.

That was the end of the subject, or so it seemed, until after supper when Adrienne retired to her sewing room, accompanied by Margot, and Jeffrey went off to his study to write a report on the conference for the Massachusetts Bay legislature, leaving Ja-gonh and Patience alone in the parlor. The young woman had no idea what prompted her devilish streak, but she took two bell glasses from her father's cupboard and poured a liberal quantity of brandywine into them. "Tonight," she announced, "you are going to break your taboo." She thrust one of the glasses at him. Her smile was mischievous, the expression in her eyes was challenging.

Ja-gonh hesitated. He was overwhelmed by the desire to respond forcefully to the challenge. He had to emerge the winner, always—his nature demanded it. What was more, Patience well knew it. His eyes flashed for an instant, and then his face became masklike, revealing nothing.

Patience was in no way surprised when he reached out slowly and took the glass from her. Eyeing her over the rim, he raised it to his lips and swallowed some of the strong brandywine.

The young woman did the same, and the potent liquor caused her to shudder. A hint of amusement flickered in Ja-gonh's eyes.

Patience was furious with herself: he was beating her at her own game. She took a deep breath, steadied herself, and again raising the glass to her lips, downed the contents. This time she made no face and managed to smile steadily, as though she actually enjoyed the taste of the brandywine, which was far from the case.

It occurred to Ja-gonh that she was winning their undeclared battle, so although he truly did not care for the taste or the effect of liquor, he emptied his own glass, and he, too, managed to smile benignly as it slid down.

Patience felt a trifle giddy, and aware that she was playing an exceptionally hazardous game, she picked up the carafe and silently refilled their glasses. This time they drank simultaneously.

All of the windows were open in the parlor, it being midsummer, but the nights were always cool at Fort Springfield, and the weather this evening was no exception. For reasons she did not quite understand, however, Patience felt that the atmosphere was stifling, and delicately, surreptitiously, she wiped a film of perspiration from her lip.

"Do you happen to find that it's very warm here?" she asked demurely.

"Very," Ja-gonh confessed. "There's no air at all."

"I—I could go up to my room for a fan," Patience suggested uncertainly. "I think it might help."

Ja-gonh shook his head solemnly. "Why don't we go out for a stroll?" he suggested. "We might find that it's cooler out-of-doors, and it's sure to be cooler in the vicinity of the river."

They rose to their feet, and as they started toward the door, Patience stumbled. Ja-gonh offered her a hand to steady her, and she grasped it, holding to it tightly as they left the house.

Perhaps it was that physical contact, however innocent it might be, that triggered such a strong response in both of them. Patience was disappointed because the young man whose company she sought had departed so abruptly; Ja-gonh was under pressure because he was deliberately abstaining from seeing a great deal of Ah-wen-ga. Although neither of them knew it, both were ripe for conquest.

The warmth of their touch did strange things to both of them; although Ja-gonh hadn't realized it before, he now desperately wanted this exceptionally attractive young woman. Patience came alive, too, and knew that she wanted this appealing young man.

They made their way in silence toward the Connecticut River, instinctively drawing closer together. The underbrush became thicker and deeper as they neared the trees on the riverbank, and Ja-gonh slid a hand around Patience's waist in order to steady her. The young woman nestled closer to him, and automatically his grip tightened.

Their thinking was already befuddled by the strong brandywine, and before either had a chance to weigh the consequences, Patience was in Ja-gonh's arms. He was kissing her, and she was straining against him.

Swiftly they went beyond the point of no return and, with one accord, sank to the soft, mossy bank of the river. Neither was to blame for what happened; they were reacting to forces beyond their control, more powerful than they could command. Neither then nor later did Patience learn how her clothes were pulled up to her shoulders; she knew only that she rejoiced fiercely in her union with Ja-gonh. Certainly he was responding as any vigorous young male would; it was a time for action, not reflection.

Not until later, when they straightened their clothing and sat up, did the full impact of what they had done strike them. They looked at each other, then hastily glanced away.

The silence that surrounded them was oppressive, but Patience could think of nothing to say. Ja-gonh's mind, too, was blank, and the more frenziedly he sought for an appropriate comment, the less readily it came to him. Nothing in the young Seneca's background had prepared him for this moment, and he was incapable of dealing with it.

Ultimately they struggled to their feet and walked slowly back to the house.

Patience drew a deep breath. "I won't pretend I'm sorry for what's happened," she said. "I'm not. I am glad, actually."

Ja-gonh nodded. "So am I," he answered truthfully. "Strange tensions have been building between us for a very long time, and now the air is cleared."

Their shoulders touched, and they smiled at each other; regardless of the consequences, they had struck a rapport.

Georges Bouchard felt great admiration for the blond young woman in Indian attire who worked so hard in the kitchen at The Maple. Never pausing to rest, never taking advantage of invitations from Georges or Philippe to relax for a time, Goo-ga-ro-no—known to her employers only as Marion, the name she was christened in the colonies—worked like an automaton, scrubbing pots and pans, washing dishes and silverware, emptying the remains of meals into huge garbage barrels that she then managed to carry to the alleyway outside the service entrance of the popular restaurant. Georges Bouchard, like his parents, lived only for the restaurant and the profits it earned, but he was a compassionate young man, and although he didn't quite recognize his own motives, he was much taken with the natural beauty of the young woman. He watched her as she struggled to clean a large skillet, and suddenly, impulsively he called out to her.

"Enough, Marion! You have done enough for the present, and the time has come for you to rest."

He dipped a ladle into a huge caldron of onion soup and filled a bowl with it. Then adding a large crust of bread and a sprinkling of cheese to the mixture, he carried it to the young woman and placed it on the table before her. "Here!" he commanded. "Stop working and eat!"

Goo-ga-ro-no was grateful for his intervention and his kindness. She was dead tired but forced herself to keep working because she needed the money, as well as desperately needing to forget all the bleak events of the last several months.

Georges looked at her curiously. She was not of French descent, he knew that much. He suspected from her accent and her fair coloring that she might be English, but on occasion he had heard her talking to herself in a strange, alien tongue that he could not identify. Not for a minute did he suspect she was an Indian; but he did know that, whatever her background, she was troubled, and he wanted to help.

Goo-ga-ro-no muttered her thanks and began to eat the onion soup, which, like all food at The Maple, was as delicious as it was simply prepared.

Georges regarded her curiously. "Why do you work so very hard?" he demanded. "Of all the people who have worked for us here, none has ever shown your zeal or your energy."

"I must work hard," she said, hoping he would accept a partial explanation for her unceasing labors. "Prices are exorbitant in Quebec, and I need every penny. I was hoping to save some money from my wages, but so far I haven't been able to save very much."

Georges digested her statement in silence and pondered for a time. "You have no family, then?"

"Not in Quebec." Goo-ga-ro-no didn't mean to sound brusque, but it hurt her too much to discuss or even think about her family. She had erred gravely when she had run off with Pierre Fanchon, and now she was paying a heavy price for her folly.

"Perhaps," Georges said, "I can speak to Mama and Papa and obtain somewhat larger wages for you. How far is your home from here?"

Goo-ga-ro-no realized she had to satisfy his curiosity, inasmuch as he was one of her employers, but she didn't want to reveal too much to him. Certainly she had no intention of telling him she was a Seneca. "I would be very happy," she said, "if I had the money that would make it possible for me to travel to Massachusetts Bay." Surely the Wilsons would take pity on her and give her refuge.

Georges smiled broadly. "Massachusetts Bay, eh?" he said. "I have long wished to visit there myself. I understand that Boston is a grand city, larger by far than Quebec, and I've been told on good authority that Fort Springfield, also, is very attractive."

"Fort Springfield is where I hope to go," Goo-ga-ro-no confessed.

Again he pondered, scowling as he tugged at the apron that covered his ample stomach. "That should not be too difficult to arrange," he said. "Perhaps I could escort you there."

Goo-ga-ro-no stared at him, hope suddenly flaring within her. "Really? You would really do that?" she demanded.

Georges wanted no misunderstanding regarding his motives. He knew that she was not only an attractive woman—though her scullery maid garb belied that fact—but also that she was a great asset to The Maple. No one, least of all his parents, would believe that his motives for escorting her were purely altruistic, and he knew he would have a hard time convincing them.

"I would escort you to where you want to go on the clear understanding that the journey would be strictly impersonal," he declared. "I would even make sure that we were accompanied by an appropriate chaperon."

A wave of relief swept over Goo-ga-ro-no. It was almost too good to be true that here was a man who was making her an offer out of kindness and wasn't demanding her body as a payment.

Georges Bouchard grinned. "Fortunately," he said, "France and England are at peace now, so the border between us is open, and we are free to travel as we please, with no one to hamper or delay us. The trails would remain open," he continued, "until the snow falls in November and December and makes travel through the wilderness very unpleasant."

Goo-ga-ro-no nodded and deliberately made no comment. She was able to travel through the wilderness at any time of the year, and certainly she would not be hampered by snow or cold, but she couldn't reveal that without admitting her true identity.

Georges patted her clumsily on the shoulder. "But there is still one problem to overcome, Marion," he said. "You are a good worker, and it will be difficult to part with you. But I will tell my parents that escorting you to Fort Springfield is a small price indeed to pay for all you've done for us, and in due time I'm sure they will agree." He leaned back in his chair, folded his hands over his ample middle, and beamed as he watched her consume the rest of her onion soup.

Roger Harkness went directly with his escort to Boston from Fort Springfield, and there he took passage on a barque, a former merchantman now heavily armed, that had been enlisted in the service of Massachusetts Bay. Carrying a small variety of objects to trade, it set sail for Quebec as soon as he went on board. Entering the mouth of the Saint Lawrence, the barque moved serenely upstream and arrived without incident at the capital of New France. There it would remain only until its trading mission was accomplished, and it would depart without Roger, who had already planned with Ja-gonh to leave Quebec on foot.

Roger, resplendent in his blue and white uniform of a captain of the Grenadier Guard, went ashore and soon was exchanging salutes with French officers and men as though he had been doing it all of his life. He obtained quarters at an inn not too far from the Citadel, and he not only signed the register with his full rank but he also took care to call at once on the adjutant at the Citadel, where he presented his peacetime military identification papers to the French officer.

With that done, he was free to go as he pleased, and he wandered up and down the great cliff that formed the core of Quebec, quickly making himself familiar with the town. As he soon learned, there was little of extraordinary interest here, and only a few businesses predominated. First and foremost was the garrison, made up of regulars of the French army who lived in barracks in the Citadel. A number of brothels existed in the town, as did a number of inexpensive eating places, including an establishment called The Maple. Since Quebec was a great shipping center and her harbor always boasted at least four or five ships from France and other European countries, there were numerous saloons in the town that catered to the seamen, with signs indicating that these establishments were out of bounds for members of the garrison. The brothels were unrestricted.

The local business that outshone all others was the fur trade, and trappers came to Quebec from the interior in large numbers, most of them carrying their merchandise in long, sturdily built canoes, paddled by frontiersmen who were a breed apart. These men, who wore buckskins and were bearded, had great contempt for civilization and its ways. They were avoided like the plague by both the merchant seamen and the soldiers. Roger soon learned that these men had a reputation for loving liberty and were willing to fight anytime they felt their liberties were in jeopardy. He was curious about them and watched them surreptitiously as they ate at The Maple, drank in local taverns, and boisterously visited the brothels. They reminded him of the frontiersmen he had met in the English colonies, everywhere from the Maine District to South Carolina and Georgia, and he marveled at the similarities that made these English and French colonists—supposedly sworn enemies—so very much alike.

On his third day in Quebec Roger returned to his inn and found a brief note penned on expensive parchment awaiting him. Major de Bienville, he was informed, requested the honor of a call from Captain Harkness at his earliest convenience.

Roger went directly to the Citadel and, presenting the communication at the main gate, gained admission at once from the officer of the watch. A sentry was assigned to him and led him across a large parade ground lined with cannon that peered out over the heights overlooking the Saint Lawrence River. Roger also noted that many stone buildings were occupied by the military. His practiced eye told him that the current garrison had to number at least two thousand to twenty-five hundred trained troops. This was a very large force, indeed, to be kept inactive in peacetime, and he considered its mere size significant.

A troop of cavalry passed in the opposite direction, its commander saluting him smartly, and as Roger returned the salute, he studied the troops surreptitiously. They were the excellent saber-bearing French light cavalry that had become famous during the reign of Louis XIV, and their presence in the New World startled and surprised him. He could imagine no reason for the French high command in Paris assigning expert light cavalry to New World duty, unless the units were going to be utilized to the fullest. These men, as well as their horses, underwent rigorous training, and the results were highly disciplined cavalry units that were second to none as offensive instruments of warfare. Every French general coveted as many such troops as he could get, and Roger felt certain that those assigned to New World duty had not crossed the Atlantic by accident or whim.

Major de Bienville received his guest in his office and, the soul of genial hospitality, offered him his choice of tea or a splendid French wine. Roger elected the wine, and his host nodded. "You are wise, Captain," he said. "Obviously you know my country's product."

"Who does not know the glory of French wine, Major?" Roger asked lightly.

They chatted about inconsequentials for a time, and Bienville satisfied himself that his visitor was indeed a professional soldier, but he learned virtually nothing else about him. Finally he had to become direct.

"May I ask your purpose in coming to Quebec, Captain?" he asked politely.

Roger's smile was both bland and innocent. Sipping the excellent red wine he had been given and enjoying its bouquet, he leaned back in his chair. "I suppose you might say I was motivated by sheer curiosity, Major," he said. "I was assigned to New World duty as aide to Governor Gooch of Virginia, and in recent months I've traveled extensively throughout the English colonies. Now, when I had an opportunity to take a furlough, I thought I would like to see for myself the sites of so many battles and other engagements. Quebec, you know, has achieved quite a name for itself in Britain. I've been obliged to study four different engagements that we fought with you here, and I didn't want to miss the opportunity to see all this for myself."

His explanation was glib—almost too glib—and Bienville, as an experienced intelligence officer, well realized it. He could not protest the young Englishman's presence, however, for fear of creating an international incident, and he didn't want to give away ulterior French planning by appearing to be less than hospitable.

"Then I must take you on a tour of the artillery bastions myself," he declared. "They're rather extraordinary, you know." He was eager to impress his visitor with the fact that the French garrison was very proud of its artillery, and with good cause. The protection afforded to the Citadel and to the ships in the harbor below was exceptional. He hoped that whatever ulterior purpose this British officer had in mind, he would take due note of the power of the French guns.

Roger suspected the Frenchman's aim and became convinced of it after he had been taken on a tour of the gun sites. Nevertheless, he thanked his host at length, and they parted on the best of terms, with both men insisting that they dine together soon.

Roger was well satisfied with his day's efforts. He had no doubt that Bienville was the chief of French intelligence and that he intended to keep an eye on Roger and his activities. Very well, let the French snoop to their hearts' content, so much the better. All he had to do now was to continue to observe and make mental notes on the fortifications and troops that he encountered in the capital of New France as he waited for Ja-gonh to join him.

After his English visitor left, Henri de Bienville entertained still another guest, Gray Fox. But if his interview earlier with Roger Harkness had been restrained, Bienville's meeting with the Huron was downright acrimonious.

"I am disappointed, very disappointed," Bienville said as he paced his office, his arms clasped behind his back. "You assured me there would be a war between the Seneca and the Mohawk, a war that would so unsettle the colonies that the New World would be France's for the taking. But now it seems as if the two nations have resolved their differences and the Iroquois League is stronger than ever. Indeed, it seems now as if New France has come under suspicion for attempting to create problems in the colonies, as a recent visit with a young Englishman would indicate."

The cunning Huron remained as unperturbed as ever. Although his attempts to abduct the sachem's daughter had ended in failure, he had scored any number of victories over the Seneca, not the least of which was Pierre Fanchon's taking of Goo-ga-ro-no from her homeland. So Gray Fox still felt very sure of himself, and he said to Bienville, "Never fear. Though the war I had envisioned between the Seneca and the Mohawk never came to pass, I have another kind of war in mind." Gray Fox paused for dramatic effect.

"Well, out with it!" Bienville stormed. "I find your air of mystery exasperating!"

"There will be a war," Gray Fox said calmly, "and it will be a war between the French and the English, between the Huron and the Iroquois. But the French will not have to enter into combat, and the Huron will defeat the Seneca without having to fight any of their warriors."

Bienville was both angry and perplexed. "Whatever do you mean by that?"

"It is simple. France has built up a very large force in the New World. That is all to the good. The Indian allies of the French—especially those tribes that live near the border of New France and the English colonies—will be reassured by the presence of all the French ships and soldiers and will be willing to do their fighting for them. Then, when the enemy is weakened, the French can step in and do whatever they wish."

"I see," Bienville said, becoming interested. "Now perhaps you will tell me what you mean when you say the Huron will defeat the Seneca but will not have to fight any of their warriors."

"That part of the plan I intend to keep to myself. All you have to be concerned with is making sure that French troops and ships are kept in prominent display. I will arrange for the rest."

The French major was impressed. The half-breed's schemes were audacious, to say the least, but they also seemed destined for success. The beauty of the plan was that France, which was ostensibly at peace with England, would not have to become involved directly, thereby avoiding being called the aggressor.

"Brilliant, brilliant," Major de Bienville couldn't help saying. "If what you plan succeeds, France will take possession of the New World."

"And the Iroquois League will be no more," Gray Fox added. Then he said, "But such an endeavor does not come cheaply. Have you remembered what we discussed about my reward?"

The major knew this was coming, and he had indeed already received word from King Louis that gifts of gold, silver, and gems would be paid to the Huron half-breed. "Yes," the major said, "you shall receive the gifts you requested. But only on the condition your plan succeeds. If it does not, the King will no doubt want something from *you*—your head."

Gray Fox continued to look at the other man without emotion. "Do not worry," he said. "My plan will not fail."

Renno notified each of the nations of the Iroquois League of the attempted perfidy of the Huron and their attempt to split the Seneca and the Mohawk. The chiefs of the other tribes reacted predictably and were wildly angry.

So when Renno quietly asked for volunteers for a forthcoming campaign against the Huron—and in all probability the French and the Ottawa at the very least—the other Iroquois replied forcibly and promptly. So many volunteers offered to join the new Great Sachem that he had his choice and took only the most experienced and seasoned warriors from each of the nations. Appointing El-i-chi as his deputy, he made a careful plan, intending to march with a total of two thousand warriors, a force as large or larger than any the Iroquois had put into the field in some years. He and his brother conferred daily and agreed that their precise campaign would have to await the decision of the English colonists regarding their own participation.

Renno and El-i-chi were discussing the matter one

morning in Renno's house, and they sat facing each other, their arms folded, as they gravely outlined the various possibilities that they might adopt. They were interrupted by the arrival of Sun-ai-yee, and both raised their left arms in greeting. He saluted them in turn and then sat down.

"I have decided," he said, speaking to both brothers but looking at neither, "that I will accompany the warriors into the field myself. I have not participated in a campaign in a great many moons, but I feel it is appropriate for me to avenge the honor of the Seneca personally."

Renno had a heartbreaking task awaiting him now. He had anticipated that the war chief would come to him to make this request, but he also knew that Sun-ai-yee was simply too old. The sachem was unable to move quickly, had lost the sharp reflexes that had made him renowned in earlier battles, and he would be a hindrance—and would be in great danger himself—if he joined in this latest campaign. So Renno spoke carefully, having already prepared what to say.

"It is more seemly," the Great Sachem said, "if Sun-ai-yee remains in the town and governs the Seneca. The government of our people is always more difficult in time of war, especially when we have a military expedition that is gone far from home." He had done rather well, he thought, and was slightly relieved.

Sun-ai-yee's expression did not change, and his face remained wooden, a sure sign that he had been hurt to the quick. "Is it possible," he demanded with typical bluntness, "that the new Great Sachem of the Iroquois thinks I am too old to take part in a military campaign?"

The question had been direct, and Renno knew he had to reply in kind. "It is true," he said, "that wars are fought by the young. That is their business. I do not mind telling you that when I led the column that visited various English settlements, it was not easy for me to keep up the pace of the young men who marched with me."

Sun-ai-yee shook his head. "Renno," he said, "can march longer than any other warrior in all of the lands of the Iroquois, and at the end of his march, he will be as fresh and tireless as he was at the start."

That was true, unfortunately, so Renno tried another tack. "Sun-ai-yee has earned many honors in many battles," he declared. "The Seneca sing many songs praising his valor."

There was a leaden silence, and then Sun-ai-yee asked, "You have discussed this with the sachems of the other Iroquois nations?"

Renno glanced swiftly at his silent brother, then nodded. "I have had words with all of them," he said, "and we are agreed that Sun-ai-yee has earned the many laurels he has won."

Sun-ai-yee tried to smile, but his voice cracked as he said, "It has been decided that I am too old."

El-i-chi looked pained, but Renno replied with his customary aplomb. He looked at Sun-ai-yee and said with great sympathy, "What has happened to you happens to all who live long, honorable lives. You have no cause for shame. You have done more than your share for the Seneca in your lifetime."

Sun-ai-yee swallowed hard and replied, "I knew this day would come, and I have long dreaded it. Now it is upon me. So be it. I accept the decision of my brothers on the Iroquois Council, and I bow to the authority of the Great Sachem of all the Iroquois."

In spite of his courageous words, he looked stricken, and both Renno and El-i-chi knew how painful the experience had to be for him. He was obviously bitterly disappointed and was trying to make the best of the situation.

But when he rose and started back to his own house, his confident walk had become the shuffle of an old man. The fact that he had outlived his usefulness in war was such a crushing blow that he seemed to age before the eyes of Renno and El-i-chi. Renno felt sorry for him, sorrier than he had ever felt for another human being, but there was nothing he could do to change the situation. One day, he thought to himself, he would be similarly affected.

In the south the Pimlico were still causing trouble, even though the breach between the Seneca and the Mohawk had been healed. So Colonel Ned Ridley, accompanied by his brother-in-law, Major André Cooke, went to the Williamsburg office of Governor Gooch. There Ned spoke vigorously of the options open to Virginia. "We have several choices," he said. "We can mobilize our full strength at once and crush the Pimlico to restore order to our own frontiers. On the other hand, we can mobilize all three of our regiments slowly so that we disrupt normal tobacco farming as little as possible, and wait for the other colonies to prepare for a campaign."

The governor leaned back in his leather chair and stared at a map of England's North American colonies on the wall beside him. "It strikes me," he said, "that we will do best if we coordinate our moves with those of the other colonies. The Pimlico are a nuisance, but they constitute no grave danger to our society, and I believe we can take care of them rather handily when the time comes."

"That we can," Ned replied. "Obviously, Your Excellency, you're thinking in terms of a major campaign against the French."

"It becomes increasingly evident to me that such a campaign is virtually inevitable," the governor replied. "If I understand history correctly, we English have always waited until the French have struck the first blow. This time, however, having been warned in advance by the trickery of the Huron, we are preparing to take the initiative, and that's all to the good. How soon do you suppose the other colonies will be ready to act?"

Ned frowned. "That's difficult to say," he said. "Massachusetts Bay is always prompt in its defenses, and I daresay they'll be ready whenever we're ready. New York is much slower, and Rhode Island always requires a very long time to mobilize. There's no set rule."

"I think we should prepare for an overland campaign," the governor said. "We would require too many warships to launch an attack on Quebec by water, so it seems rather obvious to me that we'll be sending our troops over land."

Ned nodded, as did André. "Let me just point out to you, Colonel," the governor added, "that we don't have unlimited time. We will want to conduct a campaign this year rather than give the French time to mobilize all their resources for battle next spring. So we're reduced to mere weeks, rather than months. Autumn comes far earlier to Canada than it does to these parts."

"We should know within the next fortnight," Ned declared, "just when the other colonies will be ready to move. A lot depends on what we learn from Ja-gonh and Roger Harkness, and they will have reported back to us by then. I have little doubt that the Iroquois under Renno will be prepared to move at any time that we give the word. We shall have to be patient for a little longer, and then, when we've learned everything we need to know from Roger and Ja-gonh, we'll have to strike boldly and swiftly. It's the only way to assure a victory and yet hold our losses to a minimum."

Chapter VII

Ja-gonh traveled swiftly and confidently as he made his way northward through the great forests from Fort Springfield. He encountered no problems in the wilderness, and he anticipated none; this was his natural habitat, and he was completely at home in it, in command of himself and of any situation that might arise.

It was just as well that he ran into no difficulties, for his mind was preoccupied. He was still stunned and surprised by his intimacy with Patience, and he realized it was going to cause many complications.

What troubled him was that he felt disloyal to Ahwen-ga, as well as to Patience. He had engaged in affairs

181

with both young women now, and even though he had not acted deliberately, he nevertheless felt that he was letting down both of them.

He was willing to grant that he was under no long-term obligation to either. He had taken care not to discuss marriage to Ah-wen-ga, and his liaison with Patience had been so unexpected that he had engaged in almost no verbal intimacies with her.

The upshot was that he was bewildered. He couldn't sift his feelings sufficiently to determine which of the two very attractive, highly desirable young women he preferred. It was all well and good to tell himself that the problem would work itself out and to put it out of his mind, but he knew better. Above all, he wanted to avoid being unfair to either woman. He was aware of his responsibilities, certainly, and he vowed that henceforth he would watch his step in his dealings with both Ah-wen-ga and Patience Wilson.

In the meantime he had a delicate, urgent mission to perform.

He crossed the border into Canada without incident, and when he approached the main town of the Huron, he disguised himself simply by smearing their war paint on his face and torso. He was unconcerned about his blond scalp lock and blue eyes: intermarriage between the Indians and the French settlers was official policy of the government of New France, and there were many half-breeds among the Huron, as well as the Ottawa. Thus Ja-gonh's white heritage would not betray him, and his Seneca background made it ridiculously easy for him to adopt the role of a Huron, just as it was a simple matter for a Huron to come and go in Iroquois lands, in Seneca disguise. It was said, in the legends of both nations, that once, long ago in the dim past, they had been one people. According to mythology, a sachem had had twin sons and had given the rule of his people to both of them, dividing the northern from the southern. As much as Ja-gonh disliked the idea of being related to the Huron, he had to admit that the story made sense.

He was accepted in the Huron town without question.

His accent, his habits, the very way he grasped his knife when cutting his meat were identical to that of the townspeople, who had no reason to think of him as being anything other than a fellow Huron.

Ja-gonh found the lodge of unmarried senior warriors and boldly joined the occupants at their fire for supper: his bravado was effective, and no one bothered to question him. As he ate his food, he listened to what the braves were saying, and he was not surprised to hear them talk of little else but the upcoming war against the Iroquois.

Renno's suspicions had been well founded, Ja-gonh realized, and now it was the young warrior's job to report to Roger in Quebec and then return as quickly as possible to Fort Springfield to report their findings to the colonial and Indian leaders. First, however, he would learn more about the Huron war preparations, including when and where they were going to strike, and he decided he would stay in the village for a few more days.

After he had eaten, he realized that a time of danger was at hand. The braves would be sure to offer their visitor a place to sleep in the lodge of the unmarried senior warriors, and sooner or later they were bound to ask him many questions about his town and his people. So far they had been content with Ja-gonh's brief explanations, but they would surely want to know more, and Ja-gonh did not want to push his good luck too far. So he wandered from one end of the town to the other, searching for an adequate place where he might rest without arousing suspicion. Suddenly he stopped; the man who had killed Ghonka was leaving a nearby hut. Ja-gonh's heart was beating fast, but he forced himself to do nothing except to watch the man with the deerlike run hurry off across town.

Gradually it occurred to Ja-gonh that he, too, was under observation. A slender Indian woman was watching him carefully from the entrance of the hut that the warrior had just left.

Examining her in return, he noted that her doeskin jacket revealed far more of her skin than was customary for either a woman of the Huron or of the Seneca, and that she also was unexpectedly heavily made-up. Her lips were stained with a deep red berry juice and a substance that she had smeared on her eyelids called attention to her eyes.

It dawned on Ja-gonh that the young woman was a prostitute. With the realization he quickly formed a plan of action. Putting it into effect immediately, he inclined his head, then walked toward her.

She eyed him with increasing interest as he drew nearer. "You would like to spend time with Rah-ser-i?"

He nodded. "That could be," he said, his plan already completely formulated. He could find shelter here in her hut, and at the same time perhaps he could learn something about the man who had murdered his grandfather and who had abducted Ah-wen-ga. Smiling at the young woman boldly, he said, "What do you charge for one who wishes to spend the night?"

She was surprised but recovered quickly, and noting that his clothes were travel stained but that they and his weapons were in good condition, she instantly replied, "One large strip of wampum that is made from the shells of small creatures of the sea."

The fee was expensive but was potentially well worth the price. Without a word, Ja-gonh reached into his belt, withdrew a strip of wampum, and handed it to her. Heartened by his refusal to bargain, she waved him into the hut.

He preceded her, then sat cross-legged on the ground and surprised her by saying, "I have spent long hours in the wilderness for many days, so my first requirement is sleep."

She was thankful for her good fortune, since she herself had had little sleep during the last day and night. But she said nothing and merely inclined her head.

"I come from a distant town of the Huron," Ja-gonh declared, "and do not know many people here. Was the visitor who just left you the sachem of the town?"

Rah-ser-i shook her head and smiled. "No," she replied. "Gray Fox is no sachem, but his manners are much grander than those of a sachem, and he thinks of himself as one of great power."

Gray Fox. That was a name that Ja-gonh could not forget, having first heard it from the lips of Ah-wen-ga. Feigning amusement, he asked, "Why does he put on these airs?"

Rah-ser-i instinctively lowered her voice. "He is the son of the Frenchman Alain de Gramont—known to our people as Golden Eagle," she said.

All at once Ja-gonh understood everything. He had heard numerous stories about Golden Eagle, his father's implacable enemy, and knew now that the attack on Ghonka had been directed at Renno personally, as well as at the Seneca as a nation. The young woman was proving to be a gold mine of information, and he reached into his belt for another strip of wampum.

She accepted the wampum readily enough but was troubled as she asked, "You are certain you seek no favors?"

Ja-gonh shook his head. "The company of a comely young lady is quite enough to satisfy me," he explained.

She heaved a long, deep sigh. "Would that Gray Fox felt as you do," she said.

Gradually, bit by bit, he gleaned her story from her. She had worked in Quebec as a prostitute for several years, earning a very good living for herself until Gray Fox had persuaded her to leave the city and come to the main town of the Huron. Since she had settled here, he had been her main support. It was obvious that she was somewhat afraid of him, and she mentioned his name with considerable discomfort.

Ja-gonh thought swiftly, and a new, daring scheme began to take shape in his mind. "What is it you seek?" he asked.

"I want only to return to Quebec and live there as I lived for several years," Rah-ser-i replied. "But Gray Fox will not permit it, and I dare not press the subject with him because he will surely beat me."

"Perhaps I could strike a bargain with you," Ja-gonh said. "I will gladly pay you more wampum for the privilege of making my home with you during my stay here in this town, and I ask nothing of you in return. But perhaps you could do a favor for me, as well."

Rah-ser-i looked at him in amazement. Most men, she had discovered, were selfish boors, and the polite attitude of the young warrior astonished her. "I will gladly do anything it is within my power to do for you," she said, "but I cannot imagine how one like me, who lives apart from her tribe, could do any favor for one such as you."

Ja-gonh spoke quietly. "I have heard of many preparations for war in this town," he said. "Braves are busy making new bows and whittling new arrows. Warriors are sharpening tomahawks and lances. Perhaps you know the war plans of the Huron."

Rah-ser-i shook her head, and her shrug indicated a basic lack of interest in the subject. She did not concern herself with such matters.

"It may be that Gray Fox knows," Ja-gonh said. "Perhaps you could learn from him when he next visits you."

The young woman brightened and clapped her hands together. "Of course!" she exclaimed. "He always knows such things." It did not occur to her to wonder why this Huron from a remote village was interested in the war plans of the nation.

Ja-gonh had the good sense not to press the subject too hard. "Obtain this information for me," he said, "and I think I can help you. I shall see you safely returned to Quebec." It did not occur to him that he was making a rash promise he might not be able to keep.

Rah-ser-i was delighted with his offer and hastened to accept the bargain. Perhaps finally her luck had changed. Here was a customer who paid her handsomely in wampum and demanded nothing in return, merely a little information to satisfy his curiosity.

That night as Ja-gonh lay on a blanket-covered bough of leaves opposite a similar bed on which Rah-ser-i rested, he thought about the scheme. It was shaky and had many potential flaws, but it was the best he could devise, and he thought there was everything to gain and little to lose by putting it into effect.

The following morning Rah-ser-i insisted on preparing a breakfast of fish and corn cakes for them, and then Ja-gonh departed for the day, intending to make a more thorough investigation of the town and its environs in order to determine more accurately how extensive the war preparations of the Huron were.

What he learned he found disturbing. Every warrior, it seemed, was busy preparing weapons, moccasins, or a feathered headdress for war. Squaws were also busy, and he saw strips of venison as well as corn that had been cut from the cob drying beneath the late summer sun. There was little doubt in his mind that the Huron were making ready for a large military campaign.

While he meandered, Rah-ser-i did her best to keep her end of the bargain. Gray Fox came to visit her, and treating her brusquely, almost contemptuously, he made love to her.

As he smeared fresh war paint on his cheeks and torso, Rah-ser-i tried to converse with him. "Is there going to be a war soon?" she asked artlessly.

Gray Fox paused in his efforts and studied her intently. Her question was totally unexpected and completely out of character. "Why do you ask?" he demanded.

She explained, rather lamely, that she had observed various preparations in the town.

Gray Fox's suspicions were totally aroused now. He had never known Rah-ser-i to be so observant, and he thought it very strange that she should develop such an unexpected interest in matters that had never before concerned her. He did not answer directly, instead giving her a vague, meaningless reply. Soon after, he left her but gave orders to a Huron brave to have her watched.

So although neither she nor Ja-gonh knew it, they were under observation, and Gray Fox became even more aroused when he learned that a Huron warrior, whom his informants did not know, was spending a great deal of time with the young woman.

Certainly he was not trying to keep the nation's preparation for war a secret; he well realized that by now the Seneca knew of the Huron treachery and would not dally in making war preparations of their own. The Iroquois and the English colonists certainly would not wait to be attacked but would be likely to strike immediately. Consequently, upon his return he had made it plain to the leaders of the Huron and the other Indian nations that bordered the colonies that they should make ready for war at once, and he had urged Major de Bienville to prepare immediately to carry out his end of the battle plan Gray Fox had so carefully devised.

Nevertheless, it was disconcerting to feel that Rah-ser-i was being used, perhaps by someone who was trying to utilize her as a medium of gaining information. Gray Fox had achieved success to date by making meticulous plans and carrying them out faultlessly. He wanted to know a great deal more about the unknown warrior who was spending his nights at Rah-ser-i's hut, and he now ordered two braves to keep watch on the place at all times.

Ja-gonh first noted the observers when he returned at dusk to Rah-ser-i's hut and saw a pair of warriors sitting, leaning against a nearby dwelling. They were smoking a long pipe, passing it back and forth. This was a common enough custom, but it struck him as odd because they were sitting in the shade rather than in the sun, which was highly unusual. So he stared hard at the pair. They returned his stare with so much interest that he instantly became suspicious, and when he peered at them more closely, they dropped their gaze and looked away. This convinced him that their interest was not accidental.

Ja-gonh slept apart from Rah-ser-i again that night, and the following morning after breakfast, when he left the hut, intending to go to the nearby lake for a swim, he saw the same two braves still sitting where he had seen them the previous evening. Once again, they did not hide their interest in him.

He pretended to be unaware of them, but when he returned to the hut, he took care to interrogate Rah-ser-i.

Learning that she had questioned Gray Fox but to no avail, he realized at once that she had succeeded in arousing the Huron's suspicions. Therefore, his own mission in the Huron village was ended. He reacted calmly and viewed the situation philosophically. He had learned what he had come to seek, namely that the tribe indeed was actively preparing for war, and although any additional data that Rah-ser-i could have gained for him would have been useful, it was not essential. Of paramount importance, Ja-gonh knew, was his need to leave the town of the Huron as soon as possible. With suspicion pointed at him, he wanted no official inquiries made as to his identity.

Obviously the time had come for him to join Roger Harkness in Quebec. Even though danger threatened, however, he was mindful of the bargain he had made with Rah-ser-i, and although he had perhaps been a trifle hasty in making her a promise, he always kept his word.

"How soon can you be ready to leave this place for Quebec?" he asked.

She looked at him in surprise, saw that he was serious, and after thinking for a few moments, she replied, "In two days I could have all my preparations made."

"I am thinking in terms of two hours," Ja-gonh replied firmly. "When the sun stands directly overhead, we must be on our way."

Rah-ser-i looked at him in dismay.

"Do you own this hut and its contents?" he demanded.

She was forced to admit that she did not, that the hut and all of its belongings were actually the property of Gray Fox.

Then he said sternly, "You need only to gather your own belongings."

Rah-ser-i considered his statement, then nodded.

"Very well," he said, "I shall be departing in two hours' time. If you wish to come to Quebec with me, I will be happy to keep my word and escort you there, provided you are ready to leave when I am." He turned on his heel and walked out of the hut. The presence of the pair who were keeping him under surveillance was disconcerting, and he knew it would be impossible for him to take any of the parched corn or jerked venison for the journey. Fortunately Quebec was only a short distance away, so neither he nor Rah-ser-i would become hungry on the trail. When he returned to the hut, he was disturbed that Rah-ser-i had attired herself in all of her finery for their departure. She was wearing moccasins decorated with dyed porcupine quills, a gaudy headdress, and tinseled earrings, which, combined with an excessive amount of makeup, made her very conspicuous. Her open-throated shirt revealed more than it concealed of her prominent breasts.

Ja-gonh stopped short and studied her for a moment. "Everyone in the town will be sure to notice you as you leave," he said curtly.

The young woman shook her head and blinked. "I have dressed for the city, not for the people of the Huron."

He patiently explained that it was essential for her to alter her appearance, and he suffered his first qualms about escorting her. Nevertheless, he had given his word and could not go back on it.

Pouting slightly, Rah-ser-i removed her headdress and earrings and scrubbed her face clean of makeup, and if she still didn't look like a demure Indian maiden, at least she did not appear so flamboyant that she would be sure to attract the attention of every Huron in the village.

Ja-gonh had learned years earlier from Renno that when one was going to be conspicuous, one made the best of it and behaved boldly, swiftly, and surely. So he gathered his weapons, told Rah-ser-i to follow him, and made his way to the palisade surrounding the town of the Huron. As he had anticipated, he attracted considerable attention, as did the companion who trailed him meekly in the accepted manner of a squaw, but Ja-gonh paid no attention to the stares of the elderly warriors and the squaws. Instead, he walked with a steady, rapid stride. When they came to the gate and passed through it, he waited for a moment or two while Rah-ser-i caught up with him, and then he glanced back very casually.

He was in no way surprised to discover that a number of burly Huron warriors were following them. Now he faced a dilemma that required a rapid solution.

If he possessed a longboat he could reach the city by way of the Saint Lawrence River in a few hours. Unfortunately, however, he would have to make his way to the city through the forest. Ordinarily he would have preferred this to all other forms of travel, but he knew that he would be burdened by Rah-ser-i's presence. She in no way resembled Ah-wen-ga or had the young Seneca maiden's sure knowledge of what to do in the forest. In fact, as they plunged into the woods together, the thought occurred to Ja-gonh that the wilderness seemed totally alien to the young woman. She might be at home in the streets of Quebec, but she knew almost nothing about the wilderness. Consequently, he was forced to reduce his pace to a virtual crawl as he helped her over fallen trees and other obstacles. Certainly it would be no problem for warriors following them to keep them well in sight and, if they chose, to attack at will.

Ja-gonh grasped his tomahawk in his free hand and hoped for the best as they marched on. Now Rah-ser-i caught a glimpse of the warriors who were on the trail behind them, and she gave in to a sudden sense of panic. Her eyes enormous, the color draining from her face, she whispered, "They are in the employ of Gray Fox."

Ja-gonh was anything but surprised. He nodded. As far as he was concerned, anytime he encountered Gray Fox now, he was prepared to obtain vengeance for the brutal, senseless murder of Ghonka.

"I never should have tried to leave without his permission," Rah-ser-i said in a shaking voice. "He often threatened to kill me if I disobeyed him, and now he will make good his threat. May the manitous of the Huron have mercy on me."

Ja-gonh did his best to calm her. "You haven't been harmed yet," he said. "We'll see whether their will or our will prevails." He searched the wilderness trail ahead for some sign of a natural redoubt where he could make a stand. Ever mindful of the fact that he would be able to keep no plans secret, thanks to the presence of Rah-ser-i, he nevertheless studied the landscape intently.

At last, directly ahead, tied to a stake driven into the ground on the near bank of the Saint Lawrence River, was a line to which was attached a bateau. This craft was actually an elongated canoe used by the fur traders to carry skins from the interior to Quebec and ordinarily required two men to operate it.

Ja-gonh was sure he could handle a bateau alone. In any event, he was willing to try. It was preferable to an interminable hike through the forest with Gray Fox's entourage on his heels. First, however, he had to reach the canoe safely before the Huron warriors could intervene and stop him.

Wondering how much he dared tell the totally inexperienced and apparently naive Rah-ser-i, Ja-gonh moved close to her and addressed her very softly in a tone she alone could hear. "You will continue to walk until you reach the bank of the river," he told her. "You see the large canoe? Wait beside it."

The badly frightened young woman nodded but looked at him, silently begging him for more information.

"I shall be behind you," Ja-gonh told her. "Let's say I intend to create a slight diversion that will delay our friends. I dislike traveling with people on my heels."

She had gleaned just enough to satisfy her and obeyed him silently, heading down the narrow path through the tall grass that led to the shore of the Saint Lawrence.

Ja-gonh reached swiftly for an arrow from his quiver, fitted it into his bow, and drew the bow taut as he whirled. There were three braves following, and as they made virtually no effort at concealment, they made an open, easy target. The arrow cut deeply into the chest of one, who collapsed and died before he struck the ground.

The attack was so sudden that the other two Huron were stunned, and they stood, rooted to the spot, as Ja-gonh charged toward them. Now he drew his tomahawk, and it was obvious from the way he bent his arm that he was intending to hurl it.

The pair did not wait for certain catastrophe to strike. Instead, they promptly took to their heels and crashed off into the underbrush, making no attempt to hide but simply seeking safety.

His immediate mission swiftly and neatly accomplished, Ja-gonh turned and sped down to the waterfront. His one worry was whether there were oars in the bateau, and when he drew close to it, he felt infinite relief to see that there were two pairs lying on the bottom. Ordering Rah-ser-i to get into the boat, he stood impatiently, holding the craft steady while she climbed into it gingerly. Then he shoved off swiftly and, picking up a pair of oars, remained close to the shore as he began to row. The tide was flowing toward the east, the direction in which he was traveling, so it was no great task for him to propel the craft.

Rah-ser-i was wildly excited. She squirmed and half stood to see where they were going, then leaned perilously out of the craft as she peered up at the woods to determine whether they were being followed.

In order to keep her occupied, Ja-gonh suggested that she, too, take up a pair of oars and begin to row. To her credit, the young woman tried, but she was totally unsuited for the task and soon proved to be more of a hindrance than a help.

Almost sorry that he had become involved with someone whose helplessness created so many problems, Ja-gonh had to order her to desist. She subsided and sat meekly, her sense of gratitude expanding as it dawned on her that she was truly on her way to Quebec in safety.

The sturdily built bateau moved quickly downstream, propelled in part by Ja-gonh and partly by the tide. The young Seneca was grateful, for he was accomplishing his goal in a small fraction of the time that would have been required on foot.

Ultimately, far ahead downstream on the left bank, he spotted the Citadel perched high above the city, its ramparts and walls proclaiming the power and majesty of France, its many cannon daring other nations to take from France that which she claimed. He could see the spires of numerous churches, and the roofs of many buildings. Soon they would reach their destination.

The change that came over Rah-ser-i was little short of miraculous. In the town of the Huron and in the wilderness she had been quiet, shy, and seemingly unsure of herself. Now, however, she was entering her element, and her manner became positive and self-assured. "I have known many men," she said. "Only one has offered to me much more than he demanded of me in return. You are that man, and I intend to show you my appreciation."

Ja-gonh, who had regarded her as inept, was too startled to reply.

"You may be sure," she said, "that we will be followed to the city by those in the employ of Gray Fox. They will follow us, and they will find us. Quebec is not so large that we can remain hidden from them."

Nodding somberly, Ja-gonh realized the problems ahead were many and complex, but the young woman grinned broadly. "Quebec is my home," she said. "I can do there what I cannot do in the towns of the Huron. I can meet Gray Fox as an equal, and I can beat him at his own game." She looked confident but offered no explanation.

When they approached the city, Rah-ser-i knew precisely where the bateau should be beached. She directed Ja-gonh to a landing at a stone jetty, and after he had tied up the boat, she stepped ashore lightly.

"Come with me," she said. "We will go now to a place where even Gray Fox has no authority and would not dare to interfere with me." She led him through the winding, twisting streets of the lower city to a large, unmarked building. Two guards in buckskins, one of them French and the other a half-breed, were on duty, armed with pistols and clubs, and both greeted her vociferously.

"Well, you're back," one of them exclaimed, while the other cried, "We thought you had deserted us forever."

She shook her head. "I am here," she said, "and I trust that the usual rules apply."

"They do indeed," the French guard declared, eyeing Ja-gonh.

"He is my friend," Rah-ser-i said. "But there are other Huron who may come here, and they are not my friends."

The half-breed stroked the stout club that he carried. "We shall give them the reception you may be sure they deserve, then."

She nodded brightly, then led Ja-gonh to the interior. At first glance he thought he was in an inn but quickly realized that this place was a brothel. A middle-aged Frenchwoman appeared and obviously was delighted to see Rah-ser-i. They conferred together at length in low tones, and the young woman seemed eminently satisfied with the conversation. Nodding happily, she beckoned to Ja-gonh and led him up a flight of stairs. There, to his astonishment, she opened a cupboard in the corridor and selected a silk gown and high-heeled shoes for herself.

"Here," she explained, "I do not dress as a Huron. The customers prefer that I look like a French lady."

He nodded dumbly as her smile broadened and she moved to another cupboard. "There are more than clothes for women here. Many men have come to this place, and they have left various items of attire. Feel free to help yourself to what you wish."

She opened the cupboard and he found himself looking at trousers, breeches, shirts, coats, and waistcoats by the score.

"You, too, will fool Gray Fox," she declared. "Your hair and your skin are the color of the men of France. If you speak French, they will believe that you are one of them, and no one will know that you are a Huron."

At last a light dawned. Her scheme was so simple that Ja-gonh wondered why he had not thought of it himself. He would change into European attire and would assume the guise of a civilized white man. Gray Fox's subordinates would be searching for a Huron, and he would be able to go unnoticed. The plan was as clever as it was simple, and he laughed aloud.

Rah-ser-i went off to change while he selected his own wardrobe from the astonishingly large variety of clothes that she had offered him. He selected a shirt of white lawn, a black broadcloth coat, a waistcoat of canary-colored silk, fawn-colored breeches, along with a broad-brimmed, plumed hat, and, astonishingly, a pair of boots that fitted him as though they had been made for him. He also was fortunate to find a wig that concealed his scalp lock, and as he looked at his reflection in a pier glass, he could not resist grinning. He no longer was an Indian but, in a matter of moments, had been transformed into a settler.

Rah-ser-i reentered the room, and Ja-gonh could only gape at her. She, too, appeared totally different in her French attire, and instead of looking at an Indian woman who wore too much makeup, he stared at a striking person on whom the lavish cosmetics appeared to be just right.

Rah-ser-i returned his grin. "It is as I expected," she said. "You do not look like the warrior who brought me here."

"Perhaps I can escape the notice of Gray Fox's friends," he said, "but what about you? You're far more noticeable now than you were before, and only the blind would fail to stare at you."

She nodded complacently. "That is true enough," she said, "but I no longer have any cause for fear or concern. The proprietors of this place protect the girls who work here, and neither Gray Fox nor the braves whom he pays would dare to touch me. The proprietors do not hesitate to use force to assure the well-being of the girls in their employ."

Ja-gonh quietly breathed a sigh of relief that he was no longer responsible for her safety.

Rah-ser-i regarded him critically. "Do you know how to use a fire stick or the weapon that the French call a sword?" she asked.

He didn't want to admit too much about his identity, so he contented himself with a nod.

Rah-ser-i hurried out of the room and returned a few moments later carrying a long sword in a scabbard, which she solemnly presented to him. "You may not need this," she said, "but everyone in Quebec carries them. You would look strange without such a weapon."

The overwhelmed Ja-gonh tried to thank her for her thoughtfulness and generosity, but she silenced him with a wave. "Your lack of selfishness toward me is unlike anything I have ever known. This is the least I can do to show my appreciation. I can help you no more than this, however. I suppose you will make your way out of the city and travel toward your own home before you change into your buckskins."

Although he nodded, he actually had other plans. He intended to find Roger Harkness, and together they would decide what to do. His one regret was that, again, he had failed to take the life of Gray Fox. His present mission was too delicate, and the safety of the English colonies, as well as the future of the Iroquois, required that he lie low for the present.

He tried to console himself with the thought that the appropriate time for him to obtain revenge from Gray Fox surely was approaching. His honor as a senior warrior, as a Seneca, and as the son of Renno and the grandson of Ghonka demanded that he end the life of the man who had killed his beloved grandfather. He silently addressed Ghonka and hoped that his words could be heard in the far-distant land of his ancestors.

"Do not be impatient with me, I beg you, O father of my father," he said. "I have not forgotten my pledge, nor am I neglecting my intention to avenge you. The blood that you shed is still fresh in my memory, and the blood of the brave who slaughtered you soon will run freely and will wipe out for all time the stain caused by the shame of your death."

Rah-ser-i was reluctant to bid him farewell. "You will find me here at any hour of the day or night," she said. "And I hope you will call on me soon. I have never before known a man who failed to make love to me, and I want to assure you I am yours for the taking."

Ja-gonh thanked her, although he had no intention of coming to see her. He knew that she would feel mortally insulted if he told her that he had no desire for her. His life was already more than sufficiently complicated by the problems he had created for himself with Ah-wen-ga and with Patience. He didn't need to make them worse by becoming intimate with someone else.

As he took his leave of Rah-ser-i and walked boldly out of the brothel into the Quebec streets, Ja-gonh took stock of the situation. His knowledge of French was rudimentary, and although he could understand almost anything said to him in that language, he could not speak it with any authority. Therefore, he would be unwise to pose as a Frenchman. It would be far better, he knew, if he adopted the guise of an English colonist. As Roger Harkness had pointed out to the militia chiefs, England and France were ostensibly at peace with each other, so there was no reason why a visitor from the English colonies could not find a welcome in the capital of New France.

Knowing something of the economy of Virginia, thanks to the shipping company that his Uncle Ned had inherited from his father, Ja-gonh also had gained considerable familiarity with the tobacco-growing industry, which had become Virginia's primary source of revenue. He would, if necessary, pose as a Virginia planter seeking outlets for his product.

But he would engage in this deception only as a last resort. His first and immediate aim was that of locating Roger Harkness as soon as possible. He realized now that the plans that he and Roger had made had been incomplete, at best. Quebec was a community of several thousand people, and he had literally no idea where to look for the young British officer. He guessed he would have to wander the streets and trust to luck.

Leaving his Indian weapons and clothes in Rah-ser-i's charge at the brothel, Ja-gonh systematically scoured the streets of Quebec, going from sea-level docks and saloons that lined the harbor facing the Saint Lawrence up to the heights of the town directly below the well-guarded gates of the Citadel. He searched the faces of everyone he saw, but he was unable to locate Roger. It occurred to him to inquire about inns, because Roger might have taken quarters in one, and he wandered into a large, well-lighted tavern. Ordering a small glass of porter, which he took care not to drink, he fell into a conversation with a bartender and obtained the names of several inns.

The burly man behind the bar looked at him curiously. "You are English, is it not so?" he asked.

"I come from Virginia, an English colony," Ja-gonh admitted.

The bartender nodded sagely. "Aha. And you seek your own kind, no doubt."

Ja-gonh nodded.

The man was lost in thought. "I know of no particular inn that caters to your countrymen," he said, "but there is a place you can go, and if the one you seek is in Quebec, he will almost certainly be there."

Ja-gonh concealed his mounting sense of excitement.

"There is an eating place in this city," the bartender explained, "that serves good, wholesome food for inexpensive prices, and unlike many of the fancier places that remember when the English were our sworn enemies, they are happy to serve anyone who has the money to pay them. Therefore, the English and the settlers from the English colonies always dine at the Maple."

As the dinner hour approached, the staff of The Maple was busily at work, and Goo-ga-ro-no was in the kitchen peeling and slicing the vegetables that would be consumed that evening. As she worked, she hummed a Seneca song she had learned from her mother years ago, and, indeed, she was happier today than she had ever been since leaving her homeland; young Georges Bouchard had obtained a promise from his parents that he could escort Marion back to Massachusetts Bay in the next few weeks. They had not given their consent readily, since Marion had proved to be such a valuable asset to The Maple, but when they saw how homesick the girl was—and when they realized that Georges would be able to procure quantities of beef at low prices—they finally consented.

Just then Etienne Bouchard came into the kitchen and

told Marion she had a visitor waiting for her out front. The young woman had no idea who it could be, but she wiped her hands on her apron, fixed a loose strand of her blond hair, and proceeded into the dining room.

She was shocked when she saw Pierre Fanchon, wearing the uniform of a French soldier, sitting at one of the empty tables. By now she had very nearly put him out of her mind for all time and thought only of her imminent return to Fort Springfield. She had no idea how he had found her here, no idea why he was in uniform, but she had no intention of finding out, and she immediately turned and headed back to the kitchen.

But Fanchon had seen her approaching, and he leaped out of his chair and shouted her name. The last thing Goo-ga-ro-no wanted was to cause any kind of disturbance, so she turned around again and slowly headed to the table where the man sat. She prayed that the Bouchards would not think anything was amiss and would not later question her, perhaps having second thoughts about the advisability of allowing their son to escort her to Massachusetts Bay. But luckily Phyllis Bouchard was nowhere in sight, and Etienne had gone to help his sons unload a side of beef.

"How did you find me?" the young woman asked quietly as she joined Fanchon at his table.

"I scoured Quebec looking for you," Fanchon said, his voice rising with emotion. "I just had to find you. Dearest, I can't live without you!" He reached over to take her hand, but the young woman immediately moved away from him.

"What do you want?" she asked without looking at him.

"I want *you!* That's what I'm trying to tell you. I tried to forget you—I even joined the army of New France in order to do so—but it's hopeless. I made a terrible mistake before, and I want you back." Fanchon hoped he sounded appropriately contrite and that she wouldn't suspect the real reason he sought her out. He had completely gone through the funds Gray Fox had given him, the meager pay he received from the army was an indignity, and he was desperate.

Goo-ga-ro-no still spoke softly, but the look of hatred in her eyes told Pierre Fanchon exactly how she felt. "I would not go back to you for all the world," she said, her eyes blazing. "And if you ever come here again, I will tell my employers that you have tried to seduce me. Then you can be sure they will throw you out into the pigsty, exactly where you belong."

With that she rose proudly and went directly back into the kitchen, where she casually mentioned to Etienne Bouchard that her visitor was merely an impolite customer who had noticed her in the kitchen and had hoped to make improper advances.

Pierre Fanchon remained at the table for a few minutes, looking off into space in a daze. He knew the young woman had meant every word she said, and now his opportunity to obtain a few francs was lost.

But not completely lost. There was still the despicable half-breed Huron, Gray Fox, who might offer some money for Fanchon's services. The thought of having to appear before the half-breed and beg for an assignment sickened him, but it seemed as if he had no choice. He certainly had no great future as an enlisted man in the French army. Well, let the Huron be damned! Pierre would pretend to abase himself for the money he would receive, and then he could do as he pleased. He would show the Huron who was the better man!

That evening, The Maple was crowded to capacity, and virtually every seat at every table was taken, with other customers waiting in line inside the entrance. The staff worked frantically to keep up with the demands of the customers, and Philippe Bouchard was upset. Although many customers helped themselves to their food, many others wanted to be served by a waitress. But two of the regular waitresses were ill tonight, and consequently the customers were taking much longer to move.

Philippe, who had been supervising the activities in the restaurant itself, went off to the kitchen determined to end the bottleneck. He looked around, and his eyes lighted when he saw Goo-ga-ro-no scrubbing vegetables. He beckoned to her. "Drop whatever else you may be doing, Marion," Philippe said, "and go to the dining area at once so you may help the waitresses there. They are overburdened, and they are falling hopelessly behind."

Goo-ga-ro-no immediately dried her hands and donned a crisp white apron. She had become familiar with almost all phases of The Maple's operation and was at home now no matter what she did.

Before she could hurry off into the dining room, however, Georges Bouchard left his stoves and, waving a large wooden spoon, confronted his brother. "What's this?" he demanded. "Where do you think you're taking Marion?"

Philippe explained that the help in the dining area were shorthanded and that he was trying to move the customers who were already seated in order to accommodate those who were waiting.

Georges, however, was furious. "You are shortsighted, as usual," he screamed. "Marion's presence in the kitchen is vital, it is necessary, it is urgent that she remain here."

The young woman had no desire to become a bone of contention between the two brothers and was uncertain what to do, so she waited for them to resolve their dispute in their own way.

Soon they were engaged in a shouting match that gained in volume and intensity with each passing moment. They were so loud, in fact, that Etienne Bouchard heard the commotion from the front of the dining room and hurried into the kitchen to see what had happened.

Both brothers addressed him simultaneously, and he was forced to silence them, then point a finger at each in turn in order to make sense of what they were saying. At last he understood the subject of their quarrel.

"In this particular instance," Etienne ruled, "Georges is correct. The preparation of food must come first and must take precedence over the serving of it. If we explain to the customers that we lack waitresses this evening, they will gladly help themselves to their food. I am sure that will create no real problem for us." He turned to Goo-ga-ro-no. "Return to your kitchen duties if you will," he said, and giving his sons no chance to argue with his decision, he bustled back to the dining room.

And so it happened that when Ja-gonh entered The Maple in his white man's attire, he came within a hair-breadth of encountering his sister. But Goo-ga-ro-no did not leave the kitchen, instead continuing to work steadily there under the direction of Georges Bouchard. Consequently, the paths of brother and sister did not cross.

Ja-gonh had to wait for a table, and when he finally sat down, he was surprised by the variety of dishes that were available to him. Noting that people were helping themselves, he walked over to the counter. Although he was hungry, he paid little attention to the display of food and instead concentrated on searching the establishment for Roger Harkness. As he was about to give up, he spotted Roger consuming a pudding. Quickly the young Seneca chose a meat pie and carried his dish to Roger's table, even though there was no vacancy there.

Roger looked up at the tall young stranger. His eyes widened as he recognized Ja-gonh. He knew better, however, than to acknowledge Ja-gonh's presence in public, so he lowered his gaze again to his own dish.

Ja-gonh, still standing, ate his meat pie hastily and hoped he had enough money in his purse to pay for his meal. Roger seemed to sense his problem, and he rose, then moved with Ja-gonh to the desk where Phyllis Bouchard collected the payments from the clients.

Roger paid for both their meals, and they walked out of The Maple side by side, neither of them speaking. When they reached the street, Ja-gonh broke the silence, telling his friend that the Huron were making extensive war preparations and that he himself was being followed by the men in the employ of the scoundrel who had killed his grandfather and had subsequently abducted Ah-wen-ga.

"I would give my soul," he said fervently, "for the chance to sink my tomahawk into his brain."

"That will need to wait for a while, I'm afraid," Roger replied. Speaking softly, he told Ja-gonh about the French troops he had seen in the Citadel.

"Their numbers are so large," Roger declared, "that if you had not appeared here within the next day or two, I was prepared to leave you to your own devices and to return to Massachusetts Bay myself as soon as possible. I think they are preparing to launch a campaign of considerable size in the immediate future. In fact, news of the outbreak of hostilities could come at any moment and wouldn't surprise me in the least."

Ja-gonh nodded solemnly. "Then we must report to Jeffrey Wilson and to my father as soon as we can," he declared.

"Indeed," Roger said solemnly, "there's no time to lose. Are you planning to travel in your present guise, or do you have your Indian attire and weapons handy?"

"They are available," Ja-gonh said, not wanting to go into detail about the role that Rah-ser-i had played in his adventure.

"Very well, then," Roger said. "Get them and we'll be on our way at once."

Ja-gonh was surprised. "Tonight?"

"Tonight," Roger declared firmly. "There's no time like the present, and certainly there's no time to be lost." He quickly told Ja-gonh about his meeting with Major de Bienville, and his certainty that the Frenchman was the chief intelligence officer for France in the New World. "Bienville's men have been watching me," Roger said, smiling slyly, "but I constantly manage to elude them. I don't want to press my luck too far, however, and the sooner we leave Quebec, the better."

"We will need food for travel through the wilderness," Ja-gonh told him. "We cannot go off into the deep forest without adequate food supplies."

Roger grinned at him. "I more or less figured that out for myself, and I've already attended to those needs. I've purchased a quantity of parched corn, another of dried venison, and yet another of dried, salted fish that should be sufficient to feed us on our journey."

They agreed to meet in a half hour and parted hastily. Ja-gonh hurried to the brothel, where he learned that Rah-ser-i was unavailable, as she was busy entertaining a client.

"Tell her that I asked for her," he said, "and tell her I shall think of her often." He gathered his precious Seneca weapons, as well as his buckskins, and departed without further ado. He loitered in the dark near the place that Roger had appointed for the rendezvous, and when Roger appeared, already dressed in buckskins for the journey through the forest, Ja-gonh joined him. They made their way through the town without incident and caught the last ferry that would cross the broad Saint Lawrence that night. Ja-gonh smiled when he thought that the cumbersome vessel had never carried passengers on a journey more vital to the New World.

Ja-gonh changed his attire after he and Roger reached the forest on the south bank of the Saint Lawrence. As they still had a considerable journey ahead of them through lands dotted with farms of French settlers, he decided it was the better part of wisdom to abstain from wearing anything that would identify him as a Seneca, so he borrowed a buckskin shirt from Roger and did not put on any war paint. That would wait.

He immediately took the lead in traveling through the countryside, and Roger proved to be a perfect traveling companion. Accustomed to the hard, grueling pace that Ja-gonh set from their previous journeys together, the English officer managed to keep up with the young Seneca and made no complaint.

They traveled virtually without halting, pausing only to take a few handfuls of food or to drink from a stream. Suddenly time was of vital importance to both of them, and they knew that the sooner they reported on the preparations of the French and their allies, the sooner the colonists and the Iroquois could send their own forces into the field for the coming war.

Ja-gonh had trained for such travel from his earliest youth and consequently was accustomed to trotting for endless hours at a time without halting for sleep or rest. Roger, on the other hand, had no preparations for making such a rigorous journey, and his stamina and endurance proved to be little short of remarkable. Ja-gonh paid him the highest of compliments when he finally stopped for a brief respite after trotting for more than twenty-four consecutive hours. "Roger does not know it," he said, grinning, "but he is truly himself a Seneca."

They ultimately crossed the border in the northwestern section of the Maine District of Massachusetts Bay Colony, leaving French Canada behind them. Ja-gonh quickly donned his own Seneca attire and put on his war paint. There was no longer any reason to conceal his identity.

They skirted the edge of Lake Penobscot, a short distance from the Penobscot River. Looming ahead was a border fort, constructed by the Maine District settlers and manned by members of the colonial militia.

The outpost was isolated and was used strictly for defense purposes, as there were no homes to be protected in the immediate vicinity. The area was so thinly populated that militiamen on duty at Fort Penobscot came from a distance of fifty miles.

A sentry in the wooden blockhouse that stood at the top of the palisade shouted a challenge, and as soon as the pair identified themselves, they were quickly admitted. Moments later they were conducted to Lieutenant Timmons, a lean, tall militia officer with a week's growth of beard on his homely face. He was dressed in buckskins, as were his men, and the military discipline they observed was extremely loose. But he listened carefully to the stories that Roger and Ja-gonh told him of the preparations of the French and their Indian allies for war, and then he nodded.

"It figures," he said. "The whole dang thing fits together."

Puzzled, Ja-gonh and Roger looked at each other.

"You lads got here just in time for a mite of action, if you're interested," he said. "I had a warning from one of my scouts not more'n a coupla hours ago that we can expect an Abnaki attack before the day ends."

Ja-gonh immediately felt a familiar stir of excitement. He had never actively fought the Abnaki, so this would be a new experience. "I believe," he said, "we can spare the time and give you a hand." Roger nodded vigorously.

Lieutenant Timmons was grateful. "That's right nice of ye, lads," he said. "I only have nineteen men here in my command, and we'll be a mite thin for defenders if the Abnaki come here in force."

"Did your scouts give any reasoning for the attack?" Roger asked.

Timmons shrugged. "Hellfire and damnation, Cap'n Harkness," he said, "them Abnaki rascals don't need no excuse. They're always aimin' to stir up trouble, and I reckon that the French didn't have to encourage them too overmuch."

Roger found the situation of great interest. The Abnaki, like other tribes, could attack the forts, homes, and farms of the English colonists, creating havoc even before the French became actively engaged. In other words, it was possible for the border tribes, encouraged by the French, to do much of the work for New France.

This was a new development in the colonies and could be of enormous significance unless it were checked and halted immediately. The only way to react was for the British colonies to smash such attacks forcefully. The French, Roger had to admit, were being clever, and the English had to be equally clever in return.

Roger and Ja-gonh accompanied Lieutenant Timmons on a tour of the fort and observed the location of the defenders. With only twenty of them, including Timmons himself, their line was abysmally thin in places. But that couldn't be helped. It was necessary to man the interior of the palisade to the west, to the north, and to the east, and they admittedly were taking a risk when they left the wall that faced to the south untended.

"When an attack comes," Timmons said, "we'll know where it's headin' from, and then we can pull all our forces together and meet 'em accordingly. Until then, however, I can't afford to take no chances, and I gotta cover every possibility."

The whole philosophy of this kind of warfare was so alien to Roger Harkness's experiences that the young Grenadier Guard officer was appalled. It was typical of frontier thinking, however, and Ja-gonh accepted it calmly. It was no great trick to move men from one sector of an interior wall, particularly when the fort was as small and compact as that at Penobscot.

"If you lads don't mind," Timmons told the pair, "I'd just as lief not give you any specific sector. I'd rather hold you back and use you wherever trouble develops."

Ja-gonh shrugged. He didn't care where he was employed or how he served. It was enough for him that a battle was pending and he was going to participate in it. He had extended himself on the long journey from Quebec, but he felt no weariness and was completely fresh, ready for the first battle in the campaign that had been building for so long.

Chapter VIII

A familiar battle fever gripped Roger Harkness, although the combat that was pending was unlike any he had ever before known on the formal battlefields of Europe. He checked his rifle and his pistol repeatedly, he made sure that his sword was easily removable from its scabbard, and as he stood on the ramparts behind the palisade at Fort Penobscot, staring out at the still, silent wilderness where nothing moved, he felt his stomach contracting.

Ja-gonh, however, remained completely calm, and his attitude was no pose. He made certain that his arrows were in good order, and he placed an extra thong for his bow around his middle, where he could grasp it easily and replace the thong already on the bow in case it frayed or broke. These preparations having been completed, he was totally complacent and seemed almost indifferent to the prospect of a hard fight against a superior force.

He glanced beyond the palisade toward the forest from time to time, his face showing no feelings, and Roger marveled at his calm. Ja-gonh actually appeared to be dozing.

Shortly before sundown, however, he stirred and called out softly to Lieutenant Timmons. "The Abnaki are here now," he said. "They are making ready their attack. They will begin their assault at any moment."

The lieutenant and Roger looked carefully but could see no sign of the enemy anywhere in the forest.

Knowing that they were not endowed with his extraordinary vision, Ja-gonh said, "They will come from that direction." He nodded toward the west. "They have few warriors. They have sent some to the north to create a diversion, but their main attack will come from the direction I have just indicated."

Lieutenant Timmons hastily rearranged his defense force, placing his entire unit inside the blockhouse facing toward the west.

Roger was mystified. "How do you know where the enemy is located and what his intentions are?" he demanded. "I can see nothing."

Ja-gonh shrugged. "The Seneca have a special talent," he said. "We have eyes that penetrate the forest."

Roger made certain once again that his rifle was loaded and that he had his spare ammunition and gunpowder easily available. Then, with nothing to do until the attack actually began, he became a trifle pensive.

"I wonder," he said, "if I could ask a favor of you in the event that I don't survive this battle?"

Ja-gonh inclined his head.

"In the many weeks that I have spent at Fort Springfield," Roger said, "I have fallen in love with Patience Wilson. She knows nothing of the way I feel, and if I should be killed, I would be grateful if you'll pass along the word to her."

"Of course," Ja-gonh replied gruffly, experiencing a bittersweet feeling of relief and regret. As an honorable man, he certainly would not stand in the way of a romance between Roger, his friend, and Patience. Indeed, he had to admit his relief was far greater than his pain. Assuming that he and Roger both survived the pending conflict, he would be free to pursue Ah-wen-ga, since Patience was now spoken for and he would not feel disloyal to her if he chose Ah-wen-ga. Not that Roger's feeling for Patience excused his own intimacy with her; far from it. But at least he knew that Roger would look after her best interests.

Tension mounted as the colonists awaited the beginning of the Abnaki attack. All were frontiersmen, experienced in wilderness warfare, and so they crouched patiently, their rifle butts resting on the ground beside them.

Suddenly the silence was broken by the sound of loud war whoops emanating from the forest to the north. This was precisely what Ja-gonh had predicted. He paid no attention, and the militiamen followed his example. The diversion was a failure.

Slowly warriors began to emerge from the deep woods to the west. They crawled on their hands and knees toward the palisade, their movements careful, in order not to attract attention to themselves.

Ja-gonh nodded toward the attacking party, and Roger counted at least one hundred braves. The militiamen were outnumbered by at least five to one.

Lieutenant Timmons nodded and smiled faintly. Like Ja-gonh, he was accustomed to the battle tactics of the Indians. Silently he signaled to his militiamen, and they raised their rifles to their shoulders. Roger did the same, and Ja-gonh quietly reached for an arrow and notched it into his bow.

Lieutenant Timmons waited as the braves crept closer, then still closer. His counterattack would be effective only if he could deal a swift, devastating blow. Timing was all important, and Timmons stood on no false pride but instead decided he would openly rely on Ja-gonh for guidance. He looked at the young Seneca, an unspoken question in his eyes.

Ja-gonh understood, nodded, and drew his bow taut.

He continued to wait until the Abnaki were no more than about thirty yards from the palisade. At any moment they would leap to their feet and would rush the defenses.

Recognizing the need to strike first, Ja-gonh waited a few more moments, then decided to make certain that he and his companions indeed struck the first blow. He nodded to Timmons and released his arrow.

"You may fire at will, lads," the lieutenant said softly, but the order was unnecessary. The twang of Ja-gonh's bow was the signal that every defender awaited, and the unit reacted accordingly.

Ja-gonh reached for another arrow and sent it flying in the direction of the invaders, then took yet another. In the meantime, the other defenders were firing, reloading their muskets, and firing again as rapidly as they could.

The havoc they created was considerable. The Abnaki were so close that even in the half-gloom of twilight they made large, visible targets, and many of them paid with their lives for their temerity. The shrieks of the dying and the wounded sounded above the musket fire that erupted steadily up and down the length of the western section of the palisade.

The battle lacked the formality, the rigid disciplines to which Roger Harkness had been accustomed in the Old World. In Europe the role of officers was paramount. Soldiers followed orders and took no initiatives of their own. Here, however, there were no such distinctions. Every militiaman was responsible for himself and knew precisely what needed to be done. The same was true of the Indians, and both sides fought with a fervor rarely seen in Europe.

The Abnaki were taking a terrible beating, and the pressure on them maintained by the defenders was firm. Ja-gonh ignored the occasional enemy arrow that whizzed past him, and sent a steady stream of his own arrows at the foe. The militiamen did the same, ignoring their own safety as they pumped shot after shot at the invaders.

Roger discovered, somewhat to his astonishment, that he was actually enjoying himself. This was a unique experience for him.

All at once the Abnaki withdrew into the forest, dragging their dead and wounded with them, and Lieutenant Timmons spoke up. "I reckon we might as well save our powder, lads," he said. "The savages are taking a breather." The militiamen promptly relaxed, and as the sound of musket fire died away, quiet again reigned.

The withdrawal had been so abrupt that Roger was confused. "Have the Abnaki left?" he asked. "Is the battle ended?"

Lieutenant Timmons shrugged. "That's hard to say," he replied. "We walloped them real good, and I'm sure they're not anxious for more combat, but I don't know if they feel they've satisfied their honor. What do you make of it, Ja-gonh?"

The young Seneca pondered for a time, weighing various factors. "It may be that the Abnaki will accept defeat now and will retire to their own villages," he said at last. "But they have done nothing to distinguish themselves as yet, and they will not want their neighbors to think that they fight like women. So I expect they will make a last desperate move before they are through."

Timmons was not surprised. "Such as?" he asked.

Again Ja-gonh pondered. "They have very few options open to them," he said. "I suspect they will charge the palisade wall and try to climb it. If they succeed, of course, they will win the battle. If they fail they will at least have proved to their own satisfaction that they are not cowards."

"I reckon you're right," the lieutenant replied. "And that brings up the question of where they're going to make their charge. My own experience leads me to expect they'll continue to drive from the west."

Ja-gonh chuckled. "It is plain you have fought many tribes," he said. "You know the way the Indian mind works. I believe you are right."

"I don't understand," Roger said.

Ja-gonh turned to him. "The war chief of the Abnaki thinks as follows," he said. "He has conducted a hard attack from the west and has dismissed its failure from

213

his mind because he is preparing his next move. He will try to surprise us from the very same location because he believes we will think it unlikely that he will come from the same direction twice in succession."

"Exactly so," Lieutenant Timmons said, and several of the other militiamen, listening to the conversation, nodded in agreement.

The Abnaki reorganized far more rapidly than a more civilized force would have done. Apparently they assigned very few warriors to tend the wounded and instead mustered every available brave for their final all-out assault on Fort Penobscot. They emerged en masse from the forest, screaming their war cry as they raced toward the western palisade.

Roger was appalled. They were totally disorganized, and although their war chiefs and senior warriors were in the lead, they seemed to be lacking in all sense of purpose and basic disciplines.

Ja-gonh moved to the inner palisade wall, notched an arrow into his bow, and waited. When several of the enemy had gathered at the base of the wall and were starting to make a human ladder, intending to scale it, he fired straight down at them, immediately reaching for another arrow.

The militiamen required no order from Lieutenant Timmons to do the same. They opened fire on the foe and were able to send charge after charge after them, without exposing themselves in any way at any time.

The one-sided battle ended abruptly and predictably. The Abnaki, suffering severe losses, limped off into the wilderness, withdrawing in great haste and leaving some of their dead behind them.

It was night now, and a cricket chirped loudly. An owl called mournfully to its mate, and then all was quiet again.

"I take it you're to be congratulated, Lieutenant," Roger said. "You appear to have won a victory."

Lieutenant Timmons shrugged. "I reckon we have," he said, "but we don't count victories and defeats on the frontier. The Abnaki won't be satisfied until they attack again, and we'll have to keep driving them off until there aren't enough of them left to bother us."

Roger Harkness felt increased admiration for these men who could withstand the pressures and were able to wage war successfully. Similarly his respect for Ja-gonh continued to grow.

But he was still capable of being shocked by Ja-gonh's behavior. The young Seneca disappeared for a short time, and when he rejoined Roger, he carried the scalps of several of the Abnaki in his belt. Apparently Ja-gonh was first, last, and always an Indian, Roger thought, no matter how much of a civilized veneer he appeared to possess.

Jeffrey Wilson listened in stony silence as the two young men reported in detail on what they had found in Canada, as well as on the attack on Fort Penobscot by the Abnaki. The Massachusetts Bay militia commander weighed the information they had given him and then finally said, "It appears that a time of reckoning is at hand."

"I don't believe there's any question about it, sir," Roger replied. "The French and their allies are encouraging the neighboring tribes along the English colonial borders to attack, and what will happen next is anybody's guess." He exchanged a look with Ja-gonh and then shrugged.

"One thing we can be sure of," Jeffrey declared, "is that the Ottawa and the Algonquian, as well as the Huron, will join the French. Then they'll have a force sufficiently large to cause real trouble. But whether they will march against this town, against Boston, or against Fort Albany we have no way of knowing, and I prefer not to take the risk of guessing."

Ja-gonh was puzzled. "What do you have in mind, General?" he asked.

"Attack the enemy before he can attack us," Jeffrey

said promptly, and Roger nodded in emphatic approval. "The Iroquois must be ready for a campaign by now, and Ja-gonh shall go on to the land of the Seneca with the news as soon as he rests a bit. As for the other English colonies, Virginia is ready, certainly, and so are New York and Connecticut. Now that you're both back and have delivered your report, we'll set a rendezvous and organize an expedition at once."

He summoned an aide and began to give rapid-fire orders for messages to be delivered to the heads of the militia of other colonies. Then he paused long enough to turn back to the pair who had brought him the initial news. "You two must be very tired after all your exertions," he said. "I suggest you go straight to my house for a meal and a good night's sleep in a feather bed. We'll discuss further developments tomorrow morning." He dismissed them with a wave.

Ja-gonh was lost in his own thoughts as he and Roger made their way to the Wilson home.

Adrienne greeted the pair graciously, as was her custom, and promptly ordered two extra places set at the supper table. The young men went off to make themselves more presentable, and when they returned to the parlor, they found Patience and Margot there.

Patience obviously was delighted to see both of them, and Ja-gonh realized that here was an unexpected opportunity for him to demonstrate his friendship for Roger. He greeted Patience abruptly, a trifle remotely. There was no rudeness in his manner, nothing to which she could point a finger, but certainly she gleaned that he was being definitely unfriendly.

Hurt by his unexpected attitude, Patience withdrew into a shell and then, as the evening meal progressed, reacted naturally by devoting more and more of her attention to Roger.

This was precisely what Ja-gonh had anticipated, and he was pleased with his strategy. Now Roger would have an open road in his pursuit of her and would face no competition.

Adrienne assigned the young men to a room on the top floor, but Ja-gonh shook his head. "If you please," he said, "I shall have to wait until another time to enjoy your hospitality. I am required to leave immediately after supper."

Adrienne stared at him, as did both of her daughters.

"I must go on to the land of the Seneca without delay," he said, "and I cannot afford to waste a whole night. I thank you, in any event, and hope you will understand."

Margot Wilson shook her head. "But you haven't had any real rest since you left Quebec," she said. "The land of the Seneca is a long way from here, and you'll collapse in the wilderness if you don't get sufficient sleep."

Ja-gonh grinned at the young woman. "Thank you for your concern," he said, "but don't worry about me. I'll have ample opportunity to rest after I fulfill my mission and carry word of the campaign to the Great Sachem of the Iroquois in the land of the Seneca."

The set of his jaw reminded Adrienne Wilson of his father. He had Renno's stubborn streak and Renno's deep pride, so she knew it would be useless to try to prevent him from carrying out what a normal person would regard as an impossible mission. "Give my love to your parents," she said simply.

Immediately after the conclusion of the meal, Ja-gonh took his leave. His wallet filled with parched corn and jerked venison from the Wilson larder, he set out at once for the land of the Seneca.

He trotted toward the west at his customary pace, and his stamina, as usual, was formidable. He was forced to admit to himself from time to time that he was tired, wearier than he had realized, but he refused to stop. Every hour was precious, and there was no excuse for a senior warrior of the Seneca to dally on the road.

War talk suddenly filled the air in Quebec, and soon the whole town spoke of little else. Goo-ga-ro-no heard the many conversations and was in despair. Georges had not said anything more to her of their proposed leave-taking, and it appeared that soon it would be too dangerous to travel. She tried hard to concentrate on her tasks, but her sense of depression was so great that she could not help herself and suddenly burst into tears.

Georges immediately materialized beside her and wanted to know what was wrong.

"Suddenly," she said, trying to control her sobs, "everyone in Quebec seems to be sure that there's going to be a new war with the English colonies. If a war should break out, we will never be able to leave for Massachusetts Bay as we planned, and I will be arrested and imprisoned here because I am an enemy alien."

Georges was quick to understand her distress. Acting without her knowledge, he held a long discussion with his parents and his brother. Then after the evening rush ended and the kitchen help were sitting gratefully to eat a bowl of onion soup or beef stew, Georges came up beside Goo-ga-ro-no and dropped into a chair next to her.

"I have been due to take a holiday for a long time," he said. "And now I am overdue. I plan to leave Quebec tomorrow morning."

Goo-ga-ro-no didn't really care about his holiday but tried to be polite. "Where are you going?" she asked.

Georges's voice was as bland as his eyes were innocent. "I'm thinking of making a journey to Fort Springfield in Massachusetts Bay," he said lightly.

The young woman stared at him. Her hand flew to her mouth, and as she gradually overcame her astonishment, comprehension dawned. "You—you really plan to escort me, then?" she asked.

Georges Bouchard was embarrassed. "If you wish to attach yourself to my party, I certainly have no objection," he said coyly. "I have spoken with my parents, and they feel the sooner we leave, the better. I am planning on buying several sides of beef at Fort Springfield because it is available in quantity there and is much less expensive than our local beef. Our customers will appreciate it, and I won't feel that I have wasted my holiday time."

It was typical of a Bouchard to think first and foremost

of the family's eating establishment, and Goo-ga-ro-no smiled. "What time are you planning to leave?"

He shrugged. "In my experience with the wilderness," he said, "it is always best to get an early start. So I would like to cross the Saint Lawrence by daybreak."

"I'll be ready," she said softly.

He looked at her, wondering if his softheartedness was going to create more problems than he could handle. Perhaps he was badly mistaken to offer to escort her through the rugged wilderness all the way to Massachusetts Bay. But there was no time for regrets as they hastily prepared for their departure. The elder Bouchards and Philippe assisted the pair as they packed their belongings and acquired ample provisions for the journey, provided, of course, by The Maple's kitchen. Then there was an emotional farewell as Phyllis Bouchard, with tears in her eyes, hugged the young woman, and Etienne and Philippe shook her hand and thanked her somewhat gruffly, not wanting Goo-ga-ro-no to see their distress over losing her.

If Georges had any reservations about Goo-ga-ro-no's ability to travel through the wilderness, he was in for quite a surprise. He had no idea of her Seneca background and consequently was unaware of her familiarity with the deep forest. So he was amazed when she proved to be far more expert than he or any of the other men in the party on the trail, even though she was wearing a dress. In fact, she was more adept than their Huron guide and seemed to have a sharper instinct for finding game than did the Ottawa hunter who accompanied them. But never did Georges realize the actual identity of the girl he had befriended.

He had elected to travel by foot, since his Indian guides did not ride horseback. He wasted no time on the trail, wanting to complete his round-trip journey and return to Quebec before the outbreak of hostilities, if there was really going to be a war. So he maintained a steady march, and at no time did he tarry anywhere. They reached Fort Springfield safely, without undue incident, and there they parted company. Georges would go

219

on to Boston, and from there he would take his purchases of beef by ship to Quebec. His Indian escorts would return to their homeland on foot.

Georges cleared his throat as he made a brief farewell address to Goo-ga-ro-no. "I don't know the nature of your business here," he said, "but I should like to make one matter very clear to you. If, for whatever the reason, your plans do not come up to your expectations and they disappoint you, I hope you will consider returning to Quebec. You are not only the best worker we have ever had at The Maple, but I have become quite—ah—fond of you." He paused, his face a fiery red, and turned away abruptly.

Goo-ga-ro-no reacted impetuously. Hurrying to him, she threw her arms around his neck and kissed him. "I shall never forget you or what you have done for me, Georges," she cried.

Soon thereafter, she was on the road to the Wilson house. She arrived just as the family and Roger Harkness, who was awaiting the arrival of Ned Ridley, were about to sit down to dinner.

They were so surprised to see her they didn't know what to say, and Margot broke the uncomfortable silence. "Don't tell us that you married the Frenchman you ran off with," she cried.

Goo-ga-ro-no promptly burst into tears, belying her lifetime training as a Seneca.

Adrienne gathered the young woman into her arms to comfort her, and when Goo-ga-ro-no grew calmer, she was able to tell her story, including the perfidy of Pierre Fanchon, her fortune in finding employment at The Maple, and the kindness shown to her by the Bouchards. The family and Roger listened to her in silence.

Looking at them through her tears, Goo-ga-ro-no could only begin weeping again. "It does me no good to realize I should have known better than to trust Pierre Fanchon," she said. "All I know is that I've made a grave mistake. I sought independence, and now I'm sure my father and mother have disowned me."

"Don't talk that way," Jeffrey said calmly. "I think I

can speak for Renno when I say that he'll be very glad to learn that you're safe and well and have come to no harm."

"That's also true of Betsy," Adrienne declared firmly. "I think you'll find in this situation that your parents are very forgiving and will support you with all their hearts."

Goo-ga-ro-no shook her head in disbelief. "You're not just joking?" she cried. "You aren't just saying these things to make me feel better?"

"That wouldn't be right of us," Adrienne told her, "because when you learned the truth, it would be doubly painful."

The young woman swallowed hard and sucked in her breath. "You mean—that I can really—go home?"

Jeffrey and Adrienne nodded in unison, and Patience said, "Of course you can! You've learned your lesson, and I'm sure you've profited by your experience. I know that my mother and father would forgive me and take me back, and I believe your parents are sufficiently similar to them that they'd feel exactly the same way."

Goo-ga-ro-no slowly composed herself, and her trembling lessened. As she folded her arms across her breasts, she resembled a Seneca for the first time in a long while, in spite of her fair coloring and the French dress that she wore. "Then I have no choice," she said. "I must go to the land of the Seneca at once."

Jeffrey grinned at Roger and then asked her, "How do you propose to get there?"

"The same way that I returned here from Quebec," she replied. "On my own feet."

Jeffrey laughed heartily. "I hope that Patience and Margot, who object if the carriage isn't available to take them into Fort Springfield, heard that statement," he said. "You seem to ignore the normal hazards of the wilderness, particularly in these difficult times."

"But I have made the trip between Fort Springfield and my village many times," Goo-ga-ro-no declared. "I could find my way blindfolded."

"Yes, but that was when conditions were stable," Jeffrey protested. "Also, you were in the company of the

Seneca. My troops are in bivouac here awaiting the regiments of Virginia, Connecticut, and New York, who are going to join us. I don't think Massachusetts Bay is so impoverished that we cannot afford to dispatch a small force to take you to the land of our strongest ally and the home of my best friend."

Goo-ga-ro-no clasped her hands in front of her and looked at him with shining eyes. "You will send an escort with me?"

"Precisely so," Jeffrey Wilson replied. "You've had quite your fill of adventure, and under no circumstances will I leave you to wander alone through the wilderness all the way to the land of the Seneca!"

The Iroquois Council was summoned into immediate session to hear Ja-gonh's report on the war preparations being made by the Huron. In addition, he shocked the leaders of the League by explaining that his theories regarding the killing of Ghonka had been accurate, and he positively identified the murderer for them.

In the excitement that followed, everyone seemed to be speaking at once, and Renno had to raise his voice to restore order.

"We will prepare an expedition to leave for New France as rapidly as possible," he said. "Our allies, the English colonists, are also planning to march there, and we will join them at Fort Springfield. But if they are not ready I do not intend to wait for them. We will go ahead of them, and we will deal with the warrior who dared to kill Ghonka." The leaders of the other Iroquois nations nodded their agreement.

Ja-gonh raised his voice. "I hope this does not displease my father and the sachems of the nations," he said, "but I remind all of you of my vow to dispose of the murderer of Ghonka myself with my own hands. This was a sacred pledge, and I fear that the spirit of Ghonka will not rest in the land of our ancestors until I have kept my word. So I beg you in his name, as well as for my own honor, to leave the warrior called Gray Fox to me."

His request was fair, and everyone present knew it. "The words of my son will be heeded," Renno exclaimed. "He and he alone will be responsible for Gray Fox. What becomes of the other Huron, the Ottawa, the Algonquian, and all those tribes stupid enough to become allies of the French will be the business of the rest of us."

The war preparations of the Iroquois moved rapidly. The sachems agreed that in order to save time their various contingents would not meet in the town of the Seneca but would go directly to Fort Springfield and would gather there. They departed for their homes at once, with a minimum of ceremony. The Seneca were in a ferment, but the progress they made was orderly, as usual. While Ja-gonh went to the home of his grandmother for the hearty meal that Ena and Betsy prepared for him, then enjoyed a few hours of well-earned sleep, Renno made his final plans. He gave direct command of the Seneca expedition to El-i-chi and named his brother-in-law, Walter, as the deputy leader. They were men he could trust implicitly, who knew his methods and his thinking, and by placing them in command, he was doing the next best thing to keeping it for himself.

Young warriors collected the parched corn and jerked venison that the expedition would carry; no other supplies were needed. Every warrior would carry his own blanket and his own weapons. Ja-gonh enjoyed a refreshing sleep for longer than he had anticipated, but when he was awakened the column was not yet ready to depart, so he went for a swim in the lake and then proudly daubed himself with the green and yellow war paint that he would wear on the trail and in combat. But he had something on his mind, and he went hesitantly to Betsy.

"Do you think Sun-ai-yee would resent it if I were to bid him farewell before we march?" he asked.

His mother shook her head. "I think he'd appreciate it very much," she said, understanding well that by going to Sun-ai-yee's house Ja-gonh also would see Ah-wen-ga.

"I know he must feel bad over being left behind," Ja-gonh said, "and I'd like to comfort him if I could."

Betsy shook her head. "That you will not be able to

do," she declared. "There's a crisis that comes in the life of every man, and Sun-ai-yee must face his problem alone. How he deals with it depends on him and on his character. I remember when my father—your grandfather—became too old to go off to war. He watched Ned and Renno go, and then he went to his room, where I know he wept alone. But whatever travail he passed through, he succeeded in overcoming, because for the rest of his life he was at peace with himself. Somehow he reconciled himself to the inevitability of his age and the limits that it placed on his activity. But go to Sun-ai-yee, all the same. He will be very pleased to see you."

Ja-gonh girded himself and went to the house of Sun-ai-yee, telling himself that it was the sachem he sought and that the fact that he would encounter Ah-wen-ga there was only of secondary importance.

He caught a glimpse of her sitting outside the building, where she was busy sewing a new deerskin cape with a bone needle and deer sinews, and to his surprise his heart beat rapidly.

Ah-wen-ga's eyes brightened, but she spoke calmly. "I heard that you had returned," she said. "How did you find the land of the French?"

Ja-gonh paused beside her. "I do not care for the French," he said, "or for their town."

She looked down at her sewing. "It is said that the unmarried women there are very attractive."

Ja-gonh did not take advantage of the opening that she presented him with. "I didn't notice," he declared.

That much certainly was true. His association with Rah-ser-i had been strictly impersonal. On the other hand, Ah-wen-ga's questions couldn't help reminding him of his intimacy with Patience Wilson before he had departed for French Canada, and he, too, lowered his eyes.

Sun-ai-yee emerged from the interior of the house, and Ja-gonh raised his left arm stiffly. The older man returned the salute, and it appeared that he was so weary that the gesture cost him considerable effort. "You fared well in the land of the French," he said.

"I did," Ja-gonh replied. "Most important was learning

the identity of the Huron devil who killed my grandfather."

Sun-ai-yee looked pensive. "Ghonka was my best friend in this world for many years," he said. "I would give much to accompany you to the land of the Huron and to sink my tomahawk into him."

Ja-gonh felt desperately sorry for him. "I shall think of the sachem, Sun-ai-yee, when I avenge the death of Ghonka," he declared.

Sun-ai-yee forced a smile, recognizing the gallantry that the younger man was displaying. "You are kind," he said. "It is not easy for one who feels strong and young to realize that time has rendered him useless and that he is relegated now to spending his days with women rather than going on the warpath."

Ah-wen-ga put down her sewing, jumped to her feet, and embraced her father. "Don't speak of yourself that way," she said fiercely. "You will be renowned for all time as one of the great warriors in the history of our people."

"That is so," Ja-gonh added quickly. "As long as the Seneca nation lives, the many exploits of Sun-ai-yee also will live."

Sun-ai-yee looked at his daughter, then at the young warrior of whom he was so fond. He straightened his broad shoulders, then forced himself to speak cheerfully. "Now the time has come," he said, "for Ja-gonh to distinguish himself at war." He nodded at the younger man's belt. "You acquired some Abnaki scalps, I see."

In an act of respect for an older man, Ja-gonh removed the scalps and offered them to Sun-ai-yee. His gesture was so unselfish and extraordinary that tears came to Sun-ai-yee's eyes, and he blinked them away angrily. Ah-wen-ga's eyes filled with tears, too, but she made no attempt to hide her feelings. Sun-ai-yee accepted the gift and, taking the scalps from Ja-gonh, slowly transferred them to his own belt.

"I pray to the manitous," Ja-gonh said softly, "that I will have the heart of the lion and the cunning of a wolf and the strength of a bear, as Sun-ai-yee has had them."

The older man was so overcome that he turned away quickly and disappeared into the house, not wanting to let anyone see how deeply moved he was.

Ah-wen-ga opened her mouth to thank Ja-gonh for his great kindness to her father but then said nothing. Words of thanks, as she well knew, were meaningless on such an occasion. They stared hard at each other, and their mutual desire suddenly came to life.

This was no time to give in to personal cravings, however; the expedition would be leaving shortly, and their dignity prohibited them from acting in haste.

As Ah-wen-ga stared hard at Ja-gonh, she was a woman bidding farewell to a warrior who was about to embark on an arduous and difficult campaign. Giving in to a sudden impulse, Ah-wen-ga reached up and removed her leather headband, on which had been burned symbols of the bear clan, to which Ja-gonh belonged. Then she gestured abruptly. He obeyed and extended his left arm as she wound the headband around his wrist twice and made it fast.

The significance of the gesture was not lost on either of them. Although they were not yet formally betrothed, they had moved close to it. Ah-wen-ga had obligated herself by offering Ja-gonh a gift, he had assumed a similar obligation to her by accepting it. Now they were bound by formal ties of deep meaning. He wanted to embrace her but knew it would be improper, particularly when he was going off to war, because such a gesture might be regarded by some as a sign of cowardice or weakness. Instead, he extended his left arm to her in farewell, her gift prominent on his wrist.

Ah-wen-ga folded her arms across her breasts and bowed her head. She, like Ja-gonh, took care to hide her feelings behind an immobile façade.

They stood for a time, neither of them moving, neither of them conscious of the swift passage of time. Then suddenly Ja-gonh turned on his heel and was gone. He did not look back as he went off to bid farewell to his mother and grandmother before joining Renno for the campaign that would be decisive in the development of the history of North America.

Goo-ga-ro-no became increasingly apprehensive as she and her escorts drew near the land of the Seneca. The militiamen accompanying her traveled at a snail's pace through the wilderness, at least according to her standards, but she made no complaint. But as the time grew near when she would confront her parents, her fears gripped her so hard that she was short of breath.

The militiamen were ever considerate of her welfare and had no idea that she was far better able to look after herself in the deep forest than they were. Not wanting the Seneca sentries to send word ahead that she was coming home, she deliberately traveled in her French dress rather than in her Indian attire, and this in itself slowed her pace, hampering her on the trail. Soon after they crossed the border that marked the land of the Seneca, she heard the booming of drums announcing that five militiamen wearing the uniform of Massachusetts Bay and an unidentified lady had reached the land of the Seneca. The sentries had observed Goo-ga-ro-no only from a distance and were fooled by her European attire, which was all to the good. She felt she had been granted a brief reprieve when the drums did not identify her.

At last the vegetable fields outside the palisade came into view, and Sun-ai-yee moved forward from the gates to greet the newcomers.

The lieutenant in command of the detail saluted the old sachem and explained that he had been assigned by Jeffrey Wilson to his present task. Sun-ai-yee started to reply, glanced at Goo-ga-ro-no, and was so startled that he fell silent in mid-sentence. Goo-ga-ro-no stood nervously, her fingers aimlessly touching at the waist of her dress. She was completely at a loss for words.

Sun-ai-yee was equal to the occasion. He called to a junior warrior, one of those too young to have accompanied Renno on his expedition, and ordered that the visitors from Massachusetts Bay be conducted to a lodge and given food and drink. Then he stared hard at Goo-ga-ro-no, with no hint of the compassion that he felt for her evident in his stern expression. "Welcome," he said to her, and beckoned.

Then, not waiting to see whether she obeyed, he turned on his heel and walked slowly toward the town. Goo-ga-ro-no took a deep breath and forced herself to follow. She noted that there was an absence of warriors, and she saw the women and girls glancing at her, expecting to see a stranger, and then talking excitedly among themselves when they recognized her. All the same, no one greeted her, no one called out to her, no one came forward to offer her a welcome. How she would be treated by the nation depended on the reaction of her parents, who had the power to accept or disown her.

The walk through the town of the Seneca seemed endless. Goo-ga-ro-no's feet felt like heavy lead weights, and she had to curb a desire to turn on her heels, flee, and hide in the deepest recesses of the woods.

Instead, she forced herself to continue to follow Sun-ai-yee, and she plodded doggedly, her eyes fixed on the ground as she tried to ignore the sensation that her presence created.

The women of Renno's family were keeping themselves occupied in a manless society. Ba-lin-ta had caught a number of large fish earlier in the day and was busy filleting them. Betsy was tending a hickory fire, which she was building higher, and Ena was smoking the fish, placing them on large green leaves about twenty-four inches above the smoke, which poured upward in a thick column.

Sun-ai-yee had done his duty and diplomatically took himself elsewhere. Saying nothing to Ena, her daughter, or her daughter-in-law, he glided away, with the same grace and speed he had shown in earlier years.

Ena was the first to recognize her granddaughter. She looked at Goo-ga-ro-no, blinked, and stood erect, folding her arms across her breasts, her wrinkled face set in stern, uncompromising lines.

Betsy became aware of the sudden tension, and all at once she, too, realized its cause. She gasped faintly, then straightened and stood beside her mother-in-law, her pose identical to Ena's.

Ba-lin-ta normally was so effervescent that she could not control herself no matter what the situation, but this was a far different matter. Her niece had defied the basic code of the Seneca in order to have her own way, and now she had reappeared, dressed like a foreigner. Ba-lin-ta swallowed hard, then forced herself to flank Ena on her free side and to emulate her stance.

The moment seemed to last forever. Goo-ga-ro-no knew that neither her mother nor her grandmother would address her until they heard what she had to say. It was her place to speak first. She slowly folded her own arms across her breasts, then lowered her head in a gesture of submission. "Goo-ga-ro-no," she said, "brought shame on the heads of her parents, her grandparents, and all her ancestors. She knew better than anyone what she wanted and how to achieve it. She failed miserably."

Betsy wanted to embrace her daughter but forced herself to make no move.

"All I can say now," Goo-ga-ro-no declared, "is that my disgrace is not as bad as it otherwise might have been. I went to Quebec with Pierre Fanchon. There I left him." She tried to continue, but her voice broke.

Ena showed her customary self-control. "Why did you leave him?"

"I discovered he wished my body but did not intend to marry me." The young woman's reply was almost inaudible.

Betsy could not conceal her relief. "Then you did not sleep with him?"

Goo-ga-ro-no shook her head, tried to reply, and, unable to speak, shook her head vehemently.

Betsy quietly thanked her own God and, for good measure, the manitous.

Speaking haltingly, Goo-ga-ro-no explained that she had been fortunate to find work in the Bouchard family's eating place and that Georges Bouchard had been kind enough to escort her to Massachusetts Bay. She struggled hard to curb the tears that threatened to overwhelm her. "I was wrong in everything I did," she said, "and I have paid the price many times over through the shame that I have suffered. I beg you now to find it in your hearts to forgive me and to allow me to resume my place as a worthy and respectable member of the family. I swear to you I will not err again." She lowered her head, staring at her feet while she awaited their decision.

There was a long silence that seemed endless. Finally Ena spoke, though her expression did not change. "Renno," she said, "has led his warriors into a campaign against the French, the Huron, and other Indians of the North. He is not here to speak for himself."

"Renno," Betsy said slowly, "will of course have to decide what is to be done, but until he returns he will accept the words and wishes of his mother in this as all things. I, too, will abide by the word of Ena and will do as she bids."

Ba-lin-ta looked uneasy for the first time. She knew far better than did anyone else that her mother was totally uncompromising, that in matters of principle Ena was even more strict than Ghonka had been.

"What has become of this man who stole you from your home and your people and who robbed you of your senses?" Ena demanded.

"I have avoided him since the day we reached Quebec and I realized that he had dishonorable plans for me," Goo-ga-ro-no replied. "I have seen him only once since that time, when he came to speak to me at the place where I worked, and I rebuffed him. He wore the uniform of a French soldier, so I assume he is going to fight with the French in the pending campaign."

"It is good that Renno and Ja-gonh do not know this man by sight," Betsy declared. "They would subject him to innumerable tortures. But, if they ever were able to identify him, he would be fortunate if he were killed swiftly. There is no man who deserves more the lingering death to which your father and your brother would subject him."

Goo-ga-ro-no nodded dumbly, but Ena was not yet satisfied. "What have you learned from your sad experience, young woman?" she asked.

"I was lonely and miserable during my stay in Quebec," Goo-ga-ro-no replied softly. "I earned my living working in an eating place of the French. During that time, people believed I was an English colonist, yet I did not feel like a colonist within myself. I missed this town, I missed sleeping on a mat of corn husks. I missed the smell of clean wood smoke and the taste of game that has been freshly killed, of vegetables that have been picked just in time to throw into the cooking pot. I missed hearing the stories told by my grandmother and by my father." Goo-ga-ro-no could control herself no longer, and tears poured unheeded down her cheeks. "I am a Seneca, but I could not acknowledge it. If I have learned one thing in all the torment I have undergone, I know my true identity now. I am a Seneca. I will always be a Seneca."

Ena absorbed her words in silence, then looked first at Betsy and then at Ba-lin-ta. Neither could read her expression.

Slowly the old woman's arms dropped to her sides, then she raised them again inch by inch and extended them.

"Welcome to the land of the Seneca, Goo-ga-ro-no," she said. "Welcome home." She folded the young woman into her arms.

The release from tension was so great that Goo-ga-ro-no could only shudder and sob. Not until Betsy embraced her and soothed her as she had done when Goo-ga-ro-no was a baby did the young woman finally grow calm and begin to collect herself.

For her part, Ba-lin-ta took the only practical approach. "We are preparing many fish," she said, "and some have yet to be cleaned. Take a knife and help us, please." She resumed her own work.

Goo-ga-ro-no didn't know whether to laugh or weep as she followed her aunt's curt suggestion and went to work at once, cleaning fish in the late afternoon sunshine. She had come home, and her great adventure had come to an end without causing her any permanent damage. For that she was grateful, and in the days, weeks, and moons to come, she would prove that she was a loyal and trustworthy Seneca.

Chapter IX

The Iroquois led the long column on the march north through the wilderness from Fort Springfield. All the nations of the League were represented, and it was not accidental that El-i-chi of the Seneca and Mi-shal of the Mohawk directly followed Renno in the line. Their mere presence side by side gave the lie for all time to the story that the mighty alliance of the Iroquois had been split.

Next in line came Ned Ridley's Virginians, all of them expert shots, all of them at home in the wilderness. Here was a regiment that could take care of itself under any conditions. Behind the Virginians came Brigadier General Jeffrey Wilson with his two regiments of Massachusetts Bay militiamen, by far the largest single contingent in the army. These men were, almost without exception, veterans of frontier warfare, and all of them were completely at home in the forest. Certainly Roger Harkness, who accompanied the militia, had learned a great deal about the North American wilderness since he had arrived in the colonies, and he was thoroughly comfortable in the forest, too.

Less able to cope, but eager to learn, were the regiments from New York and Connecticut, as well as the battalion from Rhode Island. These troops were eager to a fault and had to be restrained on the march.

At the head of the entire expedition marched a group of scouts in whom the allied high command had complete confidence. Commanding the unit was Major André Cooke, and even Renno had to admit that his wife's brother-in-law was as adept, as at home, as at ease in the forest as many of the most experienced Seneca. André had eyes and ears attuned to the wilderness as did no other white man.

André marched proudly, glad to be a part of this force of men who would fight to the death to preserve their homeland. It was his homeland now, too, and he realized that the many years he had spent alone as a young man in the wilderness had been something of a self-imposed exile. The son of a French mother and an English father, he had not been sure in those days long ago if his allegiance was with the English or the French, but after meeting the lovely young Virginia woman who was to become his wife and after witnessing the integrity and nobility of the English and their Iroquois allies, he had made up his mind. His parents were dead, his brother had vanished from the face of the earth, and for more than twenty years, he had lived with Anne in Virginia. André had become an Englishman through and through.

For this present mission he had chosen his own men, and Ja-gonh was delighted that his uncle had selected him to be one of the few. He knew the honor was based exclusively on merit, and the fact that he was related to André was irrelevant.

The scouts covered twice as much ground as did anyone else in the column, marching long distances, ranging for miles in their sweeps of the terrain so that nothing escaped their attention. They alone subsisted on emergency rations, they alone were on the march day and night without rest.

Gradually a picture of the enemy began to take shape, and André reported his findings to the high command.

"The disposition of the enemy is becoming clear," André told the group assembled around a campfire. "The Ottawa are moving in force to meet us, and the Algonquian have established a very large force, which is also heading southward from Quebec. There are, also, scattered units in the enemy column of Abnaki and several other minor tribes."

Renno asked the question that was foremost in the minds of everyone present. "What of the French?" he asked. "Are they on the move, also, and how many of them are there?"

André shook his head. "I hate to tell you this," he said, "but there is no sign anywhere of a French column."

The commanders stared at him in disbelieving silence.

Jeffrey Wilson was the first to speak. "That makes no sense," he said irritably. "The French are the cornerstone, always, of any army with which they're associated."

André again shook his head. "The various Indian tribes," he said, "are supported by a half-dozen ships of the French fleet, which carry ammunition and, I suppose, food, which is why the enemy is moving southward rather close to the Atlantic coast. I am positive the French themselves are nowhere to be seen. Ja-gonh went in search of them, and I trust him implicitly. He ranged far to the north, far behind enemy lines, and found no indication of a French column anywhere."

"I'll be damned," Ned Ridley said, and then a silence fell on the bewildered members of the high command.

"This is very odd," Jeffrey Wilson said. "What do you make of it all, Renno?"

The Great Sachem shrugged. "One man's guess is as good as another's, I suppose, but I would suggest the absence of French troops is deliberate."

Roger Harkness laughed harshly. "Of course!" he exclaimed. "You're quite right, and the French are using all their ingenuity."

Everyone present looked at him.

"The French are being clever again," he said, "and they're doing it through simplicity. By sending only Indians into the field against us, they can claim that they have no part in this new war. They are still at peace. They can find any one of a dozen excuses to explain the coincidence of their fleet's appearance off the coast at the same time and in the same neighborhood as the Indian warriors, who are cooperating with them. The important thing to remember is that we are taking the field with official troops, with militiamen who represent the English colonies; therefore, Great Britain is definitely at war. But France remains totally innocent and can claim that her hands are clean, that she is waging war against no one, and that she seeks to keep the peace. The French can even pretend, if they wish, that they tried in vain to persuade their Indian allies to keep the peace. In this way they have everything to gain and nothing whatsoever to lose."

Jeffrey Wilson smiled wryly. "If you and Renno are right, Captain Harkness, and I'm sorry to say that I'm afraid you are, the French are even more cunning than you indicated. Their own troops are probably on guard at the Citadel in Quebec. This gives them a double advantage. If we defeat their Indian allies and go on to Quebec, we become aggressors in the eyes of all Europe and in the eyes of the colonists. They have professional soldiers to defend their city against us and can muster support because they can claim—with apparent proof—that we, not they, are the real aggressors."

As the others began to grasp the strategy the French were employing, they nodded and became glumly silent. As usual, although the English colonies and their Indian allies were numerically superior to their foes, French cleverness more than made up the difference and equalized the odds.

"What in thunderation do we do now?" the New York militia commander asked testily.

Renno remained even-tempered. "It seems to me," he said, "that we carry on precisely as we planned. We force a battle with the Ottawa, the Algonquian, the Abnaki, and any other tribes who care to meet us. We push north, along the coast, and if the French troops are hiding in the Citadel, we attack them there and flush them out. It was my father's theory that success always speaks for itself. If Ghonka were here now, he would tell us to attack and attack and attack. Let the French claim that they are innocent and that we are the aggressors. If we succeed in taking Quebec and forcing them to sue for peace on our terms, let them claim what they will, in any way they choose. We will hold the upper hand, and that is the purpose of fighting a war."

Ned grinned broadly. "Hear, hear," he declared. "That's the kind of talk I like."

Soon everyone was clamoring for combat. The strategy of the French seemed to be backfiring, and the enthusiasm of the Iroquois and the English colonists carried the day.

Renno remained thoughtful. "André," he said, "I don't know whether this is a deliberate omission on your part or not. You've talked about the Ottawa in some detail, about the Algonquian, and even the Abnaki and the lesser tribes. How does it happen that you haven't mentioned the tribe that concerns us most: the Huron?"

André Cooke frowned. "I wish you hadn't asked me that question just yet, Renno," he said, "because I'm in no way prepared to answer it. Frankly, there is no indication of the whereabouts of the Huron, and we're badly perplexed."

The elation of the others was tempered, and they listened carefully to the conversation.

"Perhaps they're being held in reserve in Quebec, too," Ned suggested.

André shook his head. "I traveled myself as far as Quebec earlier this week," he said, "and I actually crossed the Saint Lawrence two miles more or less from the main town of the Huron. I can tell you categorically that they are not in Quebec. The French troops obviously are in garrison there, and they're making no attempt to budge, but the Huron have vanished from the face of the earth."

Renno frowned. The colonists were not inclined to take the information as seriously as he was, but they hadn't grown up with the enmity of the Huron an ever present force in their lives. Something was very much amiss. "It seems to me," he said, "that we'd best hold our specific plans in abeyance until we locate the Huron and know what they're up to. I don't trust them, and they're sufficiently powerful that they could cause us a great deal of trouble if they chose to."

Jeffrey Wilson, the senior officer present, who by virtue of his rank was the commander of the English colonial force, agreed with great reluctance. "As much as I hate to admit it, Renno," he said, "I suppose you're right. What do you suggest, Major Cooke?"

André shrugged. "At the risk of sounding unprepared," he said, "I have nothing in mind to tell you, but I'm getting together with Ja-gonh and several of my other lieutenants when I return to my own headquarters, in hopes that we'll have something specific to recommend before the night ends."

Everyone present accepted the delay stoically. They had no choice but to wait.

The scouts established their bivouac in the vast reaches of the wilderness and were so clever at concealing themselves that a stranger could have passed within a few feet of their encampment without knowing it. The men were baking in clay two or three large fish they had caught in the Atlantic. While their meal cooked, they sat in a circle smoking strong Indian tobacco and conversing in an undertone. André Cooke, sitting with them, thought their tobacco vastly inferior to that which was grown in Virginia, but he kept his views to himself. He puffed on the pipe that was handed him from time to time as it was passed around the circle, and he ignored the strong, bitter taste.

Ja-gonh was emphatic. "It is essential that we find out

what the Huron are up to," he said. "I never trust them, and I'm afraid that Gray Fox may be planning another of his vile tricks."

"That's all well and good," André replied, "but where do you propose to search for the Huron? The wilderness of this continent is virtually endless; it extends for thousands of miles. The Huron could be anywhere in the forest. I wouldn't know where to look for them."

"Nor would I," Ja-gonh replied grimly, "but I intend to find out."

Two or three of the other scouts thought he was involved in chest-beating, and grinned cynically; but André felt compelled to challenge his nephew. "How are you going to do it, Ja-gonh?" he demanded.

Ja-gonh smiled faintly. "No matter how secret the location and the moves that the Huron may be making," he said flatly, "it might be that someone knows what they have in mind, that someone is familiar with their plans. I've asked myself who would be most likely to be familiar with their schemes, and I've engaged in a process of elimination. The Ottawa are more closely associated with them than any other Indians and are tied to them far more closely, in fact, than are the French themselves. Therefore, the Ottawa are a logical choice. Not just the ordinary Ottawa warrior, however. I would suspect that the higher ranking members of the tribe—a war chief, for instance—would be the most likely to learn the plans of the Huron."

André nodded thoughtfully. "What you say is all very well and good and may be completely true. How do we benefit from the knowledge that an Ottawa war chief possesses?"

Ja-gonh spoke in a low, firm voice. "It seems to me," he said, "that it is necessary for us to abduct a war chief of the Ottawa. We then threaten him in various ways to tell us what he knows."

André stared at him. The idea he had just presented was audacious—so outrageous, in fact, that it was breathtaking.

Ja-gonh sensed his uncle's hesitation. "If you know of a

better approach," he said, "we can certainly adopt it, but logic convinces me that I have found a simple and relatively easy way."

Several of the scouts laughed, and André chuckled. "You call it simple and easy to abduct a war chief of the Ottawa?" he asked.

Ja-gonh shrugged. "It can be done," he replied. "It must be done. If you will give me two volunteers tonight, I shall see what I can do before daybreak tomorrow."

His scheme moved ahead swiftly. André gave him free rein, telling him to choose any scouts he wanted for his wild venture. Ja-gonh deliberately elected to be accompanied by fellow Seneca because their ways were the same as his, and they would be able to communicate without words.

He and his two companions left without further ado and hastily made their way northward to the camp of the Ottawa. They were in enemy-held territory now, so they had to proceed cautiously, but they nevertheless moved with great rapidity and took their time only when they came within earshot of the enemy bivouac.

The trick to what they hoped to accomplish, Ja-gonh explained to his companions, was to abduct the Ottawa war chief quickly and silently without harming him or, equally important, without injuring or killing any of the Ottawa sentries. If his companions knew he was missing, complications might result. The idea of Ja-gonh's enterprise was to do what he could without causing a major disturbance.

Thus, they ascertained the positions occupied by the Ottawa sentries. This took time and painstaking effort, but they wanted to reduce risks to a minimum, and they acted accordingly. Consequently, they were able to slide into the main bivouac area undetected and without creating a stir of any kind.

In the camps of the Iroquois the war chiefs invariably slept closest to the fire; their age as well as their rank entitled them to enjoy such a privilege. Therefore, Ja-gonh reasoned that the Ottawa followed the same principle.

His reasoning proved to be correct, and he nudged his

companions, who were making their way slowly through the tall grass, when he caught sight of a middle-aged man whose many head feathers designated him as a war chief. Near him, almost within arm's reach, slept fifteen or twenty of his subordinates, and at a glance it was obvious to Ja-gonh that if the war chief gave the alarm, Ja-gonh and his companions would be fortunate indeed to escape with their lives.

He had figured out his scheme in advance, and now he acted swiftly. Everything depended on his speed and on the self-confidence that he applied to his bold venture.

He crept close to the sleeping Ottawa war chief, then ruthlessly stuffed a gag into the warrior's mouth. At the same time, as the war chief began to come awake and to struggle, he swiftly bound his wrists securely behind him. Then he put his lips close to the Ottawa's ear. "Do as you are told," he murmured, "and you will live. Disobey me in just one thing and you will surely die." He emphasized his words by brandishing a double-edged knife, then prodding the war chief in the back with it.

The middle-aged Ottawa needed no urging. Recognizing the Seneca war paint of the trio, he automatically assumed that his span on earth was rapidly drawing to a close. As long as there was a chance that he might be allowed to survive, however, he was willing to take it. Certainly he knew better than to tempt the deadly Seneca and give them the excuse to murder him.

Ja-gonh motioned for the warrior to stand, and then Ja-gonh's companions fell in silently on either side of him. Holding the knife steadily against the small of the Ottawa's back, Ja-gonh guided his captive past the sleeping ranks of the war chief's subordinates. It was a relatively easy matter to evade the sentry outposts, and within a remarkably short time the four men were traveling at top speed through the forest toward their own camp.

Ja-gonh did not pause until they passed safely through the sentry lines of André Cooke's scouts. Then he halted and drew his tomahawk, which he regarded in silence at some length before removing the gag from the mouth of his unfortunate captive.

The Ottawa war chief could not control his indignation. "I am prepared to meet the Seneca in honorable open combat," he exclaimed. "Set me free and I challenge you to a battle that will test your courage and your skill to the utmost."

Ja-gonh paid no attention to the challenge. "All men wish to live," he said softly. "Few are eager to join their ancestors in the distant lands that the manitous have reserved for them. When one has become a war chief, one enjoys many honors and privileges. That is as it should be. It would be a shame to deny the leader of the Ottawa the good things that come from his high rank."

The Ottawa was quick-witted, as well as courageous. "The warriors of the Seneca do not risk their lives needlessly," he said. "What is your wish with the war chief of the Ottawa?"

"Our scouts," Ja-gonh declared, "have watched a mighty army gather on the soil of New France. There are men of many nations who gather for a campaign against the Iroquois and the English settlers. Certainly the Ottawa are first among them. We have seen many Algonquian, we have also seen Abnaki and Micmac and the warriors of many other tribes, as well. There are no soldiers of France in this force, but we are not surprised because we know that they remain in Quebec. However, we are aware of the French fleet off the coast, providing your warriors with food and ammunition."

The Ottawa war chief listened in stone-faced silence and grudgingly inclined his head in agreement.

"We have seen, also," Ja-gonh declared, "that the Huron are missing. This is strange, indeed. The Huron have a deep hatred for the Iroquois, particularly for the Seneca. They would not willingly miss an opportunity to win glory for themselves by meeting the warriors of the Seneca in combat and sending them crushed and in disgrace back to their own homes."

The Ottawa made no comment, but the expression in his eyes indicated that Ja-gonh's words had registered with him and obviously made sense.

"Where are the Huron?" Ja-gonh demanded, his tone

becoming urgent. "I am willing to make a bargain with the war chief of the Ottawa, and I swear on the sacred names of my ancestors that if he keeps his word, I will also keep mine. I swear that I will return the war chief of the Ottawa to his own men and will leave him in the midst of his warriors, unharmed in any way, if he will freely tell me where the Huron are to be found right now."

The middle-aged Ottawa slowly crossed his arms over his chest, his face reflecting his great dignity; he clamped his jaw shut and stared off into space. Obviously he had no intention of reaching an agreement with his young captor.

Ja-gonh was not in the least surprised by his refusal to speak freely. Glancing idly at the treetops, the young Seneca declared that when one has become a war chief in a nation as illustrious as the Ottawa, it was obvious that one was endowed with great courage and had the capacity to bear pain. "I, too, am honorable, and it does not please me to contemplate the need to inflict pain on the war chief of the Ottawa."

His threat was very plain, and he further emphasized it by running a forefinger lightly up and down the length of the blade of his tomahawk.

The Ottawa war chief knew that his young abductor meant every word he had spoken. He knew that it was customary for the Seneca to gain information from their foes by any of a number of ways. First, a victim's teeth might be pulled out with the roots, one by one; he might be blinded; or else his ears might be lopped off; or he might be tortured by the application of flaming brands to his skin until he could tolerate no more and spoke freely. Unfortunately, by this time he would be rendered a helpless cripple for whom no recuperation would ever be possible. All tribes were remorseless in dealing with foes from whom they wished to elicit information, and the Seneca were by far the least compassionate and most ruthless of all warriors. They had not acquired their ferocious reputations without good cause: once they started to torture a prisoner they continued, keeping a maximum pressure on him until they were sure he would speak.

The Ottawa war chief was engaging in his last campaign prior to his retirement. He would live off the fat of the land, and he would be honored by all of the people of the Ottawa nation. He would be served the best portions of venison, bear, and elk, as well as fish and the seasonal delicacies of the wilderness. When the tribe was successful at war, he would be given first choice in his selection of a captured enemy woman to be his slave. He was entitled to demand the best skins for his clothes, and even the medicine men were required to pay him obeisance. What a pity if he would be deprived of the joys of living for which he had worked so hard for so many years. If he was blinded, tortured, and maimed, the pleasant existence that awaited him would be transformed into a miserable life.

His first loyalty was to himself. Next came the members of his immediate family, and gradually the circle was extended to include his tribe. Only the Iroquois were fiercely devoted to other members of their alliance. The Ottawa, although associated in many campaigns with the Huron, felt no particular affection for the more aggressive tribe and had no reason to go out of their way to protect them. Therefore, the Ottawa war chief reasoned, he would be very shortsighted if he failed to take the young Seneca's threats at face value and to act accordingly.

He sighed ponderously, and although Ja-gonh gave no outward show of his feelings, he knew that a breaking point was at hand.

"I believe the words of the senior warrior of the Seneca," the Ottawa declared. "I believe it is true that he will not hesitate to inflict torture on a foe in order to find out that which he wishes to learn. I also believe that he will keep his word when he makes an agreement. It is this agreement that interests me."

Ja-gonh knew he had won. "Tell me the information I seek," he said, "and you shall be returned to your camp at once."

The Ottawa war chief sighed and began to tell of the

plot Gray Fox had devised and had revealed to the Indian war chiefs. "The Huron," he said slowly, "do not intend to miss the campaign we will wage against our ancient enemies. They will join us when they are ready, but first they have another function to perform. The Huron have gone to the land of the Seneca, where they will burn, pillage, and loot and will even the score for all the humiliations they have suffered at the hands of the Seneca for so long."

Ja-gonh was thunderstruck, as were the other two Seneca who had helped him abduct the war chief. If what the man was revealing was true, the Huron were engaging in a monstrous plot against their old foes. The active warriors of the Seneca had been lured away from their homes and currently were a considerable distance from their own land; therefore, it would be an easy matter for the armies of the Huron to attack their towns, kill the old, the infirm, and the weak, enslave the women and children whom they found useful and desirable, and burn the communities of the Seneca to the ground. There was no time to lose.

Without further ado, Ja-gonh motioned to his companions, and together they hastened through the wilderness with the Ottawa war chief, traveling at a reckless speed that entailed making noise and revealing their whereabouts.

But Ja-gonh didn't care. He passed the sentry lines of the Ottawa and felt his obligation was ended. He had kept his word, so he ordered his two companions to withdraw, and he followed suit. The war chief was being left to his own devices, could notify his sentries of his whereabouts, and could request their aid in returning to his camp.

Racing back to André Cooke's command, Ja-gonh lost no time telling the chief scout what he had learned. André shared his horror. Something had to be done at once.

Perhaps it was already too late, but Ja-gonh knew he wouldn't be satisfied unless he tried. He raced back to the main camp, where he burst in on Renno, who was eating a late supper with El-i-chi and Walter. The words poured out of the young warrior, and his father and uncles listened to him in stunned silence. Renno clenched his fists but made no comment as he listened. His wife and his mother were directly involved, and both might be either dead or prisoners of the Huron at this very minute.

"It well may be," he said bitterly, "that even now as we sit here, our homes have been destroyed and our loved ones have been enslaved by the Huron."

Walter nodded solemnly, in his mind's eye picturing Ba-lin-ta being captured and led with a thong tied around her neck through the streets of the main town of the Huron, where women and children would scream at her and revile her.

El-i-chi could think only of what the Huron would do to his mother, and he had no doubt that special humiliations would be reserved for the widow of the great Ghonka.

"I accept the full blame for this catastrophe," Renno said. "I was caught unaware in one of the oldest traps known to the tribes of North America. I have no excuses to offer; I simply was not sufficiently alert."

Ja-gonh knew that his father was being overly harsh with himself. No enemy had dared to invade the land of the Seneca and attack one of their towns for several generations, and it was unlikely that any warrior in the expedition had even dreamed that the Huron had such a scheme in mind.

"Might it be possible," Ja-gonh ventured, "that the Huron have been delayed and that a relief force might reach the town of the Seneca in time to save it?"

Renno shook his head slowly. "In war," he said, "anything is possible, but that which my son suggests is not likely. Still, we cannot afford to take the risks and must prepare for every contingency."

He had made up his mind to act, and he wasted no time. He summoned his entire command, even though the hour was late, and explained to them the brutal facts of what was in store for the towns of the Seneca.

No man moved, no man spoke until Renno was done.

Then André Cooke raised his voice, speaking in the tongue of the Indians, so that all who heard him could understand him. "You propose to send a force to meet the Huron in the land of the Seneca?" he demanded.

"I propose to divide my present command and to dispatch as many volunteers as wish to go," Renno replied. "Whether they will be in time to meet the Huron or whether they will see scenes of abject woe and tragedy remains to be seen."

Scores of Seneca volunteered, of course, as did a great number of their allies, including the Mohawk and the Oneida. André surprised the Indians by insisting that he, too, intended to march with this special expedition.

Fortunately Renno was able to weaken his force for the simple reason that the Huron had not yet appeared to join forces with their allies. If the Huron had not yet attacked the town, these braves would hold them; if the Huron hastened to join their allies, the relief column would do the same and would return at once to the main army, where it would be reunited with Renno's other men.

Renno acted with dispatch as he assigned the men who would take part in this special expedition. Without exception all were senior warriors well able to deal with any emergency. The majority were Seneca, but he deliberately included a number of Mohawk, Oneida, Onondaga, and Tuscarora as well. In all, nearly half of Renno's command would be taking part in this crucial mission. André Cooke would be an exceptionally valuable member of such a group, and Renno unhesitatingly agreed that his brother-in-law should accompany the expedition.

The biggest question that remained now was that of who would command the relief party. Renno wasted no time and gave the assignment to El-i-chi. His brother was needed with the main force, but his services were more urgently required on this special mission, and Renno unhesitatingly gave him the assignment.

Ja-gonh was rewarded for having discovered the Huron plot by being included in the company, and Walter, remaining behind, was given the great honor of leading the braves who had originally been under El-i-chi's command.

Renno spoke hurriedly with El-i-chi. "I have no idea what you'll find when you reach home," he said, "and there's no point in wasting time speculating. If the Huron have already attacked, I'll expect you to follow them and recapture as many prisoners as you can. If they have not yet attacked, hold them at bay, and whenever they commence their march in this direction to join the main body of the Indian allies of the French, hasten back here to me with all possible speed. The men in your command will be missed sorely, and they will be badly needed when full-scale hostilities begin here."

El-i-chi was concerned. "Will you fight a major battle while we're away?" he asked.

"Not if it can be helped," Renno replied. "I'll use delaying tactics as long as I can until my army is whole again. Until then, may the manitous guide you."

Gathering the men assigned to him, El-i-chi addressed them briefly. "We go to the land of the Seneca under forced march," he said. "We will not rest; we will not sleep on the journey. Every moment is precious, and I pray that we shall arrive in time to be of help to the elderly warriors, the women, and children who otherwise will be victims of the Huron. Let no man who is unable to keep up the pace we will set on the trail remain with this company. Let him retire now with honor. We will permit no stragglers on the trail, and every effort will be devoted to reaching the land of the Seneca as quickly as possible."

That ended his address. There was no need for him to make a more elaborate speech; every warrior who had enlisted in his company knew what was at stake and was sharply aware of the odds. The column started out at once, and André Cooke gravitated naturally to a position in advance of the main body.

Ja-gonh unthinkingly joined him and remained close by him as he jogged for hour after endless hour through the wilderness. The possibility that the town of the Seneca had actually fallen to the Huron was so ghastly that

Ja-gonh could not allow himself to contemplate it. The lives of his mother and grandmother were at stake, and equally important was Ah-wen-ga, whose future also was hanging in the balance.

It was very quiet in the land of the Seneca after Renno and his warriors had departed, and the tenor of life was uneventful and smooth as always. The return of Goo-ga-ro-no created no commotion, since her acceptance or rejection was strictly a family matter. Her mother and her grandmother had taken her back, that was that, and her adventure was no one's business but her own.

A number of her contemporaries were curious and wondered what had happened to her, particularly as rumors about a handsome Frenchman abounded, but no one dared ask any questions. Certain parts of an Indian's life were regarded as strictly private.

Goo-ga-ro-no confided in Ah-wen-ga, to whom she told the whole, dismal story of her experience, but she made no mention of her trials to anyone else. Ah-wen-ga was duly sympathetic but privately felt that her friend had shown very poor judgment. She herself, she thought, was far too intelligent and stable to be fooled in such a manner by any man. On the other hand, remembering her intimacy with Ja-gonh, Ah-wen-ga wondered. Perhaps affairs of the heart complicated matters and clouded one's vision. Seeing Goo-ga-ro-no's adventure in that perspective, Ah-wen-ga felt a far greater sense of rapport with Ja-gonh's sister.

The two young women worked side by side in the vegetable fields, concentrating on removing weeds from the rows where the corn was growing straight and tall. The season was well advanced, the corn was almost ripe, and there was no question that the Seneca would enjoy a bumper crop this year. The stalks were taller than either of the two women, and both looked in admiration at the bushy silk tassels on the ears of corn. No one in the land of the Seneca would go hungry that winter.

All at once a drum sounded and gradually increased in volume as the sentry manning an outpost sent his message.

The two women were busy chattering and gossiping, making up for time they had lost during Goo-ga-ro-no's absence, and at first they paid no attention to the sound of the drum. But little by little it intruded on their consciousness, and the message they heard was so startling that it stunned them.

The sentry was claiming that a large force of Huron warriors had invaded the land of the Seneca and was even now marching against the main town. Never in the lifetimes of young women like Goo-ga-ro-no and Ah-wen-ga had any such disturbance occurred, and they looked at each other in blank disbelief, unable to grasp the full significance of what they heard.

One person who understood the import of the message instantly was Sun-ai-yee. His expression did not change, and an outsider looking at him well might have guessed that he had anticipated just such a development. His seeming calm concealed the fact that his mind was already operating at a furious pace. For the moment, the size of the enemy force was not important to him. What was important was that he had only retired warriors, junior warriors, and women to defend the town. He wasted no time wishing he had a more efficient force; he had been taught to make do with what was on hand and that was precisely his intention right now. He listened carefully to the drum and then summoned two junior warriors, boys in their early teens who had only recently been granted the status of warrior.

"Go to the lodges of each of the clans," Sun-ai-yee told them, "and at each ask those warriors whose abilities to walk upright have not been impaired by age to join me at once at the main gate. Then go to the lodge of the junior warriors and spread the word there that I wish all those junior warriors of seventeen summers also to join me. Then go to the fields beyond the palisade and spread the word there to the women. Tell them that all who can shoot and who do not hesitate to shoot to kill should join me, also."

The two youths hastened to do his bidding, and Sun-ai-yee walked to his own house as rapidly as his arthritic knees would allow. There he donned his war bonnet, the symbol of his rank as sachem of the Seneca, picked up his quiver of arrows and a bow, and put a tomahawk into his belt. Then he hastened to the main gate, where the crowd of the elderly, of seventeen-year-olds, and a scattering of young women were already gathering in response to his plea.

He was a trifle surprised to see Ah-wen-ga and Goo-ga-ro-no in the group. He might have known that they would be among the first to seek adventure. Well, he could not halt them now, and he did not feel it would be appropriate to deny them the privilege that he was extending to others.

"Hear me," he told the motley assemblage. "A great force of Huron is even now marching on this town intending to destroy it. We must halt them! Our best way of accomplishing this is through surprising them. Therefore, I propose the following. We will march at once to the vegetable field, and we will conceal ourselves in the tall corn. When the enemy approaches, we will deal with them according to a specific plan that I will outline to you when we have taken up our battle positions."

Several of the elderly warriors looked at each other in obvious alarm.

Sun-ai-yee smiled at them wryly. "Never fear, my friends," he said. "I do not intend to waste lives or to subject our people to needless risks. Let no one taking part in this venture be fooled. This little force that is assembling here is in no way—in no manner of speaking—the equal of the powerful force of Huron warriors whom we will face. We will employ very simple tactics. We will strike a blow at them. We will, with the help of the manitous, strike hard and, above all, swiftly. Then, when I give the word, we will withdraw immediately into the town. We will actively seek the protection of the palisade. The first to go will be the women among us. They will be followed by the junior warriors; the elders will bring up the rear, and because they cannot move as rapidly as can those who are younger, our withdrawal will not be too rapid. Of that you can be sure."

Everyone laughed at his joke, and Ah-wen-ga felt great admiration for her father. That he could indulge in humor at such a critical time was astonishing and indicated what an extraordinary person he was.

Sun-ai-yee led the group toward the cornfield at a speed that belied his own words. When two of the teenage boys whispered to each other and started to giggle, he frowned at them, his manner so ferocious that both fell silent and looked abashed instantly. This was a matter of gravest concern, and the retired warriors well knew it.

When they reached the cornfield, they took up positions according to Sun-ai-yee's specific instructions, and he spoke crisply and succinctly to all of them, treating the young women and the junior warriors with the same seriousness that he accorded the old men. He spoke to several of the boys, who ran at full tilt to the town, returning shortly with armloads of weapons, which they had gathered in the lodges. Bows and arrows were distributed to all who lacked them.

When Ah-wen-ga and Goo-ga-ro-no received arms, they became aware for the first time of the grim seriousness of the situation. Sun-ai-yee had not asked for volunteers for the sport of it.

As the sachem made his way slowly up and down the lines of his motley force, it was unnecessary for him to instruct the old warriors, but the young women and the boys received his special attention. He urged them repeatedly to make no unnecessary move, to speak to no one, to await instructions, and to do exactly as they were bidden.

The elderly sachem smiled when he reached his daughter and Goo-ga-ro-no. "I know it's fashionable for young women to be independent," he said, "and I well realize that both of you often feel you know more than your parents, but I wish to make myself very clear. You are not expected to think for yourselves. In fact, you are not expected to think at all. You have both been taught to use bows and arrows; I hope each of you will kill a Huron warrior. Just remember, do what you're told and nothing more!"

He paused for an instant before moving on, and then he turned away abruptly and became busy talking to the next group. Goo-ga-ro-no tested an arrow in her bow and was glad that she had been given the bow of a young warrior, which was light enough for her to handle. "I thought," she murmured, "that your father was going to embrace you before he moved on."

Ah-wen-ga nodded. The same thought had occurred to her, and she knew Sun-ai-yee had refrained because he disliked shows of emotion, particularly in times of stress. Just thinking about him caused a lump to form in her throat; he was meeting the impossible challenge of the Huron with an inadequate force but was determined to do his best and to put on an exhibition of marksmanship that would slow the enemy, even though it did not halt them.

The drum sounded again, warning of the approach of the Huron column. Certainly the Huron would have silenced the Seneca sentry had they been able to do so, but they had no way of locating him in the deep woods. The Seneca had developed the hiding of their sentries into a fine art, and no one else had ever been able to master their technique. So the sentinels knew the precise location of the enemy column, and as the message was sent in code, it had no meaning to the Huron. When the message throbbed out on the drum to the effect that the vanguard was almost within reach of the town, the ill-assorted group of defenders knew that their moment of crisis was at hand.

The Seneca behaved admirably, with great restraint. Not one defender moved, uttered a word, or did anything else that would give away their presence in the cornfield.

Sun-ai-yee felt his pulse race as he notched an arrow into his own bow. This was the moment he had always relished: the precious seconds of tension and excitement just before a battle began. Miraculously, he felt now as he had felt so many countless times in the past, even though his command was made up of old men, young women, and junior warriors and he was horribly outmanned.

Those things didn't matter to him now. He peered between the cornstalks, saw a Huron war chief, whom he recognized by his feathered bonnet, and promptly put his arrow directly between the man's eyes. The Huron war chief had the dubious distinction of being the first on either side to die in combat.

The stir that Sun-ai-yee's shot created immediately signaled the other elderly warriors that their turn had come. They unleashed a barrage of arrows, which sang through the air, and that sound was all that the junior warriors and young women needed. They, too, took aim and let loose their arrows.

Ah-wen-ga was conscious of her years of training by her father and of the fact that ammunition well might run short before the battle ended, so she took very careful aim and used all of her strength to bend the warrior's bow with which she had been provided. Her arrow found its mark, and the scream of the senior warrior of the Huron whom she wounded was reward enough for her.

Goo-ga-ro-no was aware of her heritage as she, too, stood with her bow poised, ready to fire. She reminded herself that she was the daughter of Renno, the granddaughter of Ghonka. No other woman in all the world could claim such a heritage, and she felt deeply satisfied when the arrow penetrated deep within a man's shoulder, completely incapacitating him. She reacted like a veteran, taking another arrow from her quiver. Ah-wen-ga did the same.

The invaders were taken completely by surprise. As a consequence, the Huron drive was stalled, at least temporarily, and the leaders were nonplussed. This gave the defending force the opportunity to fire repeated shots, and Sun-ai-yee did not lose the opportunity. His old men knew what was expected of them and took the lead, the young men and the women following their example.

All the same, Sun-ai-yee recognized the fact that the opportunity was being exploited to the utmost and that he would be unwise to try his luck too far. Eventually the Huron would recover and would retaliate in great strength against those who were assaulting them. So far he had been lucky and had suffered no casualties, while throwing the invader off stride. That was more than enough to satisfy him, and he passed the word to retreat to the palisade.

Then the huge gate was slammed and bolted, and the opening phase of the battle came to an end. There was no doubt that the Seneca had scored an emphatic, sudden victory in this initial phase of the battle. They had taken their foes by surprise and had inflicted a number of casualties on the enemy while they themselves escaped intact.

Now, however, the battle was entering a far more serious phase for the defenders. The Huron needed time to regroup, but their leaders nevertheless had the good sense to throw a cordon of warriors around the entire palisade, and the town was surrounded. The Huron could not linger too close to the walls, to be sure, because the Seneca had taken the precaution of clearing away all underbrush and all trees from the immediate vicinity of the wall. Therefore, at no place could the attackers approach closer than about seventy-five feet.

This, as Sun-ai-yee well knew, made a surprise attack on the fortress that he now commanded almost impossible. However, the siege raised severe problems for him.

Not the least of them was that of obtaining enough food and water to supply the needs of the citizens who were crowded within the gate. After posting sentries around the entire perimeter, with instructions to notify him the moment that the enemy tried to advance or launch an assault anywhere, the grizzled sachem then sent a junior warrior to fetch his daughter and Goo-ga-ro-no, who appeared at once. "I want you to go to everyone in town and deliver—yourselves—a message to them from me. No one is to partake of any food, including that which may be in his own personal larder, without permission. No one is to bathe or otherwise waste water. We have no way now of obtaining fresh water supplies from the lake or from the river, so we will have to make do with what we have on hand."

Ah-wen-ga and Goo-ga-ro-no hastened to obey him and soon were conscientiously passing on his orders to the residents of the town.

Meanwhile, Sun-ai-yee sent for Ena and conferred with her in private. "You have more authority than any other living Seneca," he told her. "Because you are the widow of Ghonka, you have the respect of our people second to none. Therefore, I would like to ask you to accept a grave responsibility."

Ena was seemingly unflustered by the Huron siege and nodded complacently.

"I would like you to take charge of all food and water supplies," Sun-ai-yee told her. "Put to work as many of the junior warriors as you wish. Gather all food and water into one place and ration it accordingly."

Ena was quick to understand what he had in mind, and agreed to do what she was bid. "How long do you anticipate the siege will last?" she asked.

Sun-ai-yee returned her gaze without flinching as he replied, "Only the manitous can answer that question. I have no idea how long we will be able to hold out against them."

Ena nodded gravely. "I see," she murmured.

"It is possible," Sun-ai-yee said, "that we can survive for many days. It is also possible that we will fold and be forced to surrender very quickly. I do not fool myself; the odds against us are very great. We are facing hundreds of trained warriors, men who are skilled in the arts of war. Our defenders are old men, women, and children."

Ena considered his statement for a few moments, and then a tight-lipped smile appeared on her face. "Do not forget," she said, "that the old men, the women, and the children are Seneca. That well may make a difference between victory and defeat."

Sun-ai-yee was encouraged. Her refusal to recognize the overwhelming odds against them reminded him of Ghonka at his best. His widow was a worthy mate of the Great Sachem. He grinned and nodded, but further words were unnecessary. They understood each other, and if the Seneca who were trapped in the town felt as they did, it was possible to achieve victory.

El-i-chi was encouraged. His column raced through the wilderness, never pausing to rest, and the volunteers from the various Iroquois nations were somehow goaded into exerting themselves to the utmost and were therefore able to maintain the blistering pace set by their Seneca comrades. So far all was going precisely as El-i-chi had hoped, and he anticipated reaching the land of the Seneca in three to four days.

He was heartened also by another totally unexpected development. A messenger had come to him soon after he had started out on his seemingly impossible mission with word that a volunteer militia force led by Captain Roger Harkness and numbering two hundred and fifty to three hundred volunteers—most of them from Massachusetts Bay and Virginia—was closely following his unit. These troops would not be able to travel at the speed his warriors attained but instead were intending to follow him and hoped to join him in battle against the Huron. Certainly they would be welcome whenever they appeared and would be a valuable addition to his force.

No one was more eager for combat than was Ja-gonh, and he prayed that Gray Fox would be a member of the Huron unit threatening the town of the Seneca. The half-breed had already created more than his share of vicious mischief, and Ja-gonh wanted nothing more than to settle the score with him for all time.

Trotting in his place near the head of the column, Ja-gonh thought it symbolic that El-i-chi and André Cooke should be leading this expedition. El-i-chi was his father's brother, a son of Ghonka who had more than his share of personal stake in the outcome of the battle. André Cooke was his mother's brother-in-law, and to Ja-gonh he represented the best of all that was good in the English settlers. André had no personal stake in the quarrel of the Seneca and the Huron, and he had nothing

personal to gain by taking part in the combat. Nevertheless, he had volunteered his services because he recognized at once the enormous significance of what was at
stake. Like so many far-sighted colonists, he knew that,
just as the Iroquois made the English colonial cause their
cause, so colonists had to make the goals of the Seneca
their goals.

André was highly capable in the forest, and as Ja-gonh
watched him make his way through the wilderness, the
young warrior could not help being deeply impressed. The
Seneca liked to think they were unique in wilderness
travel, that they were at home and able to look out for
themselves anywhere in the forest. But André demonstrated that he was even as adept as El-i-chi, a war chief
whose experience was unmatched by any other Seneca in
the party. It was encouraging to Ja-gonh to know that he,
a Seneca by choice rather than by blood, was able to
emulate both of his uncles and enjoy the best of both of
their worlds.

In the far north, near the Atlantic coast, the Ottawa led
the advance, creeping forward at night and taking up
positions closer to the line of the Iroquois and the English
colonists. They were followed by the vast bulk of the
Algonquian, a huge nation that had contributed more
warriors to the enterprise than had any other Indian
nation. The other allies of the French followed suit subtly,
and the Micmac, who were not particularly noted for
their boldness, marched forward about four miles and
took up their positions almost head to head with the
Iroquois. Meanwhile, warships of the French fleet were
anchored in the waters along the coast, a sign to the
Indian allies that New France was lending its support
with food and arms.

Renno was concerned by these movements and discussed them with the high command, to whom he outlined the enemy advances in detail.

"It seems to me," he said, "that they're trying to force

a confrontation with us. They're pushing hard, demanding that we fight them and throw them back."

Jeffrey Wilson nodded. "There's little question of it in my mind," he said. "I would have thought that they would wait until they were joined by the Huron, but for whatever their reasons, they've decided to act now."

"It's odd when you think about it," Ned declared. "They would be in a far better position to achieve a victory if they did wait for the Huron, who are among their best fighting men."

Renno was lost in thought. Finally he said, "I think the enemy are trying to force a battle with us for a very specific reason. They believe they're strong enough to withstand defeat, and that is good enough to suit their purposes. With the presence of the French fleet off the coast, they know they can hold out for as long as they have to. They aren't necessarily interested in achieving a victory."

Ned stared at him incredulously. "I don't follow you in the least."

"Their intention," Renno said, "is to weaken the Iroquois and to punch holes in the militia. If they can deprive us of winning a definitive victory now, they will have achieved a great deal in combat against us. We'll be badly weakened, and when the Huron do arrive and join them, they should be far better able to achieve a truly sweeping victory."

Jeffrey stuffed his pipe slowly. "Much as I hate to admit it," he said, "I'm afraid that Renno is quite right. They're trying to bleed us little by little until we weaken and become an easy prey."

The head of the New York militia frowned. "That raises an interesting question for us," he said. "Do we fight, or do we stall and await the return of our own warriors, who have gone off to relieve the Seneca?"

There was a silence, and no militia leader was prepared to offer a solution to the dilemma.

Renno, however, suffered no doubts regarding what needed to be done. "If I had my way," he said, "I would do two things. First I would stall as long as possible. I would establish my lines in such a way that I would strengthen my flanks even at the expense of my center. In other words, I would deploy in a U-shaped formation. Then I would strike, and strike hard. The entire strategy of the Indian allies of the French collapses and crumbles if they suffer a severe defeat at our hands in the near future. By the time they are reinforced by the Huron, it well could be too late for them to win any battle of significance."

The furrows in Jeffrey Wilson's brow eased. "Of course," he said softly as he shook his head. "You have a knack for simplifying the complex, Renno, and for seeing problems clearly in the proper perspective. I cast my vote in favor of adopting your plan."

Ned added his endorsement of the scheme, too.

That was all that was needed, and the other militia leaders promptly fell into line. For better or worse, the Iroquois and English colonists would lure the Indian tribes allied with the French into a U-shaped trap, and when they initiated the fight, they would do their best to destroy the ability of the French allies to wage war.

The leaders of the Huron were nervous, and had good cause for their apprehensions. They had expected to win a quick victory and had anticipated that when they first struck, they would capture the main town of the Seneca. Instead, an ambush had been laid for them, and now, as nearly as they could judge from their vantage point in the cornfields, the wooden walls of the town bristled with defenders.

Ah-ha-ri, the war chief in charge of the Huron expedition, peered hard at the defense line, his eyes narrowed to slits, and finally he turned to Gray Fox in annoyance. "You told me," he said, "that the warriors of the Seneca were gone. You told me that all of their active fighting men had marched off to aid the English colonists in war and that we would be unopposed here."

"That is true," Gray Fox muttered, conscious of the glares of Ah-ha-ri and of several other Huron war chiefs.

"It appears to me," Ah-ha-ri said bitterly, "that there are ample warriors still in the town to defend it. We lost several men needlessly in the ambush, and if we attack again now, our casualties are likely to mount still higher."

As usual, Gray Fox thought, the Huron were their own worst enemies, and the war chief in command was too conservative for his own good. "We have marched a very long distance from our homeland," he said. "I assured the French and I assured you that victory would be ours if we follow my plan. I still insist that we will win! But we must proceed my way. We cannot deviate from my scheme if we expect to be the victors."

Pierre Fanchon, attired in buckskins, his head shaved on both sides of a center scalp lock, more closely resembled a Huron than a Frenchman. But he had been given no choice. This was the assignment Gray Fox had chosen for him, and though he felt himself thoroughly abased, at least he would be much better paid than if he had remained an enlisted man in the French army.

Now, despite his contempt for the Huron half-breed, he had to admit that Gray Fox was right, although he was afraid to speak up in the presence of the Huron high command. Gray Fox was still regarded with some suspicion as something of an outsider, and Fanchon knew that he himself was not accepted by the Huron. So it was best to let Gray Fox fight his own battle and reach whatever decision he and the Huron could. He would be wise not to interfere.

"We have come far into the land of the Seneca at great peril to ourselves," Ah-ha-ri said emphatically. "We left our comrades of the Ottawa and the Algonquian because Gray Fox assured us that we would win a great victory and would take many slaves, but we are far beyond the borders of the Seneca, and we are very vulnerable. If a striking force is launched from the town and forces us to retreat, we can be cut to ribbons before we reach the border. I wonder if we would not be wise simply to abandon this scheme and to join our brothers for the main battle against the English colonists and the Iroquois."

Gray Fox replied forcefully, concealing his contempt for the war chief. "We have come a great distance," he declared. "We have made many sacrifices. The other tribes are envious of us and await news of our great victory over the Seneca. Will you have us become a laughingstock? Will you have the Ottawa and the Algonquian and even the Micmac and Abnaki snicker when a warrior of the Huron walks past them? No, I say. No. Let us hold to our original scheme and let us take the town that is so ripe for the taking."

Ah-ha-ri was not convinced. "Perhaps it is right, perhaps it is not," he said. "From what I have seen tonight, the defenders are well prepared."

Another war chief entered the conversation. "Perhaps it would be wise," he said, "if we do nothing until daybreak. Then we will be able to better see the defenders clearly and to judge them for ourselves."

Virtually the entire group nodded in assent, but Gray Fox was furious. "If we wait until daylight," he declared, "we miss an opportunity to capture the town with a minimum of bloodshed to our warriors. Several hours remain of the night before dawn. I say that we attack now, and when daybreak comes, we will have occupied the town."

He was so forceful, so positive, so sure of himself that the Huron hesitated. They knew that he was held in high regard by the French, particularly by Major de Bienville, and none of the older men, among them Ah-ha-ri, could forget for an instant that he was the son of the distinguished Alain de Gramont—Golden Eagle—the finest and most courageous fighting man in the long history of the Huron.

Ah-ha-ri sighed as he capitulated. "Very well," he said. "We will do as Gray Fox suggests. It is only fair to him, as he himself has said, to follow his whole plan if we hope to achieve the victory he has promised us. Therefore, I command you to pass the word to our warriors that we will attack the town of the Seneca now!"

Ah-wen-ga peered out through the darkness from her vantage point behind a chink in the palisade. She stared steadily at the vegetable field and toward the wilderness beyond, knowing that the Huron were there lying in wait, but she was unable to see a single warrior. The strain of looking was so great that occasionally her eyes watered, and she brushed away the tears angrily. How she wished that on this one occasion, at least, she were endowed with the extraordinary eyesight with which Ja-gonh was blessed.

Goo-ga-ro-no, it appeared, enjoyed the advantages of her father and her brother. She remained motionless beside Ah-wen-ga as she, too, peered out into the night, and suddenly she said softly, "Ah, the enemy is stirring."

Ah-wen-ga could see no sign of action in the enemy camp. "Are you sure?" she demanded.

"Of course," Goo-ga-ro-no replied firmly. "There are dozens of warriors who look as though they're preparing to act." Following the careful instructions she had been given, she awakened a junior warrior who was asleep beside her, and the moment the boy opened his eyes, she sent him off to Sun-ai-yee with the news.

Ah-wen-ga sighed. "If I were endowed with your eyesight," she said, "I would put my fair share of arrows into their midst."

"If I were as accurate with bow and arrows as you, I wouldn't hesitate to use them," Goo-ga-ro-no confessed.

Ah-wen-ga felt compelled to act. Seizing her bow, she took an arrow from her quiver and notched it. "Where are they?" she demanded. "Give me a guideline."

"Very well," Goo-ga-ro-no replied. "Can you make out the first row of the cornstalks? They stand quite high, and they form an uneven smudge on the horizon."

Ah-wen-ga squinted hard. "Yes, I see them."

"Very well," Goo-ga-ro-no told her. "There are many enemy warriors in the midst of that row of corn."

Ah-wen-ga pulled her bow taut and let fly with an arrow, aiming it at the high cornstalks.

Goo-ga-ro-no gasped softly and clasped her hands together. "A perfect strike," she murmured. "Don't ever complain to me about your lack of vision. I'm sure you killed an enemy warrior."

"So," Ah-wen-ga replied calmly, then picked up another arrow. She had enjoyed great good luck but saw no need to dwell on that fact. She fired the second arrow without further ado, aiming it roughly as she had the first, and this time she was rewarded by Goo-ga-ro-no's chuckle.

"You've done it again," Goo-ga-ro-no whispered. "Not even my brother is a more accurate shot than you are proving to be."

Ah-wen-ga blushed for an instant at the reference to Ja-gonh, but she didn't hesitate long. She took full advantage of her good fortune and sent one arrow after another flying in the direction of the cornfield.

She was so intent on what she was doing that she failed to see Sun-ai-yee come up behind her. He stood for a moment or two, his expression bemused as he watched his daughter. His eyes soon registered astonishment, and then he shook his head. "I have rarely seen any warrior shoot more accurately than that, my daughter," he said in wonder.

Ah-wen-ga shrugged, and Goo-ga-ro-no said in awe, "I think every arrow you shot found its target!"

Ah-wen-ga still could not see clearly and had to take their word for what was happening. Sun-ai-yee peered out at the enemy for some little time. He, too, had difficulty seeing the distant figures, but he was an experienced enough warrior to recognize a retreat when he saw one, even if it was far away. "They're drawing back," he announced with satisfaction.

"So they are," Goo-ga-ro-no said. "I think they were planning to assault the palisade, but your fire caused them to change their minds."

"That it did," Sun-ai-yee said. "They're obviously afraid to attack us in force."

Ah-wen-ga felt compelled to admit the truth and told her father that she had merely responded to what Goo-ga-ro-no had described to her.

Sun-ai-yee laughed softly. "Whatever the cause, and for whatever the reason, you've done us a great service tonight," he said. "You saved us from an attack at an hour when we would be at our most vulnerable. I would say that Goo-ga-ro-no's eyesight and your marksmanship have won us a signal victory. This marks the second time that we have defeated the invaders at their own game. If we can keep up the good work and continue to perform these miracles, we may yet turn the tide."

Chapter X

Ja-gonh appeared to be oblivious to the normal human needs for food and rest. He trotted endlessly for hour after hour, occasionally eating a handful of parched corn or dried beef and rarely stopping long enough to drink from a stream. Otherwise, he stayed in motion, keeping up his same grueling pace endlessly.

André Cooke marveled at his nephew's stamina and strength, but he knew that all members of the relief party were not endowed with the special characteristics with which Ja-gonh was blessed. He moved into place beside El-i-chi.

"It might be wise," André said, "to call a halt before we reach the land of the Seneca. It well may be that many of our warriors will need to refresh themselves with a hearty meal and a few hours of sustained sleep. A difficult battle awaits them when they confront the Huron, and they should be in good shape—the best of all possible shape—when they go into combat."

El-i-chi listened carefully, and André's words made sense to him. As a son of Ghonka, he saw nothing unusual in his nephew's speed, but he was willing to concede that few warriors had Ja-gonh's endurance.

So, much to Ja-gonh's bitter disappointment, El-i-chi halted the column. Ja-gonh still had sufficient energy left to go hunting, and his uncles were not surprised when he shot a pair of deer, a large buck and a fair-sized doe. The carcasses were prepared immediately, and the warriors had fresh meat to eat when they awakened, before they resumed their journey. Ja-gonh was unhappy over the delay but could see that others indeed might need greater rest. He was himself filled with such zeal for the enterprise that his own bodily needs meant nothing to him. This time he would meet Gray Fox face to face and would vanquish him, this time he would keep his pledge to his grandfather and would avenge his death.

The column started forward again, most of the men responding with new vigor, and El-i-chi knew he had been wise to grant them a respite.

Ja-gonh was so anxious to reach home now that he took the lead and had to be restrained from increasing his speed and outstripping the rest of the company. As he trotted, he looked around him, his gaze encompassing everything in sight in the wilderness ahead as well as in the sky above. Suddenly he stopped short. In the far distance, high above the horizon, he saw a tiny speck that seemed to be growing larger. He examined it, and his heart hammered against his rib cage when he realized it was indeed growing. There was no longer any doubt in his mind: a hawk had come into view, and Ja-gonh was convinced that the bird was a messenger intended for him alone by the manitous.

As he gazed up at the sky the bird came closer, sweeping the sky in great circles. Ja-gonh stood very still, his feet together, conscious only of the presence of the hawk.

Certainly El-i-chi and André Cooke knew the significance of the hawk's presence. They were familiar with the signs that Renno had received through the years, and they knew that his son was being similarly favored. Many of the Seneca in the expedition were aware of the meaning of the hawk as well, and they were awe-stricken. Here was proof positive that their venture was being favored by the gods. The hawk seemed to come to a standstill almost directly overhead. Then suddenly it was in motion again, gathering speed so rapidly that the eye of a human being could scarcely follow it. It flew higher and still higher in great sweeping circles, then vanished from sight as swiftly and as dramatically as it had appeared.

Ja-gonh made no comment to anyone, not even to his uncles, but his expression told its own story. His face was still set in stern lines, but his eyes glowed like live coals and reflected the certain knowledge that he was on the right track.

He knew beyond all doubt that he was destined to meet the Huron in battle and that he would do combat with Gray Fox. The manitous were giving him the opportunity to avenge the death of his grandfather and the mistreatment of Ah-wen-ga. His anxiety vanished, and he no longer feared that unless he hurried he would miss his meeting with the Huron. The appearance of the hawk had assured him of his rendezvous with destiny, and he was very certain that the outcome of that confrontation would be favorable.

Captain Roger Harkness and his troop of volunteers traveled at a pace that the young officer would have regarded as blistering had he still been in Europe. Indeed, even by New World standards, their pace was extraordinary, and although Roger recognized the fact that they could not match the speed of the Seneca, he hoped that El-i-chi's column would not outdistance them too greatly.

He was eager to join in the combat with the Huron, and he guessed that if his troop of volunteers maintained their present speed, they would reach the town of the Seneca in less than half a day after the Indians.

He was as much concerned about the status of the troops he had left behind as he was with the possibility of arriving in time to do battle with the Huron. Certainly, as he well knew, Renno and the English militia commanders had lost their great advantage when they had decided to split their forces. The refusal of the French to commit troops to combat had given the Iroquois and the colonists a distinct advantage, but that was lost now, and they would be fighting the Indian allies of the French on more or less even terms.

It was impossible for Roger to predict the outcome of that battle. He had come to know Jeffrey Wilson and Ned Ridley well enough to feel great confidence in the abilities of both men, and he assumed that their militia regiments were steady and that the troops could be trusted to carry out their assignments in combat.

The great unknown factor was the contribution that the Iroquois would make. Roger had seen enough of Ja-gonh in action to appreciate the strength and cunning of the Seneca. What he could not judge were the talents of Renno. All he knew was that everyone acquainted with the white sachem spoke of him with awe, so it was likely that he was a man of no mean ability.

Roger couldn't help wishing that he could be in two places at once. Since that could not be, however, he supposed he was just as glad that he would be taking part in the combat that would take place in the land of the Seneca. The fact that Ja-gonh and other warriors like him would be taking part in the battle made it more exciting than it otherwise might have been. If Roger Harkness had learned one thing in America, it was that the Seneca had a magnetic quality. No wonder so much depended on them, no wonder that their success or failure dictated whether an enterprise would succeed or fail. The Seneca were the center of every action in which they participated.

Certainly no one was more aware of these basic facts than were Renno and the militia leaders. As the enemy gave increasing evidence that it was preparing for a major assault, the defense lines were established and made solid. The colonial militia regiments held the line in the center, in the deepest part of the U. Renno assigned all of his Iroquois other than the Seneca to serve on one leg of the U and kept his decimated Seneca for duty on the remaining leg. Had his entire force been available, there would have been no question that it would have been strong enough to repel any attacker. Under the circumstances, however, with approximately half of his own warriors having gone off to the land of the Seneca with El-i-chi, his lines were drawn perilously thin.

No one needed to tell Renno that his Seneca would prove to be an irresistible target. The Ottawa and Algonquian, in particular, would be strongly tempted to attack his warriors and, outnumbering them by three or four to one, would be far more likely to win a victory of considerable significance. If that happened, their reputation would be secure for many years to come, and they would be known as the tribe that had actually defeated the feared and dreaded Seneca.

What Renno relied on were the ferocity, courage, and skill of the warriors who remained in his command. There was no need for him to address them or to remind them in any way of the grave responsibility they carried. As they were Seneca, he assumed that they knew what was needed and what was expected of them.

He was summoned to General Wilson's tent one evening as he was finishing supper at his own campfire, and he hurried to the quarters of his old friend. There he found all of the militia leaders gathering.

"It appears," Jeffrey Wilson declared, "that our time of waiting has come to an end. I've had a dozen identical reports from our scouts in various sectors of the front tonight, and they all say the same thing. The enemy is preparing to launch an all-out attack very soon."

Renno nodded. "You can expect the attack to take place at daybreak," he said. "That is the traditional time for the Algonquian to initiate an engagement, and as they make up more than half of the enemy force, their routines will be followed, you may be sure."

No one doubted his word. Jeffrey hastily reviewed the disposition of the defending forces and requested that all units hold firm under enemy fire.

"Right there," Ned Ridley said, "is the key to our success in tomorrow's battle. The enemy outnumber us by perhaps two to one, but we hold the advantage because none of them, with the possible exception of the Ottawa, are particularly distinguished fighters. The French are missing, and the Huron are missing, and both are sorely needed. We needn't engage in any great shows of heroics, lads. If we hold steady under fire and refuse to retreat, I think it very likely that the enemy will be drawn into our trap."

The New York and Connecticut commanders agreed with his analysis.

"Renno," Jeffrey asked, "will you require any assistance from the rest of us?"

Renno smiled as he shook his head. "I think not," he replied without elaboration.

"You are outnumbered far worse than the rest of us," Jeffrey persisted, "and I have no doubt that the attack will be concentrated on your sector. I am prepared to advance my troops into your territory if you wish it, in order to bolster you."

Renno shook his head. "That would be a grave error, I think," he said. "Once we begin to move troops out of their assigned positions, we create holes; the Algonquian have enough warriors on hand to take full advantage of such movements. They can pour reinforcements of their own into any gaps that we create in our lines."

The militia commanders had no alternative but to accept his word and to go along with what he requested. It was plain to Jeffrey Wilson that the Seneca had bitten off a large chunk, perhaps more than they could digest, but it was impossible to say that to Renno without mortally insulting him. As Jeffrey told Ned privately, he was prepared, if need be, to come to Renno's aid, regardless of any request or lack of it that the Great Sachem might make. But he also knew that Renno and his Seneca could do things that were beyond the abilities of lesser men. Renno had become a legend in his own time, and if anyone could win against seemingly insurmountable odds, it was the Seneca Great Sachem.

Gray Fox was in serious trouble with his immediate superiors, and well he knew it. What Major Henri de Bienville would say, Gray Fox did not care to speculate. Not only had his initial plan of attack on the town of the Seneca ended in abject failure, but his suggested follow-up, a predawn assault in force, had also failed miserably. A number of Huron warriors had been killed by arrows from behind the palisade and had forced Ah-ha-ri to call off the attack.

The whole thing was too much for Gray Fox. He could not understand how the Seneca had learned that the predawn assault was going to take place, and he had no idea where they had acquired the services of warriors who could handle bows and arrows with such expertise. He knew his information that Renno had departed for the border of New France, taking virtually all of his effective warriors with him, was accurate. Where, then, did the current defenders of the town come from? That they were present behind the palisade and were defending the town and its people so vigorously was disconcerting, to say the least. The only solution that Gray Fox knew was to redouble the efforts of the attackers. There was no doubt in his mind that the Huron force was superior to that defending the Seneca, and if he were in command, he would pound hard the defenders and would force them to capitulate. Ah-ha-ri was far too conservative for his taste and well might jeopardize his overall plan.

But Gray Fox had his own neck to consider. As a subordinate of the war chief in command, he was required to obey Ah-ha-ri without question, and he knew better than to make too much of an issue of his own desires.

Instead he busied himself, dropping words to the lesser war chiefs and senior warriors of the Huron before they joined Ah-ha-ri in conclave. In this way he hoped they would foster his views without making it necessary to call undue attention to himself yet again.

The meeting took place deep in the wilderness, out of earshot and out of sight of the Huron force, much less of the defenders. Gray Fox elected to remain inconspicuous and took a place quietly at the rear of the assemblage, sitting beside Pierre Fanchon, who knew better than to say a word.

As the half-breed had hoped, he had expressed his views with sufficient force to enough of the Huron leaders that they clamored for action and wore down the caution that marked Ah-ha-ri's approach to the problem.

"I say we attack in full force," a junior war chief shouted. "Let us bombard the town with incendiary arrows. Let us set fire to every building standing there, even to the palisade itself. Then when the defenders can tolerate no more, we send our bravest warriors to climb the walls and enter the town. Surely there are not enough warriors among the defenders to stop us."

"That is true," a senior warrior added loudly. "We will not give them a chance! If we overwhelm the enemy, we will win the day."

Their enthusiasm sparked similar feelings on the part of their comrades, precisely as Gray Fox had hoped. Soon almost all of the Huron leaders were clamoring for a full-scale morning attack.

Ah-ha-ri objected to such a plan, but his normal protests were swept aside in the enthusiastic avalanche, and the issue was soon resolved: the Huron attackers would launch a full-scale assault this very morning.

The beleaguered defenders of the Seneca town knew that a major effort would be made against them, but they had no idea of what was in store. Certainly no one in the community slept late. Ena, her daughter, and her daughter-in-law arose at dawn and, obtaining small quantities of food and water, prepared a meager breakfast. Ena was lost in thought throughout the meal, and when it was done, she spoke very firmly. "I think it would be wise," she said, "if we went to the Lodge of the Masks."

Betsy was surprised. In all of the years that she had been married to Renno, she had seen the interior of the Lodge of the Masks on no more than five or six occasions. The place was the equivalent of a church to the Seneca, but it was much more than a church. It was regarded by all of the Indians in the village as a holy place, and they treated it accordingly. Betsy and Ba-lin-ta exchanged brief glances and nodded their acquiescence. It wasn't often that Ena exercised her privileges as a family matriarch, but when she did, she expected immediate, unquestioning obedience.

Just before the three women started out, Goo-ga-ro-no returned home, intending to sleep briefly before resuming her vigil on the palisade. Her mother instructed her to accompany them, and the young woman obeyed meekly.

The Lodge of the Masks was a vast structure with walls made of thick animal skins, and as there were no windows, it was very dark inside. On each of the four walls were two enormous, hand-carved masks representing figures that were part human, part animal. No one had ever seen creatures like the eight characters depicted in the masks.

It was not known how long the masks had been on display. Certainly they had been there when the oldest living Seneca had been very young, and it was probable that they extended back far beyond the lifetimes of the grandparents of the oldsters.

The significance of the masks had never been precisely explained to Betsy, who was uncertain whether they were supposed to be representations of manitous or whether they had lives and powers of their own. All she knew was that they were treated with the greatest respect by all Seneca and that the people prayed to them as though they were themselves gods.

Ena prostrated herself on the hard earth floor of the building before two of the largest of the masks. Ba-lin-ta and Goo-ga-ro-no followed her example. Betsy noted that her daughter, who had demonstrated a lack of patience in the Lodge of the Masks prior to her unfortunate adventure, was as solemn as was her grandmother now.

In spite of the many years of her marriage, Betsy did not believe that the masks exercised supernatural powers of any kind; but she never mentioned her views in the presence of her mother-in-law. It was enough, in her way of thinking, that Renno knew how she felt. This was not the time, however, to question the authority of the masks. The residents of the Seneca town desperately needed help from any source, and as Betsy followed her mother-in-law's example, she found herself praying with a fervor that equaled that of the Seneca women.

No one spoke aloud, no one made any comment, and when Ena finally rose gracefully to her feet and bowed low to the masks, the younger women did likewise. Then they silently filed out into the open.

A change had taken place in the weather during the short time they had been in the Lodge of the Masks: the sun had been rising in a slightly hazy sky, but now it had vanished behind thick, black clouds, and there was a strong hint of rain in the air.

Ena was practical as always. "Ba-lin-ta," she said, "go to the lodges, if you will, and tell the residents to prepare to put out gourds to catch the rainwater. It appears as though we're going to have a heavy shower before the morning ends."

Her daughter hastened to do her bidding, and in the meantime Goo-ga-ro-no returned home and fell onto a corn-husk mat for a brief nap.

Ena and Betsy returned to the warehouse where all the town's food had been gathered for the emergency, and as they approached it Betsy suddenly gasped. A flaming arrow soared over the palisade wall and landed quivering in the ground nearby. It burned brightly, but it was harmless and quickly burned itself out.

That arrow, however, was a harbinger of what was in

store for the community. Suddenly the air was filled with
burning Huron arrows. The danger to the town was very
great, and Ena and Betsy recognized it instantly. They
hurriedly set up a brigade of young girls, arming each of
them with a bucket of precious water.

"Every time you see a burning arrow anywhere in the
town," Ena instructed the youngsters, "pour water on it.
Be sure the fire is put out. If you cannot reach a fire because it is too high for you, notify the nearest adult, and
he will act for you."

These makeshift tactics were helpful, but everyone was
very worried, and Sun-ai-yee was especially concerned.
One arrow could set fire to a lodge, and soon the whole
town could be destroyed. The Huron were being exceptionally clever, and there was nothing that the defenders
could do to stave off this onslaught.

Suddenly, however, there was a distant rumble of
thunder off to the north, and the breeze freshened. The
thunder grew closer with surprising rapidity and was so
loud that it drowned all conversation. The sky overhead
grew dark, and all at once a torrential downpour began to
fall.

The rain was heavier than anyone could remember it
being. Huge drops seemed to descend from the sky in vast
numbers, soaking the buildings, causing rivulets in the dry
ground, and drenching those who were out-of-doors.

Sun-ai-yee chuckled as he stayed at his vantage point
on the palisade; he appeared to be well satisfied with
himself. Ena paid no attention to the rain that made her
doeskin dress soggy. "The manitous," she said above the
sound of the thunder, "have heard our prayers."

Betsy had to admit that the rain had effectively halted
the bombardment of the town by the Huron. No arrow
could burn during such a downpour, and the flow of
arrows being directed over the palisade soon dwindled
and halted.

Betsy ignored her own discomfort as she pondered this
mystery. It seemed inconceivable to her that prayers directed toward aged, grotesque carved masks could have
been effective in any way, yet she could not deny that a

true miracle had taken place. The attack of the Huron, which had threatened to destroy the town by fire, had been halted in the only possible way that it could have been stopped. What was more, the weather had changed abruptly during the time that she and her mother-in-law had visited the Lodge of the Masks. She could not explain what had happened, but she knew what Renno would tell her if he were present. He would urge her to accept what had happened for its own sake and not seek an explanation for it. It was enough that the need of the Seneca had been great and immediate and that the forces of nature had rallied to the Seneca cause and had met that need. Certainly Betsy did not intend to make light of the beliefs of these devout Indians.

From his command post, concealed in the wilderness, Renno watched the legions of the Algonquian pour past him into the hollow U-formation. He had no idea what strategy the war chiefs of the large and powerful nation were employing, but he did not care. The Algonquian were playing into his hands, and he could ask for nothing further. Pleased, he ignored the silent looks of subordinates who were begging him to begin the battle.

His patience was monumental. As Ghonka had taught him, he knew that half the battle was learning when to forbear and when to strike. He was willing to wait for a long time until the appropriate moment arrived.

A Mohawk messenger approached him after making the long journey from the opposite, outer tip of the U, having traveled the entire distance around the semicircle in order to avoid being captured by the enemy.

"The Ottawa," he announced, "are following the Algonquian, and so are the Micmac and the Abnaki."

Renno nodded and seemed indifferent to the news. Actually, however, he was highly pleased. He truly saw an opportunity to trap the enemy.

Leaving his command in temporary charge of Walter, he hurried to the base of the U in order to see and speak to Jeffrey Wilson. The Massachusetts Bay commander was undecided whether to strike at the forces that were approaching him in ever-increasing numbers, but Renno hastily told him the situation.

Detecting the note of pleasure in his voice, Jeffrey looked at him. "Apparently I'm missing something that should be obvious to me in the development of our strategy," he said.

Renno grinned at him. "We will open the battle simultaneously," he said. "You will commence your fire here, and we will come alive at the same time on both flanks. I will send my warriors straight across the open end of the U, and I shall expect the other Iroquois to launch a similar drive toward me. In that way we can bottle up the enemy and slam the gate shut. With no escape possible, we should be able to inflict very heavy casualties on them."

Jeffrey grasped the import now of what his old friend had in mind. The tactics that the Great Sachem was suggesting were very bold, and their success depended on the perfect timing necessary as all three wings coordinated their efforts.

"I will send word to Mi-shal, who commands the open end opposite my position," Renno said. "Wait for about one hour until my messenger reaches him, then begin the fight whenever you please. We will hear your muskets speak, and we will know what to do accordingly." He was gone again before General Wilson could reply.

The allies of the French continued to pour into the gap. Surprised that they were meeting no opposition, they advanced in great strength.

The hour that Renno had asked for was up, and the enemy was deeply into the U. All at once musket fire cracked, breaking the silence, and then became a steady, muffled roar as the militiamen from the English colonies settled into the battle, selecting their targets, firing, and reloading again quickly.

Renno needed no further encouragement and at last gave his warriors the signal to join in the combat. They pushed forward eagerly, unleashing whole clouds of arrows as they moved, and they swiftly cleared the ground ahead of them.

Meanwhile, Mi-shal also was active, and his Mohawk, Oneida, Onondaga, and Tuscarora began to fire their own arrows as they moved to join forces with the Seneca.

The Algonquian were dismayed when they discovered, to their utter astonishment, that they were totally surrounded by their foes. They fought furiously in an effort to open a path by which they could retreat, but they were unsuccessful, due to the tenacious ferocity of the Seneca, who set an example for the warriors of the other Iroquois nations by throwing themselves over the mouth of the U, closing off any chance of retreat. Even when the Algonquian applied heavy pressure against them, the Seneca warriors still refused to budge. Their lines held steady, and they gave far better than they received, maintaining an even fire that decimated the ranks of their foes.

The Micmac, the least belligerent of all the Indian nations taking part in the conflict, were the first to panic. Aware that they were cut off, facing enemies on every side, they hurled themselves toward the combined lines of the Seneca and the other Iroquois behind them, and when those lines did not yield, they advanced at random, battering against the flanks and directly in front of them, but to no avail.

Panic and the fear of defeat were contagious. Every warrior on the French side knew that the Seneca were involved and quickly discovered that the stories they had been told about the impotence of the once proud and powerful nation were totally false. The Seneca were demonstrating all too well that they had lost none of their prowess, none of their instinct for victory, none of their keen appetite for combat.

So the panic grew worse, and the militiamen continued to mow down their foes methodically, while the warriors of the Iroquois continued to fight with great zeal.

The major break took place when the Micmac suddenly abandoned their weapons and scattered, with every man seeking safety for himself. The Abnaki did likewise, and then the fatal contagion spread to the ordinarily disciplined ranks of the Algonquian. Only the Ottawa continued to conduct themselves honorably and remained a cohesive fighting force.

Renno knew that his outnumbered warriors deserved a major victory, and he made no attempt to curb them. They slaughtered their foes rapidly and zealously, and the carnage was so great that the regiments of militia ceased fire.

As far as Ned Ridley was concerned, the battle was won, and he saw no need to engage in needless, senseless killing of the foe. Jeffrey Wilson felt the same way, and he, too, ordered his regiment to cease fire.

Renno promptly demonstrated that his code of combat was far different from that of his brother-in-law and of his oldest and best friend. He made no attempt to curb his warriors but allowed them to indulge themselves as much as they pleased; every member of his force engaged in the heavy slaughter of the enemy and acquired a rich harvest of scalps.

Renno was not insensitive to the positions taken by the commanders of the Massachusetts Bay and Virginia militia, and to an extent he agreed with them. When victory was assured, there was little reason to continue to kill, but he gave his warriors free rein for two reasons. In the first place they expected such an indulgence and would have felt bitterly disappointed—robbed of their rights, in fact —had he curbed them. Equally important, he had the reputation of the Seneca always in mind. The survivors among the Algonquian, Micmac, Abnaki, and Ottawa would remember the fearful carnage and would contribute their horrified whispers to the legend that the Seneca were bloodthirsty and invincible.

Meanwhile, the French warships rode at anchor, with the officers on board receiving news about the course of the battle from messengers. As soon as they learned that the allies of France were taking a merciless drubbing, they ordered the entire fleet to weigh anchor and withdraw, sailing off to the north in the general direction of Quebec. One moment the vessels were firmly at anchor, supplying their allies with food and arms; the next moment they were withdrawing in far more haste than dignity, putting as much distance as possible between themselves and the scene of defeat, disassociating themselves from it.

The victory gave Renno no sense of achievement, no feeling of gratification. In his lifetime he had fought in so many battles that he could no longer count their number, and the shedding of blood no longer gave him any feeling of fulfillment. It had been imperative that the allies of the French be severely beaten, and that goal had been accomplished. In addition, it would be a very long time before any of the northern tribes dared to raise their hands against the Seneca and the other nations of the Iroquois.

Now that the conclusive defeat of the French allies had been accomplished, General Wilson, Colonel Ridley, and the other militia commanders favored granting their men a respite for a day or two. Jeffrey Wilson suggested to Renno that he might want to do the same.

"Your warriors are human beings, you know," he said. "They'll enjoy a couple of days of doing nothing but hunting and fishing."

Renno shook his head. "You forget," he said, "that our homeland is in danger. We are leaving at once, and we'll go by forced march to the land of the Seneca."

Jeffrey knew that it was senseless to point out to him that the issue would in all probability be resolved between the Seneca and the Huron long before Renno's column arrived there, but he could understand the Great Sachem's concern, and so he merely extended his hand. "Good luck," he declared. "If you find that you need help from the militia, we'll be making our way south again by easy stages, and your messenger will have no difficulty in finding us."

"Thank you, my friend," Renno replied grimly, "but I will require no assistance. In the unlikely event that El-i-chi fails to teach the Huron a lesson, I assure you I shall finish them. I don't believe I'll need any assistance in reducing them, now or ever."

Rain fell steadily for the better part of the day, hampering possible military operations, so the defenders of the Seneca town had little to occupy them other than to keep watch on their foes from the palisade and watch the Huron being soaked by the downpour. By late afternoon the rain subsided, becoming a slight drizzle, and Sun-ai-yee called Ah-wen-ga and Goo-ga-ro-no to his command post.

"Tonight," he told them, "is going to be a critical time for us. The Huron will look foolish in the eyes of their countrymen and of themselves unless they capture this town very soon. So you can rely on them to make a major, concerted effort tonight. We will have to prepare a reception for them that will perhaps cool their ardor for victory somewhat."

The young women waited expectantly.

"Go to the shed where firewood is kept for the whole town," Sun-ai-yee told them. "There, at the far end, you will find roots of the white pine."

Ah-wen-ga nodded. "The roots that we use as kindling?" she asked.

Her father nodded. "Exactly so. Tie a bundle of roots to the base of arrows. Prepare at least fifty arrows in such a manner, and know that I will feel much more secure if you return to me with one hundred such arrows."

Ah-wen-ga and Goo-ga-ro-no exchanged puzzled glances but knew better than to question the renowned sachem. Sun-ai-yee expected his orders to be followed and became very annoyed when his directions were questioned, so the two women hurried off to do his bidding. By the time they completed the task he had given them, dusk was falling.

Sun-ai-yee exhibited considerable pleasure when they returned to him and showed him the arrows they had prepared according to his instructions. He immediately asked several of the older retired warriors to join them.

"I need tell none of you that we are in perilous danger," he said. "We can hold off the Huron only by relying on ruses, and I have a plan now that will delay their next attack."

"Surely the sachem realizes that the enemy is certain to attack this very night," an elderly senior warrior declared.

Sun-ai-yee nodded. "There's little question about it, and what I have in mind will, I hope, reduce their appetite for combat." He picked up one of the arrows and tapped the dried, sticklike roots that were tied to it. "At the appropriate time," he said, "I will ask for help from these maidens, who are excellent marksmen. They will make a fire and then will light the roots attached to each arrow. They will send their arrows one by one in the direction of the enemy concentrations, firing high into the air, as high as they can."

Several of the retired warriors were quick to understand and nodded, grinning broadly. Ah-wen-ga and Googa-ro-no, however, were totally bewildered.

"My plan," Sun-ai-yee explained, "is very simple. We will transform night into day with the flaming roots attached to each arrow. The light that is shed will aid the vision of warriors whose eyesight has been dimmed by age, and they will shoot as many of the enemy as they can. If you do your part and they do their part, I think we can hold off the foe for another night."

Ah-wen-ga nodded her head as she gazed at her father. His trick was simple but promised to be effective, and the confidence of the elderly warriors encouraged her. Her father was remarkable, she thought. Not only was he unwilling to bow to the odds and admit the possibility of defeat, but he also continued to rely on his long, varied experience to provide him with means of halting a foe who, all things being normal, should have captured the town many hours earlier.

The elderly warriors took places on the palisade and prepared their bows and arrows for immediate action. Meanwhile, Ah-wen-ga lighted a small fire at the base of the palisade. When Sun-ai-yee gave his signal, she dipped the pine roots attached to one arrow into the small flames, and they caught fire almost immediately. Holding the arrow gingerly, she managed to fit it into her bow and let fly with it, remembering to elevate it as much as she could to achieve the maximum height possible.

The arrow soared into the air over the cornfields, its motion causing the flames of the burning kindling to flare more brightly. Ah-wen-ga was amazed, as was Goo-ga-ro-no, to see how much light a single arrow cast. It continued to flare as it reached its apex, and the two young women could make out the rows of Huron warriors below, waiting to launch their drive.

Taking advantage of the light, the old warriors let loose a barrage of arrows into the massed ranks of their enemies. The Huron were packed together so tightly that no great expertise was necessary, and the arrows took a deadly toll.

"Again!" Sun-al-yee commanded.

This time Goo-ga-ro-no had an arrow ready, and after holding it over the fire until the pine roots caught, she managed to send it on its way high over the enemy position. Again the elderly warriors fired at the enemy.

Directing every move with precise timing, Sun-ai-yee continued to have the young women send flare after flare into the air, and the retired warriors did their part by directing their arrows at the foe.

Caught off guard by the unorthodox technique employed by the Seneca, the Huron tried desperately to break their concentrations and make a less obvious target, but the more they scrambled, the greater became their confusion. They took a heavy beating.

Ah-ha-ri watched warrior after warrior either die or suffer incapacitating wounds. The toll was too great, and he knew that mere dispersal was not enough. He ordered his force to withdraw, and the Huron were forced to suffer the indignity of pulling back into the safety of the wilderness. War chiefs and senior warriors alike smarted and felt humiliated by this latest ridicule to which they were being exposed. It was highly improbable that there were any active warriors in the town because no attempt had been made to break out and disperse the attackers.

That meant, therefore, that the Huron were being held at bay by women, old men, and children. The Huron would never live down the blot on their good name.

Gray Fox was well aware of the position of his colleagues and deliberately stayed away from Ah-ha-ri. He was more responsible than anyone else for this expedition, and its failure so far could be laid at his feet. But it was impossible for him to avoid the Huron leader, and ultimately he was summoned to the war chief.

Ah-ha-ri eyed him coldly. "So far," he said, "your advice has brought disgrace on our heads. Can you think of anything that will restore the good name of the Huron?"

Gray Fox was well prepared to answer the question. "The Huron are being humiliated," he said, "because we are too timid. We must strike hard and boldly and in great force. Let the war chief who leads us not forget that we have a strength much greater than that of our foes."

"That is true," Ah-ha-ri replied, sounding somewhat hurt and bewildered.

Gray Fox became even more aggressive. "The autumn is almost upon us," he said, "and the weather is changing. The air is still damp, although there is no moisture or rain falling, and I call your attention now to the treetops." He gestured toward the vaulted dome of the forest above them.

Ah-ha-ri gazed up at the tops of the tall oaks, elms, and maples but could see nothing unusual.

There was a hint of scorn in Gray Fox's voice as he said, "The first fog of autumn is gathering. Don't you see?"

Ah-ha-ri shrugged.

Gray Fox knew now that his will would triumph again. "By daybreak tomorrow morning," he declared, "a thick fog will be everywhere. It will cover the vegetable fields of the Seneca and will hide the whole town. That fog will provide us with a perfect shield. We can advance noiselessly, and at the last moment we can rush the palisade, open the gate, and send our warriors swarming into the town. If we are positive and bold, we cannot be denied the victory for which we have waited so long."

Ah-ha-ri could not help grinning at him. He recognized the greater cunning of Gray Fox and was willing to acknowledge his acumen. "So be it," he declared. "When day comes and the fog is thick upon the ground, we will strike with all our might. We will kill the defenders, and we will return to the land of the Huron with many prisoners."

Gray Fox nodded in satisfaction. Within a very short time Ah-ha-ri would be convinced that he had originated the plan of attack, and that would be all to the good. The success of the enterprise would do Gray Fox far more good in French circles because the rulers of New France knew that he was responsible for the expedition, and they would give him the lion's share of the glory.

Chapter XI

The night passed slowly, and as Sun-ai-yee, who seemed to require little or no rest, studied the weather with great care, his face became set in long, deep lines. Shortly before daybreak he visited Ena. "I'm afraid," he told her solemnly, "that we have done all we can. We have held off a superior party of active warriors for far longer than I had imagined possible, but now we are in for real trouble."

Ena listened calmly. "How so?"

Sun-ai-yee's voice became grim. "The weather is perfect for a surprise assault in force," he said. "The Huron can creep very close to the palisade without detection and and launch a furious attack at almost any point in our line. It would take a true miracle—something that even

289

the manitous might be reluctant to perform—to preserve us safely now. We will fight to the end, of course, but that end is definitely in sight. I'm afaid that the survivors among us will be forced to capitulate before this day's battle ends."

Ena thought long and hard about what he said. Then she shrugged. "If it is the will of the gods," she murmured, "so be it. I know only that the Huron will not take me alive. How they would love to march the widow of Ghonka through their towns and villages. How they would enjoy mocking and reviling me. But I will not give them the opportunity. I will fight them as long as there is a drop of blood left in my veins and a breath left in my body."

Sun-ai-yee had expected nothing less from the widow of Ghonka. "I, too, expect to join my ancestors in the land that is reserved in all eternity for them," he declared. "I will not reveal this to Talking Quail because she will grieve needlessly, but I, too, have no desire to be exhibited as a prisoner of war who has been captured by the Huron."

He returned slowly to his command post and then went about strengthening his defenses. He assigned an elder, a young woman, or one of the older junior warriors to a place every few feet along the palisade, cautioning each of them to keep as sharp a watch as possible, and urging all not to hesitate to give a general alarm the moment they noted any foes about to attack. "They will assault us in force," he warned. "There's no question about it. We will gather all of our effectives to the point that is threatened, and we will fight as best we are able." But something in his tone revealed to his listeners that he believed the end was in sight.

Dawn broke, but the fog was so thick that it obscured the sky, and the passage from night to day was very slow, with the sky brightening only a little. The Seneca sentries peered out of the chinks between the logs but could see nothing. Ah-wen-ga realized that a foe could creep as close as ten feet from her vantage point without the risk of being seen. The dangers inherent in this situation were obvious.

At last the tense silence was broken. A long, sustained scream uttered by Goo-ga-ro-no alerted the defenders that the moment of attack was indeed imminent. It was unnecessary for Sun-ai-yee to order reinforcements sent to her sector of the wall; older warriors made their way there instinctively, and the juniors were quick to follow their example.

Sun-ai-yee soon arrived and peered out, trying to distinguish shapes in the thick fog. He caught glimpses of motion and knew that Goo-ga-ro-no had not given an alarm in vain. The enemy indeed was approaching the palisade. Dealing with the crisis as best he could, Sun-ai-yee ordered a volley of arrows fired at the invaders, even though the Huron still could not be seen plainly. The arrows were sent on their way, and they, too, disappeared into the fog. The silence that greeted this effort was eerie; there was literally no way of determining how effective the defense effort had been.

The Huron were unwilling to make their challenge in silence, and a loud, shrill war cry rose up out of the fog to notify the defenders that they were in for the fight of their lives.

To the astonishment of Sun-ai-yee and of everyone else in the town, the cry was answered not from within the high wooden wall but from without. And there was no doubt in the mind of anyone who heard it that the response was a Seneca war cry!

The totally unexpected development stunned most of the tired defenders. Ah-wen-ga felt tears well up in her eyes, and she blinked them away angrily, only slightly mollified when she discovered that Goo-ga-ro-no was in tears, too.

Sun-ai-yee seemed to be totally placid, unmoved by the development that no one could have predicted.

What had happened, of course, was that El-i-chi's column had arrived at the town and had managed to work its way forward without being observed by the enemy. Now, however, El-i-chi himself challenged the Huron with the shrill, sustained cry of the Seneca, the most feared sound in battle that any warrior could hear.

The confrontation between the Huron and the veteran warriors of the Seneca progressed slowly, the fight taking shape tentatively because it was so difficult for both sides to see clearly.

Ja-gonh had the honor of being the first to strike a blow. His extraordinary vision enabled him to make out the war bonnet of a Huron war chief in the gloom, and he promptly sent an arrow toward its target. The arrow pierced the throat of the chief, and he died on the spot. The loss of a senior leader at the very outset of the fight was a major blow to the Huron, but most of them didn't know it because they still were unable to see clearly.

The defenders inside the town knew only that the greatest miracle that could have happened had taken place. A relief column of their own had materialized, literally out of nowhere, and had come to their rescue at a time when all had been lost. There were smiles on the faces of those who stood on the palisade, but they did not relax their vigil. The danger was far from ended, and it was possible that the town might still be overrun.

André Cooke approved highly of the members of the relief column who had accompanied him on the long march from the Canadian border. The warriors forgot their weariness and reacted as though they had been resting for days in anticipation of this climactic battle. They threw themselves into the fray with zeal and energy. It was their discipline, however, that was most impressive. Aware of the confusion they would cause if they strayed from their formation and engaged in individual combat, they held their ranks without being told, fighting as one man.

Advancing slowly, but applying great pressure, they began to cut a path through the teeming lines of the Huron. Ah-ha-ri had heard the original war cry of the Seneca, as had all of his subordinates, but he had been reluctant to believe that a force of competent Seneca warriors had indeed arrived on the scene. His first thought was that he was again being tricked by the wily defenders of the town. It soon became evident, however, that he was very much mistaken. The arrows being fired so methodically by the force attacking his could be dispatched only by trained warriors in large numbers.

Aware that the battle could be lost before it really began, Ah-ha-ri hastily took pains to rally his men. The overall situation was vastly changed, and it was to the credit of the Huron that they did not flinch from the task that now awaited them. Instead of trying to capture the town of the Seneca from women, children, and old men, the Huron expedition now faced a competent column of their ancient adversaries. Rather than be dismayed by the sudden change in their fortunes, however, the warriors met the new circumstances eagerly and were anxious to prove that the so-called invincibility of the Seneca in warfare was a myth. A Huron victory would explode that myth for all time, and the victors would be honored as few warriors ever were honored.

Therefore, in spite of the limited vision enjoyed by both sides, the battle was joined explosively, and it was understood in both camps that no quarter would be expected and none would be given. It was a fight to the death.

André Cooke, armed with a sword in one hand and a tomahawk in the other, ranged ahead of the main body of Seneca as he searched for a suitable foe to engage in personal combat. He did not have long to wait. A buckskin-clad figure loomed up out of the fog and hurled a knife at his head.

André ducked just in time, and the knife sang as it passed him harmlessly. Then as he made out his opponent, who stood almost within arm's reach, his blood ran cold. The coincidence was a joke of fate so cruel as to be almost unbearable.

"Pierre!" he gasped.

Pierre Fanchon stared at the other man, and color drained from his face. "My God!" he cried. "André!"

Even now, André Cooke could scarcely believe his eyes. Pierre was his younger brother, whom he had not

seen in many years, and when last he had heard of him,
the younger man had been calling himself Fanchon, after a
French uncle. That they should meet now on a field of
battle—on opposite sides—was an unendurable irony.

A feeling of deep gratification welled up within Pierre
and threatened to overwhelm him. It was too good to be
true that he was actually confronting André. He had
hated his older brother with a vengeance as far back as
he could remember. His contempt had only become
stronger the last time he had seen André—when the latter
had been doing some trading in the East—and Pierre had
considered it a deliberate insult that André had chosen to
cast his lot with the English settlers rather than with the
French. Now Pierre had the perfect opportunity to do
away with his brother for all time.

Slowly he drew his own sword, and André was quick to
recognize the challenge inherent in that gesture. "Must we
fight?" he demanded softly. "We share the same blood,
the same flesh. We are brothers who sprang from the
loins of the same mother. It might be best if we go our
separate ways."

Pierre replied through clenched teeth. "This meeting
was inevitable," he declared. "It is right that only one of
us should survive this day. I defy you, André, and I swear
to you if you do not try to kill me, I shall surely end your
life."

André knew his brother was so filled with hatred that it
was impossible to reason with him. Pitying him, André
nevertheless realized that he had to fight Pierre. There
was no other way. Perhaps his brother was right, perhaps
it was their destiny to meet as enemies in a strange land
where the family saga would be determined for all time.
He sighed and said softly, "Very well, then, have it your
way. We shall fight, and may the Almighty have mercy
on both of our souls."

Pierre had always been an accomplished swordsman,
and he lashed out confidently, lunging at his brother with
the point of his blade aimed at André's heart.

The move was so sudden it caught André almost by

surprise, and he barely managed to deflect the blow in time.

Thus began a bizarre duel to the death. Pierre handled his blade with great finesse, but André had two advantages: his strength was infinitely greater than that of his brother and his natural reflexes were quicker. So he more than compensated for his lack of expertise as a duelist.

Steel clashed against steel as the brothers thrust and parried, and the sounds of the duel were magnified by the fog. André retreated slowly, repeatedly preventing Pierre's blade from striking a mortal blow. He knew beyond all doubt now that regardless of his own feelings, he had to kill Pierre or be killed by him. Pierre was so determined that he left his older brother no alternative.

So André squeezed himself dry of all emotion. He put out of his mind his memories of the times when he had tried to advise and help a younger brother who had been perpetually dissatisfied with everything he encountered in life. That youth no longer existed. In his place was a surly, ambitious man who, for his own obscure reasons, was determined to do away with André Cooke.

Vaguely aware of Indians who loomed up out of the fog momentarily, André realized that if he and his brother were seen by a Huron warrior, his own life would quickly be forfeited. Certainly the Huron would not respect the privacy of a duel, and a warrior of the tribe would be quick to come to Pierre's aid. Furthermore, he realized that Pierre would gladly accept such assistance, unorthodox though it might be.

So André coolly awaited his chance. He could tell by the way Pierre handled himself that his brother was self-confident and felt sure that he would be the victor. Therefore, inevitably, he became careless. His guard slipped, then slipped again.

André seemingly paid no attention to these errors and pretended to be unaware of them. When the slippage became sufficiently great to give him a clear opportunity to strike a fatal blow, he took full advantage of it. Drawing in his breath sharply, he poised on the balls of his feet, took careful aim, and praying to his late mother and father to forgive him, he lunged.

Pierre Fanchon stared death in the face and was not afraid. He saw the needle-sharp point of his brother's blade pointing at him, poised for a strike, and he knew he could not parry the thrust in time. Suddenly, inexplicably, he laughed aloud. There was no scorn in the sound; on the contrary he sounded rather pleased that his worldly torment was coming to an end; he would be an outsider no longer, trying in vain to improve his lot in life. Instead, he welcomed a long rest, the long rest that André's sword promised him.

The blade cut into Pierre's flesh, and he expired with a slight gasp, a broad smile still on his lips.

The ultimate irony of his death was that Goo-ga-ro-no, whom he had dishonored and cheated, was only a few yards away at the time he expired, though she was unaware of the duel and its outcome. Still, she had, in the final sense, triumphed over him.

Gray Fox was deeply concerned over his future. He had gambled heavily on the almost certain success of the Huron raid and had relied on the gratitude of the French officials in Quebec to advance his interests. Now, however, the inexplicable had happened. A column of seasoned Seneca warriors had appeared out of nowhere after the defenders of the town had managed, in one way and another, to hold their attackers at bay. All at once the odds were drastically changed. The issue was very much in doubt, and in viewing it in that way, Gray Fox knew that he was being optimistic. Man for man the Huron were no match for the Seneca warriors. The only advantage that they continued to enjoy was a distinct numerical superiority, for they outnumbered the relief column by about two to one. Although Gray Fox didn't realize it, the Huron also enjoyed yet another advantage: they were far less weary than were the foes who had marched such a long distance to meet them.

Gray Fox was of two minds. He could do his best to

rally the Huron and try to save the day. That obviously was the best approach, for it still carried the promise of reward. If necessary, however, he was prepared to abandon the enterprise and to look out only for himself. He regarded his relationship with the Huron as a convenience and felt he owed them no loyalty. For that matter, the French cause meant equally little to him, and he favored it simply because it, too, was convenient, because as the son of Alain de Gramont he had a natural, sympathetic audience to whom he could play. So if it should become necessary, he was prepared to leave his comrades at once and make his way back to New France, where he would be forced to seek a new beginning, a new approach, a new plan.

What would happen when he arrived there was an entirely different issue. Major Henri de Bienville would be incensed over the failure of New France to accomplish her goals. Indeed, the major had already said that King Louis would want Gray Fox's head if the Huron's plans failed. But the crafty half-breed would not worry about that now. He was too clever—he was, after all, the son of Alain de Gramont—and he would be able to manipulate Henri de Bienville still another time.

He tried hard to rally the Huron warriors, well realizing that their confrontation with the dreaded Seneca was numbing them and was responsible for the signs of panic they were already exhibiting. If they could only convince themselves that their foes were ordinary Indians, not beings endowed with supernatural powers and strengths, they could probably win the day. But to convince them of this was difficult, and he knew that he had little time at his disposal.

"Huron to me! Huron to me!" Brandishing a tomahawk over his head, Gray Fox shouted defiantly, repeatedly. The Huron warriors responded, and soon he was surrounded by a score of them, who followed his example and gave a good exhibition of themselves. For the moment, at least, they were holding their own.

Ja-gonh heard the shouts, realized that the enemy fighters were becoming firmer as they held their ground, and he edged closer, intending to disrupt their lines if it proved possible to do so. Moving cautiously through the fog, he advanced very slowly, halting when he caught a glimpse of Huron war paint ahead.

All at once he saw the warrior who was rallying the enemy, and looking at him, he felt a chill of grim satisfaction when he recognized Gray Fox. Here, at last, was *his* enemy. Here, at last, was the murderer of Ghonka, the abductor of Ah-wen-ga, the man whose life he had sworn to take.

Drawing his tomahawk, Ja-gonh continued to edge forward. His heart hammered against his ribs, and he felt momentarily giddy. The moment of vengeance that he had sought for so long had come at last.

Gray Fox, busy forming his warriors into a solid line, did not become aware of the proximity of his foe until he and Ja-gonh stood only a few feet apart.

Then their eyes met, and for a long moment, time halted.

During this suspended moment, each knew beyond all doubt that the other was his mortal enemy and that there would be no peace, no rest until one or the other was victorious. In a strange, almost eerie way Ja-gonh and Gray Fox were echoing, repeating the patterns of the enmity between Renno and Alain de Gramont. Just as only one of them could survive, so was it with their sons. Either one or the other would emerge the victor in a relentless, merciless struggle.

The other Huron in Gray Fox's party became aware of the nearness of a senior warrior of the Seneca, and they, too, transferred their attention to him. Ja-gonh became the target for knives, tomahawks, and spears, and he was forced to withdraw hastily into the fog.

Pausing just long enough to catch his breath, Ja-gonh circled to his right and then pushed forward again. Through the fog he could see the formation of the Huron warriors, and he looked beyond them for Gray Fox.

But he searched in vain. The half-breed, as elusive as always, had vanished into the thick mist.

Later Ja-gonh remembered nothing of the next half

hour or more. Losing all perspective, he temporarily went mad as he searched the area outside the town of the Seneca for his hated foe. Recklessly indifferent to his own life, he took repeated risks as he scoured the area for Gray Fox. Not until the mist finally began to clear and the opposing forces engaged in a vicious, pitched battle did he finally recover a measure of his sanity and devote himself to fighting the enemy and leaving his meeting with Gray Fox to be settled later.

The development of the battle entered a new, grave phase. El-i-chi knew, as did André Cooke, that the Seneca under their command were mere mortals and not gods, and for a time they feared their outnumbered forces would be overrun and trampled by the numerically superior foe.

Then, as Sun-ai-yee later said, the second miracle of the day took place. A shrill whistle sounded in the distance, informing the Seneca that the second relief column, the militia volunteers commanded by Roger Harkness, had arrived on the scene.

Roger pushed forward, his men's muskets blazing, and it took him relatively little time to break through the enemy lines and to effect a liaison with El-i-chi and André.

"I'm glad I'm not missing the excitement," he said.

El-i-chi's calm matched the young English officer's. "No," he said, "you have the chance to get in your share of combat."

André noted with approval that Roger had learned new tactics to fit New World conditions. European armies were accustomed to parading openly onto a field of battle and formally engaging their foes in combat. Any soldiers who conducted themselves in that manner in the New World would lose their battle and their lives. Roger's men took advantage of the terrain, concealing themselves behind the trunks and branches of trees, firing their muskets whenever they had a clear view of a foe, and then rapidly advancing again to the next tree. In a fight such as this, every man was on his own, and success depended on the individual; but the whole was equal to the sum of its parts, and it was necessary for the individual militiaman not only to demonstrate his own repeated initiative but also to be conscious always of the need to cooperate and work in unison with his comrades. This, Roger's veterans achieved with consummate skill. Their firearms were far from the best, but they were, nevertheless, vastly superior to the bows and arrows of the Huron, and although the unit was relatively small in numbers, it was vastly influential in turning the tide of battle.

It was significant that the victory was won by the warriors of the Seneca and by the militiamen acting in unison. One group or the other alone could not claim to have routed the Huron, but together they accomplished that feat. It was a victory that El-i-chi savored, as did Roger Harkness. Here was proof positive that the alliance of the English colonists and the Iroquois was effective.

One moment the Huron were still putting up stiff resistance, the next moment they crumbled and fled from the field. Only their discipline prevented them from giving in completely to panic that would have totally destroyed them, and they drew back in formation, keeping up a brisk fire of arrows that covered their retreat.

Only the exhaustion of the Seneca and the colonists, all of whom had marched so far in such a short time, saved the Huron from complete destruction. Had their foes been less tired and able to follow them, the survivors would have been very few in number. As it happened, however, the Huron were able to withdraw from combat in relatively good order.

Ja-gonh was aware only that Gray Fox again was escaping with his life, and the young Seneca was enraged. He, more than any other Seneca, followed the retreating column, hurling tomahawk and knife, shooting arrows and bringing down a number of the enemy. No matter how many warriors he killed, however, no matter how many scalps he won, he felt no compensation because of the escape of Gray Fox.

Ja-gonh followed the defeated, retreating Huron for several miles and gave up the chase only when it became all too plain to him that Gray Fox had disappeared earlier when the fog had still been thick. His belt laden with fresh scalps, Ja-gonh returned to the positions held by El-i-chi and André Cooke, who were directing the final stages of the operation.

Bitterly Ja-gonh told his uncles what had happened, ending his brief recital on a bleak note. "So the killer of Ghonka has again escaped and goes free," he said, clenching his fists.

André was inclined to be philosophical. "It is not our place to question the will of the Eternal, be there one God, as I believe, or be there many, as you believe." He then related the details of his unexpected tragic duel with his brother, Pierre Fanchon.

El-i-chi was deeply impressed, as was Roger Harkness, who joined them, but Ja-gonh still had only one thing on his mind. "I realize that we have saved the town of the Seneca and those who dwell here," he said, "but I am not satisfied. I cannot rest; I will not rest until I fulfill my solemn pledge to my beloved grandfather."

El-i-chi glanced at him briefly. "Ghonka," he said, "would have been the first to tell you to leave such matters to the manitous."

Ja-gonh shook his head fiercely. The fires of youth burned within him, and he could not reconcile himself to an endless wait to obtain vengeance.

But such matters were soon forgotten, at least for the moment. The gates of the town of the Seneca were opened, and the grateful residents poured out into the fields to greet their deliverers.

El-i-chi saw his mother and enveloped her in a bear hug. Ena clung to him. "I am fortunate," she said, "that I have such sons as you and Renno. I ought to know by now that no harm can befall me when you are both active."

Ja-gonh was close behind El-i-chi, and after greeting his grandmother, he hugged and kissed his mother, grateful that she had been saved from Huron captivity. Then he saw Goo-ga-ro-no standing nearby, and he was elated that she had returned safely to the town after her adventures. She told him briefly what had happened to her, and

André Cooke, overhearing the conversation, decided to await a more appropriate moment, perhaps later that night, to tell her that Pierre Fanchon, who was responsible for her deep trouble, would never cause further distress for her or for anyone else.

In all the excitement of the smashing victory achieved by the Seneca, only one man remained completely calm. Sun-ai-yee behaved as though such a victory was an everyday occurrence. Gradually the leaders of the relief expedition learned of the wonders he had performed in holding the Huron at bay, and El-i-chi tried to find appropriate words to express his feelings.

"You are unique among the warriors of the Seneca," he declared.

Sun-ai-yee smiled and shook his head. "For an old man," he said dryly, "I have not done badly."

Chapter XII

E l-i-chi immediately sent two junior warriors as messengers to inform Renno of the victory that had been achieved at the last possible moment over the Huron.

The Iroquois had left the site of their own victory and were marching south again when the messengers arrived. Renno quickly sent one of the messengers to the north, where the English colonial militia allies had remained to rest for an extra day, and then the Great Sachem called a halt to the forced march of his own column. There was no need to press his braves needlessly, now that the Huron had been thoroughly repulsed, and Renno decided to wait in the wilderness until he was joined by Ned and Jeffrey.

303

Then they would have a chance to discuss the recent campaign.

While he waited for the others, Renno retired to the privacy of the wilderness. There, in a quiet ceremony, he thanked the manitous for preserving the lives of his mother and his wife and for saving the main town of the Seneca from complete destruction.

For all practical purposes the campaign was at an end. The realization dawned gradually the next evening after Jeffrey and Ned had arrived and sat with Renno around a campfire, eating a simple meal together.

"We're a little like Alexander the Great," Jeffrey said, smiling. "Apparently we have no more worlds to conquer."

Ned chuckled. "I'd give a great deal," he said, "to fight the French, but apparently they're not going to give us that opportunity. We've beaten all of the surrogates they've sent against us, so I suppose we'll just go home now."

Renno nodded and agreed that the campaign indeed had been a strange one. No official declaration of war had been issued, so no official end of the hostilities had to be proclaimed either. The informality of the situation left a great deal to be desired.

"If we could," Jeffrey said, "I'd insist on making an issue with the governor of New France and the commander of his military forces, and I'd compel him to recognize our victory. But I'm afraid they'd merely laugh at us if we went to them now. They would claim to be totally innocent, totally unaware of what took place."

"Of course," Ned said. "That's the beauty of their arrangement. They had everything to gain and relatively little to lose."

Renno smiled quietly. "For whatever consolation it is to us," he said, "they have lost far more than they had hoped to gain. The Algonquian and the lesser tribes are in no position to take part in another campaign and thus have been removed from the field of participants in any active war for some time to come."

"That's true enough," Ned Ridley said. "Now the Ottawa will be none too anxious to heed the call of the French for another campaign, and from what little we've gleaned from the messengers El-i-chi sent, the Huron have also learned a lesson and will keep the peace for some years to come."

"That means," Jeffrey Wilson declared, "if the French want to resort to force of arms in order to expand their colonies and take over the English settlement, they'll be obliged to fight alone, and I can't imagine the French ever entering into combat single-handed. They're far too clever and wily for that."

Renno stared thoughtfully into the fire. "I wouldn't want to predict," he said, "that our victories will produce a new era of real peace. I don't believe that we're about to enjoy any such era. The most I can say is that I believe it's unlikely that any more wars will be fought for several years to come, but that doesn't mean that the French will relax their efforts."

Ned nodded vigorously. "You understand the French, I believe," he said. "They'll resort to nonmilitary means to gain their ends. I have no idea what they'll attempt next, and for the moment, I refuse to worry about it."

"So do I," Jeffrey said heartily. "We won a victory, and we deserve the opportunity to celebrate it. If the French are up to any of their tricks, I'm sure we'll find out about them in due time."

"I'll be satisfied just so we learn what they plan in time to thwart them," Renno said. He paused and grinned at his companions. "I extend an invitation to you and to your families to join us in the land of the Seneca. This victory binds the Iroquois League tighter than ever before, and the people of our nations deserve the right to mingle with each other and to feel as one. I would like to extend that same privilege to you who are close allies."

"I accept with great pleasure," Jeffrey said. "My wife and daughters love visiting the Seneca and won't need a second invitation, you may be sure."

Ned smiled. "I'll come, of course, as will my troops, and I'll arrange passage for Consuelo on a ship sailing from Virginia to Boston."

"While you're about it," Renno said, "invite your governors to join in the celebrations with us, as well. We have been united in this campaign as never before."

They agreed, and that same night Renno sent messengers ahead of the column to inform Betsy of what he had in mind. The warriors already at home in the land of the Seneca would be kept busy now, hunting, for there would be hundreds of mouths to feed. The celebration would be memorable, an occasion that no one who attended would ever forget.

That night, Renno fell into a deep sleep, and once again the manitous came to him to foretell the future. In his dream he found himself once again in the Lodge of the Masks.

"Renno has done well," the ugliest of the masks declared. "He has prevented the destruction of the Iroquois League. The spirits that guide the Iroquois are pleased."

"They are pleased," the other masks echoed.

"But an even greater danger faces the Seneca and the other nations of the Iroquois," the homely mask said, and suddenly a voice arose out of nowhere and sounded like a crack of doom.

"Beware, O Seneca," the voice said. "Beware, O Iroquois. You have lived in the land of your fathers for many moons and many years. Your whole existence is threatened. Heed our words or you shall perish, and the Seneca shall be no more, the Iroquois shall be no more."

"I listen to your warning and I heed your words," Renno said, but to his consternation his voice made no sound. His lips moved, but there was absolute silence.

This had never happened to him before in any dream. He, who had faced countless foes in battle without fear, without flinching, had to fight a sense of panic that welled up within him. This was an experience that was unique in all his dreams, and he didn't know what to make of it.

He tried again to speak out his reply but could make no sound.

As the dreaming Renno watched in wonder, the roof of the lodge opened wide, and there, revealed in a bright, cloudless sky, was the figure of a proud hawk, flying rapidly. Suddenly, to Renno's horror, the hawk split in two, from head to tail, as though struck by the blade of an exceptionally sharp tomahawk. Renno was horrified, but to his amazement the hawk did not bleed. The two halves of the hawk floated gently toward earth.

Then in a way that was never clear to the dreamer, they came together again. The hawk was whole and unharmed, and it proudly soared in magnificent flight.

Then again the deep, disembodied voice spoke. "Renno, Renno," it called. "Here I am," a stranger's voice called out, and to Renno's astonishment the speaker was a young man no more than half his age, who wore the war paint of the Seneca and whose feathered headdress identified him as a war chief.

He stared incredulously at this stranger whom he had never before seen. The young man bore a distinct resemblance to him, he could tell that much. At the same time, and this was very confusing, the stranger was not white-skinned, as was Renno himself. His hair was darker, and his eyes were dark brown, those of a born Indian.

As nearly as Renno could judge, he was being afforded a glimpse of one of his descendants, a warrior who had not yet been born, and who was, Renno guessed, part white and part Indian. As he watched, a great golden eagle suddenly dropped down and attacked the hawk, and the young man—who apparently bore his name, Renno—produced a bow and arrow, which he handled with familiarity. He shot an arrow high into the air, and it pierced the breast of the eagle, which fell in death toward earth. Then the strange young Renno smiled as he saw the hawk, still proudly flying against a bright, cloudless sky.

All at once the mask faces began to laugh, and as they faded from view, their laughter echoed through the endless vaults and corridors of time and space. Renno awakened from his dream and discovered that he was in a cold sweat. The manitous had shown him that at some future time the entire Seneca nation would be in grave danger of dissolution and that a young man named Renno—presumably his descendant—would take firm action of some sort to prevent the catastrophe.

The dream raised more questions than it answered, and Renno knew he could repeat it to no one. Perhaps, if he was patient, the truth would be revealed to him in due time. He had to content himself with that knowledge and had to be grateful to the spirits who watched over the Seneca for raising the curtain on the future for his benefit, even if they had not given him the ability to fully understand that which he had seen and heard.

The tribes of the Iroquois accepted Renno's invitation with alacrity and pleasure, and all of the nations of the League promised to send their leaders and scores of warriors to attend the festivities. The column parted company with the militia troops, and they, too, promised to send delegates to the land of the Seneca to participate in what promised to become an occasion on which the pledge of mutual allegiance would be renewed by all of the partners.

The Seneca increased their pace as they reached their homeland, and the drums of the sentries told the nation that the balance of the victorious army had returned.

Betsy and Ena walked alone to the far side of the cultivated vegetable gardens and waited there for the column to appear. At last the warriors arrived, trotting easily. Renno, who was in the lead, saw his wife and mother and immediately sent the warriors on without him. He grinned as he approached them. Never had he been so glad to see either of them.

Betsy was thoroughly grounded in the ways of the Seneca: as her husband drew near, she folded her arms across her breasts and bowed her head. Ena did the same.

Renno wanted to kiss both of them, but there were proprieties that had to be observed, so he merely halted and raised his left arm stiffly in greeting. Then he lifted an eyebrow. "Surely you didn't leave the town to extend to me a formal greeting," he said. "I rejoice that you are safe, and I thank the manitous day and night for your deliverance."

"We're equally grateful," Betsy said, exchanging a significant glance with her mother-in-law. "Renno," she began, "we don't know how much you've learned of what's happened since you left, but we thought it best to prepare you for the fact that Goo-ga-ro-no is home."

He was stunned, as both of them realized, although his expression remained unchanged. He looked first at his wife, then at his mother, and waited in silence to hear more of what they had to say before he passed judgment on his daughter.

Betsy hastily told him all she knew of Goo-ga-ro-no's adventures and the reason she engaged in them. "I'm convinced," she added, "that she has learned her lesson. She was very contrite when she came home prior to the Huron attack, and her attitude has not changed since."

Ena knew that Renno was remarkably like Ghonka, and consequently she realized what would impress him, so she related at length the story of the heroism that Goo-ga-ro-no had displayed during the enemy siege of the town. Renno listened in stone-faced silence.

Betsy concluded by telling him what she had learned from André Cooke about his unexpected, tragic duel with the brother he had not seen in so many years. "So the man responsible for Goo-ga-ro-no's degradation and misery has paid the supreme penalty for his follies," she said. "Otherwise, Ja-gonh would have gone off to Canada at once and would have killed him in order to cleanse his sister's good name, but that is unnecessary now."

Ena became brisk. "We wished to speak to you before you greeted the members of the family. Goo-ga-ro-no will be present with them, and we wanted you to be prepared to see her."

Renno nodded but did not reply.

Betsy was annoyed but hid her feelings. Even now, after all her years of marriage to Renno, there were times when his Indian nature proved to be too much for her. Certainly this was such an occasion, but she knew it did not occur to him to express his feelings about accepting or rejecting Goo-ga-ro-no.

The truth of the matter was that Renno did not know how he felt. He was still absorbing what his wife and his mother told him, and he had no idea as yet whether he would open his arms to his daughter or would bid her to absent herself from the family. All he knew was that, like Ghonka, he would not face the issue until he came to it. Then, he felt certain, his instinct would tell him what was right and what was wrong. That instinct never failed him, and he felt certain it would not desert him today.

They walked into the town, with the two women following Renno by the customary several paces. Ja-gonh appeared from the direction of his parents' hut, and in his arms he carried his father's embroidered buffalo robe, the mark of his high office.

Father and son extended their left arms in greeting, and when their eyes met, both felt a great sympathetic satisfaction. Renno knew that Ja-gonh rejoiced in his victory, just as Ja-gonh knew his father was pleased with the role he had played in the dispersal of the Huron. He would have to talk privately with Renno about the escape of Gray Fox, but that meeting could wait until the whole family had an opportunity to welcome its head appropriately.

He draped the robe over Renno's shoulders, then fell in beside him, and they walked together to the hut. There the blood relatives were gathered in front of a fire burning in the cooking pit, where Betsy had begun preparing Renno's favorite dishes as soon as she had received word from the messengers of his arrival.

El-i-chi came forward to greet his brother and was followed quickly by André Cooke and by Walter Alwin. Ba-lin-ta, whose spirits were as irrepressible as when she had been much younger, could not control herself and grinned broadly at Renno, her eyes dancing, but she managed sufficiently to bow sedately. Renno returned the greetings, one by one.

Standing alone at the far end of the fire was Goo-ga-ro-no. She suspected that her mother and grandmother had intervened with Renno on her behalf, although she didn't know for certain. She realized that her father had been instantly aware of her presence, although he gave no sign of it. Now, with his greeting to others in the family disposed of, he turned to her.

Unsmiling, his face grave, Renno slowly advanced toward his daughter.

Goo-ga-ro-no slowly folded her arms across her breasts and even more slowly lowered her head in a gesture of obedience. This was not the moment to apologize, to explain, to say a word about anything.

Renno halted within arm's reach of his daughter and stared at her, his expression unfathomable.

As well as Betsy knew her husband, she had no idea what might be going through his mind at this moment. She was desperately afraid he would order Goo-ga-ro-no to take herself from the land of the Seneca. His decision would be final, so she caught her breath.

Ena braced herself and was prepared to brave Renno's wrath if need be in order to come to Goo-ga-ro-no's assistance. Renno might be the Great Sachem of all the Iroquois, but he was still her son, and she could clearly recall carrying him when he had been too small to walk.

Renno cleared his throat and astonished his entire family by raising both arms and extending them to his daughter. Never within the memory of any relative had he shown his emotions so clearly.

Betsy was so relieved that she felt weak-kneed. Ena smiled to herself. Renno was more like Ghonka than even he knew.

Goo-ga-ro-no clung to her father and could not hold back the tears that cascaded down her cheeks, but not one relative criticized her behavior. As Ba-lin-ta later commented, "There are limits as to what can be expected from the conduct of a Seneca maiden."

Renno again cleared his throat and knew that he would have to risk speaking. "I expect to be here for a long time to come," he said, "so we will have the opportunity to speak of many things in the moons that are ahead."

Goo-ga-ro-no caught her breath. "We shall, my father," she said. "You shall speak, and I shall listen. I think you will find that I shall be the first to heed your voice from this time forward."

For an alarmed moment Ja-gonh was afraid that Renno would weep, which would be unforgivable, so he hastened to his father's rescue. "Perhaps the Great Sachem has not heard," he said, "that his daughter deserves a place of honor in the ranks of the family's warriors."

El-i-chi laughed aloud. "That is true," he said cheerfully. "Renno's daughter conducted herself with great spirit and with great success during the siege."

Walter laughed, too. "I have heard that she and Ahwen-ga were both entitled to take and wear as many as a dozen Huron scalps. But for reasons that are beyond me, they have both refused."

A twinkle appeared in Ja-gonh's eyes, and he nodded solemnly. "I offered to obtain the scalps for my sister," he said, "but she would not hear of it."

They were teasing Goo-ga-ro-no now, as Renno well knew, and he promptly came to her rescue. "I will hear the report of Sun-ai-yee of those who served under his command in the battle against the Huron," he said, "and will commend those whom he deems worthy of commendation." He looked at Ja-gonh and then at the other men of the family, daring them to further haze Goo-ga-ro-no. No one elected to challenge his authority.

Laughing happily now, Goo-ga-ro-no hurriedly joined her mother and grandmother in making the final preparations for the meal and in passing out the gourds to everyone. Renno seated himself in his customary place directly in front of the fire, and as he arranged the folds of his ceremonial buffalo robe around him, he caught Betsy's eye.

They looked at each other for a long moment, and Betsy was content. Never had she seen such love, such happiness etched in Renno's face. He and his beloved daughter were reconciled, and all was right in his world.

* * *

Certainly no one was busier at the grand Seneca conclave than Governor Gooch of Virginia, who made it his business to become acquainted with every sachem and the more prominent men of every Iroquois tribe. He distributed gifts of Virginia tobacco to them with a lavish hand and further stunned them by presenting them with "special firesticks," handcrafted dueling pistols that were far more accurate than were most firearms of the period.

Roger Harkness had little time to himself during the opening phases of the conclave, but gradually, as the pace became less frenzied, he was left to his own devices. That suited his purposes perfectly, particularly after the arrival of the Wilson family from Massachusetts Bay. On the afternoon after they reached the town of the Seneca, he invited Patience to walk with him, and she consented gladly.

He led her into the forest to a clearing whose whereabouts he had learned while hunting with Ja-gonh. The spot was isolated. A small brook gurgled pleasantly, and several large boulders promised security.

When the couple reached it, Roger removed a handkerchief from his pocket, opened it, and spread it on the top of a flat rock before inviting Patience to sit. She smiled as she made herself comfortable, delighting in Roger's sophisticated, mannerly behavior.

Roger did not return her smile. "I have been looking forward to the chance to speak with you in private," he said. "I have spent many months in the New World, and in a sense, my original mission here has come to an end. If I wished, I could be transferred back to England at once."

"I see," she said. She realized that she would miss him very much if he went back to England.

"I've weighed the consequences carefully, and I've had many long discussions," he said. "I've tried to look at every angle, and I've conferred with the governor, with Colonel Ridley, and even with Renno, who may be the wisest of all of them. In any event, for better or worse, I've decided to stay in the New World."

Patience inadvertently broke into a broad smile.

Roger felt heartened. "I shall be resigning my commission with the army, of course, but I'll have no trouble obtaining a post in the Virginia militia. Colonel Ridley has assured me of that."

"What will you do?" Patience asked.

"I've been searching the countryside, and I've decided to claim a plot of land for myself. As a matter of fact, it lies adjacent to some land that Governor Gooch is claiming, so I'll be his neighbor."

The young woman nodded gravely and was secretly very relieved.

"I don't intend to spend all my life as a man of war," Roger continued. "The time has come to devote myself to peaceful pursuits. I know virtually nothing about the growing of tobacco, other than the little that I've learned in the recent weeks, but André Cooke has offered to teach me all that he knows, and he assures me that the soil and climate are right on the property that I've chosen, so I should have a bumper crop in a short time."

Patience merely nodded, calmly waiting for him to make his point.

"One of the wonderful things I've discovered about this continent is the spirit of cooperation that exists here," Roger went on. "When I return to Virginia after these festivities, some of my neighbors have offered to help me build my new house, and with their help, it should be ready in no time."

Patience was surprised and made no attempt to conceal her reaction. "My," she said, "you intend to sink roots rather quickly."

"Well," he replied, grinning, "I am trying to make up for lost time, I suppose. I've never had a home I could call my own." His manner changed as he rose from his seat on the ledge opposite her and stood, looming over her. "I truly want to sink roots," he said. "That means I want to marry and raise a family."

Patience was uncomfortable as she felt his eyes boring into her. "I see," was all she could say.

Suddenly he began to fidget, unnerved by her proximity. "Forgive my bluntness," he said, "but I know of no subtle way to express what's on my mind. Have I—ah—your permission to speak to your father and request the right to ask you to become my wife?"

She had been anticipating such a request, but now that he'd actually made it, she felt somewhat flustered. Roger Harkness was a splendid catch, and any young woman in the colonies would be fortunate to become his wife, but Patience had a problem—she was still undecided as to how she felt about Ja-gonh. Remembering their intimacy on the bank of the Connecticut River, she had no way of knowing whether that had occurred because of the potent brandywine they had drunk or whether it had had a truly deep meaning. She wanted to know for certain how she felt about Ja-gonh before she could commit herself to anyone else.

"I am flattered," she said, "sincerely, deeply honored by your request. But I ask one favor of you in return. Please give me a little time before I reply to you."

"Of course," he said, trying to hide his disappointment.

"My father and mother would be delighted, I know, to have you for a son-in-law," she said. "My father will automatically grant you the permission you seek and will give it as soon as he checks with me, but I want to make sure—very sure—of my own feelings before I commit myself for life. I beg you to be patient and not to question me too closely. Let me find my way through the maze myself, in my own way."

"Of course," Roger murmured, because he had no choice, and he prepared himself for a long wait. At least he knew better than to ask why she needed time to ponder.

Their conversation became desultory and eventually they meandered back toward the town of the Seneca. Before they reached the clearing where both were residing in temporary quarters, however, a small group of warriors suddenly emerged from the wilderness directly in front of them. The Seneca had been hunting, obtaining fresh meat for the many guests attending the celebration. There were a number of warriors in the party, which was headed by Ja-gonh.

This was the first time Patience had seen him since her arrival in the land of the Seneca, and the sudden confrontation with him was abrupt, totally unexpected. She had not braced herself for it, and she was in no way prepared for a face-to-face meeting.

Ja-gonh greeted her in the Seneca style, raising his left arm, then did the same to Roger.

Patience stared at him silently, finding it hard to realize that she had been intimate with this buckskin-clad warrior in full Seneca war paint. She noted that there were some smears of blood on his knife, undoubtedly caused by his carving the carcasses of the animals that several of his companions carried, and she shuddered inadvertently. Then all at once she noted something that turned her stomach.

Hanging from his belt was a cluster of scalps he had taken in the final battle with the Huron. They had not yet dried and shrunk, and it was all too apparent that they had been carved from the tops of human heads.

In that instant Patience knew beyond all doubt that Ja-gonh was not the man for her. Granted that she had grown up in a frontier settlement and had been accustomed to the ways of Indians all her life, she was incapable of marrying any man who was savage enough to collect scalps.

No matter how civilized Ja-gonh appeared when he spoke English and wore the attire of a colonist, he was a barbarian at heart. He might be the son of a white woman and a white man, yet he was a Seneca in every sense of the word, and she knew he would never change.

Patience rewarded Ja-gonh with an unexpectedly dazzling smile. He did not know it, but he had done her a great favor; he had enabled her to solve her dilemma far more rapidly than she had anticipated.

Roger Harkness could not help noting the warm smile she bestowed on Ja-gonh; he had already suspected that Patience's interest in Ja-gonh was the reason for her doubts. But Patience continued to smile as she turned to the young Englishman and placed her hand on his arm. "If you wish," she told him, speaking softly, "you may make that request of my father whenever you please. There's no need to wait now, not for a day and not for an hour."

Roger was totally bewildered. She had reversed herself so completely that he was confused. He stared at her, trying to make certain that he understood her completely.

"It's a lady's prerogative to change her mind," she said, offering him the only explanation that she would ever give him. "But if your new neighbors are going to help you build your new house, I should be in Virginia beside you as your wife when that house rises from the ground. It will be my house, too, and I shall have some definite ideas as to what I do and don't want."

She linked her arm through Roger's, and they increased their pace, walking rapidly now as they searched for Jeffrey Wilson. That evening the friends of the young couple would have cause for additional celebration.

It was not easy to find Renno alone long enough for a private conversation, but Ja-gonh managed the feat and cornered his father in his house shortly before the first major banquet for the many guests.

Knowing there was no time for subtleties, the young warrior came to the point at once. "How long is it necessary for me to remain in the town, my father?" he asked. "When do I have your permission to go off to the land of the Huron to find Gray Fox and avenge the death of my grandfather?"

Renno frowned, then hesitated. Many matters were crowding his mind, but he put them all aside, knowing that nothing was more important than the question his son had just asked him. "You are a host to our fellow Iroquois and to the English colonists, my son," he said. "You have fought in battle shoulder to shoulder with all of them, and therefore you owe it to them to display hospitality to them."

Ja-gonh nodded and then tried to keep a note of impatience from his voice as he replied. "I am well aware of my obligations, and I will do my best to be hospitable," he declared, "but my heart is heavy within me because my obligation to the memory of Ghonka is unfulfilled. I cannot rest, I cannot celebrate until I have wiped clean the blot on his good name. I must kill his murderer, preferably with my bare hands, and then I will be free to do as I please again."

"That is so," Renno acknowledged solemnly. "I sympathize fully with your plight, my son. I am well aware of your sacred pledge, and I understand your determination to honor it. That is as it should be. Ghonka was a great man, and his memory is precious to all who inherited so much from him. As long as I live in this world, I shall be proud that I am his son. I know you will be proud that he was the father of your father. That is as it should be. I, too, feel a knot of terrible hatred within me for the Huron who murdered him. That knot will not dissolve until the blood of the Huron melts it, so no one is more anxious than I that you fulfill your pledge. But you cannot leave behind the many guests on whom the future of the Seneca depends. The Iroquois League has been shaky, and now it is strengthened. Nothing must interfere with the tightening of those bonds. The friendship that exists between us and the English colonists has grown greater with each passing moon. So it continues to grow now, and it is your function as a senior warrior of the Seneca to further that relationship in every possible way. Therefore, I must command you to remain here in the town until the festivities are at an end. Once they are done and the guests depart, you are free to seek Gray Fox and to kill him. While guests remain, however, your place is here."

Ja-gonh was bitterly disappointed but had no choice: any decision made by the Great Sachem of the Iroquois was final and irrevocable.

As he watched Ja-gonh leave the house, Renno thought again of the dream he had had in the wilderness outside the lands of the Seneca. There was going to be great strife in the future, and the Iroquois League would be challenged as it had never been. But somehow a descendant of Renno would be there to preserve the dignity of their people.

Renno felt great hope for the future and great pride in his son. Ja-gonh was truly a Seneca, was truly the rightful heir to the lofty principles that Ghonka had lived by and that Renno continued to believe in. In Ja-gonh dwelt the Indian future.

That same evening at dusk the Seneca and all their guests gathered for the first of the great banquets that marked the celebration. No one thought it strange that Consuelo Ridley and Adrienne Wilson wore off-the-shoulder silk gowns that would have been appropriate at the King's court in Whitehall, and it was taken as a matter of course that their husbands wore their full-dress blue uniforms trimmed with gold.

Betsy, as was her custom, refused to compromise. Her doeskin dress was decorated with dyed porcupine quills, and her headband, which had been made for the occasion, contained symbols extolling the virtues of the Iroquois. Renno wore his huge feathered bonnet and the buffalo robe that were the symbols of his unique rank among the Iroquois.

André Cooke was delighted that Anne had accompanied Consuelo from Virginia. The couple were joyfully reunited, and Anne listened solemnly as her husband told her about his terrible confrontation with his brother.

"It was fated to happen, my darling," she told him as she reached for his hand. "Now you have exorcised all the ghosts of your past and can live your life—and our life together—as an Englishman to the last."

Junior warriors and maidens of the Seneca had been pressed into service in large numbers and completed the preparations of the meal that would be consumed by so many. Ena had been in charge of preparing the first course, which was her favorite soup, a bubbling mixture of corn, beans, and relatively small quantities of squash, which had simmered for many hours in a stock with a buffalo-flavored base, to which wild garlic and onions had been added.

Young warriors turned sides of deer, elk, and buffalo on huge spits, and in the coals were enough potatoes, which the young particularly favored, to serve every guest.

The final course had been supervised by Betsy and was one of her family's favorites. It was a simple dish of corn bread to which chunks of fresh fruit were added, and the whole was drenched in the fresh, sweet syrup that flowed from the maple trees in the spring.

Speechmaking was kept to a minimum. At subsequent events there would be ample opportunity for the sachems of all of the Iroquois nations to engage in the long, interminable harangues that they relished. On this occasion, however, Renno spoke for all of them and confined his remarks.

"On behalf of all the nations of the Iroquois," he said, "I welcome our cousins from the English colonies. We have vanquished the common foe together in a war. May we prosper side by side also in peace."

Sir William Gooch replied on behalf of all the colonies, and he was equally succinct. "I bring greetings to our brothers, the Iroquois, from the mighty King who lives in England, across the sea. Most of all, however, I salute you on behalf of the men, women, and children who are making new lives for themselves in the New World and have learned the value of friendship with you. Long may our relationship prosper, long may our relationship continue!"

Some of the medicine men objected because that was an end to the speechmaking, but the vast majority of those present, including the Seneca, the other Iroquois, and the white guests, approved. The meal was delicious, and the atmosphere was convivial.

Betsy had decided that the entertainment should consist of nothing more and nothing less than a typical Seneca dance, and a half-dozen drums began to throb very softly in unison, their volume increasing slowly, consistently. As was only proper she and Renno inaugurated the evening's dancing, and the close bond between husband and wife was nowhere more evident than in the way they moved together and looked into each other's eyes. Many of the warriors grinned when the couple was followed into the open field by the determined Talking Quail and Sun-ai-yee, who had been given no choice in the matter by his equally determined wife. The grins faded, however, when the portly Sun-ai-yee proved to be an extremely accomplished dancer and matched Talking Quail gyration for gyration.

The Wilson family had been enjoying a private celebration of their own, the betrothal of Patience and Roger Harkness, and they applauded when the engaged couple rose to their feet and moved into the field.

"I have literally no idea what to do," Patience said. "I've never engaged in an Indian dance before."

"Neither have I," Roger told her, laughing. "But it doesn't matter. As long as we're doing it together, we'll manage somehow."

She bestowed a dazzling smile on him. "Yes," she said, "as long as we're together, nothing else matters."

They soon entered the spirit of the occasion and danced with the zest of the most accomplished Seneca.

White Deer was disturbed when she concluded her work distributing food to discover that Ah-wen-ga was not dancing in the field but was sitting with the other unmarried Seneca women. Similarly, she searched in vain for Ja-gonh in the field and finally spotted him sitting stolidly with a number of other senior warriors. The young girl jumped to the conclusion that her sister and Ja-gonh had quarreled, but apparently that was not the case; both of them looked completely at peace, which mystified her.

Ja-gonh's failure to participate disturbed other people besides Ah-wen-ga's little sister. Betsy glowered at him, as did Ba-lin-ta, and he was forced to avert his eyes in order to pretend not to see them or be aware of their displeasure. When Ena chose to intervene, however, she was so insistent that he had to acknowledge her. She glowered at him and made such a point of being annoyed that Ja-gonh knew there was only one course open to him. He rose swiftly to his feet and walked to the place where Ah-wen-ga was sitting. He did not address her but merely looked at her.

Ah-wen-ga returned his gaze, and she did not speak, either. Instead, with one accord, they walked onto the field and began to dance.

Their performance was extraordinary. Even Patience, who was completely devoted to Roger Harkness, could not help noticing the remarkable rapport that existed between Ja-gonh and Ah-wen-ga.

The young couple danced as one. Without exhanging a single word, each had the ability to communicate thoughts and desires to the other, so they seemed to fly across the open field, zooming and dipping, stomping and swaying in perfect unison.

They were so expert that many of the dancers stopped in order to watch them. Betsy and Talking Quail glanced at each other for an instant; their eyes met, and both smiled quietly. Their dearest wish appeared to be on the verge of materializing.

At last Ja-gonh and Ah-wen-ga were satiated and left the field. Instead of returning to their places, however, they made their way some distance into the forest, pausing in a small clearing that the moonlight had made almost as bright as day. There they looked at each other for what felt like a very long time.

Ja-gonh folded his arms. "I am not free to speak freely or to relate that which is close to my heart," he declared.

Ah-wen-ga, in no way surprised, nodded quietly. "I know," she replied.

"That which I wish, and that which is, are two very different matters," he declared harshly. "I cannot satisfy my own desires until I fulfill a sacred obligation."

Ah-wen-ga looked as wise as she was lovely. "It would not be seemly," she said, "for Ja-gonh to seek his own happiness before he has avenged the murder of his grandfather. The manitous would disapprove, and their curse would spoil his future and would ruin his happiness and that of the woman who became his wife."

He felt instantly relieved and thought it miraculous

that she had such a complete understanding of him, of his needs, and of the demands made on him as a warrior of the Seneca.

"I crave the patience of Ah-wen-ga," he said.

She inclined her head.

"When the visits of our brothers in the Iroquois League and the English settlers come to an end," he said, "I must perform my mission. I will go alone to the land of the Huron and make sure that he who killed my grandfather mercilessly and in cold blood meets the fate that he deserves."

"I feel certain," Ah-wen-ga replied firmly, "that you will not only do your duty as you see it but that you will also cause great pleasure for Ghonka in the land of your ancestors, where he now resides. The manitous will rejoice!" She was so positive in her manner that he felt strongly encouraged.

"I hope the words of Ah-wen-ga come to pass," he declared. "I shall think of them often on my journey."

Her smile remained steady. He felt a complete sense of rapport with her, and his grin broadened. "When I return from the land of the Huron," he said solemnly, his words belying his expression, "I shall be free to do that which I wish more than all else in the world. I shall be free to unlock the bars that bind my tongue and make it impossible for me to express that which lies closest to my heart."

Ah-wen-ga's smile grew broader, too. "I shall eagerly await the return of Ja-gonh from the land of the Huron," she said. "I feel certain that the scalp he wants more than all others will hang from his belt. When he comes back to the town of the Seneca, I shall be here. I shall be waiting for him. I shall listen for the words I know he wishes to speak and shall reply to them with my own words, which will cause Ja-gonh and Ah-wen-ga to rejoice."

He refrained from taking her in his arms then and there because he knew the manitous were watching him and were subjecting him to their greatest test. He inclined his head, then stood aside for the young woman to pass him.

Ah-wen-ga brushed against him as she started back to the celebrants, her touch feather-light. Just that slight touch, however, was enough to inflame both of them, and she, too, had to fight temptation as she slowly walked away. Ja-gonh followed her and prayed to the manitous to hasten the day when he would obtain his revenge and would be free to live his own life as he wished to live it.

The future was bright with promise, but that promise could not yet be fulfilled.

★ WAGONS WEST ★

A series of unforgettable books that trace the lives of a dauntless band of pioneering men, women, and children as they brave the hazards of an untamed land in their trek across America. This legendary caravan of people forge a new link in the wilderness. They are Americans from the North and the South, alongside immigrants, Blacks, and Indians, who wage fierce daily battles for survival on this uncompromising journey—each to their private destinies as they fulfill their greatest dreams.

☐	24408	**INDEPENDENCE!**	$3.95
☐	24651	**NEBRASKA!**	$3.95
☐	24229	**WYOMING!**	$3.95
☐	24088	**OREGON!**	$3.95
☐	24848	**TEXAS!**	$3.95
☐	24655	**CALIFORNIA!**	$3.95
☐	24694	**COLORADO!**	$3.95
☐	25091	**NEVADA!**	$3.95
☐	25010	**WASHINGTON!**	$3.95
☐	22925	**MONTANA!**	$3.95
☐	23572	**DAKOTA!**	$3.95
☐	23921	**UTAH!**	$3.95
☐	24256	**IDAHO!**	$3.95

Prices and availability subject to change without notice.

Buy them at your local bookstore or use this handy coupon:

Bantam Books, Inc., Dept. LE, 414 East Golf Road, Des Plaines, Ill. 60016

Please send me the books I have checked above. I am enclosing $_____
(please add $1.25 to cover postage and handling). Send check or money order—no cash or C.O.D.'s please.

Mr/Mrs/Miss _____

Address _____

City _____ State/Zip _____

LE—3/85

Please allow four to six weeks for delivery. This offer expires 9/85.

**FROM THE PRODUCER OF WAGONS WEST
AND THE KENT FAMILY CHRONICLES—
A SWEEPING SAGA OF WAR AND HEROISM
AT THE BIRTH OF A NATION.**

THE WHITE INDIAN SERIES

Filled with the glory and adventure of the colonization of America, here is the thrilling saga of the new frontier's boldest hero and his family. Renno, born to white parents but raised by Seneca Indians, becomes a leader in both worlds. THE WHITE INDIAN SERIES chronicles the adventures of Renno, his son Ja-gonh, and his grandson Ghonkaba, from the colonies to Canada, from the South to the turbulent West. Through their struggles to tame a savage continent and their encounters with the powerful men and passionate women in the early battles for America, we witness the events that shaped our future and forged our great heritage.

	24650	White Indian #1	$3.95
	25020	The Renegade #2	$3.95
	24751	War Chief #3	$3.95
	24476	The Sachem#4	$3.95
	25154	Renno #5	$3.95
	25039	Tomahawk #6	$3.95
	23022	War Cry #7	$3.50
	23576	Ambush #8	$3.50
	23986	Seneca #9	$3.95
	24492	Cherokee #10	$3.95

Prices and availability subject to change without notice.

TALES OF BOLD ADVENTURE AND PASSIONATE ROMANCE FROM THE PRODUCER OF WAGONS WEST

A SAGA OF THE SOUTHWEST
by Leigh Franklin James

The American Southwest in the early 19th century, a turbulent land ravaged by fortune seekers and marked by the legacy of European aristocracy, is the setting for this series of thrilling and memorable novels. You will meet a group of bold, headstrong people who come to carve a lasting place in the untamed wilderness.

- ☐ 23170 Hawk and the Dove #1 $3.50
- ☐ 23171 Wings of the Hawk #2 $3.50
- ☐ 20096 Revenge of the Hawk #3 $3.25
- ☐ 22578 Flight of The Hawk #4 $3.50
- ☐ 23482 Night of The Hawk #5 $3.50
- ☐ 24361 Cry of The Hawk #6 $3.50
- ☐ 24659 Quest of The Hawk #7 $3.95

Prices and availability subject to change without notice.

"FROM THE PRODUCER OF WAGONS WEST COMES YET ANOTHER EXPLOSIVE SAGA OF LEGENDARY COURAGE AND UNFORGETTABLE LOVE"

CHILDREN OF THE LION

SPECIAL
MONEY SAVING
OFFER

Now you can have an up-to-date listing of Bantam's hundreds of titles plus take advantage of our unique and exciting bonus book offer. A special offer which gives you the opportunity to purchase a Bantam book for only 50¢. Here's how!

By ordering any five books at the regular price per order, you can also choose any other single book listed (up to a $4.95 value) for just 50¢. Some restrictions do apply, but for further details why not send for Bantam's listing of titles today!

Just send us your name and address plus 50¢ to defray the postage and handling costs.